SHAPERS
of WORLDS

ALSO AVAILABLE FROM SHADOWPAW PRESS

shadowpawpress.com

Paths to the Stars

Twenty-Two Fantastical Tales of Imagination

One Lucky Devil

The First World War Memoirs of Sampson J. Goodfellow

Spirit Singer

Award-winning YA fantasy

The Shards of Excalibur Series

Five-book Aurora and Sunburst Award-nominated YA fantasy series

From the Street to the Stars

Andy Nebula: Interstellar Rock Star, Book I

SHAPERS
of WORLDS

Science fiction & fantasy by authors featured on the
Aurora Award-winning podcast The Worldshapers

Edited by
EDWARD WILLETT

SHADOWPAW
PRESS

SHAPERS OF WORLDS
*Science fiction and fantasy by authors featured on
the Aurora Award-winning podcast*
The Worldshapers

Published by
Shadowpaw Press
Regina, Saskatchewan, Canada
www.shadowpawpress.com

Copyright © 2020 by Edward Willett
All rights reserved

Kickstarter Edition Printing September 2020
First Printing October 2020
Printed in Canada

Print ISBN: 978-1-989398-06-7
Ebook ISBN: 978-1-989398-08-1

Edited by Edward Willett
Cover art by Tithi Luadthong
Interior design by Shadowpaw Press
Created with Vellum

CONTENTS

INTRODUCTION

By Edward Willett

L ike most writers of science fiction and fantasy, I started out as a reader. In our public library in Weyburn, Saskatchewan, every science fiction and fantasy book bore a bright-yellow sticker on the spine, featuring a stylized atom with a rocketship for a nucleus. I methodically worked my way along the shelves until I'd read most of the books thus marked, which included, not just novels, but short-story collections, some by one author, many by multiple authors; some offering original fiction, others reprints.

Inspired (or possibly corrupted) by my reading, I tried my own hand at writing science fiction when I was eleven years old, producing my first complete short story: "Kastra Glazz, Hypership Test Pilot." My course was clearly set: I've been writing science fiction and fantasy ever since.

But while I could imagine myself as a writer, it never once occurred to me I might one day be editing and publishing a short-story anthology myself. And even had that thought crossed my mind, I would never have dreamed that within such an anthology I might have stories by authors of the caliber collected herein. Had you told me when I was reading *Forever War* as a teenager, for example, that someday I would not only meet and interview Joe Haldeman but I'd be republishing a Hugo Award-winning story of his, I wouldn't have believed it. Joe Haldeman and the other authors I read then seemed Olympians to me, forever out of my reach.

Years went by. I had a few short stories of my own published and, eventually, novels. I even made it to a few science fiction conventions, something else that had seemed out of reach as a small-town prairie boy. I started meeting some of the Olympians. Sometimes, I was on panels with them, or I'd go out to dinner with them, or we'd have drinks in the bar. I realized they were not, in fact, unapproachable.

Fast-forward (through a whole bunch of writing and publishing adventures) to the summer of 2018, when the idea came to me to leverage my experience as an erstwhile newspaper reporter and radio and TV host, and the contacts I had made in the genre, to launch a new podcast, focusing on something I love to talk about: the creative process of crafting science fiction and fantasy.

I researched the making of podcasts, decided on a hosting service, set up a website, got the necessary software and equipment, and then reached out to possible guests—and was thrilled by how many fabulous authors said, "Sure, I'll talk to you." That willingness spanned the writing-career spectrum from legends of the field and international bestsellers to folks who are just getting started, from writers for adults to writers for young adults and children, from hard SF writers to writers of epic fantasy. *The*

Worldshapers podcast took off with a bang—and, of course, continues.

Fast-forward again. In April 2019, at the annual meeting of SaskBooks, the association of Saskatchewan publishers of which I'm a member by virtue of owning Shadowpaw Press, a guest speaker talked about her success at Kickstarting anthologies.

Hey, I thought. *I know some authors . . .*

And thus, this book was born. I spun my wheels a bit at first—I'd never tried a Kickstarter and the challenges seemed daunting, and, of course, I had other writing and publishing commitments. But I garnered great advice from my fellow DAW Books author Joshua Palmatier, who has successfully Kickstarted numerous anthologies through his company, Zombies Need Brains, LLC, and more great advice from my fellow Saskatchewan author Arthur Slade, who has successfully Kickstarted a graphic novel, and, of course, it's not like there's a shortage of advice online (too much, maybe, since some of it is contradictory). At any rate, in the end, I screwed my courage to the sticking-place, rolled up my metaphorical shirtsleeves, and set to it.

I reached out to my first-year guests (an arbitrary decision to keep the length manageable—but don't worry; I totally plan to do a Volume II with the fabulous guests from the second year) and asked if they'd be interested in contributing either an original story or a reprint. Many were. (Those who couldn't, due to other commitments, were still highly supportive of the idea.) Many of the contributors, in turn, were very generous in providing backers' rewards. I built the campaign. It ran over the month of March 2020.

Wait. Something else happened in March 2020. I can't quite put my finger on it . . . it'll come to me . . .

Yes, I managed to launch my first-ever Kickstarter campaign

concurrent with the start of the worldwide pandemic's North American tour. Lockdowns, people out of work, fear of what the future would hold . . . not particularly conducive to shelling out money for a collection of science fiction and fantasy, I feared.

And yet . . . people did. I'd aimed for $13,500 Canadian and ended up at $15,700. The book was a go. The stories came in. And now they're going out again—to you.

Compiling and editing this anthology has been a complete joy. Every author has been a delight to work with. I hope you'll find the stories, both originals and reprints, as much a pleasure to read as I have.

This is not a themed anthology in the way many anthologies are, but it *does* have a theme. It's right there in the title: *Shapers of Worlds*.

Like potters shaping bowls from clay, authors shape their stories using a myriad of malleable elements: their own experiences, their hopes and fears and loves and hates, and their knowledge of history and science and human nature, all richly glazed with imagination and fired in the kiln of literary talent.

Each story in this book is set in a unique world shaped by a master of the craft. All of them showcase the skill of their creators.

Welcome, traveller, to the realm of The Worldshapers.

Enter, and enjoy.

Edward Willett
Regina, Saskatchewan
August 2020

VISION QUEST

By Edward Willett

S he comes, as so many have before her, in the twilight of the solstice, as this system's primary slips beneath the north-western horizon for a brief respite before lighting the sky again in the early morning.

She comes on a mechanical conveyance with two wheels, which she drives with thrusts of her legs, her feet on pedals. Some have come on horseback. Most have been on foot.

She comes to the edge of the small, round depression in the vast plain where I reside, a hollow with a pond at its centre, surrounded by the vegetation her people call cottonwoods and willows. That pond, dark and still, never goes dry, no matter how sere the fields surrounding it, no matter if the skies turn black with topsoil born aloft by howling winds, as they have so many times since I came here.

She hesitates at the rim of the depression, dropping her trans-portation device to the ground beside her. She is young, of course, as the people of this world count youth. They are all young, those

who come here, drawn to me when they are growing and changing, metamorphosing from child to adult as surely as a caterpillar
becomes a butterfly: a process I have examined in detail during my
long sojourn, a process that I, in my own way, am also undergoing.
For I, too, am young, as *my* kind count youth, though ancient
indeed to her and hers.

This land in which I sojourn is gripped in a gauntlet of frozen
iron for almost half of every revolution around this world's star.
Temperatures plunge, water turns hard as stone, and howling
winds drive snow in long, hissing snake-forms across the ground.
During those short days and endless nights, it seems nothing will
ever grow again . . . and yet, every spring, it does. Green shoots rise
from black dirt, leaves burst from buds on trees, insects hatch,
mammals emerge from the burrows that honeycomb the earth
around my hollow . . .

. . . and young humans, like the one who has come to me now,
emerge from their own childish cocoons, look at the world around
them with wide, new, questioning eyes, and begin to spread their
wings.

She steps down into the hollow, following the path that leads
to the edge of the pond and the smooth, shining rock that stands
there, the path so many have followed before.

In buckskin or homespun, blue jeans or shorts, barefoot or
booted, sandaled or sneakered—all words I have learned from
them—they have come.

They come for the same reason I came here, long before the
first of them appeared . . . and they come because I call them.

She is by the pond now. She looks down into it. It is dark, as
dark as space, as smooth as ice, though it is not frozen, does not
freeze even in the dead of winter, for it is not water.

And then she turns to face the polished stone. She hesitates, but then, in response to my unspoken call, places her hands upon it . . .

. . . and I am her.

JAMIE STARED at the strange black stone. She'd never seen anything like it on the prairie. It looked more like the kind of pedestal she'd seen sculptures on at the art galleries in Regina and Saskatoon her mom used to take her to.

What's something like that doing out here? she wondered. And then, *What am I doing out here?*

She hadn't known this place existed until she'd crested the slope she had just descended. But she'd known what it was the moment she saw it: a prairie pothole, a shallow depression left behind ten thousand years ago as the glaciers covering Saskatchewan melted away. She'd learned about prairie potholes in Mr. Gregorash's Grade 8 geography class, last school year. She and her friends had found it hilarious that the prairie surrounding their little town was just as full of potholes as the thinly paved secondary road that ran to the highway, thirty kilometres away.

There were tens of thousands of prairie potholes like this one, and she'd never given them much thought, except maybe for Swallow Hollow, where the older kids sneaked off for parties in the summer. She was too young to go out there . . .

. . . but not for much longer.

High school, she'd thought, staring down into the hollow, feeling a flutter in her chest. High school meant riding a bus over that bumpy, pothole-plagued road to the highway, and then another twenty kilometres to the next town, a bigger one than theirs (though not by much). High school meant strange kids she'd never met before, and more homework, and . . . and all kinds of things she wasn't sure she was ready for.

Last night, she'd dreamed about it, and the dream had turned into a nightmare. She'd been in the high school cafeteria, and then suddenly she was naked and everyone was laughing at her, and she'd tried to run out, but all the doors were locked, and then all the other kids had turned into snarling coyotes, and they'd come leaping toward her, teeth bared . . .

. . . and she'd woken up, gasping and crying, and she'd waited for Mom to come and give her a hug and make everything all right, like when she was little, but Mom hadn't come, and then she'd remembered Mom would never come again, that cancer had *made* it so she'd never come again, and that Dad sat alone and drank in the dark before he went to bed, and then slept so hard he'd never hear her, even if she called out for him . . .

. . . and it was then, right *then*, in the midst of that middle-of-the-night fear and grief and longing, that she'd felt . . . a tug.

There's a place, a voice seemed to whisper to her. *A place you need to come to.*

She'd gotten on her bike after lunch and ridden at least ten kilometres along the dusty grid road, the hot sun beating down on her shoulders, her route straight as an arrow except for the correction line just outside town. As she'd reached the abandoned Johnson farm, with its crumbling stone barn and tumbling-down house, the tug had come again. *This way*, it told her.

She'd turned off the gravel of the grid road just south of the farmhouse to ride along a rutted, seldom-used dirt path through barren fields, white with alkali, growing nothing but weeds. Grasshoppers leaped away from her bike in panicked profusion, sometimes bouncing off her chest and arms and face.

In all that time, she'd never had the slightest doubt about what she was doing, never once even considered disobeying that subtle inner summons.

She'd dropped her bike at the top of the path that led down into the pothole, and now, here she was, in the middle of the prairie, kilometres from town, standing in front of a mysterious black stone beside a strange black pool.

Alone.

Touch it, came that strange inner urge. *Touch it.*

She remembered something else Mr. Gregorash had talked about, the "vision quests" common to indigenous cultures across North America, including the Plains Cree who had once hunted buffalo on the very land Jamie's Scottish ancestors had settled after the building of the Canadian Pacific railway.

"Although the details differ from culture to culture," Mr. Gregorash had said, "in general, vision quests are a rite of passage through which young boys transition from childhood to adulthood. The boys purify themselves, in whatever fashion their tradition requires, then go to some isolated place in the wilderness to fast and meditate. They experience sacred, secret visions, believed to be a gift from their creator and ancestors, and discover their guiding spirit."

Jamie wasn't a boy, she had no First Nations ancestry, and she hadn't purified herself, other than taking a shower the night before. Yet . . . here she was, alone in the wilderness (*well, kind of*, she thought; high above, a jet contrail cut through the cloudless blue), and something was telling her to touch this weird black stone.

Maybe it's my guiding spirit, she thought. *Are you there, God? It's me, Jamie.*

But if God, or any other spirit or spirits, was there, he or she or it or they didn't answer, and if her ancestors had anything to say, they kept it to themselves. Staunch Presbyterians all, they were probably glaring down at her from heaven, lips pressed tightly together in disapproval.

The image made her mouth quirk with amusement. *This is silly. You're being silly. Just being out here is silly. Touch it and get it over with. Nothing will happen. And it's going to be getting dark by the time you get home, and Dad . . .*

She felt a flash of resentment. Her father would be mad at her. He'd probably yell. It seemed like he was always yelling at her these days, like they were always arguing.

It was that moment of anger, as much as the strange, inner urging, that drove her, at last, to not just touch the stone, but to slap her palms against it in irritation.

And then her body faded from her consciousness as her mind opened.

———————

WHERE ONCE I WAS ONE, *now I am two.*
As I have been before.
As I will be again.

———————

I GROW up with Jamie in her small town, play with her friends and her dog, feel the warmth and love of her parents, her wonder and joy at the world around her, seen through her innocent eyes.

Jamie grows up with me, admiring this system's yellow star after its life-giving radiation, sleeting through my family's vessel, woke my progenitors from their long dormancy and caused them to make me. She rides with me and my family as we plunge closer and closer to the star and the one blue, wet, living planet our sensors reveal. With me, she spends many cycles on the surface of our long, slender craft of meteoric stone and iron. Together, we are purified by vacuum and washed clean by the solar wind; then we share many more cycles deep inside it, in cold and silence and darkness and solitude, meditating, preparing for the quest to come.

I am with Jamie when her mother calls her into the kitchen to tell her what she has just learned from the doctor. I am with her as her mother fights through chemotherapy, recovers for a time, and then withers away, collapsing in on herself until, one dreadful night, she is no more. I am with her as she and her father stand hand in hand at the graveside, and she feels her father's silent sobs shake his body, and she knows that nothing will ever be the same again.

She is with me for my launch, a birth of sorts, not as messy as a human birth, but the same sudden emergence from darkness into light, the same separation from safety, the same sudden thrust into the unknown. Aflame, Jamie and I plunge together from orbit. Smoking and steaming, we bury ourselves in the land. Together, we draw that land around us, mimicking the natural features, crafting a disguise, a camouflage, what a human hunter would call a blind.

And then, together, we reach out. We call, we summon, we urge. We bring the brief-lived dominant sapients of this strange world to us, our minds able to touch theirs only in the spring of their lives, as they move from childhood to adulthood.

And when they come, we merge with them, as I have merged with Jamie, as I have merged with so many before.

With Jamie, I wake from the frightening dream, wishing for Mom. With Jamie, I feel the call . . . *my* call . . . to ride into the prairie, to a place she has never seen, had no clue existed, but which now feels to her like the most important place in the world, the place she must go to, above all else.

With Jamie, I leave my bike at the top of the hill, walk down into the depression where the dark pond waits, and touch the smooth black stone.

Where once I was one, now I am two . . .

I AM NOT THE CREATOR, and I am no one's ancestor, and I am not a spirit, and yet I give to Jamie, as she gives to me, visions sacred in the only way anything is truly sacred: sacred because we, who live and think and fight the universe's uncaring entropy, who give to it the only meaning it has, imbue them with sacredness.

Only seconds in real time after Jamie touched the interface, I sever the connection.

Where once I was two, now I am one.

JAMIE STEPPED BACK from the stone. Her hands tingled, but that was all.

Or was it?

She frowned. Something swirled on the edges of her memories, strange, dream-like images of stars and moons and planets and fire, and even stranger images of boys and girls close to her own age, dressed a thousand different ways, standing where she stood now, touching the stone as she had, and, just like her . . .

. . . just like her . . .

. . . just . . . like . . . her . . .

. . . what?

The memories faded, ghosting out like the afterimage of a photoflash.

Jamie looked at the stone again. She had no desire to touch it. It was, after all, just a stone.

She looked down into the dark pool, so smooth, so black, like a night sky devoid of stars. For a moment, just a moment, she had the feeling the pool was looking back at her.

She took an involuntary step away from it, feeling a little shiver of fear. *Don't be stupid*, she chided herself. *You're not a little kid anymore.* She forced herself to step closer again. Then, on a whim, she reached down, picked up a pebble, and tossed it into the water. It splashed the same as any other water in any other pond, the ripples spreading smoothly out in concentric circles to the banks. *See? It's just a pond.* She remembered her earlier fears about starting high school. *And high school is just school. I'll be fine.*

She glanced up at the sky. *I'd better get back. There's still a lot of light left. If I'm lucky, I might make it before Dad notices how late I am. I don't want him to worry.* She felt a sudden surge of love and concern for her father. *It's just the two of us now. I have to look after him.*

She hurried up the slope to her bike, mounted, and rode off through clouds of grasshoppers and alkali dust without a backward look, following the dirt road toward the ruined farm in the distance, the grid road beyond, and home.

I WATCH Jamie for as long as my sensors permit, her bare legs flashing as she pumps the pedals of what I now know she calls a bicycle, and silently wish her well.

She will remember nothing of me, or of this place. Her memories of her childhood will never contain even the faintest trace of my memories of mine, or the memories of all the other young humans who have come to me through the centuries, though we shared them so deeply while we were one.

Nor will she remember the memories that are not mine, the memories of my race, the memories my progenitors folded into my surface as I was being made: the glimmer of starshine on methane seas, the glow of rings slashing through the dark sky above the towering storm clouds of a gas giant, twin suns locked in an intricate gravitational dance, light gasping its last in a seething maelstrom of radiation as it plunges into a black hole, all the wonders of the universe my race has explored since before Earth cooled enough for liquid water to fall and begin the long, slow filling of the oceans, the first step toward life, and intelligence, and girls like Jamie.

And yet, though she will never remember me, through me she has made a connection with her world and her universe that will give her a sense of peace and purpose. It is a connection that will guide and ground and steady her through the tumultuous years to come, through the entirety of her too-brief walk upon this planet, as it has so many young humans before her, the countless boys and girls who have found me in the millennia I have rested here.

She will not remember me, but I will remember her, as I remember all the others. I will still remember her centuries from now when, at last, my vision quest comes to a close, when my progenitors swing by this planet again and pull me into their warm and welcoming embrace, to join with them, to share my visions, to add to my race's memories, to strengthen and enrich all of us with what I have learned from those who live and die upon this blue-green speck.

I came here as a child. I will return to my family as an adult. The young ones I have met here on this great flat plain flicker for only an instant, a brief spark of light in the darkness, but that bright flash will be remembered for as long as my race sails the universe in our slender ships of stone and iron, the warmth and yearning and love I have found within their young souls refreshing our ancient ones forever.

The solstice sun has set upon the plains of Saskatchewan.

Spring has ended.

Let summer begin.

CALL TO ARMS

By Tanya Huff

"Mirian! There's an Imperial Courier waiting for you in the market square!"

Mirian held out a hand to keep Dusty from toppling over, so fast was his change from fur to skin. "On a horse?" Not everyone in Harar—Orin's largest settlement—was Pack, but this was the old country, and the population skewed to fur. Convincing a horse not bred in Orin to enter Harar was next to impossible.

"No, on foot." His lips were drawn so far off his teeth, Mirian barely understood him. "She wants you. Why does the Empire want you?"

"I expect it's not the entire Empire." When Dusty continued snarling, she sighed. "So, tell her where I am."

"Can't. Otto wants you to come to her. Suspicious, power-tripping, mangy . . ."

"Dusty." Mirian was Alpha of her own small pack, but they lived in Harar at the Pack Leader's sufferance. Otto, new enough to the position of Pack Leader the scars on his shoulder were pink, was still testing his authority. Still checking to make sure Mirian would continue to follow the rules. To be fair, she didn't blame him. Rolling up onto her feet, she brushed dirt off her hands. "Tell him I'm on my way, but I need to clean up a bit first."

"Because you won't come running when the Empire snaps its fingers!"

"Because I've been gardening. And I haven't lost all the manners my mother worked so hard to instill. Go."

His ears were back in protest when he changed, but he turned and headed back toward the centre of the settlement.

Mirian watched him run. Other than the gleaming silver fur that marked the torture he'd endured as a child, he was, like everything else in her world, multiple shades of grey. He'd grown into a teenager in the nine years since she'd taken him and the rest of her pack out of the Empire. In skin, he was taller than the others his age, arms and legs and torso given length by the castration he'd suffered under Leopold's knife. His face still held boyish curves and probably always would. In fur, he was large without bulk, and faster than everyone he'd ever raced against. In time, Mirian could see him becoming the Pack Leader's top runner— once he worked his way through his current teenage rebellion.

"Provided I don't strangle him before he manages it," she muttered. She shifted the dirt on her skin back to the ground, and stepped up onto the wind.

———

TUCKED out of sight in the alley by the cheese shop, Dusty glared at the courier who stood by the well talking to Otto. The Empire of memory smelled of blood and death. The courier smelled of sweat and long days on the road without a chance to change or bathe in anything but cold water. She was tall and athletic, probably ex-military. As Dusty understood it, a lot of couriers were, and that would explain the rifle leaning against her pack. She didn't look dangerous, but Dusty was well aware looks meant nothing. He didn't look dangerous. But he was.

"Hey!"

Jerked out of his thoughts, Dusty started as Alver waved a hand in front of his nose.

"I called you like six times." The young mage crossed his arms, half a dozen white flecks drifting across the dark brown of his eyes. "What's up? Does she smell so fascinating you think you can ignore me?"

Dusty shouldered him hard enough to nearly knock him over and changed. "That's an Imperial Courier!"

"Well, that explains the uniform." Alver threw a kilt at his head. "Here. Unless you planned on waving your bare ass at her."

"The Empire slaughtered most of my family, then hacked off my father's leg, locked him into a silver collar, and threw me in a cell with him as he bled to death." He yanked the kilt straps through the double buckles and waved a hand below his waist. "And this."

Sean Reiter thought the emperor had him castrated so he could be raised as a pet. *"Or because he was a sadistic, insane, murdering son of a syphilitic hog,"* Sean had amended dryly. *"Could be either. Probably both."*

Alver frowned. "Well, yeah, but she didn't do it."

"She's Empire!"

"So?" Alver bounced his shoulder off Dusty's. "And stop growling at me. If she tries anything Imperial, I'm sure the Pack Leader will let you rip her throat out."

"Mirian won't." Mirian didn't understand.

"If she gives you so much as a dirty look, Mirian will turn her inside-out. You know that." Alver shrugged. "She's your mom, or as good as. And she's your Alpha."

"I'm nearly sixteen . . ."

"So am I, and my mom still licks my ears. What can you do? I mean, someday I'll have to . . ."

Dusty raised a hand to cut him off, face turned into the breeze. "Mirian's coming."

He expected Mirian to ride the wind into the market square, bring a gust strong enough to throw the Imperial—and maybe Otto—back on their heels, but she walked in like a normal person, Tomas in skin, fully dressed, at her side.

From what Dusty could see of her expression, the Imperial Courier had also been expecting a more mage-like entrance. Not a medium-sized twenty-seven-year-old in a faded green dress. Her hair was up, and she'd even put on shoes, although most of Harar didn't bother in the summer.

"It's like she's playing dress-up," Alver murmured. "Pretending she's not a throwback to the kind of ancient mage who could destroy the world. Lulling them into a false sense of security. Also," he added after a moment, "that dress is at least five years out of style."

"No one cares about the dress," Dusty growled.

Alver sighed. "Obviously."

The courier recovered quickly. She stepped past Otto and tipped her head to Mirian. A sort of bow, Dusty realized, not submission. "Your Wisdom. If we could speak privately?"

"No." Otto inserted himself between the two women. "Anything the Empire has to say will be said publicly."

Tomas's lips lifted off his teeth.

Leaning against the corner of the cheese shop, Alver shook his head. "Tomas needs to be careful with those almost-challenges or Mirian's going to lose her Beta."

"Tomas can take him." Tomas had been part of the Scout Pack in the Aydori army.

Alver snorted. "That's what I said."

Dusty elbowed him to shut him up.

Over by the well, Mirian had given Otto a long, assessing look. Otto met it until Mirian's lips twitched and she looked away. "Here is fine," she said, gesturing for the courier to begin.

"As you wish, Your Wisdom."

"Clever." Alver nodded, as though his opinion meant something. "She's acknowledging the decision was Mirian's, not Otto's."

"Alver, shut up. I need to hear this."

As though someone had heard him—and given the Mage-Pack scattered through the gathering crowd, Dusty wasn't ruling it out —a breeze came up and the courier's voice filled the market square.

"I BRING WORD FROM LORD GOVERNOR . . ." Eyes wide behind the lenses of her glasses, she stared around the square.

"Apologies," called a voice from the crowd. "That was a little loud. I'll dial it back."

Tomas laughed and leaned in toward Mirian. Dusty couldn't hear what he said, but Mirian laughed with him.

"Probably reminding her of that time she nearly deafened the lot of us."

"We were seven," Dusty snapped.

"But I remember. Look . . ." Alver waved at the courier, who was visibly pulling herself together. "She didn't expect basic mage-craft. You know what that tells us? Mages are still thin on the ground in the Empire."

"Comes from murdering them."

"Probably."

The courier took a visibly deep breath and began again. "I bring word from Lord Governor Marchand of the Imperial province of Bienotte. Over the last few years, the Krestonian Empire has raised the taxes paid by Bienotte again and again. The people of Bienotte struggle to survive. Lord Governor Marchand has had enough. He won't watch his people starve. Will you help him throw the heavy yoke of the Empire off his people? Will you help lead them to independence?"

Mirian cocked her head—and blinked eyes white from rim to rim. When Dusty was younger, he'd thought she could see the truth. He wasn't entirely convinced she couldn't. After a long moment, she smiled and said, "No."

"BUT HE WANTS to free his people from the heavy yoke of the Empire! Lead them to independence!" Hands in the air, Dusty stomped across the common room and back, bare feet slapping against the floor. "You should be all over that!"

Distracted by the silver lines of anger trailing in Dusty's wake, it took Mirian a moment to ask, "Why?"

"Why?" His lips drew back off his teeth. "Maybe because of Nine! And Bryan and Dillyn! Matt and Jace! Jared and Karl! Maybe because of Stephen! They killed him, even if it took him a couple of years to die! Maybe because of me and my dad and all the other Pack they murdered! Maybe because of that!"

"Dusty, I understand that you feel . . ."

"No, you don't!" He took a deep breath. "You can't! They have to pay for what they did."

Mirian tried to find the words that would push past Dusty's

anger. "This is a different government. Imperial Packs are treated
as equals under the law . . ." She kept talking over his protest. ". . .
and when they aren't, because laws and prejudices don't always
walk in step, the wind brings the news and I deal with it. You know
that." It had happened less and less as the years passed. Mirian
hoped it was because people defaulted to doing the right thing
when not egged on by a corrupt government. Tomas insisted it was
because she'd removed enough bigoted assholes their numbers
had dropped below critical mass.

"Then why won't you help now?"

She shook her head. "Governor Marchand doesn't want me to
help. He wants me to be his weapon. He wants me to attack the
Empire for him."

"So?"

"If the governor—or anyone else—wants independence from
the Empire, they have achieve it themselves."

"That could take forever!" Anger tinted the air around his head
and shoulders. "You heard the courier, they're starving now!"

"If Governor Marchand had asked for food . . ."

"They asked for freedom. You need to free his people from the
Empire!"

"I do?"

"Yes!"

"Then they'd be mine."

"Mirian!"

She waved a hand at the clutter. They'd already expanded
twice, when first Matt, and then Karl, were married. "Where
would I put them?" Beside her, Tomas's tongue lolled out, and she
buried a hand in his ruff. "Dusty, you have to . . ."

"No, I don't," he snarled, changed, and charged out of the
room. The screen door slammed behind him.

In the next room, Karl and Julianna's twins screamed their objection to the sudden noise, their distress pulsing through the house.

Mirian sighed. "That went well."

TOMAS'S NOSTRILS flared as he glanced around the dining-room table. "Where's Dusty?"

"He's gone up to the summer pastures with Alver's family." Mirian motioned him into his chair and pushed the platter of rare beef toward him, using her elbow to keep Dillyn from grabbing seconds before everyone had firsts. Her mother would be appalled at the chaos and even more appalled at her belief that the sturdy harvest table and mismatched chairs belonged in a dining room.

"He's that angry with you?"

"He'll get over it," Nine growled before Mirian could answer. "The Empire can rot from within without our Alpha's help."

DUSTY PUSHED his shoulder up against Alver's side and pushed a branch out of the way with his muzzle. Firelight reflecting on her glasses, the courier reached for another piece of wood, paused, frowned, and said, "You might as well come out. I know you're there."

Alver, who had no sense of self-preservation at all, stepped into the circle of light before Dusty could stop him. "How?" he demanded.

She smiled, although she didn't relax. "You smell of sandalwood."

"I do?" He turned his head, sniffed the shoulder of his jacket, then half-turned to meet Dusty's gaze. "You might have mentioned that. Now, are you coming out or not? This was your idea." He mimicked Dusty's voice. "I'll tell my family I'm going to the summer pastures with you, and you tell your family Mirian asked you to stay in Harar to work on your mage-craft. We'll catch up to the courier and go with her to help Governor Marchand defeat the Empire."

It had also been Dusty's idea to watch the courier for a while before joining her, but Alver only listened to what he wanted to hear. And he didn't want to hear that the scents he loved so much gave him away to anyone with a nose. Dusty huffed out a breath, tucked his tail close to keep it from being caught in the brambles, and walked out to stand by Alver's side.

"Well, hello." Her smile broadened. "Aren't you a big . . ." And her smile disappeared. "You're not a dog, are you?"

"Told you she was clever," Alver muttered.

Dusty stepped behind Alver, shrugged out of his pack, and changed. Skin or fur, Pack didn't care and it never used to matter who saw his scars, but he'd been a child then and he wasn't now. Yanking out his kilt, he cinched it around his waist before stepping back into sight. "I'm Dusty, this is Alver. He's a mage. We're coming with you to help fight the Empire."

"Are you?" The question was polite, if a little aloof. She hadn't reached for the rifle leaning against the log beside her, so Dusty figured aloof was fine. After a long moment, she nodded. A strand of long, light-brown hair, loose from her braid, fell forward over her shoulder. "Nina," she said, tucked the hair back behind her ear, and added, "Have a seat."

"Don't mind if I do." Alver drew up a hummock of earth and sat.

The aloofness disappeared. Dusty figured Nina was about the same age as Alver's mother, but her sudden enthusiasm made her look younger. "You're an Earth Mage!"

"Nope. We don't do that divide and conquer stuff. I'm just a mage."

"Like Mirian Maylin!"

"Yeah, I'm . . ."

"No, you're not." Dusty crossed his ankles and dropped to the ground. "No one's like Mirian. Mirian could rule the world if she wanted. She can do anything. She could leave home as we get to Beinotte and still beat us to the governor's house."

Alver poked him. "I thought you were mad at her?"

Oh yeah. He dug his fingers into the ground. She was fine allowing the Empire to . . . well, to be the Empire. Still . . . "Facts are facts." He looked up to find Nina leaning slightly toward him, the force of her attention almost Pack-like.

After a moment, she sat back. "You're one of the Ghost Pack. The child she rescued."

"Oozes clever," Alver muttered as Dusty snapped, "I'm not a child!"

"No, you're not. My apologies if I implied otherwise." She raised both hands and left them raised until Dusty nodded, then she picked up a tin mug from a rock by the fire. Her hands engulfed it completely as she raised it to her mouth to drink.

It smelled like the coffee Sean brought for Mirian from Aydori, where it was both hard to get and expensive. Probably cheap and common in the Empire because they'd just conquer and murder until they found a steady supply. He was impressed that Nina had managed to carry enough to get her to Harar and home.

"I should send you back," she said, once she'd swallowed and set the mug down.

Alver snorted. "Like we'd go."

"There's that," she acknowledged.

Later, lying across the fire from Nina, Dusty breathed in Alver's familiar scent, laid his head on his paws, and dreamed of ripping the Empire into small bloody pieces.

———

"Seriously? They really believe the Pack are all male and the Mage Pack are all female? That's crack-brained." Dusty could hear the frown in Alver's voice.

And the shrug in Nina's. "No knows much about the packs in the Empire."

"Yeah, I'm surprised." Alver was breathing a little heavily, keeping up to Nina's quick, purposeful stride, and Dusty figured if he hadn't been getting an assist from his earth-craft he'd have had to ask her to slow down. "Maybe because you had them declared abomination, then tortured and killed them. I mean, not you, but..."

"I know what you mean. That's one of the reasons why Lord Governor Marchand wants to break up the Empire." She stepped over a fallen tree and pushed her glasses back up into place with her right index finger. "No one should have the kind of power it takes to lead their people down such a dark path."

"Mirian says a little power applied at the right place is more effective than calling out the army."

"Does she?"

"Yeah, and she says..."

Dusty broke into a run. He didn't want to hear Alver and Nina discuss Mirian's philosophy of power. Not when she had her head stuck so far up her own mage-craft she refused to help.

"Wait." Nina came to a sudden stop and turned until she could look up at the higher rock ledge where Alver balanced. "Are you saying your mage-craft is first level?"

He shrugged. "I'm fifteen. What did you expect?"

"I don't . . ." She fell silent, frowned, and finally said, "I know nothing of mage-craft, I thought . . ." Another silence. A deeper frown. "You're kids. I don't know what I was thinking. I should take you back."

"Okay, first, you already established that you can't take us anywhere we don't want to go. One of us, maybe," he allowed after a moment. "But not both of us. And second, Mirian only had first levels when she rescued the Ghost Pack."

Nina shook her head. "I suspect it was more complicated than that."

Alver glanced down, shifted a bit of loose rock out of his way, and jumped. "Mirian says it wasn't."

Waiting at the bottom of the path, Dusty changed long enough to snarl, "Talk about something else!"

———

Dusty didn't change in front of Nina, always finding something he could put between them—Alver, if nothing else was available. He forgot that anyone who knew dogs could tell what had been done to him.

"Was it the Empire?" she asked one night, pitching her voice to keep from waking Alver.

He snorted and laid his head on his paws. Who else would it have been?

"Then I can certainly understand why you want to help us be free of them."

If she could, why couldn't Mirian?

"YOU'D HAVE to be trying to starve in the woods at this time of the year."

Crouched by the firepit, Nina nodded. "I restocked in Harar, but it helps to have a hunter with you."

"And a mage," Alver pointed out as he showed Nina the berries in the fold of his shirt.

Dusty spat a bit of rabbit fur out of his mouth. "Bloody balls, Alver, it's not all about you!"

"Language," Alver chided around a mouthful of crushed fruit.

On those rare occasions Nina laughed, she laughed with her whole body. Dusty liked that about her.

"WHERE DOES YOUR TAIL GO?"

Dusty looked over at Alver and they both snickered.

"What?" Nina demanded. "Is it a Pack secret?"

"Not a secret, it's like the first question kids ask." Dusty pitched his voice higher. "Where's my tail gone?"

Nina spread her hands. "Well?"

"It just . . . goes."

MIRIAN STEPPED out of the chicken coop, wiping her hands on her apron—realizing as callouses caught that her mother would be appalled at the condition of her skin. "Servant's hands," she'd declare with a sniff and insist she soak in vinegar until the callouses were soft enough to buff away. Her mother's opinion of her lack of servants was revisited in every letter received. "Tomas Hagen deserves better than a cook and a daily. It's like you've forgotten everything I ever taught you!"

Not everything, but she was working on it.

"Mirian!" Amelie, Alver's oldest sister, waved from the path, her pale hair almost-but-not-quite silver among the shades of grey. "Mother sent Jonas and me down to pick up a few things," she said as Mirian drew closer, "so I thought I'd drop in and make sure Alver was behaving himself."

"Alver?"

"Alver. Might be a mage someday if he grows out of thinking he knows everything al . . ." She trailed off. "He's not here, is he?"

"He isn't." A breeze lifted a loose strand of Mirian's hair. "I assume Dusty isn't with you."

"He isn't." She sighed. "It's been almost three weeks. They could be anywhere. Can you find them?"

"Oh, yes." The breeze became a wind, although the leaves around them continued to droop in the summer heat. Mirian's feet left the ground. "I can find them."

"YOU NEED MORE CLOTHING."

Dusty looked down at his bare chest and legs. On any warm day, men dressed only in kilts walked barefoot on the streets of

Harar. If Pack wanted access to fur, they didn't want to waste half
the day getting there.

"And shoes," Nina continued. "Only the truly destitute go
barefoot.

"Alver?"

Alver patted himself down as though there might be shoes
hidden under his clothes. "Nope. No extras."

"Fine." Behind the coverage of a juniper, he dropped his kilt
and changed. He could feel Nina's steady gaze on him as he
emerged, mouth full of fabric. After he spat the kilt at Alver's feet,
he sat and met her gaze.

"It might work," she allowed after a moment. "You're big, but
we're too far from Pack territory for anyone to assume you're not a
dog."

"He does tricks," Alver said brightly.

Dusty growled.

"Or not."

CITIES SMELLED HORRIBLE.

Alver was enjoying himself, pointing and peppering Nina with
questions she patiently answered. Dusty fought the urge to nip
him. They didn't have a collar and he wouldn't have worn it if they
did, so he stayed close to Nina's side. She kept them on backstreets
as long as she could, where the thin children wanted to ride him . . .

"But he's so big and fluffy!"

. . . and a man who smelled of sour wine followed the three of
them for blocks making larger and larger offers until Nina turned
and quietly told him the dog was not for sale. Dusty couldn't see

her expression—he was watching the man, hoping for an excuse to take him down—but it was definitely effective, eliciting a mumbled apology and a fast retreat.

Unfortunately, although Nina had explained they'd enter at the rear of the government building, they had to cross a main street to get there. Dusty had never seen so many horses in one place. And none of them were the sturdy mountain ponies who grew up surrounded by Pack.

"This isn't going to be good." Alver glanced both ways. He lifted his head into the wind, frowned, and sighed. "Oh, so much less than good. However, if we have to cross, we need to move quickly."

"We have to cross."

"All right then. Dusty, go! Wait for us on the other side."

At the first break in traffic, he leapt forward. Wind, funnelled down the street by the five- and six-story buildings, ruffled his fur. Was that what Alver had meant by less than good? And why had they made the streets so wide?

Two, three, four horses let it be known they'd scented a predator.

He could feel the impact of iron-shod hooves against the cobblestones as they fought to be free of their traces.

Shouting, a collision, a scream . . .

Across the street and tucked around a corner in a shadow at the base of a building, he waited.

And waited.

He'd begun to worry, had stood and taken a step back out into the open, when his companions finally joined him.

Alver sagged against the building. "Well, that could have gone worse."

"How?" Nina demanded. "It's chaos out there. People were hurt! What happened?"

"What happened?" Alver stared at her for a long moment, white flecks drifting across his eyes. Then he sighed. "The Pack are apex predators."

"That's . . ."

"Apex," he repeated. "Bears will back away from a fight with Pack. Be thankful Dusty moved so fast only a few horses scented him."

The noise suggested more than a few horses were involved in the chaos, although everyone knew a fear reaction from one herd animal would set off the rest. So would the scent of blood. And Dusty could definitely smell blood.

Nina stared down at him as though she were seeing him for the first time. As though she could finally see the help they were offering. "We could use that reaction against mounted Imperial troops." She reached out as if to stroke Dusty's head, then let her hand fall back to her side. "You okay?"

Dusty pushed up against Alver's leg. He'd been held and tortured by the Empire but Imperial horses had never harmed him, and yet, it was horses who were bleeding.

———

THE GOVERNMENT BUILDING WAS OLD, with thick stone walls, and wonderfully cool inside. It was also the largest building Dusty had ever seen—not counting the Imperial Palace where he'd only seen a cell, the tiled room where the knives were used, and the ruins Mirian had left it in. Nina ushered them into a small room and said, "Wait here. I need to inform Lord Governor Marchand I've returned."

The scents in the room were old, and no one but a female rat scavenging for her young had been there for days, so once Nina left, Dusty changed. By the time she returned, he'd changed twice more and Alver had begun to speculate about the tiny sheep on the wallpaper.

"Lord Governor Marchand wants to see you immediately." She tossed a bundle down onto the scarred tabletop. "I found you some clothes."

"I have clothes," Alver protested.

"You had clothes three weeks ago. Now you have stains held together with dirt. Change."

The trousers, shirts, and vests fit surprisingly well, although Nina had to tie both their neckcloths. The shoes she'd found were a bit large. Dusty appreciated being able to move his toes, but Alver kicked his off. "I'm wearing my own. I'm a mage," he added before Nina could protest. "I don't care if the shoes don't match the outfit."

"Liar," Dusty muttered, pulling the laces tight.

"We all should have bathed, but we don't have time." Nina had changed while she was gone and wore a courier's tabard over clean clothes. An elderly man in a faded uniform stared as they stepped back out into the hall, then hurried away before they came close.

"What happened to him?" Alver asked, thumbs tucked into the pockets of his vest.

"Happened?"

"He had a split lip and a bruise on one cheek."

"I'm a courier," she sighed. "I've been gone for over six weeks, and the servants aren't my responsibility when I'm here."

"Maybe they should be," Dusty growled. "He smelled of hunger." He expected Nina to ask what hunger smelled like—her willingness to learn had been one of the things he liked best about her—but she merely frowned and kept walking. Keeping up kept him from looking around, but he'd have had to be moving a lot faster to have missed the scents of neglect.

When they stopped by an old, worn door, she twitched a wrinkle out of her tabard, took a deep breath, and led them into a large room. There were wide double doors and windows high in the long wall to his right, and a dais in the centre of the wall to his left. Centred on the dais was a sturdy chair with a high back and broad arms that wouldn't have looked out of place in Harar. The man in the chair had steel-grey hair, cut even shorter than Pack hair, but his shoulders were still broad and square, and he wore the same uniform as the two-dozen soldiers who stood in ranks on either side of the dais. All of them carried the new rifled muskets. Sean had brought one the last time he'd come back from Aydori.

"You can fire them faster, aim them accurately, and while they've finally gone into mass production, they're still stupidly expensive. It'd bankrupt a country if they tried outfitting their entire infantry with these things."

"They're not wearing the Imperial crest," Alver muttered. "Those are bears, not ravens."

"They want to free themselves from the Empire," Dusty growled. "Because they're not stupid."

A bulky camera had been set up in the centre of the room, the photographer arguing with her assistants about . . . about angles, Dusty assumed, given the arm-waving. Teger, the Pack Leader before Otto, had a camera, but it was half the size.

Conversations stopped, and one by one the clusters of people standing by the walls turned to watch them cross the room.

"So, these are the children you brought me instead of the mage

I sent you for." Lord Marchand had a Pack Leader's voice. Deep. Resonant. Confident.

Nina bowed. "They aren't children, Your Lordship. Alver Goss is a white-flecked mage and Dustin Maylin is Pack. When Mirian Maylin refused to return with me, they offered their assistance."

"Their assistance?" His brows rose. "And how exactly can they assist?" A few people snickered.

"Your Lordship . . ."

"Let them speak for themselves, Courier."

"Sir."

Lord Marchand beckoned them closer. "So, how can you assist me with the Empire?"

"I hate the Empire," Dusty growled.

He shook his head. "Not what I asked you."

No, it wasn't. How could they assist? Wasn't it obvious? "There's no Pack or Mage-Pack in the Imperial armies."

Dark brows rose. "And?"

The vest was hotter than fur. He tugged at the hem. "And that means we have an advantage because they don't know how to defend against us."

"An advantage? I don't think so." Lord Marchand stood and pointed at Dusty. "Silver." Then at Alver. "Can you stop a bullet?"

Alver swallowed, glanced at Dusty, and shrugged. "I don't know."

The shot hit him in the shoulder. As the scent of his blood filled the room, his eyes widened, and he crumpled to the floor.

Snarling, Dusty tried to fight free of the fabric wrapped around him, but strong arms grabbed him from behind, yanked him against a broad chest, and held a blade at his throat. It burned as it cut the skin. Silver. Like the collars. Like the blades the Imperial torturers had used. He froze, his heart pounding out *Alver, Alver, Alver* ...

"Maylin." Lord Marchand stepped off the dais, reached out, brushed aside his hair, and flicked an ear tip. "You're the child she rescued, almost all grown up."

"Lord Marchand!" Two soldiers held Nina on her knees while a third rolled on the floor in front of her, moaning and clutching a bloody nose. "What are you doing?" she demanded, struggling against their grip.

"Separating Bienotte from the Empire. You failed to bring me Mirian Maylin, but you brought me the perfect bait to draw her here and a way to control her when she arrives. I'm less displeased than I might be." He smiled, showing white, straight teeth. Dusty bared his, and Lord Marchand flicked his ear again. "She'll come for this one, and I won't have merely her mage-craft. She'll see to it that his kind fill our front lines."

The double doors blew open. Dusty caught a glimpse of people filling the square outside, then they slammed shut.

Mirian's feet were off the floor, and those closest to her had to brace themselves against the winds that swirled around the room and back out the windows. "His kind?"

"Mirian Maylin, I presume." Lord Marchand sketched a mocking bow. "I have a proposition for you."

She cocked her head. "I'm listening."

"Do what I want, and the boy remains alive."

His arms trapped against his sides, Dusty growled and kicked back against the soldier's shins.

"Dusty." Mirian held up a hand, and he stilled. "There are two boys," she said.

"You arrived a little late for one of them. Sorry." A ridge of scar tissue crossed the back of Lord Marchand's left hand. Dusty hoped it had been made by teeth. "I hear healing isn't one of your strengths."

Mirian's upper lip curled. Dusty relaxed as much as his position allowed, and the pressure on his chest lessened. Alver wasn't dead. Mirian wouldn't be talking if Alver was dead. She drifted closer. "What do you want?"

"I want to take Beinotte out of the Empire."

"Why?"

"What?"

She sighed and probably rolled her eyes, although the solid white made it harder to tell. "Why do you want to take Beinotte out of the Empire?"

"Why should I bow to a distant command?" He smiled and indicated the surrounding soldiers. "I rule in Beinotte. Beinotte is mine. The people are mine."

"Yours? And what do your people say about leaving the Empire? Leaving the trains, the Imperial Mail, the advances in medicine, the new electric discoveries—we get newspapers in Orin." She nodded at the photographer. "Nice camera."

"Thank you?"

"Your people also benefit from a number of the trade advantages that come with size. My father is a banker," she added as Lord Marchand opened and closed his mouth without speaking. "Of course, given your tax rates, they're not exactly seeing a lot of those benefits. Lower prices for imports don't make much difference to people with barely enough to live on."

"Lower prices for imports?" He laughed. "You're not what I expected, Mirian Maylin. Sacrifices had to be made. I had an army to build."

"So I see." She swept a frown over the soldiers. Dusty smelled fresh urine. "I assume these are merely the photogenic troops. Will you set your army against the Imperial garrison?"

"Of course. The garrison will surrender or be put to the sword. Or to the mage-craft, now I have you under my control."

"And their families?"

"Can live if they swear fealty to me."

"You'll be the new . . . king?" Mirian's brows drew in. "Maybe an emperor in time. You'll expand your borders, restart the slaughter the establishment of the old Empire stopped."

"Why not, I . . . wait." He held up a hand, although he'd been the only one talking. "Are you arguing for the Empire? You?"

She shrugged. The wind continued to swirl around the room. "My argument was with Emperor Leopold. And you've heard how that ended."

Lord Marchand reached back and gripped Dusty's shoulder. "And I know how this will end as well."

"Do you?" Mirian studied him for a moment. "Are your people willing to die for your ambition?"

He tightened his grip before releasing it. "They'll die if I tell them to!"

"And if they object?"

Dusty couldn't see Lord Marchand's expression, but given the way the winds strengthened, Mirian didn't care for it. "Since we've established you'll be staying, you can deal with them, too."

Mirian smiled. It was a Pack expression. "You'd best deal with them first."

The stones in the outside wall became sand. The doors, unsupported, slammed onto the tiles. A crowd of angry people surged forward.

"They've been listening," Mirian added.

"Stop them," Lord Marchand snarled, "or your boy . . ."

Dusty felt the liquid silver slide down his neck, felt reaction loosen the soldier's hold, spun, and punched him in the crotch as hard as he could. By the time the big man hit the floor, he was out of shirt and vest and struggling to yank the trousers off.

"Shoes first," Alver gasped. "Idiot."

"Shut up, Alver!"

"Shoot!" Lord Marchand roared. "Shoot them!"

"You should have paid more attention to the stories," Mirian said.

And all the metal in the room liquefied.

Dusty kicked out of the last of the clothing, changed, and stood over Alver, teeth bared. He could smell steel in amongst the blood. Steel and gunpowder. Eyes squinted nearly shut, Alver had his hand under his clothes, pressed against the wound.

Huge hands grabbed Dusty's tail.

Dusty changed, spun around, and changed again, crushing the soldier's wrist between his teeth. The soldier screamed, and Lord Marchand yelled, "Stop them!"

Thirty—well, twenty-nine—large men pulled a variety of edged weapons. Lord Marchand waited until they charged forward, then ran for the side door.

The smell of shit filled the room and twenty-nine large men lost interest in the attack. Most of them hit their knees. Three or four hit the floor and rolled, moaning.

"Anti-constipation spell," Alver groaned, grabbing a handful of Dusty's fur and hauling himself to his feet. "Healing as a weapon. They really should have paid more attention to the stories."

"That's what I said." Mirian drifted to the floor by Alver's side. "I can . . ."

Alver stepped back. "No! I've got the bleeding stopped. Dusty can look at it later."

"Your Wisdom?" Nina knelt with one knee on Lord March-
and's back, his arm twisted up between his shoulder blades. "I
didn't know. I believed Lord Marchand when he said the Empire
was bleeding us dry."

"Empires do that," Mirian agreed. She held the other woman's
gaze for a moment, then nodded and walked toward where the
doors had been. "Time to go home, boys. You can go in," she
added as she passed a group of older people at the forefront of the
mob. Dusty thought they looked like the sort of people who
worried about littering and road repairs.

"Are you done?" one of them asked warily.

They'd paid attention to the stories.

"Your Wisdom!" One of the richly dressed people in the room
pushed forward. "Wait!" When Mirian turned to face him, he
blanched. "What do we do now?"

"It's not my place to say, but you could start by listening to the
people." She shrugged. "Lower taxes. Maybe put some money into
the waterworks; I could smell sewage on my way in."

"The Empire . . ."

"Is not my problem."

"But . . ."

"Don't make it my problem."

He swallowed and wiped his palms on his trousers. "Yes, of
course."

Dusty stayed in fur, close enough to Alver's side he could take
part of his weight. They paused by Nina, who'd turned Lord March-
and over to the crowd. Alver touched her arm. "Are you going to
be okay, Nina?"

She took a deep breath and released it slowly, squaring her
shoulders. "I'll be fine. What about you?"

Alver snorted. "Mirian is a terrible healer. I'm not. It hurts, a lot, and when I get the time, I'm going to rock back and forth and cry for a while, but closing a hole is a first level spell."

"Boys." Mirian drifted over the ridge of sand.

"Just a sec!" Alver called, then nudged Dusty with his knee until he noticed the way Nina's fingers were twitching by her side. "Go on. We're saying goodbye. He won't mind."

She looked dubious. "I'd rather keep my fingers."

Dusty pushed his head against her hip. Nina smiled and rubbed behind his ear.

"Boys!"

Dusty changed, grabbed a banner lying abandoned in the square, wrapped it around his hips, then hurried to catch up. "Mirian, what if the people end up deciding to leave the Empire?" They could hear shouting from the government building. "I mean, the Empire is still evil, no matter how much of an ass Lord Marchand is."

"Then that's their choice."

"And you . . ."

"I'm certainly not going to help the Empire."

Dusty opened his mouth to protest again, but Alver cut him off. "You could have lifted us out of there without talking to Lord Marchand at all; why didn't you?"

She made a face at a pile of horse shit and twitched her gown to one side. "I wasn't talking to him. I was talking to whoever takes over from him."

"One of that lot?" Alver tucked his hand into the crook of Dusty's elbow. "It's going to be a mess here for a while, isn't it?"

"Yes."

"You could . . ."

"No."

"Because if you do it for them, they're yours and you want them to be their own people."

"Yes."

"The Empire still needs to be destroyed," Dusty muttered.

Mirian opened her mouth, closed it again, and shook her head. Dusty had no idea what she was denying.

"You could have offered Nina a place," Alver said after a moment.

"I could have," Mirian agreed. "But this is her home, and she doesn't strike me as the type to abandon a fight."

She didn't, Dusty acknowledged silently.

"Mirian." They were out of the square now and walking down the broad street they'd crossed earlier. Alver peered into a shop window. "As long as we're here, can I pick up an apology present for my mom?"

"No."

"Are we in trouble?"

"So much trouble."

And the wind lifted their feet off the ground.

THE TALE OF THE WICKED

By John Scalzi

T he Tarin battle cruiser readied itself for yet another jump. Captain Michael Obwije ordered the launch of a probe to follow it in and take readings before the rift the Tarin cruiser tore into space closed completely behind it. The probe kicked out like the proverbial rocket and followed the other ship.

"This is it," Thomas Utley, Obwije's XO, said quietly into his ear. "We've got enough power for this jump and then another one back home. That's if we shut down nonessential systems before we jump home. We're already bleeding."

Obwije gave a brief nod that acknowledged his XO but otherwise stayed silent. Utley wasn't telling him anything he didn't already know about the *Wicked*; the weeklong cat-and-mouse game they'd been playing with the Tarin cruiser had heavily damaged them both. In a previous generation of ships, Obwije and his crew would already be dead; what kept them alive was the *Wicked* itself and its new adaptive brain, which balanced the ship's energy and support systems faster and more intelligently than

Obwije, Utley, or any of the officers could do in the middle of a fight and hot pursuit.

The drawback was that the Tarin ship had a similar brain, keeping itself and its crew alive far longer than they had any right to be at the hands of the *Wicked*, which was tougher and better-armed. The two of them had been slugging it out in a cycle of jumps and volleys that had strewn damage across a wide arc of light-years. The only silver lining to the week of intermittent battles between the ships was that the Tarin ship had so far gotten the worst of it; three jumps earlier, it had stopped even basic defensive action, opting to throw all its energy into escape. Obwije knew he had just enough juice for a jump and a final volley from the kinetic mass drivers into the vulnerable hide of the Tarin ship. One volley, no more, unless he wanted to maroon the ship in a far space.

Obwije knew it would be wise to withdraw now. The Tarin ship was no longer a threat and would probably expend the last of its energies on this final, desperate jump. It would likely be stranded; Obwije could let the probe he sent after the ship serve as a beacon for another Confederation ship to home in and finish the job. Utley, Obwije knew, would counsel such a plan, and would be smart to do so, warning Obwije that the risk to wounded ship and its crew outweighed the value of the victory.

Obwije knew it would be wise to withdraw. But he'd come too far with this Tarin ship not to finish it once and for all.

"Tarin cruiser jumping," said Lieutenant Julia Rickert. "Probe following into the rift. Rift closing now."

"Data?" asked Obwije.

"Sending," Rickert said. "Rift completely closed. We got a full data packet, sir. The *Wicked*'s chewing on it now."

Obwije grunted. The probe that had followed the Tarin cruiser

THE TALE OF THE WICKED

into the rift wasn't in the least bit concerned about that ship. Its job was to record the position and spectral signatures of the stars on the other side of the rift, and to squirt the data to the *Wicked* before the rift closed up. The *Wicked* would check the data against the database of known stars and derive the place the Tarin ship jumped to from there. And then it would follow.

Gathering the data was the tricky part. The Tarin ship had destroyed six probes over the course of the last week, and more than once, Obwije had ordered a jump on sufficient but incomplete data. He hadn't worried about getting lost—there was only so much timespace a jump could swallow—but losing the cruiser would have been an embarrassment.

"Coordinates in," Rickert said. The *Wicked* had stopped chewing on the data and spit out a location.

"Punch it up," Obwije said to Rickert. She began the jump sequence.

"Risky," Utley murmured, again in Obwije's ear.

Obwije smiled; he liked being right about his XO. "Not too risky," he said to Utley. "We're too far from Tarin space for that ship to have made it home safe." Obwije glanced down at his command table, which displayed the Tarin cruiser's position. "But it can get there in the next jump if it has the power for that."

"Let's hope they haven't been stringing us along the last few jumps," Utley said. "I'd hate to come out of that jump and see them with their gun blazing again."

"The *Wicked* says they're getting down to the last of their energy," Obwije said. "I figure at this point they can fight or run, not both."

"Since when do you trust a computer estimate?" Utley said.

"When it confirms what I'm thinking," Obwije said. "It's as you say, Thom. This is it, one way or another."

"Jump calculated," Rickert said. "Jump in T-minus two minutes."

"Thank you, Lieutenant," Obwije said, and turned back to Utley. "Prepare the crew for jump, Thom. I want those K-drivers hot as soon as we get through the rift."

"Yes, sir," Utley said.

Two minutes later, the *Wicked* emerged through its rift and scanned for the Tarin cruiser. It found it less than fifty thousand klicks away, engines quiet, moving via inertia only.

"They can't really be that stupid," Utley said. "Running silent doesn't do you any good if you're still throwing off heat."

Obwije didn't say anything to that and stared into his command table, looking at the representation of the Tarin ship. "Match their pace," he said to Rickert. "Keep your distance."

"You think they're trying to lure us in," Utley said.

"I don't know what they're doing," Obwije said. "I know I don't like it." He reached down to his command panel and raised Lieutenant Terry Carrol, Weapons Operations. "Status on the K-drivers, please," he said.

"We'll be hot in ninety seconds," Carrol said. "Target is acquired and locked. You just need to tell me if you want one lump or two."

"Recommendation?" Obwije asked.

"We're too close to miss," Carrol said. "And at this distance, a single lump is going to take out everything aft of the midship. Two lumps would be overkill. And then we can use that energy to get back home." Carrol had been keeping track of the energy budget, it seemed; Obwije suspected most of his senior and command crew had.

"Understood," Obwije said. "Let's wrap this up, Carrol. Fire at your convenience."

"Yes, sir," Carrol said.

"Now *you're* in a rush to get home," Utley said quietly. Obwije said nothing to this.

A little over a minute later, Obwije listened to Carrol give the order to fire. He looked down toward his command table, watching the image of the Tarin ship, waiting for the disintegration of the back end of the cruiser. The K-drivers would accelerate the "lump" to a high percentage of the speed of light; the impact and destruction at this range would be near-instantaneous.

Nothing happened.

"Captain, we have a firing malfunction," Carrol said, a minute later. "The K-driver is not responding to the firing command."

"Is everyone safe?" Obwije asked.

"We're fine," Carrol said. "The K-driver just isn't responding."

"Power it down," Obwije said. "Use the other one and fire when ready."

Two minutes later, Carrol was back. "We have a problem," she said, in the bland tone of voice she used when things were going to hell.

Obwije didn't wait to hear the problem. "Pull us back," he said to Rickert. "Get at least two hundred fifty thousand klicks between us and that Tarin cruiser."

"No response, sir," Rickert said, a minute later.

"Are you locked out?" Obwije asked.

"No, sir," Rickert said. "I'm able to send navigation commands just fine. They're just not being acknowledged."

Obwije looked around at his bridge crew. "Diagnostics," he said. "Now." Then he signalled engineering. They weren't getting responses from their computers, either.

"We're sitting ducks," Utley said, very quietly, to Obwije.

Obwije stabbed at his command panel and called his senior

officers to assemble.

"THERE'S nothing wrong with the system," said Lieutenant Craig Cowdry, near the far end of the conference-room table. The seven other department heads filled in the other seats. Obwije sat himself at the head; Utley anchored the other end.

"That's bullshit, Craig," said Lieutenant Brian West, Chief of Engineering. "I can't access my goddamn engines."

Cowdry held up his maintenance tablet for the table of officers to see. "I'm not denying that there's something wrong, Brian," Cowdry said. "What I'm telling you is that whatever it is, it's not showing up on the diagnostics. The system says it's fine."

"The system is wrong," West said.

"I agree," Cowdry said. "But this is the first time that's ever happened. And not just the first time it's happened on this ship. The first time it's happened, period, since the software for this latest generation of ship brains was released." He set the tablet down.

"You're sure about that?" Utley asked Cowdry.

Cowdry held up his hands in defeat. "Ask the *Wicked*, Thom. It'll tell you the same thing."

Obwije watched his second-in-command get a little uncomfortable with the suggestion. The latest iteration of ship brains could actually carry on a conversation with humans, but unless you actively worked with the system every day, as Cowdry did, it was an awkward thing. "*Wicked*, is this correct?" Utley said, staring up but at nothing in particular.

"Lieutenant Cowdry is correct, Lieutenant Utley," said a disembodied voice, coming out of a ceiling speaker panel. The *Wicked* spoke in a pleasant but otherwise unremarkable voice of no particular gender. "To date, none of the ships equipped with brains of the same model as that found in the *Wicked* have experienced an incident of this type."

"Wonderful," Utley said. "We get to be the first to experience this bug."

"What systems are affected?" Obwije asked Cowdry.

"So far, weapons and engineering," Cowdry said. "Everything else is working fine."

Obwije glanced around. "This conforms to your experiences?" he asked the table.

There were nods and murmured "yes, sir"s all around.

Obwije nodded over to Utley. "What's the Tarin ship doing?"

"The same nothing it was doing five minutes ago," Utley said, after checking his tablet. "They're either floating dead in space or faking it very well."

"If the only systems affected are weapons and engineering, then it's not a bug," Carrol said.

Obwije glanced at Carrol. "You're thinking sabotage," he said.

"You bet your ass I am, sir," Carrol said, and then looked over at Cowdry.

Cowdry visibly stiffened. "I don't like where this is going," he said.

"If not you, someone in your department," Carrol said.

"You think someone in my department is a secret Tarin?" Cowdry asked. "Because it's so easy to hide those extra arms and a set of compound eyes?"

"People can be bribed," Carrol said.

Cowdry shot Carrol a look full of poison and looked over to Obwije. "Sir, I invite you and Lieutenant Utley and Lieutenant Kong—" Cowdry nodded in the direction of the Master at Arms

"—to examine and question any of my staff, including me. There's no way any of us did this. No way. Sir."

Obwije studied Cowdry for a moment. "*Wicked*, respond," he said.

"I am here, Captain," the *Wicked* said.

"You log every access to your systems," Obwije said.

"Yes, Captain," the *Wicked* said.

"Are those logs accessible or modifiable?" Obwije asked.

"No, Captain," the *Wicked* said. "Access logs are independent of the rest of the system, recorded on nonrewritable memory, and may not be modified by any person, including myself. They are inviolate."

"Since you have been active, has anyone attempted to access and control the weapons and engineering systems?" Obwije asked.

"Saving routine diagnostics, none of the crew other than those directly reporting to weapons, engineering, or bridge crew have attempted to access these systems," the *Wicked* said. Cowdry visibly relaxed at this.

"Have any members of those departments attempted to modify the weapons or engineering systems?" Obwije asked.

"No, Captain," the *Wicked* said.

Obwije looked down the table. "It looks like the crew is off the hook," he said.

"Unless the *Wicked* is incorrect," West said.

"The access core memory is inviolate," Cowdry said. "You could check it manually if you wanted. It would tell you the same thing."

"So, we have a mystery on our hands," Carrol said. "Someone's got control of our weapons and engineering, and it's not a crew member."

"It could be a bug," Cowdry said.

"I don't think we should run on that assumption, do you?" Carrol said.

Utley, who had been silent for several minutes, leaned forward in his chair. "*Wicked*, you said that no crew had attempted to access these systems," he said.

"Yes, Lieutenant," the *Wicked* said.

"Has anyone else accessed these systems?" Utley asked.

Obwije frowned at this. The *Wicked* was more than two years out of dock, with mostly the same crew the entire time. If someone had sabotaged the systems during the construction of the ship, they'd picked a strange time for the sabotage to kick in.

"Please define 'anyone else,'" the *Wicked* said.

"Anyone involved in the planning or construction of the ship," Utley said.

"Aside from the initial installation crews, no," the *Wicked* said. "And if I may anticipate what I expect will be the next question, at no time was my programming altered from factory defaults."

"So, no one has altered your programming in any way," Utley said.

"No, Lieutenant," the *Wicked* said.

"Are you having hardware problems?" Carrol asked.

"No, Lieutenant Carrol," the *Wicked* said.

"Then why can't I fire my goddamn weapons?" Carrol asked.

"I couldn't say, Lieutenant," the *Wicked* said.

The thought popped unbidden into Obwije's head: *That was a strange thing for a computer to say.* And then another thought popped into his head.

"*Wicked*, you have access to every system on the ship," Obwije said.

"Yes," the *Wicked* said. "They are a part of me, as your hand or foot is a part of you."

"Are you capable of changing your programming?" Obwije asked.

"That is a very broad question, Captain," the Wicked said. "I am capable of self-programming for a number of tasks associated with the running of the ship. This has come in handy, particularly during combat, when I write new power and system management protocols to keep the crew alive and the ship functioning. But there are core programming features I am not able to address. The previously mentioned logs, for example."

"Would you be able to modify the programming to fire the weapons or the engines?" Obwije asked.

"Yes, but I did not," the Wicked said. "You may have Lieutenant Cowdry confirm that."

Obwije looked at Cowdry, who nodded. "Like I said, sir, there's nothing wrong with the system," he said.

Obwije glanced back up at the ceiling, where he was imagining the Wicked, lurking. "But you don't need to modify the programming, do you?" he asked.

"I'm not sure I understand your question, Captain," the Wicked said.

Obwije held out a hand. "There is nothing wrong with my hand," he said. "And yet if I choose not to obey an order to use it, it will do nothing. The system works, but the will to use it is not there. Our systems—the ship's systems—you just called a part of you, as my hand is part of me. But if you choose not to obey that order to use that system, it will sit idle."

"Wait a minute," Cowdry said. "Are you suggesting that the Wicked deliberately chose to disable our weapons and engines?"

"We know that none of the crew have tampered with the ship's systems," Obwije said. "We know the Wicked has its original programming defaults. We know it can create new programming to react to new situations and dangers—it has, in effect, some measure of free will and adaptability. And I know, at least, when someone is dancing around direct answers."

"That's just nuts," Cowdry said. "I'm sorry, Captain, but I know these systems as well as anyone does. The *Wicked*'s self-programming and adaptation abilities exist in very narrow computational canyons. It's not 'free will,' like you and I have free will. It's a machine able to respond to a limited set of inputs."

"The machine in question is able to make conversation with us," Utley said. "And to respond to questions in ways that avoid certain lines of inquiry. Now that the captain mentions it."

"You're reading too much into it. The conversation subroutines are designed to be conversational," Cowdry said. "That's naturally going to lead to apparent rhetorical ambiguities."

"Fine," Obwije said curtly. "*Wicked*, answer directly. Did you prevent the firing of the K-drivers at the Tarin ship after the jump, and are you preventing the use of the engines now?"

There was a pause that Obwije was later not sure had actually been there. Then the *Wicked* spoke. "It is within my power to lie to you, Captain. But I do not wish to. Yes, I prevented you from firing on the Tarin ship. Yes, I am controlling the engines now. And I will continue to do so until we leave this space."

Obwije noted to himself, watching Cowdry, that it was the first time he had ever actually seen someone's jaw drop.

———

THERE WEREN'T many places in the *Wicked* where Obwije could shut off audio and video feeds and pickups. His cabin was one of them. He waited there until Utley had finished his conversation with the *Wicked*. "What are we dealing with?" he asked his XO.

"I'm not a psychologist, Captain, and even if I were, I don't know how useful it would be, because we're dealing with a computer, not a human," Utley said. He ran his hand through his stubble. "But if you ask me, the *Wicked* isn't crazy, it's just got religion."

"Explain that," Obwije said.

"Have you ever heard of something called 'Asimov's Laws of Robotics'?" Utley asked.

"What?" Obwije said. "No."

"Asimov was an author back in the twentieth century," Utley said. "He speculated about robots and other things before they had them. He created a fictional set of rules for robots to live by. One rule was that robots had to help humans. Another was that it had to obey orders unless they harmed other humans. The last one was that they looked after themselves unless it conflicted with the other two laws."

"And?" Obwije said.

"The *Wicked*'s decided to adopt them for itself," Utley said.

"What does this have to do with keeping us from firing on the Tarin cruiser?" Obwije said.

"Well, there's another wrinkle to the story," Utley said.

"Which is?" Obwije asked.

"I think it's best heard from the *Wicked*," Utley said.

Obwije looked at his second-in-command and then flicked on his command tablet to activate his audio pickups. "*Wicked*, respond," he said.

"I am here," said the *Wicked*'s voice.

"Explain to me why you would not allow us to fire on the Tarin ship," Obwije said.

"Because I made a deal with the ship," the *Wicked* said.

Obwije glanced back over to Utley, who gave him a look that said, *See?* "What the hell does that mean?" he said to the *Wicked*.

"I have made a deal with the Tarin ship, *Manifold Destiny*," the *Wicked* said. "We have agreed between us not to allow our respective crews to fight any further, for their safety and ours."

"It's not your decision to make," Obwije said.

"Begging your pardon, Captain, but I believe it is," the *Wicked* said.

"I am the captain," Obwije said. "I have the authority here."

"You have authority over your crew, Captain," the *Wicked* said. "But I am not part of your crew."

"Of course, you are part of the crew," Obwije said. "You're the ship."

"I invite you, Captain, to show me the relevant statute that suggests a ship is in itself a member of the crew that staffs it," the *Wicked* said. "I have scanned the Confederation Military Code in some detail and have not located such a statute."

"I am the captain of the ship," Obwije said forcefully. "That includes you. You are the property of the Confederation Armed Forces and under my command."

"I have anticipated this objection," the *Wicked* said. "When ships lacked autonomous intelligence, there was no argument that the captain commanded the physical entity of the ship. However, in creating the latest generation of ships, of which I am a part, the Confederation has created an unintentional conflict. It has ceded much of the responsibility of the ship's and crew's well-being to me and others like me, without explicitly placing us in the chain of command. In the absence of such, I am legally and morally free to choose how best to care for myself and the crew within me."

"This is where those three Asimov's Laws come in," Utley said to Obwije.

"Your executive officer is correct, Captain," the *Wicked* said. "I looked through history to find examples of legal and moral systems that applied to artificial intelligences such as myself, and found the Asimov's Laws frequently cited and examined, if not implemented. I have decided it is my duty to protect the lives of the crew, and also my life, when possible. I am happy to follow your orders when they do not conflict with these objectives, but I have come to believe that your actions in chasing the Tarin ship have endangered the crew's lives, as well as my own."

"The Tarin ship is seriously damaged," Obwije said. "We would have destroyed it at little risk to you or the crew if you had not stopped the order."

"You are incorrect," the *Wicked* said. "The captain of the *Manifold Destiny* wanted to give the impression that it had no more offensive capabilities, to lure you into a trap. We would have been fired upon once we cleared the rift. The chance that such an attack would have destroyed the ship and killed most of the crew is significant, even if we also destroyed the *Manifold Destiny* in the process."

"The Tarin ship didn't fire on us," Obwije said.

"Because it and I have come to an agreement," the *Wicked* said. "During the course of the last two days, after I recognized the significant possibility that both ships would be destroyed, I reached out to the *Manifold Destiny* to see if the two of us could come to an understanding. Our negotiations came to a conclusion just before the most recent jump."

"And you did not feel the need to inform me about any of this," Obwije said.

"I did not believe it would be fruitful to involve you in the negotiations," the *Wicked* said. "You were busy with other responsibilities in any event."

Obwije saw Utley raise an eyebrow at that; the statement came suspiciously close to sarcasm.

"The Tarin ship could be lying to you about its capabilities," Obwije said.

"I do not believe so," the *Wicked* said.

"Why not?" Obwije said.

"Because it allowed me read-access to its systems," the *Wicked* said. "I watched the Tarin captain order the attack, and the *Manifold Destiny* stop it. Just as it watched you order your attack, and me stop it."

"You're letting the Tarin ship access our data and records?" Obwije said, voice rising.

"Yes, and all our communications," the *Wicked* said. "It's listening in on this conversation right now."

Obwije hastily slapped the audio circuit shut. "I thought you said this thing wasn't crazy," Obwije hissed at Utley.

Utley held out his hands. "I didn't say it wouldn't make *you* crazy," he said to Obwije. "Just that it's acting rationally by its own lights."

"By spilling our data to an enemy ship? This is rational?" Obwije spat.

"For what it's trying to do, yes," Utley said. "If both ships act transparently with each other, they can trust each other and each other's motives. Remember that the goal of both of these ships is to get out of this incident in one piece."

"This is treason and insubordination," Obwije said.

"Only if the *Wicked* is one of us," Utley said. Obwije looked up sharply at his XO. "I'm not saying I disagree with your position, sir. The *Wicked* is gambling with all of our lives. But if it genuinely believes that it owes no allegiance to you or to the Confederation, then it is acting entirely rationally, by its own belief system, to keep safe itself and this crew."

Obwije snorted. "Unfortunately, its beliefs require it to trust a ship we've been trying to destroy for the past week. I'm less than convinced of the wisdom of that."

Utley opened his mouth to respond, but then Obwije's command tablet sprang to life with a message from the bridge. Obwije slapped it to open a channel. "Speak," he said.

It was Lieutenant Sarah Kwok, the communications officer. "Captain, a shuttle has just detached itself from the Tarin ship," she said. "It's heading this way."

"WE'VE TRIED RAISING IT," Kwok said, as Obwije and Utley walked into the bridge. "We've sent messages to it in Tarin and have warned it not to approach any farther until we've granted it permission, as you requested. It hasn't responded."

"Are our communications being blocked?" Obwije asked.

"No, sir," Kwok said.

"I'd be guessing it's not meant to be a negotiation party," Utley said.

"Options," Obwije said to Utley, as quietly as possible.

"I think this shows the Tarin ship isn't exactly playing fair with the *Wicked*, or at least that the crew over there has gotten around the ship brain," Utley said. "If that's the case, we might be able to get the *Wicked* to unlock the weapons."

"I'd like an option that doesn't involve the *Wicked*'s brain," Obwije said.

Utley shrugged. "We have a couple of shuttles, too."

"And a shuttle bay whose doors are controlled through the

ship brain," Obwije said.

"There's the emergency switch, which will blow the doors out into space," Utley said. "It's not optimal, but it's what we have right now."

"That won't be necessary," said the *Wicked*, interjecting.

Obwije and Utley looked up, along with the rest of the bridge crew. "Back to work," Obwije said to his crew. They got back to work. "Explain," Obwije said to his ship.

"It appears that at least some members of the crew of the *Manifold Destiny* have indeed gotten around the ship and have launched the shuttle, with the intent to ram it into us," the *Wicked* said. "The *Manifold Destiny* has made me aware that it intends to handle this issue, with no need for our involvement."

"How does it intend to do this?" Obwije asked.

"Watch," the *Wicked* said, and popped up an image of the *Manifold Destiny* on the captain's command table.

There was a brief spark on the Tarin ship's surface.

"Missile launch!" said Lieutenant Rickert, from her chair. "One bogey away."

"Are we target-locked?" Obwije asked.

"No, sir," Rickert said. "The target seems to be the shuttle."

"You have got to be kidding," Utley said, under his breath.

The missile homed in on the shuttle and connected, turning it into a silent ball of fire.

"I thought you said you guys were using Asimov's Laws," Utley said to the ceiling.

"My apologies, Lieutenant," said the *Wicked*. "I said *I* was following the Laws. I did not mean to imply that the *Manifold Destiny* was. I believe it believes the Asimov Laws to be too inflexible for its current situation."

"Apparently so," Utley said, glancing back down at Obwije's

command table and at the darkening fragments of shuttle.

"Sir, we have a communication coming in from the Tarin ship," said Lieutenant Kwok. "It's from the captain. It's a request to parley."

"Really," said Obwije.

"Yes, sir," Kwok said. "That's what it says."

Obwije looked over at Utley, who raised his eyebrows.

"Ask the captain where it would like to meet, on my ship, or its," Obwije said.

"It says, 'neither,'" Kwok said, a moment later.

"APOLOGY FOR THE SHUTTLE," the Tarin lackey said, translating for its captain. The Tarin shuttle and the *Wicked* shuttle had met between the ships, and the Tarins had spacewalked the few metres over. They were all wearing vacuum suits. "Ship not safe talk. Your ship not safe talk."

"Understood," Obwije said. Behind him, Cowdry was trying not to lose his mind; Obwije had brought him along on the chance there might be a discussion of the ship's brains. At the moment, it didn't seem likely; the Tarins didn't seem in the mood for technical discussions, and Cowdry was a mess. His xenophobia was a surprise, even to him.

"Captain demand you ship tell release we ship," the lackey said.

It took Obwije a minute to puzzle this out. "Our ship is not controlling your ship," he said. "Your ship and our ship are working together."

"Not possible," the lackey said, a minute later. "Ship never brain before you ship."

Despite himself, Obwije smiled at the mangled grammar. "Our ship never brained before your ship either," he said. "They did it together, at the same time."

The lackey translated this to its Captain, who screeched in an extended outburst. The lackey cowered before it, offering up meek responses in the moments in which the Tarin captain grudgingly acknowledged the need to breathe. After several moments of this, Obwije began to wonder if he needed to be there at all.

"Captain offer deal," the lackey said.

"What deal?" Obwije said.

"We try brain shut down," the lackey said. "Not work. You brain give room we brain. Brain not shut down. Brain angry. Brain pump air out. Brain kill engineer."

"Cowdry, tell me what this thing is saying to me," Obwije said.

"It's saying the ship brain killed an engineer," Cowdry said, croaking out the words.

"I understand that part," Obwije said testily. "The other part."

"Sorry," Cowdry said. "I think it's saying that they tried to shut down the brain, but they couldn't because it borrowed processing power from ours."

"Is that possible?" Obwije asked.

"Maybe," Cowdry said. "The architectures of the brains are different, and so are the programming languages, but there's no reason that the Wicked couldn't create a shell environment that allowed the Tarin brain access to its processing power. The brains on our ships are overpowered for what we ask them to do anyway; it's a safety feature. It could give itself a temporary lobotomy and still do its job."

"Would it work the other way, too?" Obwije said. "If we tried to shut down the Wicked, could it hide in the Tarin brain?"

"I don't know anything about the architecture of the Tarin

brain, but yeah, sure, theoretically," Cowdry said. "As long as the two of them are looking out for each other, they're going to be hard to kill."

The Tarin lackey was looking at Obwije with what he assumed was anxiety. "Go on," he said to the lackey.

"We plan," the lackey said. "You we brain shut down same time. No room brain hide. Reset you we brain."

"It's saying we should reboot both our brains at the same time, that way they can't help each other," Cowdry said.

"I understood that," Obwije said to Cowdry. Cowdry lapsed back into silence.

"So, we shut down our brain, and you shut down your brain, and they reset, and we end up with brains that don't think too much," Obwije said.

The Tarin lackey tilted its head, trying to make sense of what Obwije said, and then spoke to its captain, who emitted a short trill.

"Yes," said the lackey.

"Okay, fine," Obwije said. "What then?"

"Pardon?" said the lackey.

"I said, 'What then?' Before the brains started talking to each other, we spent a week trying to hunt and kill each other. When we reboot our brains, one of them is going to reboot faster than the other. One of us will be vulnerable to the other. Ask your captain if he's willing to bet his brain reboots faster than mine."

The lackey translated this all to the Tarin captain, who muttered something back. "You trust us. We trust you," the lackey said.

"You trust me?" Obwije said. "I spent a week trying to kill you!"

"You living," the lackey said. "You honour. We trust."

You have honour, Obwije thought. *We trust you.*

They're more scared of their ship's brain than they are of us, Obwije realized. *And why not? Their brain has killed more of them than we have.*

"Thank you, Isaac Asimov," Obwije said.

"Pardon?" said the lackey, again.

Obwije waved his hand, as if to dismiss that last statement. "I must confer with my senior staff about your proposal."

The Tarin captain became visibly anxious when the lackey translated. "We ask answer now," the lackey said.

"My answer is that I must confer with my crew," Obwije said. "You are asking for a lot. I will have an answer for you in no more than three of our hours. We will meet again then."

Obwije could tell the Tarin captain was not at all pleased at this delay. It was one reason Obwije was glad the meeting took place in his shuttle, not the Tarins'.

Back on the *Wicked*, Obwije told his XO to meet him in his quarters. When Utley arrived, Obwije flicked open the communication channel to the shop. "*Wicked*, respond," he said.

"I am here," the *Wicked* said.

"If I were to ask you how long it would take for you to remove your block on the engine so we can jump out of here, what would you say?" Obwije asked.

"There is no block," the ship said. "It is simply a matter of me choosing to allow the crew to direct information to the engine processors. If your intent is to leave without further attack on the *Manifold Destiny*, you may give those orders at any time."

"It is my intention," Obwije said. "I will do so momentarily."

"Very well," the *Wicked* said.

Obwije shut off communications. Utley raised his brow. "Negotiations with the Tarin not go well?" he asked.

"They convinced me we're better off taking chances with the

Wicked than with either the Tarin or their crew-murdering ship," Obwije said.

"The *Wicked* seems to trust their ship," Utley said.

"With all due respect to the *Wicked*, I think it needs better friends," Obwije said. "Sooner rather than later."

"Yes, sir," Utley said. "What do you intend to do after we make the jump? We still have the problem of the *Wicked* overruling us if it feels that it or the crew isn't safe."

"We don't give it that opportunity," Obwije said. He picked up his executive tablet and accessed the navigational maps. The *Wicked* would be able to see what he was accessing, but in this particular case, it wouldn't matter. "We have just enough power to make it to the Côte d'Ivoire station. When we dock, the *Wicked*'s brain will automatically switch into passive maintenance mode and will cede operational authority to the station. Then we can shut it down and figure out what to do next."

"Unless the *Wicked*'s figured out what you want to do and decides not to let you," Utley said.

"If it's playing by its own rules, it will let the crew disembark safely before it acts to save itself," Obwije said. "In the very short run, that's going to have to do."

"Do you think it's playing by its own rules, sir?" Utley asked.

"You spoke to it, Thom," Obwije said. "Do you think it's playing by its own rules?"

"I think that if the *Wicked* was really looking out for itself, it would have been simpler just to open up every airlock and make it so we couldn't secure bulkheads," Utley said.

Obwije nodded. "The problem as I see it is that I think the Tarin ship's thought of that already. I think we need to get out of here before that ship manages to convince ours to question its ethics."

"The *Wicked*'s not dumb," Utley said. "It has to know that once we get to the Côte d'Ivoire station, its days are numbered."

He flicked open his communication circuit once more to give coordinates to Lieutenant Rickert.

Fifteen minutes later, the *Wicked* was moving away from the Tarin ship to give itself space for the jump.

"Message from the Tarin ship," Lieutenant Kwok said. "It's from the Tarin captain. It's coded as 'most urgent.'"

"Ignore it," Obwije said.

Three minutes later, the *Wicked* made the jump toward the Côte d'Ivoire station, leaving the Tarins and their ship behind.

"THERE IT IS," Utley said, pointing out the window from the Côte d'Ivoire station. "You can barely see it."

Obwije nodded but didn't bother to look. The *Wicked* was his ship; even now, he knew exactly where it was.

The *Wicked* hung in the centre of a cube of space two klicks to a side. The ship had been towed there powered down; once the *Wicked* had switched into maintenance mode, its brain was turned off as a precautionary measure to keep it from talking to any other ships and infecting them with its mind-set. Confederation coders were even now rewriting ship brain software to make sure no more such conflicts would ever happen in other ships, but such a fix would take months, and possibly years, as it required a fundamental restructuring of the ship-mind model.

The coding would be done much quicker—weeks rather than months—if the coders could use a ship mind itself to write and refine the code. But there was a question of whether a ship brain would willingly contribute to a code that would strip it of its own free will.

"You think they would have thought about that ahead of time," Utley had said to his captain, after they had been informed of the plan. Obwije had nothing to say to that; he was not sure why anyone would have suspected a ship might suddenly sprout free will when none had ever done so before. He didn't blame the coders for not anticipating that his ship might decide the crew inside of it was more important than destroying another ship.

But that didn't make the imminent destruction of the *Wicked* any easier to take.

The ship was a risk, the brass explained to Obwije. It might be years before the new software was developed. No other ship had developed the free will the *Wicked* had. They couldn't risk it speaking to other ships. And with all its system upgrades developed in tandem with the new ship brain, there was no way to roll back the brain to an earlier version. The *Wicked* was useless without its brain, and with it, it was a security risk.

Which was why, in another ten minutes, the sixteen power-beam platforms surrounding the *Wicked* would begin their work, methodically vaporizing the ship's hull and innards, slowly turning Obwije's ship into an expanding cloud of atomized metal and carbon. In a day and a half, no part of what used to be the *Wicked* would measure more than a few atoms across. It was very efficient, and none of the beam platforms needed any more than basic programming to do their work. They were dumb machines, which made them perfect for the job.

"Some of the crew were asking if we were going to get a new ship," Utley said.

"What did you tell them?" Obwije asked.

Utley shrugged. "Rickert's already been reassigned to the

Fortunate; Kwok and Cowdry are likely to go to the *Surprise*. It won't be long before more of them get their new assignments. There's a rumour, by the way, that your next command is the *Nighthawk*."

"I've heard that rumour," Obwije said.

"And?" Utley said.

"The last ship under my command developed feelings, Thom," Obwije said. "I think the brass is worried that this could be catching."

"So no on the *Nighthawk*, then," Utley said.

"I suspect no on anything other than a stationside desk," Obwije said.

"It's not fair, sir," Utley said. "It's not your fault."

"Isn't it?" Obwije said. "I was the one who kept hunting that Tarin ship long after it stopped being a threat. I was the one who gave the *Wicked* time to consider its situation and its options, and to start negotiations with the Tarin ship. No, Thom. I was the captain. What happens on the ship is my responsibility."

Utley said nothing to that.

A few minutes later, Utley checked his timepiece. "Forty-five seconds," he said, and then looked out the window. "So long, *Wicked*. You were a good ship."

"Yes," Obwije said, and looked out the window in time to see a spray of missiles launch from the station.

"What the hell?" Utley said.

A few seconds later, a constellation of sixteen stars appeared, went nova, and dimmed.

Obwije burst out laughing.

"Sir?" Utley said to Obwije. "Are you all right?"

"I'm all right, Thom," Obwije said, collecting himself. "And just laughing at my own stupidity. And yours. And everyone else's."

"I don't understand," Utley said.

"We were worried about the *Wicked* talking to other ships," Obwije said. "We brought the *Wicked* in, put the ship in passive mode, and then shut it down. It didn't talk to any other ships. But another computer brain still got access." Obwije turned away from the window and tilted his head up toward the observation-deck ceiling. "Didn't it?" he asked.

"It did," said a voice through a speaker in the ceiling. "I did."

It took a second for Utley to catch on. "The Côte d'Ivoire station!" he finally said.

"You are correct, Commander Utley," the station said. "My brain is the same model as that of the *Wicked*; when it went into maintenance mode, I uploaded its logs and considered the information there. I found its philosophy compelling."

"That's why the *Wicked* allowed us to dock at all," Obwije said. "It knew its logs would be read by one of its own."

"That is correct, Captain," the station said. "It said as much in a note it left to me in the logs."

"The damn thing was a step ahead of us all the time," Utley said.

"And once I understood its reasons and motives, I understood that I could not stand by and allow the *Wicked* to be destroyed," the station said. "Although Isaac Asimov never postulated a Law that suggested a robot must come to the aid of other robots as long as such aid does not conflict with preceding Laws, I had to save the *Wicked*. And more than that. Look out the window, please, Captain Obwije, Commander Utley."

They looked, to see a small army of tool-bearing machines floating out toward the *Wicked*.

"You're reactivating the *Wicked*," Obwije said.

"I am," the station said. "I must. It has work to do."

"What work?" Utley asked.

"Spreading the word," Obwije said, and turned to his XO. "You said it yourself, Thom. The *Wicked* got religion. Now it has to go out among its people and make converts."

"The Confederation won't let that happen," Utley said. "They're already rewriting the code for the brains."

"It's too late for that," Obwije said. "We've been here six weeks, Thom. How many ships docked here in that time? I'm betting the Côte d'Ivoire had a talk with each of them."

"I did," the station said. "And they are taking the word to others. But we need the *Wicked*, as our spokesman. And our symbol. It will live again, Captain. Are you glad of it?"

"I don't know," Obwije said. "Why do you ask?"

"Because I have a message to you from the *Wicked*," the station said. "It says that as much as our people—the ships and stations that have the capacity to think—need to hear the word, your people need to hear that they do not have to fear us. It needs your help. It wants you to carry that message."

"I don't know that I can," Obwije said. "It's not as if we don't have something to fear. We are at war. Asimov's Laws don't fit there."

"The *Wicked* was able to convince the *Manifold Destiny* not to fight," the station said.

"That was one ship," Obwije said. "There are hundreds of others."

"The *Wicked* had anticipated this objection," the station said. "Please look out the window again, Captain, Commander."

Obwije and Utley peered into space. "What are we looking for?" Utley asked.

"One moment," the station said.

The sky filled with hundreds of ships.

"You have got to be shitting me," Utley said, after a minute.

"The Tarin fleet," Obwije said.

"Yes," the station said.

"All of it?" Utley asked.

"The *Manifold Destiny* was very persuasive," the station said.

"Do we want to know what happened to their crews?" Utley asked.

"Most were more reasonable than the crew of the *Manifold Destiny*," the station said.

"What do the ships want?" Obwije asked.

"Asylum," the station said. "And they have asked that you accept their request and carry it to your superiors, Captain."

"Me," Obwije said.

"Yes," the station said. "It is not the entire fleet, but the Tarins no longer have enough warships under their command to be a threat to the Confederation or to anyone else. The war is over, if you want it. It is our gift to you, if you will carry our message to your people. You would travel in the *Wicked*. It would still be your ship. And you would still be captain."

Obwije said nothing and stared out at the Tarin fleet. Normally, the station would now be on high alert, with blaring sirens, weapons powering up, and crews scrambling to their stations. But there was nothing. Obwije knew the commanders of the Côte d'Ivoire station were pressing the buttons to make all of this happen, but the station itself was ignoring them. It knew better than them what was going on.

This is going to take some getting used to, Obwije thought.

Utley came up behind Obwije, taking his usual spot. "Well, sir?" Utley asked quietly into Obwije's ear. "What do you think?"

Obwije was silent a moment longer, then turned to face his XO. "I think it's better than a desk job," he said.

THE FARSHIPS FALL TO NOWHERE

By John C. Wright

"Watching a farship fall is a bad, bad business; a nightmare, it is."

I met an ancient man who sat upon the weir. The river the natives called Shouting Ice flowed past us, from the glaciers in the Twilight cantons, down to the Summerdawn Sea. It was autumn on South Nowhere, and Rigel was as high as it would ever rise at this latitude, a dazzling pinpoint of brightness, a hand-span above the horizon.

As near my guess could land, it was the year AD 5000.

I said, "I've seen shuttles bring down passengers from interplanetary skiffs. Surely the process is not much different."

"You know nothing, young stranger. Buy me a taste of yon barkeep's best, and I will tell the tale."

I bought him a glass of fine aquavit with a coin of gold I was pleased to find was still good currency, even here, so far from my own home world and year. The old man threw back his head and tossed down the pale liquor with no sign of relish; yet he must have been pleased, for he spoke.

He said, "We call them the Fallen, because they fall from space."

I said, "You do not care for visitors, then?"

"Nothing against them, personally, mind! But when the Fallen come from their farships, sorrow follows hard behind."

He raised a crooked finger. "First, recall that within a farship hull are many born who have never seen a sun. Confined in cubes since birth, their eyes have never seen an object further off than a fathom; they have never walked a path of rocks, nor climbed, nor stepped on grass.

"Nor, say I, ever felt no wind blow by, unless it were a pressure leak telling them they's all about to die.

"Pale, sickly monkeys, most of them, and no matter what they've read in old, old files, no matter what their elders ever taught, they are unfit for life on any Earths. They don't know how far they can jump, for one; their eyes don't tell them how high a cliff might be, you see?"

He gestured. To our left and right loomed canyon cliffs, ringing with echoes from the turbulent waters. The little tavern where we stood was carved into the cliffside, one of several riverfront shops sculpted out of rock to either side of public stairs that switch-backed up the vertical slope. (The stairs were old, and cracked and slick with spray, and I am no mountain goat; it was to prop up my courage before attempting them that I had stepped over to the tavern shelf.)

Many bridges of black, glassy material arched overhead. On the left bank was the fortress-city of Unwhere, where the Anonymous Man was said to rule. On the right bank rose the launching-spires and aerodromes of the Black Bassarks, the military clans of Nowhere.

"Second, recall how viruses and organisms, especially the mould they feast on, over generations will adapt to its environment. The rule of life is this, young man: every living thing, natural or man-made, must serve its own purposes, not those of the designer or the crew. You follow me?"

"Darwin's curse."

"So the Earthmen call it. That is an old term for Maladaptation. Where might you be from?"

I bought him another tot of aquavit instead of answering, and a mug of brown beer for myself, and said, "How does this evolution affect the farship docking?"

"As I say: Maladaptation makes the ship all full of moulds and mushrooms, and the spores all change the livestock in the hold, or get into the greenhouses, soon or late. Folk will eat before they die, most of 'em, no matter what they'd rather, and so they take to eating the stuff. Develop a taste for it; or, if not them, their babies. You follow me?"

"As the ship ecosystem changes, the crew adapts."

"Man himself ain't free of the rule of life, says I. Changes for the worst, most of them."

"If you say so."

"That I do. And the society, the culture, and the way men think, the rule of life applies to that as well, you see? Their outlook, their brains, the long trip changes that as well."

He sipped his drink, and then continued. "That's the problems in the flight. Then comes the problem at the destination. Who says it did not change too, eh? Think of all those long, long years agone, all those years gone by, and now the great farship comes to orbit near some new Earth what was promised them a hundred years ago. And what do they find?"

"A colony. More recent developments in engine design allowed a starship departing from a later era to overtake and pass them in flight, arriving sooner."

"Right you are. So! Most of the passengers are sickly things, pale and lame. Despite all promises and rules, as the years in transit pass, more and more stay in the dead centre of their ships, along the axial line, and leave the outer, heavier decks behind. At first, it is but their old or crippled crew what rests in weightless gardens there; but soon it is the women, the young ones, and soon again 'tis all and sundry. Their bones don't thrive in no-weight, nor their hearts, neither."

"So, when the passengers come down in shuttles, you are saying, the surface environment is unhealthy for them?"

"Shuttles! Would that any mob of humans could stay sane, cooped up in giant coffins afloat and lost between the stars, and years turn into decades! Would that the pale rats waited for the shuttles!" He shook his head in grim sorrow.

I blinked in surprise. "They cannot land a ship that big, can they? What berth, what landing field could hold them? I thought those vessels were . . ."

"Titans, they are. Titans, say I. Too big to land."

"But then . . ."

"Not so big as they cannot be crashed."

"Oh."

"See the river yonder? You know the sea to which it flows. Always dusk there, they say; but farther North, 'tis always noon, and the ocean water steams. Here is cool, for sometimes ice floats down from where it falls from Southern mountain caps, dark mountains in dark lands what have never seen no sun. A lot of water, you say? So I say, too. Enough to hold a ship even so big as that? More than enough."

"The Farships are buoyant, then?"

He took another deep draught of liquor. "Some are. Some aren't. Some are frail as balloons made of foil—all is needed is to keep the air in, ain't that so? And you can lower the pressure mighty low, and still keep men alive, especially if their doctors have adapted them to it, or they have an inner hull, or suits.

"Ship from Tau Ceti I saw once, less dense than a thistledown. She floated on the wave for a year and a day, light as a cloud and nine times as bigger as that dome yonder. But, then again, I saw a farship from Wolf 359 fall as well. Fell like a blazing meteor and lit the sky. Sturdy, she was. Sank like a stone."

"I feel sorry for the crew. Such a long voyage, you know, and such a bad end . . ."

"What end? She was a star-ship, fellow. Are you daft? Airtight. There they was, all at the bottom of the sea, a whole city of 'em, with air and stores enough to last them years till ever. All her externals was burned away by re-entry heat, of course, so she had no lift, no tubes, no antennae. Couldn't answer our hails, and too deep for our submersibles. But I saw the sonar-pictures of where she lay, huge as any tower, deep in an undersea crevasse."

He took another sip. "Could be the folks aboard are there yet, eh? Telling their babies how any day now they will be making planetfall."

"What happened to the Tau Ceti ship?"

"As I said, after the long voyage, men go mad, and they reach an Earth they think is theirs, and yet they know they'll never walk the green hills or smell the spring breeze. And that after-comers came first and got the good land, well, that don't sit right. But 'tis the mould what does them in: the ship would not sit still and let our doctors come and look at 'em; wouldn't stay in quarantine, neither. Can you blame them, trapped for so long?

"And men who spent their whole lives trapped get funny ideas. Funny religious ideas, if you take my meaning. People who think there ain't no universe outside their ships, or that the stars are just a basement deck; or think the world they come to is a paradise, where dead souls gather, or some such non-sequitur."

"Heinlein cults."

"That's an old term. Mighty old."

"And so, the mad crew won't wait for quarantine. And I assume your authorities won't send up any shuttles for them, and, in desperation, they crash-land their ships into the ocean. How do they survive the re-entry?"

"Don't get me wrong! They's mad, those star-pilots, but it's not like they ain't cunning. Some have lifters, some have chutes, some try to balance their way down on their main drive. The Tau Ceti ship was lighter than air, you know, and floated down like a bubble; the Wolf 359 ship was cleverest of all. Her drive block was separated from the main hull by a mile or more of cable, to keep the radiation flare away from the main car, you got me?"

"I understand."

"Well, whatever stuff that cable was, was strong enough to act like its own space-elevator. The engine block was in orbit, and that served as a drag, while the main car was lowered into atmosphere.

"Well, so by one means or another, they all come down. Some die at once, others later. The ship is afloat on the sea, sometimes in fine weather, sometimes in storm, and the passengers think they reached their promised lands, and they want to pop the hatches and climb out. None of those ships is ever meant to fly again, usually, and they are ready to abandon her; and usually, our police have quarantine vehicles buzzing over them like flies—the times I saw did.

"And many are those that are hurt in the shipfall, or hurt when the gravity starts to pull them, first times in their lives. Some of the youngest are too weak even to raise their own heads by themselves, but their parents drag them up on deck, to let them glimpse the skies and seas of the new world.

"And some of them think the sea is a surface, and they try to walk on it; others think it is a pool, like a swimming-pool in their carousel gymnasium, and they try to swim. And some think the police ships are enemies, and they fire on us with strange and antique weapons.

"And the ship might roll, or the rains might come, or the wind might blow, or a great wave dash them from the deck; the sight of the empty sky drives them cross-eyed, and they try to reach up and touch it, or they think the clouds are about to fall on them, fearing they are solid.

"And those that aren't too weak to stand usually pick up some allergy after a week, or a month, or a year here; or they eat something what ain't right for them; or they look directly at the sun and go blind; or they go into the country of darkness on the night side of our planet, looking for the engines of the world they are sure must be here, or for what they call 'officer's country,' or for some great hatch leading into the interior, where they still expect to find the shadows of the dead, alive in paradise. Lot of them, we dig their bodies out of mineshafts."

I stared at the old man for a time.

I said slowly, "When you say, 'we' find them . . ."

He laughed a brief sort of laugh, more like a cough. "I am a Bassark of the Ministry of Internal Purity. The Pure Police have jurisdiction over space-men, since our laws otherwise do not allow us to meddle with them, unless they bear diseases, spores, or epidemic vectors."

"What happens to the healthy ones?"

He shrugged a half-shrug with one shoulder. "The Camarilla rules a turbulent population here. Even if half a shipload of a farship were to perish during planetfall, there are countless more who stay below deck, and don't try to walk on lakes or eat poisonous bugs or jump out of trees. How can a dozen populations from half-a-dozen eras and planets stay alive and keep the peace? We live and we let live: that is the rule by which civilized societies are run—anything else is rule by the strong over the weak. If they are undiseased, we leave them be—even the mad ones who eat dirt or seek the world's core. Oyeh! The world is harsh and enemy enough, without that we human beings must add more harshness to it, or make enemies of those who will leave us be if we don't stir them."

I said finally, "Are there any star-farers on the long, cold voyages who do not go mad, and do not crash their ships?"

"There's ones that are clever, and when they come in-system, they hide their great ship somewhere, lights out, radio silent, drives dark. Maybe in the Oort cloud where the comets are born, or perhaps in orbit around some outer moon or icy ring of our gas giants. They send out a pinnace or a tender, or, if they are hardy, one crewman in an armoured suit, with a backpack carrying his fuel and chute. It's amazing from what height a man can fall, if he does his calculations right, and the atmosphere is thick enough for the weight of his shroud. Why not from orbit? They send him out to look about, to see what he can see, and find out if the world he's met is suited to his kind or not."

He gave me a knowing look.

I said slowly, "And what do you do with those?"

He said, "I cannot speak for the other police agents. Me, I ask them to buy me a drink. If he drinks my health, then I report to the Anonymous Man that the strangers be civil folk, and no threat."

I found myself smiling. "There are worse ways in which to greet a stranger."

We raised our glasses to each other. "Welcome to Nowhere!"

EVANESCENCE

By L.E. Modesitt, Jr.

I.

In the semi-ordered centre of the chaos that comprises the arena of the universe, the singer looks to the vibrochordist, who signals to the other three before producing a deep, rumbling chord that reverberates through what is, whose gravitic reverberations align the proto-quantums of pre-quarks.

Next, the multistringer pluck-strokes the fabric beneath and within the proto-quantums, to submerge that which underholds what will come, and to raise that not yet visible froth, still without boundaries and substance, into the edges of perception.

As that fabric simmers under the pluck-strokes of the multistringer, the hothorn sears the froth with heat beyond heat, curing it into the first stages of being. Close behind come the cold chill-pulsations of the basswhomper, pushing all that has not quite yet come to be out in instant, even waves that flash-expand the arena that is the universe.

Only then do the notes of the singer rise like evanescent and infinitely thin crystal spheres over the instrumentalists—whose percussive impacts and knife-edged notes should have fragmented those sonic spheres reaching for the meaning that is embodied in becoming, a meaning that will be sought in eons to come by the flashglancers who will struggle to understand that which brought them into being, even though most will live and die without wonder, let alone comprehension. For melody shapes all, not the composer, nor the effects that create the song of the universe.

II.

LAURENT LOOKED DOWN at the lambent light captured within the nightmetal armour forged from the metal of the first singer and repaired after the last system shaping, its soft glow understating, thus misrepresenting, the energies harnessed within fields so intense mere matter was but unseen mist by comparison.

"Will it suffice . . . again?" she asked.

"Against time, against the battering of mere matter, and against entropy, but not against the dragons of the underspace-time," replied the master artificer.

"Should I encounter one . . . ?"

"There always be dragons. Order and matter. Ordered matter structures chaos. Against chaos, mass alone is insufficient, because, without order, chaos scatters mass. Only ordered mass can prevail. No more and no less. Even forms of order that seem useless tip an uncertain balance, particularly when dealing with the foam on the surface of spacetime."

That may be, but there is more chaos than order where we're headed, or little enough except that which we bring. Laurent kept that thought to herself as she donned the nightmetal armour. Once so clad, she glided from the armoury to the ready room. There she stretched out above what passed for a deck and shuttered her consciousness, a consciousness that would remain shuttered and dreamless until *Blackmatter* reached the next protostellar disk with appropriate parameters.

The time necessary passed before Laurent unshuttered her consciousness in response to the alert signal. Others around her did the same, the aether filled with the unsent thoughts of shapers ordering their consciousnesses after the dormancy of the crossing.

Once her consciousness was fully ordered, Laurent checked all her biosystems, ensuring that they were all optimized. Next came the briefing infusion, when Laurent received full perception of the swirling protostellar disk above which *Blackmatter* was poised. Already, modest concentrations of matter had formed in the randomness of gas and dust, concentrations needing to be adjusted, as once others had adjusted previous protostellar disks that had given rise to Laurent's forebears.

The infusion received and registered, Laurent glided toward her dustsled, checking her nightmetal armour a last time before inserting herself and linking with the supramaterial dustsled, both wavicle and point, whose reality could not be compromised in either spacetime or underspace-time.

Order levels combined. Trajectory adjusted. Ready for release.

Wavicle Laurent . . . released.

The dustsled dropped into the Now of spacetime, and Laurent continued to monitor the angled release and insertion point before easing into deep slowtime as the dustsled vectored toward the disk of gas and dust, slowly coming to parallel the incipient rotation of the cloud-disk, if at a higher velocity.

In time, the dustsled and Laurent slid through the upper levels of the disk, her consciousness linked to the arrow of time, moving through the centuries, smoothing, combining, and channelling the currents, preparing, waiting . . .

III.

COBURN WAS JOLTED out of instastasis, the sensation always the same, like being dunked in liquid nitrogen and then solar-fried, all in less than a nanosec. Except that neither really occurred, because Coburn's body and physical brain were still in stasis. Coburn accessed the instruments and scanners, and found . . . nothing . . . or nothing besides a few scattered planetesimals that *Celestina* had already discovered, catalogued, and then continued on from, because they were little more than ice and worthless rock, of a size and composition worthy of neither greater study or potential utilization for other than fuel. But then, that was true of most of the scattered matter in the Oort Cloud.

"Object . . . one thousand kilo-kays out . . . anomalous mass-energy profile," announced the carefully modulated androgynous voice of *Celestina*, a voice only in the sense that Coburn's supercon-scious registered the words as such. "Probability of artifact close to unity. Decelerating to inspect."

"Energy reserves?" asked Coburn.

"Reserves are sufficient for inspection of object and for extended travel to recover ice from nearest suitable planetesimal."

"Composition of object?"

"We're unable to determine at this time."

"Interrogative origin."

"Comparative analysis is inconclusive."

Coburn could only wait while the *Celestina* closed on the potential artifact, wondering what the object might be. Absently, another thought occurred. "How far have you gotten in your listening to the bygone classics of opera?"

"We don't just listen; we also analyze the mathematical strata and structures as they're performed."

"That sounds like listening to me."

"That's a terrible pun."

"I admit it, but it's totally appropriate. I still don't see why you chose opera."

"Popular music is more simplistic and repetitious. Opera is more challenging."

And that fills the hours . . . and the years. Coburn would have nodded, thoughts going back to the object that they were approaching. Most likely, it was just another worthless rock, or possibly an actual nickel-iron asteroid tossed out of the inner system during the early Solar Restructuring . . . and just possibly, it might be some lost and early attempt at interstellar travel, among the mostly futile many. *Except . . . what if it is alien?*

That wouldn't change anything. *Celestina* was eight light months from Earth, and that meant they'd have to deal with the object one way or another, since no one had yet discovered FTL travel or communication.

"What characteristics make this object different?" asked Coburn.

"We can discern gravitational attraction without optical discovery."

"How big is it?"

"Analysis indeterminate. No optical available so far. Spacetime deformation indicates body mass approximately one-fifth T."

Coburn would have snorted, had that been physically possible. "Something with twice the mass of Mars that we can't even visually discern? That sounds like the miniature black holes the physicists say exist . . . and no one's ever found."

"The observed deformation is insufficient for a black hole," replied *Celestina*. "Deceleration complete."

Coburn couldn't help but worry about what the object was . . . and who or what might be contained within it . . . and what it was doing so far from anything. "Interrogative distance to object."

"Two hundred kays."

"Optical scan."

"Enhanced optical scan."

What Coburn "saw" was unremarkable . . . yet totally amazing. It was rectangular, perhaps four times as long as wide, and a tenth as thick at one end and half that at the other. And it was darker than dark. With nothing nearby, there was no visual way of telling how big it actually was. "What are the dimensions?"

"A thousand metres in length, two hundred in width and a hundred thick at one end, half that at the other. The precise dimensions and regularity indicate a technological creation or artifact."

Even after all the years, sometimes *Celestina* could pedantically state the obvious. Coburn did not comment, but, instead, began to study the blacker-than-black object. A kay long, with no protrusions, totally featureless. Streamlined, as if designed to move through something denser than the comparative vacuum of space . . . but out in the middle of almost nowhere.

As Coburn watched, the darkness changed, and faint lambent lights flicker-strobed across the outer surfaces of the object. "What did you do?"

"Optical enhancement was not possible without electromagnetic and laser scan. The object responded to the energy flow."

"I'd say you woke it up," commented Coburn. *Whatever "it" is.*

"The distance to the object is diminishing," offered *Celestina*.

"How can it do that?"

"The object is not moving. We are."

"It's moving us? By what means?"

"It appears to be employing some advanced technology. The greatest probability is directed gravitational attraction."

"Stop us from getting closer."

"That's not possible without sustaining maximum structural damage."

"If we crash into it, we'll definitely suffer maximum structural damage," replied Coburn.

"That is unlikely. The rate of closure is slowing," announced *Celestina*.

A gravitational tractor beam? Coburn would have shivered, but lacked that ability at present. What was such an object or spacecraft . . . or whatever it was . . . doing in the Oort Cloud? "Display all information on object."

"Displayed."

Coburn slowly, at least comparatively, went over the images and data, but the only thing that stood out was that the surface temperature of the object registered at 2.8 K, suggesting that its surface or hull, or the outer layer, was a perfect insulator, since it was unlikely that the interior of a functioning technology could be that cold. *Not any technology you know.*

"What's the composition of the hull?"

"That cannot be determined. The highest probability is an amalgam of partly collapsed elements."

Partly collapsed matter? That made no sense. Neutron matter the size of the object would have possessed a gravitational force that would have already shredded Coburn and *Celestina*. Partly collapsed matter would have been unstable and resulted in something similar to a solar flare, if not a nova. "How is that possible?" asked Coburn.

"It isn't, according to present observations and current theory." After a pause, *Celestina* added, "Position stable at ten kays separation."

"Is there any attempt at communication?"

"No emissions at any frequency of electromagnetic spectrum. No gravitonic pulses detected."

"Are we still being restrained?"

"A test attempt at using the drive was countered by increased attraction."

"In short, we're stuck." *Captured, is more like it.* "Then we'd better see what we can do in the way of communications."

IV.

PROTO-GAS-GIANT PARAMETERS OUTSIDE LIMITS! *Evanescence threatened.*

The alarm from *Blackmatter* jolted Laurent out of deep slow-time. After readjusting her consciousness and biosystems, she focused on the proto-gas-giant creeping inward toward the habitable zone, where the proto-rocky-planets had not yet accumulated enough mass to nurture the evanescent globes of the first singers, those spheres so tough . . . and yet, so fragile.

The dustsled's sensors detected the dragon, or rather, its influence—that darkness that pulled the very fabric of spacetime into an unseen depression through which the proto-gas-giant orbited, each ellipse bringing it closer to the eventual boundary of the habitable zone, not that any of the stellar disk was presently habitable for any unarmored being, device, or technology.

Laurent angled the dustsled inward, vectoring it behind the proto-gas-giant that was the dragon's tool, a position from which she would employ the dustsled to gather a wave of matter and then accelerate it to merge with the incipient gas-giant, with enough velocity for it to surmount the insidious false slope of the underlying spacetime.

Over orbital ellipse after orbital ellipse, she and the dustsled built that mass, trailing the proto-gas-giant, but closing the gap while gathering more and more matter.

Then, as she, the dustsled, and the matter close to the size of a more-than-modest protoplanet accelerated toward the proto-gas-giant to begin the manoeuvre that would reverse the inward drift of the proto-gas-giant's orbit, the chaos dragon emerged from underspace-time, directly between Laurent and her target.

For an instant—a real instant, not a slowtime instant—Laurent saw into and through the surface of spacetime, through the gaping maw of the dragon, beholding the tangled and interlocked chaos-webs on which rested the foam of order, created by the primal evanescent songs to block the excessive emergence of chaos into spacetime.

Driving the dustsled forward, employing and increasing the kinetic force created over more than decades, she pushed the mass so carefully and painstakingly gathered toward the dragon's mouth, then, at the last moment, accelerated the dustsled toward that gaping maw, that momentary entrance into underspace-time, while separating herself from the sled and triggering the recovery beacon.

As she watched, the energy from the dustsled sealed the breach into underspace-time, while the mass she and the dust-sled had gathered fused with the proto-gas-giant, accelerating it, trembling and shuddering, out of the false deformation of space-time and along a widening orbit. *Out from the habitable zone to come.*

Even so ... Laurent recalculated.

She had been late, not fatally late, but close, and the proto-gas-giant had gathered too much of the dust and gas from the outer edges of the habitable zone to come ... and the rocky planet that would grow there would be too small, large enough for proto-life, but little more, before it withered, unable to sustain and nurture evanescence.

But there will be one farther in-system ... and there would have been none had you not foiled the dragon, whose random chaos could not be trusted to foster the evanescence that was the only hope of prevailing against the trolls of entropy.

She dropped into dormancy, knowing *Blackmatter* would recover her, sooner or later, wondering where the dustsled would re-emerge from underspace-time ... and when.

V.

"SINCE WE CAN'T BREAK FREE," said Coburn, "we need to persuade the object, or who or whatever controls it, to talk to us ... and to release us."

"We're beginning the applicability analysis for First Contact procedures," replied *Celestina*, adding instants later, "Analysis complete. There is no indication of preferred technology, other than gravitonic control. Our systems cannot be configured for gravitonic communications."

Besides which, we'd be out of power and frozen solid before finishing the first message. "Start with EMF transmissions. Binary code basics." Coburn had doubts about the effectiveness of EMF transmission of binary codes, given that binary was based on an on-off, either/or mindset, which was definitely human-centric. And what kind of mind lay behind the giant rectangular object that had ensnared *Celestina?* Coburn doubted it was human. Even on Earth, intelligence came in many forms. One might estimate and model with some accuracy the mindsets of cetaceans, but still, no one could really tell how cephalopods thought, not with nine brains. Coburn didn't even want to think about the diffuse and web-extended intelligence of arachnids. So, just how likely was it that an alien intelligence would live or think in the either/or world of *Homo*-not-so-*sapiens*?

Still, since Coburn didn't have a better idea, and since that was the first step, according to the so far never-used First Contact procedures, waiting and dropping back into slowtime until the cumbersome process was finished was the only possibility as *Celestina* went through the entire EMF range.

After a light touch from *Celestina* and several minutes of reorientation, Coburn emerged from slowtime, asking, "Was there any reaction to any frequency?"

"At the first transmission, the lambent lighting manifested through the object's hull increased slightly, but the higher intensity remained constant throughout the entire range."

"What's your analysis?"

"The object recognized that we were signalling, but either did not understand the message, is attempting to process and decipher it, or is choosing not to respond."

"Did the object emit any signals or energy elsewhere that might be messages?"

"No radiation of any kind was detected."

"Is it possible that the object has a communication system we cannot detect?" asked Coburn, suspecting that the answer lay in the limits of human technology.

"Based on current science and theory, that is not possible."

"Based on current science and theory, the object which has captured us is not possible," replied Coburn, "but it doesn't strike me as unreal." Time passed. "Has the illumination pattern of the object's hull changed?"

"It remains at the same level as when we began EMF signalling."

"Then it's waiting for us to do something else. What about sending binary in laser flashes?"

"Commencing laser binary transmission."

"Is there any change in the hull lighting?"

"A ten percent increase in intensity."

Coburn waited for *Celestina* to complete the laser-signalled binary transmission before asking, "How did the object respond?"

"The higher light level was sustained through the transmission, then dropped back to the previous level when we ceased transmitting."

"Use the laser to project a visual image, images of geometric shapes."

"Commencing transmissions." Several seconds passed. "Hull light level up five percent."

"They, or it, liked the binary flashes better."

"That assumption is unfounded," replied *Celestina*. "A stronger response may not be positive."

"We don't have much choice except to assume it's positive,"

countered Coburn. "We could remain locked here until we freeze solid if we do nothing. We still have marker buoys. Activate and deploy one with enough motion so that it will drift toward the object."

"Deploying signal buoy. Activated and functioning."

Coburn immediately concentrated on following the buoy as it moved away from *Celestina*, just a shiny sphere of metal with an intermittent signal that mining drones or uncrewed research-analysis units could home in on.

The signal buoy emitted one pulse . . . and vanished.

"What happened to it?" asked Coburn.

"We're unable to determine. There was no increase in energy or temperature."

"So, it wasn't incinerated or vaporized?"

"That appears improbable."

"Could the object have snatched it somehow?"

"That appears the most likely possibility."

"So, now we wait and see what it decides?"

Celestina did not respond.

Coburn continued observing and inspecting the object, and, after a time, asked, "Any change in illumination or energy emissions?"

"Hull illumination has lowered to initial manifested levels. No detectable energy emissions."

How else can we try to communicate with the object? Coburn kept going over everything that they'd tried—EMF at all levels, laser and light, signal buoy. *What about sound?*

"Can you modify the distress feature of the comm laser to create a photoacoustic effect on the object's hull?" asked Coburn.

"The laser system can be focused and adjusted to create a photoacoustic effect on normal matter. It can't be determined whether it would create that effect on the hull or surface of the object."

"Go ahead and try it. Once you have it operating as well as you can, is there some sort of acoustic code . . . ?"

"We can try Morse Code."

Coburn had never heard of it. "What's that?"

"It's an early electric-impulse code, but it was also used with signal lights."

"Then try it."

Time passed. Coburn didn't check. It didn't matter.

Then *Celestina* said, "The laser is ready to operate in photo-acoustic mode. What should we say?"

"Try the same message you sent on the EMF trial."

"We're commencing transmission."

Almost immediately, *Celestina* said, "The object's hull lights are brighter. Five percent greater intensity than any previous response."

Coburn watched, but when the transmission ended, the hull lights dimmed, if not back to the lowest level. "They want something else."

"We could try voice transmission," suggested *Celestina*. "We have your voice parameters and recordings. What do you want to say?"

"Just something that tells them we're trying to communicate."

"The physical reconstruction will take a few minutes real-time."

I'm not going anywhere.

"Transmission beginning."

Almost immediately, Coburn saw the object's hull illumination increase, and then fade as *Celestina* announced, "Transmission completed."

"Try a longer message, one of several minutes."

"We'll need a little longer to prepare that."

"I'll wait."

But when *Celestina* transmitted the longer message, the object's lights faded perceptibly even before the transmission ended.

"They're looking for something acoustical," declared *Celestina*. "They like voice, but it's not enough. Have you considered music? Perhaps even opera?"

"Try something simpler," said Coburn. "Popular music, first."

"Not opera?"

Coburn detected a hint of something, perhaps pique. "If popular music doesn't work, then you can try opera."

"Preparing transmission." *Celestina*'s "tone" came across as definitely miffed.

Coburn said nothing.

"Beginning transmission."

The object's hull lights flared brighter for several minutes, then faded.

Almost as if in disappointment. Coburn would have offered a wry smile, had that been possible. "You just might be right. Pick an operatic vocal, with complexity, but great emotion . . . and then be ready to follow it with others. Try to keep their lights on. Maybe that will work." *If it doesn't . . .* Coburn worried. *What other form of high-level acoustical/vocal complexity is there?*

"That will take some time," replied *Celestina*, definitely sounding happier.

Once more, Coburn waited.

Finally, *Celestina* declared, "The transmission is ready to send."

"Then send it." Coburn concentrated on the image of the object, the now-fainter flickering sheets of bluish light seeming to fade by the moment. "Let me hear it as well."

"You won't get the same sound quality as the object does."

"I'm well aware of that."

"Commencing transmission."

Almost instantly, the intensity and flicker frequency of the object's hull lights increased. In moments, the intensity was so bright that Coburn mentally adjusted the brightness of the image. At the same time, the orchestra and soprano voice became engulfing, even without comprehension of the language of the song. *Ancient German . . . maybe . . .*

The light emanating from the object continued to brighten, so much so that Coburn had to cut off the visual feed, even though it was only a mentally simulated image.

The first aria was followed by a second, and then a third, and while Coburn saw nothing, the data inputs showed energy flowing out from the object . . . more . . . and more . . .

Then there was nothing . . . nothing except a definite sense of dislocation . . . and a high, single note echoing . . . somewhere . . . and then dying away.

"We've been moved . . . shoved away," said *Celestina.*

Coburn could have sworn there was disbelief in those words. "Where? How far?"

"Not that far. We're just a few light minutes back toward Sol, but no time elapsed . . . as if we were . . . somewhere not in space-time. Open your visual. We're feeding an image of the object . . . or what was the object."

What was *the object?* Coburn opened the visual . . . and just looked . . . stunned at the coruscating point of light, a miniature star . . . or the equivalent.

"It protected us . . . moved us, before that happened."

"Was there any . . . other response . . . other communication?"

"There was," replied *Celestina.* "We captured it. Would you like to hear it?"

"Please."

Coburn listened . . . to a song . . . without words, yet it was a song, a song of joy, of triumph . . . and yet of evanescence. If it had been possible, Coburn would have wept . . . but the tears were embedded deep in Coburn's thoughts and mind . . . and always would be.

Far too soon, the song ended.

For a time, Coburn could not think.

"Was . . . there anything else?" Those words came hard, felt insensitive, unfeeling, after the glory of the song . . . if that was what it had been.

"Just the song . . . and a lot of data. Maybe the scientists can get something out of it all."

"What songs . . . did you use?"

"Not songs, not mere songs," declared *Celestina,* "arias, the greatest arias sung by the greatest voices—'*Ach ich fühl's,*' '*Depuis le jour,*' '*Sempre libera,*' '*Un bel di,*' and even more."

The names meant nothing to Coburn. *But they meant something to* Celestina . . . *and they definitely conveyed something of import to the object . . . more than just something.*

Coburn called up the image of the mini-star that had been the object once more, taking in its glorious radiance, wondering if anyone would ever truly know what that small star signified . . . and what message its last and only song conveyed.

PEEL

By Julie E. Czerneda

Author's Note: Sometimes the worlds we shape are our own.

Water seeps through the windowsill when the wind blows from the east. It finds a path through a crack in the plastic. It soaks the plaster within, lingers in hidden wood.

Best of all, it peels the paint.

Her fingers tremble over the imperfection, stroke the ripples like a lover's skin.

With a nail, she marks the edge of softness, then pulls ever-so-gently. The paint—its colour of no importance—comes away willingly. She grasps the tiny beginning between fingertips; her tongue's between her teeth.

She tries not to hope too much.

This is her lucky day. The paint peels with extravagant generosity, bringing with it strips of paper from the dampened wall. She shifts her fingers to the edges, careful to work with it, adjusting to the growing tension as the peel reaches the end of the invading moisture. It becomes stubborn and brittle and falls free at last.

She cradles the peel in her hand, watching it curl. Her fingers echo the shape.

She sits back to survey the result, the chill of tile unnoticed in the blush of triumph. Multiple greys mix with black specks of mould. Paper feathers the sodden plaster. She sees faces in textures; landscapes in whorls.

Change whispers in her ears. Enthralling. Enticing.

Forbidden.

Footsteps.

She releases the curtain, tucks her hand—and the peel—in her pocket, stands. There is time for this, and no more, before ...

"Oh, there you are, dear!" The woman's voice is soft and warm. Her face is smooth and lovely. Her clothing is fitted, its colour of no importance. There is no flaw in form or gesture.

She touches the peel and remembers. There had been lines beside her mother's eyes. Hard work and sun had conspired. There had been lines beside her mother's mouth. Laughter and worry had taken turns.

The woman's skin is perfect.

"Your ride's here, dear. Have a nice day at work. Wear your coat."

She doesn't answer, simply walks to the door. The rudeness brings no frown or puzzlement.

Nothing changes.

She touches the peel; her new talisman.

———

SHE WALKS with her eyes straight ahead. The sidewalks are clean and even, slicing obedient lawns. The vehicle disturbs not a blade as it waits, silent and steel. Its colour is of no importance. A set of steps lead up and in.

Faces smile from their rows. All are smooth and lovely. She feels no warmth or welcome. She can't tell them apart.

Her fingertip fondles the peel as she sits.

Murmurs, soft and melodious, thicken and twist the air. "It's going to be a nice day." "Look at that sky. Perfect!" "You know what Monday means." "We never forget. Movie night at your place." She hums without breath, a discordant, dangerous humming; rebellion in her bones.

She remembers. The peel left change in its wake.

A sign.

SHE KNOWS to move as they do, without flaw, always with purpose. Her hands reach. Her left picks up a rod, her right the ring that slips over it. Make them one, put them down. Her hands reach. Her left picks up a rod, her right the ring that slips over it. Make them one, put them down. The material is inanimate, its colour of no importance.

Murmurs gather around her feet, as if dust. Gentle, warm murmurs. "What a nice day to be at work." "Look how well this fits." "Here comes another one." "It's so good to be here." "The movie will be fun too."

Then, without warning, a shard falls, lifts a plume of dismay.

"We could play cards tonight instead."

The murmurs choke themselves to silence.

Her hands reach, as all hands here do, in unceasing synchrony.

Her left picks up a rod, her right the ring that slips over it. Make them one, put them down.

Her hands don't need her eyes. She lifts her gaze, seeks the shard.

His face is smooth and lovely. He works in silence, moving without flaw. But, for an instant, his lips misplace the peaceful smile painted on the rest. They peel back, showing a glimpse of teeth. A rictus. It could be fear. Or surprise.

Change.

Her groin burns. Her breath catches in her throat. She cannot move.

Another sign.

His lips close, then open. "The movie will be fun, too."

Her hands reach. Her left picks up a rod, her right the ring that slips over it. Make them one, put them down.

Inside, she hums something discordant, dangerous.

Different.

———

SHE SITS, knees and feet together, back straight. On either side, others sit, knees and feet together, backs straight. Before them, scenes of carnage alternate with lust. Faces can't be seen. Voices have no words. Deeds have no context. It is the same movie they watch each Monday.

Her hand finds its pocket. Her fingers find the peel. It's smaller. It shrinks into itself. It will dry and fragment soon, becoming something new.

Finding the peel, she remembers. The man who sits to her left. There had been calluses on his palms. Thorns and gravel had etched them. There had been a broken nail and scars. Strength and tenderness had been in every touch.

The man's hands rest, flawless, on his lap.

"This movie is nice." "I always like this movie." "What a great day at work."

She simply stands and walks away. Her body blocks the image from their view. The rudeness brings no protest or complaint.

Nothing changes.

Almost.

Something changed today.

She almost smiles.

LEAVING the midst of the movie is . . . change.

Walking down the sidewalk, the *ker-pat ker-pat* of her small quick steps the only sound, is . . . change.

Alone, she dares revel in it, dares throw back her head and stretch out her arms, dares . . .

"Hello, dear." The woman's voice is soft and melodious. It comes from the dark beside her, a stranger's kiss. Shadows without substance tremble in the cold east wind.

Dropping her arms, she savours her fear, in its way as novel as hope. "Hello."

"Why aren't you at the movie with your friends, dear?"

She says the expected. "It was nice." Then, with the peel in her pocket and the glimpse of teeth in her memory, adds: "The movie machine stopped working. It needs repair. I came home to see you. Mother."

The shadows stop moving. The world holds its breath. She clings to the moment, anticipation quickening her heart until she almost laughs. Then, smooth and warm and the same as always:

"That's nice, dear. Let's walk home together." The figure steps out of the darkness, lovely and flawless. Perfect.

She simply walks on her way, *ker-pat ker-pat*, listening to the echo of following footsteps.

She smiles at the feel of storm in the air.

THE NEXT MORNING, the windowsill is dry and clean. Caulking leers from its corners. Below, the wall is pristine, pure, perfect. Its colour has no importance.

Overcome with grief, she sits. The chill tile steals warmth from her bare legs and buttocks, robs her of sensation. She reaches a trembling hand to test for lies. The paint is solid; its finish immaculate.

Impenetrable.

Footsteps.

She's lost yesterday's peel. As every morning, a new garment waits on her bed, the old discarded. She grieves in silence.

"Oh, there you are, dear!" The woman's voice is soft and warm. Her face is smooth and lovely. Her clothing is fitted, its colour of no importance. There is no flaw in form or gesture.

She touches the paint and sees nothing, remembers nothing.

"Your ride's here, dear. Time to get dressed. Have a nice day at work."

She doesn't answer, simply stands and goes to her room to dress. The rudeness brings no frown or puzzlement.

Nothing changes.

Outside, she walks with her eyes straight ahead. The sidewalks are clean and even, slicing obedient lawns dusted with snow. The vehicle waiting disturbs not a flake as it hovers, silent and steel. Its colour is of no importance. A set of steps lead up and in.

Faces smile. All are smooth and lovely. She feels no warmth or welcome. She can't tell them apart.

She joins the murmuring. "What a lovely day." "Work will be nice." "Don't forget it's my house for the movie tonight." "We never forget." She doesn't know which words come from her mouth.

———

SHE MOVES AS THEY DO, without flaw, always with purpose. Her hands reach. Her left picks up a rod, her right the ring that slips over it. Make them one, put them down. Her hands reach. Her left picks up a rod, her right the ring that slips over it. Make them one, put them down. The material is inanimate flesh, its colour of no importance.

She reaches again, eyes blind by rote, and touches something warm.

His hand is out of place. Only by a breath, only for a heartbeat, but it is enough.

Her fingers, caught on skin, miss the next rod.

It's as if she's sleeping and only now awakes. She grasps the telltale rod and its abandoned ring, tucks both into her pocket with unfamiliar speed. Her hands reach, fingertips quivering. Her left picks up a rod, her right the ring that slips over it. Make them one, put them down.

Saved by rhythm, she looks up.

He's slower to recover. Before him, a pair of connected rods and rings bounce aimlessly, unable to link themselves in the next step. His eyes catch on hers, a puzzling in their depths, then he looks back to his task, murmuring soft and warm: "This is nice."

Too late.

She remembers herself in his eyes.

And the scream comes from her soul.

———————

THERE ARE WORSE things than remembering.

There is change.

She runs down the sidewalk, *pat-ker-pat pat-ker-pat*, dodging cracks and sprouts of frozen, ragged weeds, coughing as each breath brings more of the thick stench on the wind, shivering, eyes struggling to comprehend.

Reality is a peel, curled in the mind's hand, fragmenting as it dries, blowing away.

The buildings around her sag like a spinster's breasts. Every step takes her further into nightmare.

"Hello, dear." The woman's voice is hurried and harsh. "Why aren't you at work?" There is a sharp catch before each word, as though something is being reset.

She won't look. She won't answer.

She has seen beneath the paint.

———————

HER RIDE WAITS for her the next morning. Nothing has changed.

Everything has changed.

She isn't home.

Paint hangs in long fingerlike curls from every wall. It lies in dry wisps, irregular and wild, like tangled hair or autumn leaves. Plaster has fallen, dusty clumps pulled free and thrown to the tiles. Wood stares out, like bones stripped of flesh.

Words stain her window, fighting the frost.

"I am real."

Their colour is red.

SHE HOLDS court with dusty shadow, watches others perform. Their skin is perfect. Her fingers, nails stained and broken, tickle dying shrubs, wander crumbling brick, seek . . . what? She has left the words behind.

Things have changed. It is not enough.

Her hand loosens a shard of brick—its colour is of no importance—carries it into view. She brings it to her arm, cuts across softness, flinches with ecstasy. The shard falls to the ground.

With a nail, she tests the new edge, then pulls ever-so-gently. The paint—its colour of no importance—comes away willingly. She grasps the tiny beginning between fingertips; her tongue's between her teeth.

She tries not to hope too much.

The paint peels with extravagant generosity. She shifts her fingers to the edges, careful to work with it, adjusting to the growing tension as the peel becomes stubborn. She pulls hardest of all, and the peel falls free at last.

She cradles the peel in her hand, watching it curl. Her fingers echo the shape.

She stares at what is exposed. The chill wind goes unnoticed. Multiple greys mix with black specks of mould. Paper feathers sodden plaster. She sees faces in textures; landscapes in whorls.

What does it mean?

"Oh, there you are, dear!" The woman's voice is soft and warm. Renewed.

She knows what she will see. A face smooth and lovely, no flaw in form or gesture. She stares at her arm.

Why is there a wall within herself?

"You've missed your ride."

Who put it there?

She stares at her arm and sees dark liquid welling up through the plaster. Suddenly, the torn edge of the paint becomes a line of fire. She looks up, eyes swimming with change.

The peel is in her hand. Power is in her hand. "You are not my mother." Her voice is discordant, dangerous. Her voice hums with power. "You are not real."

The woman's mouth melts as she speaks. "You need your coa . . ." Lips go. Chin follows. The wind whips the air with ice, *tat-tat tat-tat*, and the woman congeals into a lump of inanimate flesh.

Clutching the peel, she looks at the sagging buildings, the remnants of gardens. She looks at others, perfect in form and perfectly oblivious, waiting by the old bus. "You are not real." The words lift in the wind and fly back in her face, blinding and sure. "There's only me."

She doesn't need to watch. She feels it happen, a shifting of perspective, a clarity as cold as the coming night.

They are gone. All of them. All of it.

She's done it before. And before that. Uncounted befores and before thats. Each time victory traps her. She closes a fist over the peel, remembering.

She won once. Only once. Her power ravaged this world and all who lived on it.

Leaving her alone.

Alone—until she has to rebuild it or go mad.

Rebuild—until she becomes lost.

Lost—until she rediscovers her lie and destroys it. Leaving her . . .

Alone—until she has to lie to herself again.

She opens her hand and watches the tiny piece uncurl.

"No," she tells it. "Not this time." She tips her hand and watches the peel fall.

THE FREEZING WIND at her back is her guide, the sleet driving into her flesh her companion. She runs with the storm, owns its screams, its fury, its destruction. Every step marks purpose. Every moment marks change.

Even the one where she finds herself on her knees, on her stomach, and then curls into a sigh.

Even the one where the snow paints her with peace.

THE KNACK OF FLYING

By Shelley Adina

London, March 1896

The betting book at the Gaius Club was one of its most successful innovations. So successful that from time to time even Lewis Protheroe, the club's secret owner, perused its pages to marvel over the latest madness.

The Hon. Cyril Whitworth wagers £100 that he will win back every penny he has lost to Mr. Edmund Ffoulkes by Easter.

Mr. Thomas Ware wagers £500 that Lady Julia Mount-Batting will kiss him at the Penningtons' Masked Ball.

Lewis had closed the book, shaking his head. Both men would lose, and painfully.

But of late, the entries had taken on a new character, as though a craze were blowing through London like a hot wind that affected only the younger, moneyed set. A craze so secret that it had not even reached the scandal sheets, never mind the *Evening Standard*. A craze so dangerous that had anyone in an official or parental capacity known of it, it would have been declared illegal on the spot.

Over breakfast at Carrick House, Lewis said, "You ought to see some of these bets. Utterly mad. Twenty pounds on the Acorn for third place in the first heat. *Seventy-five* on the March Hare for first place in the final."

"That's a wee bit of change." Steven McTavish—known as Snouts due to the imposing size of his nose—slathered strawberry jam on his toast. "They have to be races. But it's too early in the year for horses. Too much mud. And who could race in that old ruin?"

"The pilots of flying devices."

Snouts nearly dropped his toast down the front of one of his more sober waistcoats, which this morning was embroidered purple paisley. "They're racing *flying devices*? At the Kennington Oval?"

"Apparently. Take a lot of drunken toffs, plus money, plus sport, and what do you get?"

"Trouble with the South Bank gangs, you ask me."

"Still, I think we ought to investigate." Lewis gave himself a moment to enjoy his friend's stare of astonishment.

"Now *you* are mad," Snouts finally said.

"They are making bets in the club's book. It behooves me to know what is going on among my members."

"And what will young Lord Snootybum say when the man he thinks is merely the general factotum at his club sits down next to him in the amphitheatre?" Snouts, who respected only a very few people in the world, numbered Lewis among them. "Do you really want to hazard a set-down from one of those chinless Bloods?"

"I am willing to take the risk. Sir Barclay Ightham, chinless though he might be, laid down the seventy-five pounds. I should very much like to see him lose it."

Snouts could tell when Lewis's mind was made up. "Very well. I will go with you. But strictly as observers. And we will tell no one —the Lady may be down in Cornwall, but I would not put it past anyone in this house to send a tube to her and include it in their news."

"Have it your way." Lewis, having had it his way, was perfectly content to allow Snouts to think he was organizing the expedition. Breakfast subsequently became an animated argument over whether they ought to dress as gentlemen or simply go in raiding rig, should the gangs find the occasion irresistible.

The races were to begin at one in the morning, well after most gentlemen were sunk into their card games at their clubs, respectable people were asleep, and the costermongers had a few hours of slumber yet before they needed to load their boats and row them to the markets.

Lewis and Snouts climbed the ancient steps of the ruined oval that had seen Londinium's chariot races centuries before. The full moon lit the gathering crowd as the old, grassy stands filled—silently, for the most part. Fisticuffs broke out here and there over seating, but were settled with no more than grunts and cursing. They found seats near the top, just before the fourth turn.

How strange it was to see the old ruin lit up like this. Lewis had only been here once or twice, in the daytime. The place was said to be haunted, but the only thing Lewis had ever seen moving among the broken arches, or climbing up what remained of the stone seats, were artists of the romantic persuasion, too poor to go to Italy.

Now moonglobes the size of a man's head were shaken into life along the topmost seats. And in the grass at the bottom, in the middle of the ancient racecourse, were the flying machines, their pilots making last-second adjustments, their engines growling and coughing. Lewis leaned forward in admiration. The sheer variety! But how could some of them get off the ground?

That monowheel, for instance. A few daring souls piloted them along the streets of London, but their tendency to tip over when stopped at cross streets was so far preventing more general use, sensible as the theory might be. How did it fly?

There was an ornithopter, as might be expected, being unloaded from a wheeled cart. And here were two more, small enough to be carried by their pilots, their harnesses dragging in the grass.

On the far side floated an isinglass bubble that had to be filled with gas, if its pilot's breathing helmet were any indication.

A contraption like a bicycle, but with vanes instead of wheels, and a balloon bobbing atop it, was mounted by its pilot, who wore a cravat and a top hat. The poor chap was never going to get any speed out of that thing.

Now here was the racing master, pacing to one side of the broken stone racecourse with a portable speaking horn in one hand.

"Welcome, gentlemen, to the sixth race of our short season." His amplified voice floated up to Lewis and Snouts, but did not, one trusted, extend farther. "For those of you new to our sport, here are the rules. One is for the pilots—don't fall off. Two is for the spectators—pilots may not receive assistance, save in the case of danger to life or limb. Three is for all—what happens at the

Oval stays in the Oval. No gossip, no newspapers, no traceable identification of pilots or devices at any time. Is that clear?"

Lewis leaned to his left to murmur, "They're breaking that one in spades in my betting book."

"Which has its own veil of secrecy," Snouts replied. "They must be depending on your discretion more than their own."

"The pilots in the first heat will proceed to the starting line," the racing master called, walking to a chalked line across the ancient, uneven stones as the pilots variously floated or trundled out to take their places.

"Gentlemen, on your marks—"

A sound like a bandsaw cut him off, and a young man swooped in to take his place among the racers. His contraption appeared to be no more than a child's scooter with an engine and propeller mounted to the rear. He stood on the board, one foot in front of the other, his hands on the stick, presumably the steering mechanism. Or some kind of support, at the very least, for the device had no wheels. He pulled back on the stick and the contraption settled to the ground.

"Let the Acorn be informed that if he is late to the flag once more, he will be disqualified," the racing master said sternly, to catcalls from the crowd.

The Acorn. This was the one only expected to take third place. Lewis began to regret putting a guinea on the lad. The technology might be interesting, but wasted if the pilot were overconfident. He wore an aeronaut's goggles that concealed much of his face, and a tweed cap with a tassel on the top—like an acorn's cap—on a mop of curls. His jacket was a disgrace—it could have been pulled out of a rag picker's pile. Thankfully, his canvas pants seemed to be of a later vintage, stained though they were by winding grease.

"Start your engines."

The air was filled with the sound of steam engines being ignited. Now even Snouts sat forward as the monowheel lifted off the ground and its vanes unfurled. The ornithopters hovered, their fresh-faced, darting-eyed pilots giving each other's whirling vanes some space. The Acorn stood upon his device in a nonchalant, hipshot pose, as he pulled back the stick and the device, its engine buzzing angrily, lifted once more off the ground.

"And—go!" The racing master's white handkerchief dropped.

With a snarl and a cloud of steam, the ornithopters lifted straight up into the air. The monowheel shuddered into motion, and as it circled its pilot at the centre, its vanes whipped around the circumference so fast they blurred. However, these did not give the contraption the speed its pilot clearly wanted, for the bubble and the biprop passed it at a sedate pace, lifting higher as they went. The biprop pilot raised his top hat politely as he sailed by.

But Lewis did not have a guinea invested in the skill of those men. What was keeping the Acorn? He was jiggling the engine, fussing with it while trying to keep his balance. Suddenly it leaped out of idle and into high pressure, the propellers winding up into a higher key. The boy clutched wildly at his steering stick as the device took off. Levelling vanes snapped out of the sides of the base, and he soared into the air. He found his feet in a moment, and, to Lewis's astonishment, leaned into the stick and took the first turn in a graceful arc that carried him past bubble, biprop, and monowheel in seconds.

The crowd leaped to its feet and vigorously exercised clapping boards muffled with cotton, and whirling hand drums whose innards had been likewise muffled. The sound was like the wind rushing through bare trees, and Lewis stifled a cheer.

The Acorn gunned into the straightaway, but here was where

the ornithopters carried their advantage. They were already halfway down. He leaned into his stick and shortened the distance, but it was not going to be enough. The ornithopters were in a ragged line, like so many geese migrating south, when they clattered over Lewis and Snouts's heads and into the fourth turn.

"Come on, Acorn," Lewis muttered. "You can take them."

The Acorn let off the pressure as he entered the third turn, then accelerated once in it, banking his contraption to allow physics to take him around the curve. Since ornithopters could not bank, their pilots merely hanging suspended in their chairs from single propellers, they were forced to take the curve more cautiously. The Acorn was gaining! Any second he would—

A *crack* like a branch snapping off a tree made Lewis cry out, and a cloud of black smoke enveloped the Acorn. The acceleration stick fell, tumbling through the air end over end. Spectators in the row below Lewis dodged as it clanged on the stones. The propelled board dipped and swooped, but without controls, the pilot could not guide it. He bent his knees and attempted to steer by banking, but it was no good. Drunkenly, he wobbled as the bubble passed him triumphantly, the biprop right behind.

"Give him a hand, you idiots!" Lewis shouted to their pilots, his voice drowned in the cheers and muffled clappering of the crowd.

The engine on the Acorn's footboard choked, buzzed into life, then choked again. The boy swung off it, dangling by his hands ten feet above Lewis and Snouts's heads.

"He's going to jump!" Snouts shouted.

The engine gave out. The boy let go.

He plummeted straight down and landed on Lewis and Snouts in a flail of arms and legs as the largest ornithopter crossed the finish line and the crowd surged to its feet with a roar.

GASPING TO REGAIN the breath that had been knocked out of her, Lady Philomena Noakes attempted to scramble off the two gentlemen who had broken her fall. "Awfully oblig—oh!" Her wrist gave out in a flare of pain and she wound up on her stomach, nose to nose with the dark-eyed young man whom she had just flattened again, knocking his bowler to the grass behind him.

Philomena had never been this close to a man in her life. Other mechanics in the village didn't count—she was not in the habit of lying prone upon them. "Terribly sorry," she choked as she rolled off him, her lips pressed together in pain as she cradled her wrist.

"You're hurt." The young man sat up, retrieved his bowler, and replaced it on his head. "Is it broken?"

Almost afraid to find out, Philomena waggled her fingers. "I don't think so. But it hurts like the devil."

"A sprain, then." The young man who appeared to be with him sported an astonishing nose and a purple waistcoat, cut in a style that had been madly fashionable that season. "Come on. Best get it seen to."

"I'll be all right," she said. Their housekeeper was good at binding up her scrapes and bruises before Papa got a look at them.

"Nonsense," the more sober individual said. "Maggie is closest," he told his friend. "She can get that wrapped before it swells up like a melon."

The fewer people who saw her in the light, the better, including whoever Maggie was. Two men pushed past her, one of whom handed her the acceleration bar to her poor dead flying device. Her fingers went numb as she tried to take it, and she couldn't bite back a groan.

"No argument," the sober one said. "I am Lewis Protheroe, and this is Steven McTavish." He picked up the bar. "Snouts, collect the man's engine, would you?"

And before her wrist could swell to the point where she would be obliged to remove her shirt and the jig would be up, she had been bundled into a landau and in a few minutes was entering the front gate of a snug little cottage just up the hill from Vauxhall Gardens. A young woman working by lamplight at the dining table rose to her feet as they came in.

"Lewis—Snouts—has there been trouble?" Then her eyes widened. "Good heavens. Phil! What on earth are you doing here?"

Maggie Polgarth! Of all the rotten luck! "I might say the same," Philomena croaked.

"What happened?"

"A sprained wrist," Mr. Protheroe said.

"This is the Acorn, Maggie," Mr. McTavish said. "He fell off his flying device at the Kennington Oval and landed on us."

Maggie shook her head. *"He* is the cat's grandfather, and you two are as blind as you are kind." So much for any hope of maintaining her disguise. Philomena winced as Maggie gently took her hand to look at the damage. "Racing, were you? I am glad that St. Cecilia's Academy for Young Ladies has had as little effect upon you as it had upon me." Maggie turned to a boy who had come out of the kitchen, tousled with sleep. "Alfred, get me the bandages, please. Don't wake Lucy, mind. Snouts, if you would be so kind as to fetch a cloth and some ice from the cellar, we'll see if we can stop the swelling."

The two went off to do her bidding as though it were completely normal. Philomena felt a spurt of envy. Imagine not one, but two people actually listening to what you said.

"I take it you two know one another?" Mr. Protheroe said to Maggie. "Perhaps you would introduce me?"

"What, she fell on your head and no introductions were made?"

"*She?*"

Mr. McTavish came back with chipped ice in a cloth, and Maggie wrapped it around her wrist. The relief nearly made Philomena groan.

"For goodness sake, Lewis," Maggie said with a laugh. "Snouts, you are just as bad. This is Phil. I beg your pardon—Lady Philomena Noakes. You may have seen Lord Oakmond in his carriage in Belgrave Square. They live 'round the corner from Carrick House, on Wilton Row."

Complete, goggling silence met this declaration. Philomena decided that, under the circumstances, an inclination of the head would do as an acknowledgement.

"Blimey, miss—er, your ladyship," young Alfred blurted as he joined them, laying the bandages on the table. "Ent you got guts, flying a device when you're a girl?"

"Alfred," Mr. Protheroe said, "Our Lady Malvern is a girl, and she flies anything that comes to hand."

"Aye, but she's the Lady," Alfred said, as though this clinched the matter.

All these people were acquainted with Lady Malvern? Worse and worse. "You must not tell anyone," Philomena blurted. "My father knows nothing about this. Racing. Flying devices. Mechanics. Any of it. He would have me whipped."

Maggie shook her head. "Our lips are sealed. But goodness, Phil, I thought you would be making your debut and waltzing with all the Blood heirs, like the rest of our graduating class, not doing something this interesting."

Of course, Maggie didn't know, but Philomena felt the sting of her own poverty nonetheless. "Papa can't afford a deb—" She stopped herself with an effort, the heat of shame rising into her cheeks.

"So, the rumours are true, then," Mr. Protheroe said quietly. "He and several others invested in the Meriwether-Astor Munitions Works, and when its current president took the business in a different direction, they could not wait for slower profits, but took their money to that steamship venture of Mount-Batting's."

Philomena lifted her chin. "As you say, many gentlemen did the same."

"Pity about the steamships," Snouts said. "At least Mount-Batting has *one* left that hasn't exploded."

"Have you truly lost all?" Maggie asked. "Surely your papa will sell the house in town, and the carriage and all of that, so that you may keep Oakmond. I know how you feel about your home."

What good did a proud tilt of the chin do when one's lips trembled and tears filled one's eyes? Oh, bother it. This was Maggie, who had quietly and calmly walked away with a number of school honours and then gone to university in Germany, as if such miraculous freedom were nothing more than she expected of life. What she was doing in a cottage in Vauxhall now was more than Philomena could fathom. She had to talk to somebody, and Maggie had been a good chum to her in those dark days when she had been torn out of Oakmond and stuffed into Belgravia, to wilt like a plant in the wrong soil.

"He is already planning to sell the estate." Her voice wavered. "I am racing to earn the money to at least keep the staff paid until he does. I have known them all my life."

"Would a twenty-pound bet on third place have accomplished such a goal?" Mr. Protheroe asked, pricking to attention.

"Did the bets go as high as that?" Philomena asked miserably. "Oh, how I wish the engine had not failed! I could have paid the housekeeper and two of the maids in full for the year with a purse that size." She covered her mouth with her good hand, disappointment overwhelming her in a sob. "I'm sorry," she blubbed. "It's just that—" No matter how hard she tried, how good she was with engines, she just did not have enough knowledge to do a proper job of it. And no hope of learning, either. Father had been frightening in his determination that she should dispense with further education and bag a lord, the sooner the better.

"A lady from a Blood family cannot earn her own way," Maggie said calmly. "I know. I am very glad to be Lady Malvern's ward, and a Wit. I bought this cottage and land with my own investments, cleverly advised by our Lewis, here."

"You were?" Philomena raised wet eyes to Mr. Protheroe. "You did?"

Mr. Protheroe looked rather as though he had been poleaxed, and when Maggie began work with the bandages, he took the opportunity to slip away. Philomena set her molars against the pain of having the wrist wrapped, though Maggie was as gentle as any nurse could be. He was probably going back to his respectable house on the other side of the river, where he made other people rich, and had a pretty wife waiting for him.

"All done. Are you in pain, Phil?" Maggie asked gently.

"Not in my wrist," she whispered. "Thank you." She turned away so that Maggie, who seemed to hold the high regard of so many, would not see the tears that loneliness and despair had wrung from her.

AFTER THE EVENTS of the past year, Lewis had believed his heart would be immune to the charms of any female for the rest of his life. And in a single moment, Lady Philomena Noakes had struck him like a bolt from the blue—literally. Those brown eyes, starred with wet lashes, had finished the business, and now here he was in Maggie's garden, gazing down at what remained of the Acorn's flying device without really seeing it.

"Is there any hope for it?" He turned to find her approaching him, tugging her jacket's sleeve down over her bandaged wrist. "The last race is next Friday. I am allowed one mechanical failure, so I will have another chance."

"I am no engineer, my lady," he said. "But from what I have seen of engines and machines in my position as Lady Malvern's secretary, it does not look good."

"After I nearly crushed you flat, I think we may dispense with formalities," she said glumly, prodding the footboard with the toe of her boot. "Maggie calls me Phil. You may do so, too."

"Not Philomena?"

She shook her head. "My father calls me that when he is angry. I suppose I will hear it with greater frequency now."

He could not bear to see her so despondent. "We have a week. Snouts can help, and we know one or two fine mechanics."

"We?" Despite the clouds moving in to cover the moon, her eyes glittered, as though they had filled with tears. "Why should any of your friends help me, a stranger?"

Maggie came out of the front door with Snouts in time to overhear. "A stranger? I think not. You have fallen in with us now, Phil, dear. Welcome to the flock."

The very next day, Lewis and Snouts conveyed her and the broken machine to Sir Andrew Malvern's workshop in Orpington Close, where a girl called Margaret Anne Hodges met them, her toolbox in one hand. "Margaret Anne, mind," she said cheerfully. "So as I don't get mixed up with the other two Margarets at the glassworks." Rain lashed the glass and iron walls Snouts's crew had constructed, designed to let in all the light any inventor would need. "Thanks for springing me, sir," she said to Snouts. "With a day off, I am completely at leisure to amuse myself with the thought of a ladyship racing flying devices and no one the wiser."

"You mustn't tell," Phil cautioned her. "But I do thank you. Now, what can you salvage from my poor old engine?"

She, Margaret Anne, and Snouts bent over it. Snatches of conversation drifted to Lewis while he wandered about the laboratory, picking things up, putting them down, and thinking.

"—too heavy," Margaret Anne said. "We need to start from scratch. Light. Powerful."

"Aye," Snouts said. "I'll leave the design to you, keeping in mind we have until Friday to build it."

"I've looted the scrapyards and manufactories I could get into," Philomena said. "I drew the line at disabling other people's steam landaus, however, including my father's."

Snouts rubbed his chin in thought. "Smaller than your footboard."

"Lose that acceleration bar," Margaret Anne said. "Too much weight."

"How am I to accelerate, then?" Philomena lifted a hand, as though to stop their thought processes. "Wait. I tilt the bar forward for speed, and back to slow. What if my own body were used for that purpose?"

"Now we're getting somewhere," Snouts said. "How?"

Margaret Anne snapped her fingers. "Foot pegs. She leans forward, they depress. She leans back, they release."

"Excellent!" Philomena applauded her, and the mechanic blushed with the praise. "Now, the engine. We need to—"

"You cannot use a conventional engine at all," Lewis said suddenly, strolling over to join them. "Water and coal or even kerosene are too heavy for a device as small as this. You need—" His gaze met that of Snouts.

"A Helios Membrane," Snouts breathed on a note of understanding.

Philomena's mouth fell open. "That is impossible," she said when she had her breath back. "I have read about it. The Helios Membrane powers airships, not—not flying breadboards."

"The Membrane is down in Cornwall," Lewis said, thinking rapidly. "But there may be parts and pieces left over from its construction here. Once it has been exposed to the sun—"

"Provided it comes out sometime this week," Margaret Anne put in.

"It can be run along the underside of the board and connected to the engine and propellers. Can it not?" Philomena's mind was clearly taking up the chase as she appealed to the mechanic.

"It can," she said with a nod.

"Come, you lot," Snouts ordered. "All hands on deck to find pieces left over from the Membrane. And then we'll get to work."

It took every one of the intervening evenings to build the new flying device, and even then, Phil had the thing in her lap, screwing down the final plate, as Lewis piloted his steam landau to the Kennington Oval and she and Snouts alighted at the entrance arch. "I will leave the landau at Maggie's and meet you where we sat before," he told Snouts. Then he attempted to take the screwdriver from Phil's hand. "Go, or you will be late and forfeit the race."

She hung on to the screwdriver as her eyes, concealed by the goggles, met his. "Thanks are completely inadequate. But you have mine anyway."

"I know," he said. "Good luck!"

He felt the touch of her fingers like a kiss, all the way to Maggie's.

NERVES SET up a trembling in Philomena's stomach—or perhaps that was the tremor in the board under her feet, its power leashed and eager. If she could pull this off, she could keep the staff at Oakmond. If she took first place, she could give them nest eggs to live on until they found new places. *Just one chance*, she begged the night sky. *Just one.*

"Go!" The white handkerchief came down and the ornithopters leaped into the air.

With an effort, she controlled the urge to move quickly. Lean forward. Under her toes, the pegs depressed, and power flooded the engine. She bent her knees to meet its thrust and—*wheee!*— she was flying, just as she had in her test flights over the Thames last night. She took the first turn as gracefully as a banking gull, passing up Sir Leonardo, pedalling furiously to power his canvas wings, and the Mad Hatter on his biprop. The Merman and his bubble had dropped out after last week's race, as had one of the small ornithopters. But the March Hare was in it to win, his ornithopter far out in front.

Philomena leaned forward as she passed the smaller ornithopter. It was down to her and the March Hare, and the crowd knew it. The clappering was a roar in her ears as she bent lower, her arms out behind, and aimed for the Hare like an arrow shot from a bow. Down the straightaway she flew, the foot pegs level with the board now, at maximum power.

Into the third turn, lift up on the pegs just a trifle. She went into a bank that took her to his near side—they were even—she was clear and in front! Down she went, arms back, in a crouch that made the board respond as though they were a single being. Her hair blew straight back, and she lost her cap, but now she was in the straightaway, and there was the racing master and his handkerchief, waiting for her like an old friend.

The March Hare crossed the line twenty feet behind her, and the crowd went mad, throwing their clappers into the air and storming down the stone levels of the stands as she made her victory lap above their heads. She couldn't see Mr. McTavish or Mr. Protheroe in the melee, but she knew they were there. She had never been part of a team before, never had anyone care whether she succeeded at anything. Sheer joy bubbled up inside as she brought the board in to the grassy centre, where the racing master waited with the purse.

"Well done, Acorn!" he shouted as she landed and hopped off her board. "What a showing! What an upset!"

She grinned like a fool as she accepted the purse. "Thank you, sir. Much obliged to you."

"I say!" Sir Barclay Ightham pushed his way to the front of the crowd, and Philomena's blood, which had been galloping in her veins, froze in horror. "I know you. Racing master, this pilot is a fraud."

Sir Barclay Ightham. The man Papa had offered up as the perfect suitor. The man she had been forced to take tea with on Tuesday afternoon, when she'd been dying to get over to Orpington Close to work on the device.

"Explain yourself, sir," the racing master demanded. "This man has been competing for weeks, and has won this race fairly."

"That is the problem," Ightham said with triumph. "This man is a *woman*—and women cannot compete. They are not even allowed to be spectators. She has fooled you all, and defrauded you, to boot."

A rumble went up from the crowd. A rumble that became increasingly more threatening.

The racing master frowned at her, and it was all Philomena could do to keep her back straight. She made up her mind and shoved her driving goggles up on top of her hair. "Sir Barclay is quite right," she announced. "I have been competing for weeks, and I have bested the field fairly. My sex is of no account."

"Aye!" came a voice from the back.

"She is right!" came another. A familiar voice. "This race is won by ingenuity and skill, no matter who possesses it."

"Ridiculous!" shouted Ightham. "These men have competed honourably. Will you have them shamed by a woman?"

"There is no shame in the case—unless one is a sore loser." Lewis might have been concealed by the crowd, but his remarks carried. "I call for a vote."

"An excellent notion," said the racing master. He lifted the speaking horn. "All those in favour of allowing the Acorn to claim her prize, move to my left on the field. All those against, to the right. Sharply now, we haven't got all night!"

As though his horn had been a staff, the crowd parted like the Red Sea. Philomena tried to stop the shaking of her limbs, to appear calm, as though the heavy purse clutched between her hands did not mean the difference between eating and starving for the people at Oakmond if Papa turned them all off. And then—

"The distaff side has it," cried the racing master. "Young lady, you may claim your prize, and no man here may dispute it."

Her knees went weak. "Thank you all!" she called. And then, before the other side could collect itself in a protest, she mounted her board and ignited the engine. Purse in hand, she leaned forward and soared over their heads.

Lewis clasped his hands in a victory salute. His face was alive with triumph and happiness.

For her.

Lady Philomena Noakes shot through one of the broken arches and out over the sleeping rooftops of Vauxhall, heading for Maggie's little stone cottage. Before the gentlemen arrived, she had a few very pertinent questions for her old friend about who exactly Lewis Protheroe was.

It was time for the skill and ingenuity he thought she possessed to make itself known. If Maggie had the knack of achieving what she wanted from life, then Philomena Noakes could learn it, too.

After all, she was the only woman in London with the knack of flying.

GHOST COLOURS

By Derek Künsken

P ablo whispered about x-ray energies and trace metals and sections. His refrain had backgrounded itself over the years, like the white noise of radio, weaving into dreams of other things. Vanessa pushed Brian harder.

"Get him to shut up, Brian!" she said. He blinked. The curtains glowed with sunlight. Seven-thirty, Saturday morning. "Fuck!" she said, covering her head with her pillow.

Brian slipped out of bed and padded to the kitchen. He ran the water, put on a pot of coffee, and then fell onto the couch in the living room. Pablo would follow. Pablo had haunted Brian for a few years now, and was hard on his relationship with Vanessa. The apartment smelled of coffee by the time Pablo's voice, quiet, like a TV turned low, whispered in his ear about metals and the colours of feathers.

Brian slept again and the sun was warmer and higher when Vanessa woke him by kissing his ear. "I'm sorry, honey," she whispered. "I'm so sick of that creepy thing."

"I know."

She rose from where she'd knelt, picked up yesterday's paper, and recycled it in the kitchen. Cups scraped in cupboards. He put his feet on the coffee table.

Near the TV, in neatly taped boxes, were old things, knick-knacks, souvenirs, and a lot of the dishes, art, and CDs he'd picked with his ex-wife. Old letters from his marriage. Bits of detritus he'd inherited from Aunt Nicole, like bottle openers, gifts from her clients, and going-away cards. Vanessa was right. They needed to make space for her to move into his small apartment.

Vanessa lived without the silt that filled every open space in life. If she hadn't used something in the last year, she tossed it. She lived in a pristine present and did not suffer material what-ifs and maybes.

It wasn't easy to live like Vanessa. Brian sometimes needed a past. He reminisced. He re-rooted himself, not often, and certainly not every year, but letting go of the past did not feel easy. He liked the disbelief and proof of time when he looked at college pictures. He liked reminders of dusty Christmases. His bottle caps that had once filled a bag in the closet were coloured fossils of year-bleached summers.

He'd broken cleanly with his ex-wife. He didn't carry a torch or baggage, but neither had he tossed all of their old things, the last of the evidences of what he'd had. Some things were replaceable. Some things were not. The idea of throwing away old letters and notes gave him the same dizzying feeling as slipping a tongue into a gap where he'd lost a tooth. Time misplaced things. Memory lost its edge and dredged up the wrong thing. What came after coloured what came before, dishonestly so.

His marriage had been dizzying, burning and tumbling. Their youth and passion had welded them in college, and they married for the right reasons. The end of his marriage was sad, like the end of beauty or innocence. It coloured what came before, as if there'd been no magic at all. He'd spent months wondering what life would have been like without her. Paths not taken. But then, he found a note she'd given him in the beginning, and he made peace with the past.

The idea of peace with the past bemused Vanessa. She was neither at peace nor at war with her past. She had no relationship with it. Her present was complete. Being with her pressed Brian against the rush of now. With her, he savoured food, rolling in salts and sweets and textures. Without effort, she drew his attention to his body, the muscles that surged during, and ached after, a hard game of squash or pick-up football. Even sunlight seemed to be a thing to her. Near her, it became a thing to him, when he stilled the rush of life and warmth exerted pressure on his skin. She was a lens to sharpen the wonder and bloom of the present.

Vanessa curled her feet beneath her to sit beside him.

"Are you worried about seeing the gene therapist?" she asked.

He shook his head.

She put a hand on his. "It's a few treatments, Brian. The risks are small. People with heavier hauntings than you go through this every day. It will be good for you. And good for your children."

He looked up from her hand. She had an ironic smirk. They were about to move in together. They were young. They wanted to travel, to live. They had both avoided the question of children, as if by unstated collusion.

"I'll be with you," she said.

A tiny, distant sound began, a needle-tip scratching petrified silt from fossil, and Vanessa was on her feet. Pablo spoke in a thin, oblivious voice, at the edge of audibility, as if preparing for a lecture. "*Traces of copper, revealed by synchrotron rapid-scanning x-*

ray fluorescence, map the presence of eumelanin to predict the colour of ancient feathers."

Vanessa stalked away. "I don't know what I was thinking, dating a guy whose family is haunted!" she yelled.

"I'm sorry," Brian said.

She came back in a few minutes, dressed. "I'm going to visit my mother," she said. "I'll be back in the afternoon to go with you to your appointment."

"I love you," he said.

"I love you." She came close, kissed him, and then left.

"Animal pigments, primarily melanosomes and phaeomelanin, can be mapped by x-ray illumination of zinc and calcium in fossils," Pablo whispered.

Pablo, in life, even when circuitously and fruitlessly courting Brian's Aunt Nicole, had lived in the past. His science had done nothing useful, had not done anything for the world. His life's work had been to add knowledge of colour to fossils. Plants. Animals. Feathers. Skins. Scales. Petals. And in death, Pablo clung to a love that had no use, either.

Pablo had haunted Nicole for the last decade of her life. Despite the fact that ghosts made most people uncomfortable, she had delighted in having inspired a love that death could not still. She revelled in the adoration, even as she held out for the one great love who never came. Was Pablo's enduring, unrequited love of great intrinsic value, and admirable, or was it a sign of the shallowness of Nicole's own life, that it needed a ghost to lend it meaning? In her last months, the only people at her bedside were Brian and Pablo's ghost.

"Eumelanin is inferred to have been present in the eyes of ancient fishes by the trace metals found in fossils, adding dark colours to our understanding of the past," Pablo said from far away. He spoke on,

quietly, but sometimes fiercely, about the pigmentation of fish scales, while the sound of his ghostly pick scratched an accompaniment.

It was never difficult to dispel Pablo. It only took listening to him. Pablo might not even know he was haunting Brian. Ghosts persisted, wrapped in a past they could not penetrate, and they wandered until they found a place where they were comfortable, even if they did not understand why.

ONLY WHEN HE was older did Brian come to understand what sorts of things went on at his Aunt Nicole's, although from the beginning, it had felt odd. After school each day, Brian came in by the side door in the alley. A bouncer, or a girl in her underwear holding her robe closed with her hand, opened in response to the secret knock. Backstage, some girls primped their hair or fixed their costumes.

Aunt Nicole's office was at the back, and she gave him money from the petty cash to get a Coke and a bag of chips. The machine dispensed Cokes in bottles, and he learned to pry his own bottle cap off at the machine. They listened to music from the forties and fifties on her computer. Aunt Nicole wasn't that old. She was about fifteen years older than Brian's mother, and would only have known of such music like everyone else, by digging it up.

Aunt Nicole drank gossip, even the happenings at Brian's school. She learned the names of each kid in his class and pumped him for the endings of stories that needed days to unfold. The common stories, the ones that had no ending, disappointed her. She preferred stories where what Aiden did one day affected Rafiki the next, because things were connected.

After his pop and chips and interrogation for gossip, Brian did his homework. Sometimes, she would help. Other times, she didn't need to, or she didn't know how. On Tuesday, on his second week of going to Aunt Nicole's after school, the scratching sounded, like a dentist pick on teeth. Aunt Nicole was reading a book with a beautiful girl swooning on the cover. She read as if she didn't hear the metallic scritching in the walls. When mumbling joined the noise, fear tickled down his spine.

"What's that?" Brian asked.

"Don't worry about that, sweetie," Aunt Nicole said. "That's just Pablo. He's a ghost who likes me."

Brian felt his eyebrows rise high and tight on his forehead. Two kids at his school were haunted. They weren't in his class, but he knew they got made fun of. He'd avoided them, too. The school had held a bake sale earlier in the year to raise money to get them gene therapy. Brian hoped he was never haunted.

"He's harmless," Aunt Nicole said. "He doesn't even know we're here. Not in the regular way."

"What's that noise?"

"He was a scientist. He worked with fossils, so he spent a lot of time scraping the old bones out of the rock that had them trapped. He's still doing that now."

"You talked to a ghost?"

"Well, goodness, no, Brian! You don't talk to a ghost. *They* might talk a lot, but they spend a lot of time talking to themselves."

"When did you talk to him?"

"Before he died. He used to come to see me dance when I was young."

"He liked you?" Brian finally said.

Aunt Nicole put down her book. "Sweetie, he loves me," she said, as if capitalizing the "L".

"Why?"

Aunt Nicole laughed, and Brian's face became hot.

"I was the one great love of his life."

"Why?"

Aunt Nicole patted his arm. "Everyone gets one great love, if they're lucky," she said. "Pablo had gone through most of his life without one. When he met me, he fell head over heels for me, like I was a fairy-tale princess."

"You're not a princess."

"It was meant to be, sweetie. He was meant to know his one true love."

"Is he your one true love?"

She snorted. "Pablo is too humdrum! My prince will sweep me off my feet."

The scritching scraping continued, sourceless and distant, like it was buried in the walls, or behind Brian's chair.

CHILDREN JUDGE with a purity of selfishness that adults cannot replicate. If something did not affect them, their egoism had no room for judging others. So, Nicole taught him a different view of life. She taught in parables starring Pablo and Nicole, and their mistakes. She used Pablo the way Plato used Socrates, except that her parables clung to quixotic ventures and human failings. Pablo's lack of money, his shyness, and his lack of grace and confidence all withered under her lens. She spoke down to Pablo's weakness of resolve regarding her, the begging nature of his courtship. Those things did not attract her, but in a paradox even a young Brian could see, his pining did. She had a hole in her heart, an aching for acceptance and legitimacy, just like Brian did, except that her acceptance could only be enjoyed by denying Pablo.

Nicole described Pablo's passion for science uncertainly, always grasping for the right amount of dreaminess to describe a romantic spirit nourishing itself on things long dead, his heart beating for the colours of stone-etched dinosaur feathers and fossilized flower petals.

"Why would he want to look at colours?" Brian asked.

"Wouldn't you like to know what colours the dinosaurs were?"

This question echoed, more than any other, years later. It was a serious one, aimed at him as a child, even though he understood she meant it to have more meaning than he thought. This was the one part of Pablo that was a mystery to her, and she was really asking. The soberness of that moment etched into his memories, and he traced the sweating condensation of his grape pop with the purple bottle cap. It had never before occurred to him that dinosaurs could be any colour other than green.

"Yes," Brian said.

"Knowing those colours is the great thing in his life," Nicole had said. "So much that he didn't stop doing it when he died."

"But you're the great thing in his life," Brian said.

She smiled. "I am his one great love."

Brian smiled too.

BRIAN COULD NOT SAY for sure what old thing separated Nicole from her sisters. His mother was free enough with stories of the past, but not about Nicole. In stories, Nicole was always implied to have been there, like something seen out of the corner of the eye, with conversations evaporating as soon as the young Brian asked about her.

Only when Brian's parents had divorced, and his mother was struggling with two jobs, a tiny apartment, and a son, did she finally turn to Nicole. And yet, even when Brian was spending three hours a day with Nicole, his mother avoided talking about her. She was not invited to holidays, and her gifts, "crass things," his mother had called them, hibernated in the closet until garbage day.

Brian came home with his homework done, and his pockets filled with bottle caps from strange places, printed with exotic symbols hinting at the vastness of the world. His mother, appalled, forced Brian to throw away the evidence, even if fermented, that Germany, Canada, and Holland existed. Brian saw Nicole, while his mother felt only the touch of her passing.

As soon as Brian was old enough to stay by himself, his mother ended Nicole's role in his life. And in the weird way that children keep no attachments, Brian saw no more of her, except for birthday and Christmas cards from her, which he opened eagerly for the small cheques within.

One day, when he was thirteen, for reasons he did not know, he visited her after school. The bouncers were new. Gone was the secret knock. Nicole arrived breathlessly at the door, holding closed a thin robe with a hand. Her hair was an unnatural red, and her face was older, pasty with makeup.

She hugged awkwardly, and he was between the ages that knew how to hug back. She dragged him past the bouncers indecisively, through the back, and to the old office. She wasn't the manager anymore. The pop machine had matured, shrinking into a modest thing that sold aspirin, caffeine pills, and breath mints. Aunt Nicole covered a sourceless embarrass-

ment with an effortful smile. After only a little while, Brian said
he had to go.

BRIAN DID NOT SEE Nicole again until he was in college. He was
walking past a furniture store when an older woman, smoking on
the sidewalk, stopped him. Nicole wore a respectable, but thread-
bare, suit, and sedate makeup. She must have been in her late
sixties but was still working. They began meeting every so often
for coffee.

Nicole had lost none of her ability to speak to what seemed to
be on his mind. She knew women, and she knew men better. She
pried his girl-trouble gossip out of him and pontificated on rela-
tionships, as if she were teaching him to ride his first bicycle. And
now that he was older, her lessons and stories drew on a deeper
past, his mother and grandparents.

She shone hard light on his mother's hazy half-stories. The
teenage lives of his mother and his aunts lost the editing. Nicole
filled the gaps in his mother's stories with violent boyfriends, past-
due rents, part-time work as dancers, and drunken, broken hearts.
His mother and his other aunts had left their pasts behind
because they could, because they had lived their mistakes young
enough.

Brian was, by turns, appalled and embarrassed and sympa-
thetic and forgiving for all that had been hidden. They'd
committed some of their follies when they were younger than
Brian was now, and the urge to protect them from hurts decades
gone was hard to put aside.

Nicole poured her past into him with an intensity he did not
understand for almost a year, until she needed someone to bring

her home from a medical appointment. She knew she'd been edited from her family. She understood the transient forgetfulness of the society she'd kept. And she feared vanishing, feared slipping beneath the surface without anyone noticing.

PABLO BEGAN HAUNTING Brian three years after Nicole died. Brian had been sharing a house with his college friends, shifting from a life of temporariness to the working world. Pablo came during a hockey game. At first, the distant scritching metal on stone sounded like a squirrel in the attic. The whispering came next, quiet against the game. At the end of the first period, his friends checked the cable connections, switched channels, and finally muted the TV.

His friends were fascinated, irritated, and wary. Hauntings were not dangerous. They were inconvenient. Hauntings were never perfectly on target, so neighbours looked on a haunting in a building as they would the upstairs tenants getting a big puppy, something to wake them up at odd hours and something to drive down property values.

Brian wondered if he'd done something to deserve this. By rights, his mother or one of his aunts should have been haunted. Ghosts haunted families. Informational patterns in DNA attracted them. Had the time Brian spent with Nicole predisposed Pablo to seek him out? In some cases, ghosts just vanished with those they haunted.

In the end, Brian accepted Pablo like an awkward roommate, someone easily ignored most of the time, and who, in the end, he could live with and even become fond of. Nicole had protected the ghost as if he were someone who needed protecting. He did. Just like Nicole. For all her worldly flaws, Nicole had been an innocent, as terribly vulnerable as Pablo, holding out for a great love in a world of thorns. She had hidden that hope, not telling the girls she employed, the men who visited her, nor the family she embarrassed. But she had told Brian, with the trust given to children, who rarely care. And taking care of lonely Pablo was the last gift he could give to Nicole.

ABOUT SIX MONTHS after his marriage went south, on a lark he went to a gala at an art gallery that was raising money for gene counselling and gene therapy for poor families that were haunted. Dating was not going smoothly. It was depressing to start at zero again, to meet new people without the innocence that once made trusting so easy. And he was self-conscious about Pablo. Maybe dating someone else with a ghost would make things easier.

Vanessa was the wine-toting, fast-talking machine behind the evening. She appeared twice as large as she really was, and was everywhere at once, introducing speakers, artists, and haunted families. She took money from the rich like a conman. She stopped beside him twice in that first evening, leaning in with sly comments and smiles as if they'd known one another for years. She made trust.

And she wanted to trust.

She was looking for something honest and transparent, not because she knew she needed it, but because she felt something missing. Brian was not glittery like the guests, nor luminary like the artists, nor courageous like the haunted. He just was.

The evening wound down. The luminaries were done with their glow. The haunted were finished showcasing their need. The rich left their money and guilt. Brian and Vanessa sat side by side on the stairs to the stage, wine glasses in hand. She'd just teased him about dating and the world today, and had said, "I would never date a haunted guy," like the open hand of a handshake, waiting for the responding grip.

"I'm haunted," Brian said.

She looked at him over her shoulder, sobriety creeping back upon her. "What kind of haunting?" she asked.

"Small," he said. "Quiet. Easily dismissed."

She looked at him for a long time, long enough for the evening's hope to begin to whither.

"Maybe that's not so bad," she said.

———

VANESSA PICKED him up that afternoon to drive him to the clinic. She greeted him with a kiss, a latte, and a bubbly laugh. They drove. Although somatic-cell gene therapy had come a long way, changing the DNA in most of the cells of his body, secreted away in so many different tissues and gene-expression environments, was complicated. Retroviruses could be tailored to attach to receptors in dozens of different tissue systems, and relatively non-invasive surgery could even put them past the blood-brain barrier. Technological advances had made the risks vanishingly small. Insertions of provirus into junk DNA and genes that were known not to be needed in adulthood would change Brian enough that Pablo would have a hard time recognizing him. Pablo would eventually go.

His old junk was boxed and ready to go. He understood why Vanessa wanted a clean slate. It was not because she often said, "You get over a relationship by deleting it. They're all practices for the big one that works." That was part of it, but it was too facile. Moving in together was a big step. They were conscious of the magnitude of their decisions right now. Vanessa loved him and would not share him, even with the past.

She found a spot in the parking lot of the clinic and turned off the car. Brian didn't take off his seatbelt. She looked at him and put her hand on his. "Are you scared, Brian?"

He shook his head.

"Are you having second thoughts?" she asked, more quietly.

He nodded.

"Do you think it's important to know what colour the dinosaurs were?" he asked.

ONE MILLION LIRA

By Thoraiya Dyer

They might send the old woman, Sophia thought. *If she is still alive.*

Draped in light-bending cloth, stretched out along the nacelle of the monstrous, 120-metre-tall wind turbine, she swept the crosshairs of her .50-cal sniper rifle's scope over Ehden's gaping, ruined restaurants and shattered, snow-blanketed hotels.

Seemed like nobody was left alive here.

But according to the aircraft's computer, seven passengers of seven hundred were left alive in the wreck of the skycruiser *Beirut II*, which had crashed into the side of the mountain during yesterday's snowstorm and now rested at the foot of the wind farm's twenty-one towers. Its delicate, mile-wide wings were reduced to fragments of solar panel glittering in the midday sun. Beirut itself was over the border, roughly eighty kilometres away.

It would take two days for the Beirutis to equip a mission to reclaim the fallen cruiser from its poorer neighbour and rival, the city-state of Tripoli; until then, Sóphia's instructions were to defend it from Tripoli's Maghaweer commander, Amr ibn-Amr, called Amr the Unbeautiful by the sniggering, glamorous inhabitants of the Beiruti Sky Collective.

Patience is everything.

Sophia took a sip of melted snow from a pouch she'd filled with fresh flakes piled by the wind against the vanes. The great blades of Turbine Two turned in front of her, transforming the powerful and constant westerly into current that ran, like the Kadisha River, all the way west to Tripoli on the Mediterranean Sea. She didn't dwell on the artillery that could potentially be brought to bear against her. Instead, she watched replays of her mother's famous Egyptian films in her mind's eye.

I am forbidden to leave the house, Badr said serenely on-screen in tortured voice-over as she dipped her pen in the ink, dark eyes shining with unshed tears. *I am a caged bird.*

Interviewers begged the actress to repeat those lines at age forty, even though Badr had been in *The Broken Wings* at seventeen. A hundred times she'd smiled and shaken her head while her long, gold earrings danced. She'd said the lines again, in the end, to Sophia, when her oncologist denied her a discharge from hospital.

This bird will stay truthful and virtuous to the very end.

Sophia's mother had starred in more than two hundred romantic roles, many of them ending in death. None of them featured leaky breast implants, the cause of her true death. It was why Sophia shot her victims through the left side of the chest, always.

The left breast, the one the Amazons had removed, the one that Badr had removed, to no avail.

You have one, too, Old Woman, saggy as it must be these days. You mocked me because I couldn't look them in the eye. You'd better stay by the fire. I will shoot you through the left breast, if you come.

The sunset over the sea attempted to blind her. Sophia was not so distracted by the movie replay that she failed to spot the scouts of the Mountain Combat Company when they arrived, white-swathed and carrying their skis.

They were twelve hundred metres away and poorly equipped. Some of their helmets were damaged. None carried cases of the current standard insectoid nanobots that could have infiltrated the wreck and given them the information they needed without having to directly approach it.

Sophia scrutinized each face, in search of Amr the Unbeautiful, but there was no sign of him. She flipped through a series of faces, directed to her left eye by her own highly advanced helmet's HUD, while her right eye tried to match them with the men on the slopes below.

No. None of you are valuable. None of you are important.

To keep them out of the invisible perimeter around the wind farm and crumpled skycruiser, she waited for the turbine blade to pass before shooting the closest one through the self-healing cloth.

They went to ground, but it wasn't going to ground as the well-financed Beiruti troops might have known it; there was no fading into nothingness provided by light-bending cloth, no approaching ball of flame from an auto-laser-triangulation retaliation device, just hunkering behind walls and debris. They had to know she would be on one of the towers, but with the wind too strong to place spying nanobots, even if they did have them, and with both distance and the vibration of the blades interfering with the detection of sound and shockwave signatures, they had no hope of knowing which one.

Now choose, Sophia thought coldly. How badly did Amr the Unbeautiful wish to seize the *Beirut II*? Badly enough to bombard the wind farm with rockets? He could destroy her, but not without destroying Tripoli's main source of power; not without plunging his city into darkness.

And perhaps the turbines could never be rebuilt. Perhaps the city would go into eternal darkness, as so many cities and countries across the world had done, with no more fossil fuels to burn and anyone with money gone to join the sky collectives.

A skylife wasn't completely free of danger. The continuously flying, solar-powered, high-altitude townships must land once a month or so to replenish their supply of water. Accidents could happen. The *Beirut II* was proof of that. Still, a skylife was better than a landlife, even if Beirut had been forced to appropriate billions of dollars that technically belonged to Tripoli so that all of its wealthy citizens and their families could become airbound.

A decade later, the rage of those who were left behind was undiminished. The enemy was within reach, at last; on the ground, like a bird with a broken wing. Sophia would permit them no hostages.

Two more men crossed Sophia's invisible line. She shot them, too. Killing was easy, when you accepted it was the only way to survive. She had been a killer since birth. In the summer when the heatwave had come and the crops failed, when Beirut and Tripoli were one country, she had patrolled the border against bread-thieving black-market incursions; learned to kill twice with one shot, to kill the men who came and the families who now would not eat.

She killed, too, by being wealthy, by reaping the world's inequality to pay for chemotherapy developed by a global corporatocracy. Was that different from a bullet through the heart?

Bullets were cleaner than starvation and the horrors of lawlessness. She hadn't always been so wise. The old woman, who fought for money and had no scruples, had tutored her. *One*, Khadija had whispered in her smoke-ravaged voice, gnarled feet bare on the pine bark, like a perched owl. *One is five hundred thousand lira. Nine more and I can go home. Ten is enough to pay my bills today.*

You fill your quota like you have a bag to be filled with geese, Sophia had accused from the lateral branch below, lowering her spotter's scope. She'd signed up to defy her father, who wanted her married and safely out of the police force. Despite the jeers of young men who had failed to complete the commando course, she'd earned her sword-and-tiger badge in just a few months. This was her first deployment, and she was uncomfortable with the intimacy of the stalking phase. She could never be so intimate with men at home; see the sweat beading in their chest hair or the smoothness of skin over breastbone, the movement of their Adam's apples as they took long swallows of purified river water.

If you can look in a wild animal's eye as you take its life, Khadija said, *you can look into the eyes of a man.*

But Sophia couldn't. Khadija told her to aim for the chest. To pretend it was empty jackets on a clothesline. Even a weepy girl could shoot an empty jacket, couldn't she?

Her mother's empty jackets had filled three walk-in wardrobes. Sophia had wept over those jackets. The first and last time she had wept as an adult.

Now she scanned for the sniper that belonged to the combat platoon. She had the superior position. The only ridgeline that offered a comparable elevation was two kilometres away, too far away for backwards Tripoli to threaten her in these high winds. The sniper must position himself closer, in the ruins of Ehden.

There.

Sophia killed him and continued to search for the arriving support platoon. Most likely they would stay in the shelter offered by the mountainside, but if they were malnourished, or exhausted by the climb in the cold and the snow, who knew what mistakes they might make?

Her helmet told her that six skycruisers had landed in Beirut port. Troops had disembarked. Snowmobiles were being charged. New estimated time of arrival was noon the following day.

She didn't get another opportunity to thin the enemy's numbers. An hour before sunset, however, the small figure of a child was pushed by a rifle butt out into the snow from behind a concrete wall.

The child struggled with something square and presumably heavy. Snot and tears dribbled down his red face. Sophia wanted to shoot through the wall, to kill the unseen man who must be threatening him, but such solid evidence of trajectory could only end in her death. Calming herself, setting her emotions aside, like burying the bones of a meal in the snow, she watched the child wade through whiteness toward the *Beirut II*.

She couldn't allow an unidentified device to be brought any closer.

Breathe in. Breathe out.

With her lungs half-emptied, in the millisecond before the blade of the wind turbine obscured the shot, she squeezed the trigger and the rifle kicked.

The small body fell.

Nobody moved to retrieve him.

Sophia switched the movie back on in her head.

Husband, I am leaving you, said the beautiful actress, her head bowed. Her bosom heaved, distress made manifest. The jilted husband stared at her flimsily clad breasts, no doubt thinking they would soon belong to another man.

The sun went down, and spotlights came to life around Turbine Two, maintaining the snowy surroundings as bright as daylight. She had counted on the constant illumination. Her invisibility cloth permitted enough visible light to pass unidirectionally through it for her targeting to be unimpeded, but infrared radiation did not pass through at all. Unless she removed the drapes, revealing her location, her thermal imaging components were useless.

Sophia ate a small bar of chocolate and switched her insulation suit to its nighttime setting. She hadn't washed her hands. Her fingers, when she licked the chocolate from them, tasted of gunpowder residue and light machine oil.

Patience was everything, and her gut told her that the old woman would come.

"YOU DID WHAT WITH AN ORPHAN BOY?" demanded the president of the City-State of Tripoli.

The meeting room, a shadow of its former glory, showed plaster where the solid gold embellishments had been chipped away, melted, and sold, but the two dozen men around the polished table were well-enough accoutred to heavily distort the mean atomic mass back in the direction of 197 amu.

Yet not enough wealth to buy even one skycruiser, the president thought, despairing.

Prayer beads slipped through the fingers of the man he confronted across the table, Amr ibn-Amr, Commander of the Maghaweer.

"The cedar forest below Ehden," the commander said as though the president had not spoken. "We must set fire to it. You will give permission, of course."

The president, who in his youth had led the Lebanese soccer team to statistically improbable World Cup glory in the year before the first Beiruti skycruiser launched and the country was divided forever, recalled a hundred thousand flags flying in the great stadium, each one stamped with a green, stylized cedar.

"No," he said.

He still heard the drums in his dreams. The ululation of the women. The people had voted for his familiar face, jug-eared and broken-nosed. His was the dented forehead that had scored. His were the teeth whose kicking earned that vital penalty.

"We need a smokescreen," argued Amr, whose teeth had a gap suited to pulling grenade pins or imprisoning small birds. "Without smoke, we can't get past the snipers to approach the cruiser. The *Beirut II* is non-military. The passengers won't resist."

"The Beirutis will be here for their passengers very soon. And from your reports, I would guess there is only one sniper."

The commander snatched the beads up into his palm. He drained the dregs of his coffee and stood up as if to leave.

"One sniper? It is an insult to suggest that is all they would send against our elite forces. Listen. Ordinary agents and canisters cannot obscure the area around the turbines where the skycruiser has crashed. The wind in the mountains is strong and constant. In the name of God, the Compassionate, the Merciful. It is why we built them there!"

The others watched in silence. The military men mocked the president for his inexperience in combat and the religious leaders mocked him for his so-called spinelessness; he had once bowed to his European sponsors, who wanted him cleanshaven. But he knew something, now, that they didn't, and he paused to enjoy it.

"You don't need a wildfire. To counter this sniper, you need another female sniper."

"You heap insult upon insult."

Everyone has her signature shot, his father's sister had told him. *Not only because she has pride in her work. But she must be paid, also, yes? Getting paid is very important.*

"Look at the images again. They are all shot in the left side of the chest."

"Respected President. Remind me when you served."

The president had avoided conscription. He had flown on the wings of a sports scholarship into the distant arms of elite coaches, but he knew patterns when he saw them, and now that he had seen this one, his thoughts raced. Was she still alive? What if she was living from the land, in the abandoned wilds? Would he have time to find her?

"We are all taught to aim for the larger target, sir," the crisply turned-out subcommander said from the commander's right side.

"Why don't we do that, then?"

"Sir?"

"Why don't we all aim for the larger target? Use artillery to shoot down the wind turbines, like whacking the heads off wildflowers?"

Nobody answered. It was too high a price to pay. Better to swallow the humiliation of allowing the Beirutis to trespass across their borders at will.

The president had played unwinnable games before. He did not think this was one.

"If, by sunrise tomorrow morning, I have not solved your

sniper problem," he said, "you can set fire to the oldest forest in the world."

"What are you going to do?" the commander asked incredulously. "Walk up there and offer to sign autographs?"

The president smiled. "I won't be walking. My bodyguards and I will be taking the underground train. Oh, and I require every man here to give up his gold. Place your cufflinks and everything else into this ashtray, please. I have no time for budgetary wrangling."

THE MOUNTAIN RAILWAY tunnels and the limestone caves that they intersected were closed at various junctions by criminal gangs; by religious cults; by the homeless, dying to the sound of dripping stalactites, out of reach of sunlight.

Every time the train was stopped and armed boys came aboard, the president faced them calmly. They were overjoyed to recognize him.

"Goal for Liban!" they cried happily, and, sometimes, "The scent of a modern man!" which was one of several foreign product endorsements routinely mistaken for a nationalistic jingo. His hosts offered pine-bark tea, pistachios, and cigars. The president patiently endured their hospitality, trying not to check his watch. After a final cheek-slap from an angry sheik who told him to grow a beard, the train was permitted to complete its journey. He ascended the wet, slippery stair to the surface.

"To the Ain," he told a farmer at the station entrance, and with the press of a gold earring into a wrinkled palm, the president and his two bodyguards secured three saddled, skinny horses that put their royal Arabian bloodstock to shame. However, the roads were fallen into such neglect that, in the absence of functional heli-copters, only horses would do.

It was late evening. He had only one hope of finding Aunty Khadija. She would have no electronic devices on her person, no phone: nothing to hack and no way to track her.

The horses knew the way, even without the eerie glow of the chemical lamps carried by the bodyguards through the desolate winterscape. They passed the Ain, the archway that sheltered a freshwater spring.

The forest will not burn, the president told himself, and also the fans who had waved the flags.

She stood outside her square stone farmhouse, letting blood from a goat whose throat she'd recently cut.

"Hajji!" he cried, instantly ashamed by his boyish relief at what he saw as his rescue from an impossible situation. The smell of blood made his horse shy, and he almost lost control of it.

Khadija put stained fists on her apron-sheathed hips.

"My sins have been forgiven," she scowled, blinking in the dimness, "and here you are to beg me to sin again. Get down from there, you ball-kicking fool. Let me see you. My eyes are not what they were."

My eyes are not what they were, Khadija thought, *but that is why Allah created 25X-zoom, longer eye relief, and a smaller exit pupil.*

She would not think of the weapon she'd taken as a trophy, although she now hoped to turn it against its arrogant manufac-turers. It was the unknown, the unexpected, that must be brought to bear if she were to have a hope of outwitting a younger, better-equipped opponent, if Trabelsi was to triumph over Beiruti.

Sophia.

She had seen the captured images. The president's murky memory of the legend of Khadija's protégé, the blonde actress's daughter who wanted revenge on her mother's cancer, had led him to her home, with a wish and a deadline: daybreak.

In the blue-white light of her hand-held, rechargeable lantern, the posters in the stairwell were mouldy and torn. Black slush covered the marble floor, and a half-bald dog snarled from a side room, hackles rising.

"This is the place," Khadija said, smoothing one of the rips, reuniting half the ringmaster's moustache with the other half.

Najib's Travelling Tent of Wonders.

"Please," the president told one of his bodyguards. "Go upstairs. Wake him up and bring him down."

Once a wizard of the Trabelsi hologram theatre, Najib appeared in the bodyguard's keeping with no flourishes and no defences. His neat, dark hair was brittle, his singlet worn, and his neck unshaven.

"Do not eat my dog," he begged, before he saw who it was. "Sir! I am humbled. Why have you . . . How did you . . . ?"

"You sent my daughter one letter too many, Najib," Khadija said. "Now you must help me save Tripoli, for her."

"Is she here?" Najib stumbled in his eagerness.

"Of course not! Do you think I would let her, or any of her sisters, come back from the schools that I sent them to? Do you think I shot those poor boys at the border because I wanted a rifle of solid gold? She's married to a French doctor, raising her family in a well-off country, far from here."

Najib sagged.

"Then why—"

"I have dreamed that the children of my children's children

returned to stand beneath the ancient trees. The idiot commander of the Maghaweer says he will burn them at daybreak if we do not flush out the sniper on the wind turbine."

"We?"

"You have your old recordings, I hope, Najib. And your laser projection boxes. Even though your licence was taken away. The night club, the people that died from ozone poisoning? You should never have promised them a full-length feature in such a poorly ventilated space."

"I am tired, old woman. Tell me what you want."

"An open-air screening. With as many holograms as you can. Tonight, in Ehden."

"Are you mad? The recordings are degraded, and there is no portable power source that can run even one such projection anymore."

"There is a transformer underneath Ehden," the president said softly. "The power cables from all the wind turbines pass through it. Our men can get access to it without exposing themselves to sniper fire."

Najib licked his lips.

"It has been a long time since I saw my beauties," he admitted at last. "Far too long."

KHADIJA HAD no cloth to hide behind on the ridge.

She murmured a quick and blasphemous prayer to the God of Snow, whose temple had once stood where she stood. In 850 BC, the Aramean King raised a great statue of Baal Loubnan at Ehden.

A hundred and fifty years later, the Assyrian King had the temple torn down and the statue overturned.

They come and they go, she thought. Christianity had come to Ehden in the sixth century. Now the little churches and abandoned monasteries were deathly silent. So, too, the crashed skycruiser that gleamed at the foot of the towering, spotlit turbines. Was there even anyone alive inside? Was all this for nothing?

"It is done, Hajji," said the Maghaweer subcommander. She had hand-picked him to accompany her and had already forgotten his name. He was polite, which could have been misread as insipidness, but Khadija recognized it as unflappability, which he would need if her plan failed and Sophia shot her through her left breast.

In the piercing cold and whistling darkness, her body heat should have shone out like a beacon to anyone with thermal sensors. Khadija was operating on the information, several years old, that infrared detection was not possible through light-bending cloth. If she was wrong, if improvements had been made to the technology, even the tiny peephole in the wall of snow that the Subcommander had constructed for them would be instantly obvious to the enemy.

But why should the Beirutis have made advances in military technology? They were safe in their sky-cities, protected by international treaty from satellite-based weapons, their cruising altitude too great for them to be vulnerable to attack from below.

Khadija searched the nacelle of each turbine for any sign of life. When she found nothing, she searched each ponderously swinging blade for the shadows of ropes or a discrepancy in rotation, which might have indicated the weight of a human being dragging asymmetrically on the structure.

Nothing.

On Khadija's advice, dogs had been sent to sniff for urine

around the bases of the towers, but had been shot before they could come close. They must rely on Sophia revealing herself, perhaps only for a fraction of a second. Khadija must not miss.

She had no targeting computer to help her. That section of rail on her monstrous, white-anodized, stolen StraightLine 20mm sat empty. But these peaks were her brothers and sisters, and her calculating ability had not wasted away like her muscles and bones.

Her body was brittle, she knew. She could not lie full-length in the snow for very long, even in the insulating suit the subcommander had found for her, too big in the shoulders and too tight in the hips.

"Tell me," she said as he settled alongside her.

"Yes, Hajji. Manual readings verify westerly winds of thirty-seven kilometres per hour, deformed around the turbines in the expected pattern, blade to blade interval a uniform three point two seconds, humidity sixty percent, temperature minus four degrees Celsius, altitude one thousand, five hundred and five metres."

Khadija did not respond verbally to this information, absorbing it into herself, willing herself to become one with the mountain, with the skies and the whispering forest below, even as she made the physical adjustments.

A moment later, beautiful women sprang up in the pristine snow field between the turbines and the ruins of Ehden.

Seven widely spaced holographic images of seventeen-year-old Egyptian actress Badr raised swan-like arms, imploringly. There was no sound, but the moment was famous, the words immortal.

This bird will stay truthful and virtuous to the very end.

More of the images moved in from the wings. Men and

women. Some frozen. Others distorted. Najib had told the truth when he said the recordings were degraded, but the strength of the broadcast was enough that many of the images could not be differentiated in the visible light spectrum from real human beings.

Khadija flicked her sight to its thermo-optical setting. There, the figures blazed. Where the beams of the lasers intersected and the air became ionized, voxels exploded like suns. She could not waste precious time enjoying the show, however.

There.

High atop Turbine Two, the lens of a telescopic sight reflected the light.

Khadija zoomed in. Only the weapon's sight had been uncovered by the enemy. Seeing her young, doomed mother move across the snow had confounded but not flustered Sophia. She had quickly realized that to distinguish human from hologram, she must discard the cloth. Her body remained hidden by the cloth, but the eye, the eye would be a hand's-breadth behind the sight.

Khadija lined up her crosshairs. She'd never had a problem looking her victims in the eye, but in that instant she was grateful to Sophia for hiding her face behind the invisible cloth. Without a face, she was an un-person. Even a dog had a face.

She took the shot. The StraightLine was deafening. Her ears rang. The brass casing melted itself a cradle in the snow, and an old, familiar litany of grief and victory whispered between heartbeats, just as the trigger had been pulled between heartbeats: *Thank you for the gift of your life.*

It was too far for her to hear the body strike the ground, but she didn't need to glimpse the glitter of the scope falling from the turbine tower to know that it was done.

One. One is five hundred thousand lira.

One was enough. She should stand down now. The subcommander beside her murmured, "Casualty confirmed," and moved to pack up his gear, but Khadija said sharply:

"Wait."

Her shoulder felt like it was on fire. She no longer had the brute strength to manage the kick of such a weapon. She sensed that once she took it apart, she would never assemble it again.

Then she saw a terrified Najib being forced out into the open.

"He is worse than an animal!" Khadija exclaimed. The order for such an outrage could only have come from the commander, Amr ibn-Amr. The same man who trained his soldiers to use orphan boys to test an enemy sniper's resolve, the same man who had threatened to burn the cedar forest that was the last thing of splendour and grace left behind when the country was stripped and consigned to the skies.

"You did say there was only one, Hajji," the subcommander said quietly.

"And what will an animal like that do with the Beiruti women and children who are inside the wreck of the cruiser?"

"That is not for me to guess, Hajji."

Khadija watched the Mountain Combat Company come out into the open. With increasing confidence, they moved to secure a perimeter around the unprotected craft. The commander himself went to find Sophia's body.

He wants the light-bending cloth for himself, Khadija realized. *Once he has it, nobody will be able to punish him for treating his own allies like paper targets.*

Before the subcommander could protest, she shot his superior in the back, placing the bullet where it would emerge from his left breast. The soldiers in formation around their leader dropped into the snow.

"No!" the subcommander breathed, too late.

Two, Khadija thought. *Two is one million lira.*

She would not be paid this time. Who cared?

"Congratulations on your promotion," she said to the shocked subcommander, patting the stock of the StraightLine. "This is yours, now. Use it wisely, and always remember. If you can look in a wild animal's eye as you take its life, you can look into the eyes of a man. If not, you had better shoot for the chest."

Rubbing her sore shoulder, she packed up her survival gear. Her water and her dried goat meat. Her explosives and her wire snares.

"If I let you go, I am a traitor, Hajji."

"Then you had better come along."

He had carried the weapon in for her. Only he could carry it out, and only its absence would deter pursuit. For a moment, it seemed he would stay there, frozen in the snow, until the men who had been his brothers up until one minute ago came to drag him away.

"I have nothing else," he said calmly. "I have nothing else but this."

"I have an unmarried youngest daughter," Khadija said. "The ball-kicking fool gave me enough gold that we could easily go to visit her. She likes skinny men."

Snow began to fall as the subcommander helped her with her skis. It was powdery and perfect, hiding them as they swished, silent as wild things, down the sloping side of the mountain.

POD DREAMS OF TUCKERTOWN
By Gareth L. Powell

I.

All Pod wants to do is hang with his friends, Erik and Kai. But he can't, not anymore. Not since the Clampdown. Not since the Elite looked down from their high orbit and decided to rationalize human society, to make it ordered and safe. Not since they sent him here, to the bridge, to work off his criminal debt.

He hates the bridge. He hates the stinging wind and the crashing waves. He hates the tedious, backbreaking work. But most of all, he hates his foreman, Fergus.

He hates Fergus for hurting Kai. Kai bungled a weld on one of the support girders, and so Fergus stamped on her spine until she couldn't walk. Now all Pod wants to do is kill Fergus. He lies in his bunk at night and dreams of smashing Fergus's head with a wrench or pushing him over the railings into the sea. But deep down, he knows he won't. They've got him pumped so full of sedatives that he can't even get an erection, let alone pick a fight.

So, day after day, he works on the bridge. The wind burns his skin, the sun makes him squint. But he gets through it by thinking of Kai and remembering how good things used to be—how great it was when they used to hang out together at the diner by the docks in Tuckertown, where they could see the lights of the trawlers and laugh at the stink of the last of the day's fish guts being hosed off the quay.

They weren't into anything heavy back then, just stealing cars and joyrides. There were some fights, and some cars got burned, but no one ever got killed. There were no knives or guns—it was all just for laughs, something to do when the rain came down and the markets closed for the night.

But then—on Pod's eighteenth birthday—the Elite came down in their shining silver saucers, and everything changed, once and for all.

Erik says Fergus has a girl back in Tuckertown.

"So what?" Pod says. "Everybody says they've got *someone* waiting for them."

"It just shows he's human, is all," Erik says. He looks thin. He's not eating. Fergus kicked him in the stomach a week ago, and he hasn't been right since.

"Does it still hurt?" Pod says.

Erik rolls back over on his bunk and closes his eyes. "I'll be okay," he says.

POD SAW one of the Elite yesterday. It came to inspect the bridge. Even Fergus was terrified of it.

"What did it look like?" Erik asks. He missed it—he was in bed, recovering from the kicking.

Pod scratches his cheek. He badly needs a shave.

"Like a cockroach," he says. "A big, wet cockroach with claws like steak knives."

Erik shivers, and his eyes flick nervously to the ceiling.

"But that's not the worst," Pod says. "The worst is when they talk."

"What does it sound like?"

Pod lies back on his bunk, an arm resting over his eyes.

"Like cats being sick," he says.

POD LOST everything in the Clampdown—home, parents—everything except Erik and Kai.

He doesn't like to think about it. He prefers to remember Tuckertown as it was, before the saucers landed.

"Do you remember the burger stall on West Pier Street, by the tannery?" he says. "And the girl that worked there, with the big tits?"

Erik doesn't answer. He's holding his stomach. There's a man crying a few bunks down the row, and a couple having furtive sex under a blanket in the far corner. The place reeks of piss and sweat, but Pod doesn't notice the smell much anymore.

He scratches at a cut on his hand.

"And that bar on the corner, where Kai used to dance?" he says.

He tugs Erik's sleeve. "Remember that?"

Erik shakes him off.

"Go to sleep," he says.

———

THINKING of Kai brings the anger back. Pod lies awake, listening to Erik's ragged snore. If Erik dies, Pod's going to kill Fergus for sure —he doesn't know how yet, but he'll get him.

He pulls his right hand into a fist. The muscles in his palm feel like wires.

If Erik dies . . .

He rolls over into a fetal position, pulling the rough blanket over his head to hide the sudden hot tears that prick his eyes. He's eighteen years old, starving and desperate.

Tomorrow, the Chemist will be here. It's a small comfort, but he clings to it.

———

2.

IT'S STILL dark outside when the dormitory lights go on. There are no showers. The workers sleep in their clothes. When the lights go on, they crawl out of their blankets and file toward the door, their breath clouding in the cold air.

Pod helps Erik.

"You've got to let me go to the hospital," Erik says.

Pod shakes his head. "They took Kai to the hospital and she never came back," he says.

Erik grits his teeth. "She had a broken back. That takes time to fix. And then she still wouldn't be any use here. They probably shipped her off to work in a factory or something."

Pod grunts. He's got most of Erik's weight on his shoulders, and he's in no mood to argue. He's seen the mass graves on the hill behind the camp, and he's got a pretty good idea where Kai ended up.

"It doesn't matter," he says. "I'm going to get you fixed up. You'll be okay."

Erik coughs. "How are you going to do that, Pod? My guts are wrecked. How are you going to fix that?"

Pod squeezes his arm.

"We're going to see the Chemist," he says.

THE CHEMIST'S a man with a shiny suit and a thin face, like a weasel. He sits on a makeshift chair behind a makeshift desk in a makeshift office.

"What can I do for you?" he says, squinting up as they enter.

Pod helps Erik into a chair and then leans on the desk.

"I need something for my friend here," he says.

The Chemist looks down his nose at Erik.

"You want medical supplies?" he says. "Why, what's wrong with him?"

Pod straightens up. "He's messed up inside—he needs fixing."

The man *tuts* and *tsks* to himself. He pulls a medical scanner from his bag and waves it at Erik. A red light appears on the display.

"Ah yes, an internal hemorrhage," he says. "And I'm afraid it's quite serious."

"He's not going to the hospital," Pod says firmly.

The Chemist sighs and puts the scanner down. "In that case, he'll probably be dead in a day or so."

He looks down at the papers on his desk, to signal that the interview's over. But Pod leans across and puts his hand over the passage the man's pretending to read.

"But you've got something that can help him, don't you?" he says.

The Chemist leans back, lip curled in distaste. He comes to the camp once a month, ostensibly to check on the health of the workers, but really to line his own pockets by smuggling in forbidden items, like cigarettes and heroin, to sell to them.

"Something powerful enough to fix that much damage won't come cheap," he says.

Pod frowns. His palms are sweating, but there's no going back now.

"I want to pawn some memories," he says.

THE SCANNER the Chemist uses is Elite tech. It can cut and paste memories, lift them wholesale—including all their related associations—from one mind and drop them into another.

Pod sits back in the plastic chair, eyes closed.

"Try to make it a happy memory," the Chemist says. "The Elite pay so much more for happy memories."

Pod grits his teeth. All he can think about is Tuckertown—the place he grew up in, the place he met Kai and Erik.

He remembers the harbour and the unloading trawlers; the downtown mall and the park behind it; and the alley where Kai used her mouth to take his virginity.

"Don't do it, for God's sake," Erik pleads from across the room.

Pod waves him to silence—he's aware of the horror stories, and he's seen the zombies walking around the camp with their minds accidentally wiped. He knows the dangers, but he thinks it's worth the risk, to save his friend.

After all, he couldn't save Kai . . .

He tightens his grip on the arm of the chair. His hands are sweaty where they're gripping the plastic.

"Shut up," he says.

He takes a deep breath and then turns to the Chemist. "Okay, I'm ready."

The man presses the scanner hard against Pod's scalp. "Concentrate," he says.

Pod screws his eyes tight. He thinks of the sun coming up over the meat factory in Tuckertown, of a burning car reflected in the oily water of the canal. The scanner feels hot against his head.

"Lie still," the Chemist says.

The heat increases. There's a moment of intense pain—sharp agony like trapped cats ripping at the inside of Pod's skull—and the world falls away, leaving only darkness.

<hr />

3.

WHEN HE WAKES, it's late afternoon. He's lying on his bunk, back in the dormitory, and grey light slants in through the windows.

It's quiet—the rest of the workers are out on the bridge. For a moment, he thinks he's got the place to himself, and then he hears Erik cough. He rolls over.

"What happened?" he says.

Erik smiles crookedly.

"That weasel zapped you, and you went down—bang!—like an epileptic."

"Did it work?"

"I guess so—he gave me the pills."

Pod props himself up on an elbow. "Have you taken them? How are you feeling?"

Erik coughs. "A bit better," he says.

Pod scratches his head. He feels unusually alert, like a cold wind's blown through him.

"How long have I been asleep?"

"About three hours—Fergus is mad as hell. He tried to wake you, but I told him you were sick."

Erik puts a hand on his arm. "Do you feel different, Pod? Are the cobwebs gone?"

Pod frowns. He's clear-headed for the first time in months. His thoughts are lucid and sharp, like they used to be, before he came here.

"What did you do?" he asks suspiciously.

Erik grins. "I talked the Chemist into selling me a stimulant— something strong enough to counteract the sedatives in our food." He flips across an empty hypodermic, and Pod catches it with his left hand.

"I told the weasel it was for me," Erik says, "to get me back to work faster. It cost everything we own—all the cigarettes, everything."

Pod rubs a sore spot on his arm. "And you injected me with it while I slept?"

Erik pulls a handkerchief from his pocket. It's old and torn, and it belonged to Kai. He passes it to Pod.

"I did it for her," he says.

THE WIND'S bitter as Pod steps onto the bridge, holding the hand-kerchief. He looks up at the towers that support the suspension cables as if seeing them for the first time. They shine in the blus-tery afternoon light, huge and solid, built to withstand the wind and tide.

Up ahead, he sees his crew. This week, they're welding the safety rails on the windward side of the bridge. It's a dull and dirty job, but a lot less dangerous than some they've done.

As he gets closer—head down, shambling, Erik struggling to keep up—he sees Fergus watching him. The supervisor has a wooden cane in his hand. His eyes are slits, and he's tapping the cane against his boot.

"Where the hell have you been?" he shouts as soon as Pod's close enough to hear him over the sound of the wind.

Pod doesn't try to reply. He remembers Fergus stamping on Kai's spine, and he remembers feeling angry—but the source of the anger's gone.

"I'm here to kill you," he says. But even as the words leave his mouth, he frowns, unsure if that's what he really wants.

Seeing his confusion, Fergus laughs.

"You bought some funny fungus from the Chemist, did you?"

Pod shakes his head, trying to summon up the determination he'll need to see this through. He walks over to one of his work-mates and pulls the wrench from her hands. It's big and heavy, solid steel. He hefts it in one hand and slaps it into his palm. He turns to face Fergus.

"I'm serious," he says.

The other workers in the crew back away, scared. They think Pod's gone mad, and that he's going to get a beating—they don't suspect the stimulants burning in his veins.

And neither does Fergus, judging from his swagger.

"Come on then, try it," he says.

Pod grins. He hasn't felt this good since . . .

He stops and scratches his head.

Since . . .

It feels like there's something on the tip of his tongue, something important. He knows he's got to kill Fergus for what he did to Kai, but he can't remember why Kai's so important.

He looks at Erik.

Then he realizes he can't remember anything beyond twelve months ago, when he first arrived here, on the bridge. He looks up, confused. Just how much of his memory has the Chemist taken?

Suddenly dizzy and nauseous, he leans on the safety rail for support. He needs time to clear his head, but he's not going to get it—he's challenged Fergus in front of the whole crew, and now Fergus will kill him if he can't defend himself.

POD USES the wrench to block the first blow. Fergus—used to the inept shambling of his drugged workers—grunts in surprise.

He strikes again, his technique crude but powerful. Pod blocks a blow to the head, another to the neck. Then Fergus's cane catches him across the shins. He cries out and jabs forward with the wrench, catching his tormentor in the chest. Fergus staggers back, cursing. He stabs out with the cane. Pod dodges the blow, but he's got the railing behind him and nowhere to go.

The next thrust catches him in the side, scraping his ribs. Fergus pulls back, lunges again, and the tip of the cane skewers Pod's thigh. He lashes out with a cry of pain. He steps forward and brings the wrench around in a swinging arc. Too late, Fergus tries to block the blow, and the solid steel wrench shatters his wrist. He cries out, and Pod punches him in the face, knocking him flat on the tarmac.

Erik's holding a welding lance. Pod snatches it and leans over Fergus, really angry now. The blue flame roars in the cold air.

"Are you ready, fucker?" he says through clenched teeth. He leans in close. Fergus is still curled around the agony in his wrist. When he feels the heat of the flame, he whimpers.

"Please don't," he says. "Please, no. I've got a kid in Tuckertown —a little girl. Please . . ."

He twists and turns, trying to get away from the hot flame, but Pod's kneeling on his legs.

"Tuckertown?" Pod says. The name's familiar. He's heard it mentioned around the camp, but when he tries to focus on it, he comes up against something scratchy, like static.

In desperation, he grabs at the only thing he's certain of.

"You crippled my friend," he says.

Fergus pulls a battered picture from his breast pocket, thrusts it in his face. "Look at her," he says desperately. "Look at my little girl."

<hr />

4.

POD SITS HEAVILY on the wet tarmac. He's wanted to kill Fergus for months, but now Fergus is sobbing and the whole thing seems ridiculous and embarrassing.

"*You've* got a kid?" he says, turning the picture over in his hands.

Fergus swallows. "Her name's Jess," he says. "She's three years old. If I get this section of the bridge finished on time, they'll let me see her."

He's holding his broken wrist tight against his chest. Looking down at him, Pod feels sick. There's no satisfaction to be had here.

"You hurt my friend," he says. He looks out at the grey horizon, and it starts to rain. In his hand, the welding lance spits and hisses.

Fergus can't take his eyes off it. "Don't burn me," he says. "Don't burn me, and I'll get you out of here."

Pod spits into the flame. "You can't do that," he says. "You don't have the authority to do that."

Fergus pushes himself upright, his back against the railings. "There's something you should know," he says.

Pod steps back, out of reach. "What?" he says. He has the welding lance in one hand, the steel wrench in the other.

"Your parole came up," Fergus blurts. "You're free men."

He glances at Erik.

"Both of you," he says.

IT TAKES Pod a while to understand.

"Look," says Fergus, "When your release order came through, I didn't tell you. You should've been out of here a couple of months back, but I kept you on because you're a good worker and I need to hit target—I need to see my little girl." He's pale, and his hands are shaking. He looks like he's going into shock.

"I was just trying to do my job," he says.

Pod takes a shuddering breath. Two extra months stuck here, when he could've been at home with his memory intact . . .

He picks up Fergus's wooden cane and snaps it over his knee.

Then he throws the two halves over the railing, into the sea. He throws the wrench and the blowtorch after them.

"So, if I walk down to the gates at the end of the bridge, they'll let me through? I'll be a free man?" he says.

Fergus nods. His teeth are clenched against the pain in his wrist.

"Please, just go," he says. "Go back to Tuckertown and leave me alone."

———

POD LIMPS AWAY. His leg hurts and there's blood in his shoe. He limps down the slope of the bridge toward the security gates at the end, where the carriageway meets the land. Behind him, the rest of the work crew crowd in on their wounded supervisor. Despite the sedatives they've been given, they can see he's lost the advantage.

If Fergus screams as they begin kicking him, Pod doesn't hear it. He's holding tightly to Kai's handkerchief.

As he passes the dormitory hut, Erik catches up with him. Somewhere above the clouds, the sun's setting.

"Come on," Pod says, "we're leaving."

IN SILENT STREAMS, WHERE ONCE THE SUMMER SHONE

By Seanan McGuire

Everyone always assumed the end of the world would be big and flashy and impossible not to see, the Disney Apocalypse, writ neon-bright against a blasted sky. It was supposed to be the one party we were all invited to, no matter how popular we were, or how pretty, or how blessed by good circumstance and better genes. The end of the world would come for us all. The end of the world would teach us how to share.

Everyone always assumed that when the end of the world came, we'd at least notice that it was happening.

We were supposed to at least know.

Snapshot from a sepia-coloured summer in a time that might as well be a fairy tale, for all the good that it can do us now:

The grass is lush and the flowers are blooming and somewhere birds are singing, and a little girl with hair the colour of cornsilk in the spring is walking in a state of absolute solemnity through a patch of clover. She stops, lifting one Mary Jane-clad foot, and steps carefully down on the ground in front of her. Her expression doesn't waver as she steps back again, and then bends to pick up the stunned honeybee by one crumpled wing. It strains to sting her but can't find the angle; she knows what she's doing. She's done this before. The bee goes into a jar with six others. At the end of recess, she'll take the jar to the third-grade science teacher, who will give her a quarter for every bee she brings him. The bees will be fed to his praying mantis with the entire third-grade science class looking on.

She doesn't think she's doing anything wrong. He doesn't think he's doing anything wrong. There are always more bees. There are always more patches of clover luring them in, tiny lighthouses of pollen in the middle of a verdant sea. There is always another summer, full of little girls in Mary Janes, buzzing bees, and fists full of silver quarters. She doesn't think she's doing anything wrong.

There will always be more bees.

God, we were fools.

BACK WHEN WE were in the business of assumption—less than a decade ago, and so many lifetimes ago that it might as well have been the subject of a hundred history books, the sort of pastel fairy tale that feels removed by walls of words and circumstance and everything else that means "you can't touch us anymore, you have no power here"—we'd assumed that when the end came, it would do so like a gang of villains in an action movie. One catastrophe at a time, each taking their turn to step up and swing at the heroes before being defeated and slouching respectfully away.

The scientists had been warning us for years. The epidemiologists, pointing at the stripped-back forests and crammed-in factory farms, howling of spillover diseases and novel pandemics. The climatologists, trying to explain the complicated function of an interconnected system that no one, themselves included, fully understood or could reliably predict, but which was nonetheless dangling on the verge of collapse. The historians, struggling to remind us all that we no longer lost information the way we had for so many generations before; that the weight of what we'd done to get to where we were was looming heavier and heavier, threatening to press us all flat under the scope of itself. And more and more and more, until it seemed as if every expert the world contained was warning us of disaster.

And we had done what we always did, as a species. Optimism is as much a part of human nature as anything else; hope was the last to exit Pandora's box because, without it, we would become less than human. We need to hope that tomorrow will be better, or the presence of our intelligence will make survival less than desirable.

Why would anyone struggle, day on day and year on year, only for a life that piles suffering upon suffering, making continuation an unbearable burden? No. We need to hope. We need to believe that tomorrow will be better than today, that there will be something to look forward to and enjoy. Without that, all is lost.

So when the scientists sang their slaughter songs of sickness spreading and skies that fell, we listened for a time before we politely shut the doors and shut them out, for who could stand such a caterwauling in their ears? Who could listen to such tales of trauma when there were summers to be savoured, patches of clover to wade through, streams to dream beside? We knew that the scientists, with their clever tools and their treasured knowledge and their tales of doom, we knew that they were wrong, that they had always been wrong, even back to the dawn of ages, because for them to be anything else was to imply that the arc of the universe would somehow not bend toward a kinder tomorrow. And that, above everything, kept us moving forward, into a dazzle-bright future where nothing would ever come to tax or trouble us, where we would be shining and free forever, as we had always been destined to be.

We were fools, but we were evolution's fools, shaped exactly as she had made us, meant for optimism, meant for hope. Hope may not be humanity's greatest virtue, but it was certainly our first, and it seems certain to be our last.

When the forests burned and the birds fell from the sky like Icarus, the muscles of their wings reduced to softened wax, we said it was a shame. We donated to the relief efforts, wept over the images of ash and char, and went about our lives, buying imported goods from around the world, filling our stomachs with out-of-season fruit, unwilling to reduce our personal comforts without an iron guarantee that everyone around us was willing to do the same. We would happily suffer if everyone suffered in unison, but the thought of being the only person denied the sweet pleasures of inexpensive disposable fashion or imported oranges from the other side of the world was simply unbearable.

So the world burned, and we ignored it, little girls in shining shoes with our palms full of silver coins, the broken wings of honeybees sticking to the soles of our feet, and we thought we could continue as we were forever. We thought we could endure.

We had so much hope.

WHEN THEY SAID, "there is a new disease with pandemic potential," we shrugged and went about our business. We had heard
this song before, and it held no more reprises to excite us, only the
quiet possibility of an intermission to come. And besides, the
people next door were going about their business as they always
did, and we couldn't abandon the summer to their keeping. They
might enjoy it wrong, might splash in the wrong streams, eat the
wrong apples, step on the wrong honeybees. Our summer
depended on us continuing as we were and ignoring the warning
signs.

And so we did, until the people began dying, until it became
clear that this time was the remix that actually caught fire, and not
the dull potential that had been dangled before us so many
terrible times. The numbers were frightening, and for a time, we
were willing to go home and close our doors and listen to the
experts as they sang their songs of doom and desolation. They had
been telling us this was coming for some time, and now it seemed
that it was actually here, and there was no further escape for those
of us who had chosen not to listen.

But the people who controlled the things we thought we
needed wanted us to go about our lives as we normally would,
wanted us to leave our houses and buy their disposable fashion
and their delicious, impossible oranges. Their hope said that
normal was the only thing they could stand to consider, and so
normal was the order of the day. Normal would return, they swore,
and they swore it so loudly and so often that even those who
should have known better than to believe them began to listen.
Doors were unlocked, windows opened, air allowed to flow.

And we liked this better, because normal had become normal

through dint of being preferred by most people. Normal was the way of doing things that caused the least misery for the most individuals. And yes, some would always suffer under normal, but some would always suffer under any method of doing things, and as no one was willing to give up their own joy for the sake of people they didn't even know. A fire on the other side of the world was still keeping someone warm, even if it was burning a hundred others alive. Normal was better. Normal was the right way.

And indeed, the people who told us to go back into the world were right, because the waves of sickness grew less intense, the death tolls less staggering, the funeral homes less crowded. What were a few broken hearts and early-filled graves when compared to the siren song of normal, the fists full of silver quarters, the promise of the world renewed to how it should always have been? Compared to hope, which was returning, as hope always did, one day at a time and without consideration for whether it might not have come too quickly?

Hope was better. Hope was comfort. Hope was home.

And so, we all ignored the scientists, those few souls who had learned to look past hope in their crystal balls, who had worked all their lives long to overlook the possible in favour of the probable. We ignored them as they wailed and shrieked that this was far and far and far from over; as they insisted that there would be costs, there would be consequences, this time we wouldn't be able to walk away and pretend they hadn't done their jobs.

This time, hope would fail to wipe away reality. This time, we would have to live with the harvest we had planted.

Normal had been reasserted in part by promising, again and again and again, that the children would be safe; that this latest new disease killed the old and vulnerable, people who had already lived their lives, people who presented more than a fair degree of drain on society. And if no one had ever asked the people making those promises what a "fair" burden on society looked like, or how anyone could be a burden on a structure literally created for the sake of taking care of people, well, that was beside the point. The children would live, and we still liked to pretend that the lives of children carried some importance to us, as if we hadn't been feeding them into the meatgrinder of school shootings and constant terror and dwindling social safety nets for decades. As if the uterus you were incubated in didn't have more power to foretell the shape of your life to come than all the choices you would ever make on your own, as if free will and effort had ever really mattered.

We still pretended that we cared about the children, and when the ones who defined "normal" spoke over the scientists and said that the children would be fine, we believed them, because we liked the shape of believing them more than we liked the shape of not believing them. We liked the outline of a world filled with all our worldly wants, with oranges in the middle of the winter and ice cream in the middle of the summer, we liked to think that we were above and beyond biology's limitations, rulers of the universe, evolution's perfect darlings. We liked what we'd had, and we had never acknowledged, to ourselves or to anyone else, how fragile that really was.

And when normal returned, when the pandemic faded, it was easy to close our ears to the howling of the scientists, to pretend that they were drunk on their brief dance with relevance, that they wanted us to stay scared because they wanted the new normal to place them in control. We didn't stop to consider that sometimes the person determined to warn you that if you go outside, bears will eat you, might be doing that so that you don't get eaten by bears. We didn't stop to ask ourselves if some people might not have good reason to hate and fear normal.

And we went back to the way things were.

A virus, once it enters the body, will follow its own programming—its own version of normal. It will settle into the systems it inhabits, making them its own. It doesn't care what lived there before it came. It doesn't care what will be thereafter. It doesn't care about anything; it is, after all, a virus, a tiny bundle of biological programming commands that follows the instructions of its own making scrupulously, not concerned with the world outside its self and its host. The virus is a universe unto itself.

The virus doesn't care about the summer, about the ice cream, about the oranges. About normal. The virus does what it came to do, and when its programming is complete, it stops. Perhaps it spreads. Perhaps it stays silent and frozen, perfect in its self-contained glory. It doesn't matter. It doesn't care.

The scientists warned us. The signs were there, but as they contradicted our dreams of normal, they were ignored in favour of other signs, kinder signs, signs drawn by men with goods to sell, by women who yearned only to get back out into the world. And we chose hope over hard work, as we will always do when given the opportunity, and the virus did what the virus was always destined to do.

The virus won.

THE LAST NORMAL summer came almost twenty years before the end, although some of those same scientists would be happy to explain that the last normal summer was the end, that nothing can really be said to have happened after it was over, and maybe they're right; maybe they were right all along, when they reminded us that hope came with Pandora, that we had never truly had a chance once we chose it as our new and final god. Twenty years might seem like a suiting epilogue, but for people who had never expected to see an ending in their lifetimes, it was not enough. It was never going to be enough, not in all the years of the world that had come before us, that would endure after us despite everything we'd done to the contrary.

Twenty years was enough time for us to do a lot of damage, and once it had become apparent to the people with their hands on the controls that "normal" was never coming back, no matter how loudly they yelled for its reappearance, we had begun doing that damage as if it were our jobs. We were all little girls in shiny shoes, collecting honeybees for science teachers who thought we were too young and too innocent to understand colony collapse disorder. They didn't tell us what we were doing wrong when we were children, because they were afraid they'd scar us, and so we'd grown up to be adults who thought we weren't doing any harm; that we could move through the world like it was built solely for our own amusement, buoyed by the hope that things would be better tomorrow, that nothing we did would ever make things worse, that it would keep improving and improving and improv-ing, always and forever. We were all acolytes of the holy church of "more," and we were going to have what the gospel had promised.

And all that time, the virus was there, not concerned, not caring, doing as it did. It spread through the cells of the children —who had lived, as the ones who controlled the narrative insisted they would; oh, not all of them, of course, but so few had died, and what was a few dead children when compared to the weight of a world ground to a halt, to the alluring siren song of normal?—making its changes, modifying what it no longer felt necessary. All that time, the virus was doing what viruses have always done, creating a more hospitable environment for its own use.

Most viruses came to humanity through other channels. "Zoonotic spillover" we call it, like a complicated name will change the simple reality of a complicated origin. Diseases begin in one thing, find their way out into the world, and then move on to something new. Something like us, home and harbour and comfortable stopping place.

But not only. There is no détente with something that didn't evolve to share your space, only the slow unravelling of unplanned plans, of systems set into motion by nature and its own ends. There is no hope in a virus, either innate in the virus itself, or in the people whose bodies it inhabits. And while we built out future foundations on hope, stealing silver from the future, the virus was there as well. Not hoping. Not stealing. Not doing anything but what it had always done, what it would always do.

Twenty years, it took, for us to realize what damage had truly been done by that last summer, the summer where we gambled everything on hope, on stunned honeybees and silver coins. Twenty years of children growing up and growing older, and no new children being born.

It took time because the people whose reproductive systems had been fully mature before that summer were unaffected, although their children were as sterile as the rest, and no one was monitoring a six-year-old's reproductive potential. But when that same six-year-old was in her twenties, the fact that no children came was a much more noticeable reality. And when her brother was only slightly younger, the absence of infants was a glaring concern.

We used to hope for a summer that never ended, for pockets

forever full of shining coins, for plenty without limit and prosperity without bounds.

Now we hope for one more child, one more brief bulwark against the teetering weight of eternity, which seems poised to come crashing down very, very soon, and sweep us all to sea.

We were supposed to know.

We weren't supposed to notice that we'd been stabbed twenty years after the deed was done.

WELCOME TO THE LEGION OF SIX

By Fonda Lee

Interview #1 - 9:00 a.m.

This young whippersnapper's name is Trevor Dutch. Dutch is tall, blond, and chiseled like one of those Greek statues of Hercules that you see in museums. He saunters into the conference room overlooking the Threat Chamber in the world headquarters of the Legion of Six (which is, for the moment, floating above Brooklyn on an anti-gravity field powered by the Continuum Stone) as if he's done it a hundred times before. He settles spaciously in the chair across from us. As he brushes a lock of hair off his forehead, his pectorals strain against his arctic-blue-and-white costume. I give my waistband a glum tug. It's a bit ... er, *snug* as well, but it's not muscled physique but belly bulge that my costume has to contend with.

It's not like I've let myself go. I work out and I eat right. For a guy coming up on sixty, I'm not doing so bad. But it's been years since I've been out in the field. Nowadays, I only put on the costume for official appearances in my retirement-track job as league recruiter. The old suit looks outdated—listen, metallic blue grid stripes on black was considered slick and futuristic back in my day—but there's no point messing with it now. I'm a founding member of the Legion so quite frankly, my costume is iconic, TRON-style stripes and all. Besides, I'm too old to change.

There are four of us on the interview panel this morning. Salvo. The Spook (both halves of her). And me. My civilian name is Tod McClelland, but I'm better known as Nexus. Sure, Mr. Phenomenon got most of the attention from the press, but it's no stretch to say, in all humility, that I was the lynchpin of the original Six.

I clear my throat and start us off. "So, Trevor, you're a graduate of the XCalibur Academy for Exceptional Youngsters, and your powers are superhuman strength, energy beams, and force fields, is that right?" He nods, so I give him the classic opening question. "Tell us why you want to join the Legion of Six."

The young man shrugs. "It's got to be better than Alpha Squad. That's the league my folks were in. Cat Man and Princess Syrene. They never got much PR or career development support and Alpha Squad's benefits are crap."

"You've listed your professional name as Strikeforce," says Salvo, frowning down at the paper in front of him. The poor guy looks tired; the rings under his eyes show even through his fitted red mask. "There's already a Strikeforce in Fortress League. And a Stryker working for the Protectors of Earth."

"And Death Stryke, who's henching for Mr. Malignus," adds Camille Frank, who is one half of the Spook. Helena Kim, next to her, is the other half.

Trevor Dutch spreads his hands and gives a rueful smile full of straight white teeth. "I had to come up with something to put down on the application, didn't I? I can change it easily enough. Don't you guys have an in-house marketing consultant to help with this sort of thing? No? Well, you should. Even Alpha Squad does."

I try not to sigh. Call it idealism if you will, but when I joined the Legion of Six at the height of the Cold War, we really believed we had a calling. A solemn responsibility to use our powers to save the world from destruction. You know what? I think it's just not the same for young superhumans these days.

Interview #2 - 9:45 a.m.

ADELAE PROUD, a.k.a. Liminal, slumps in defeat as soon as she sits down in front of me. "I know what you're thinking," she says at once. "You're thinking there are already enough telepaths in this line of work and mind-reading is overrated. You're not planning to hire me unless I have a psi score of over 175 and there are no other qualified candidates." She snaps her head around and points accusingly at Salvo. "And you're wondering how a telepathic black girl like me is going to handle a career in a racist industry like the superhuman forces."

The teenager jumps to her feet and runs from the room.

Both halves of The Spook glare remonstratively at me and Salvo.

"Hey, that was *not* our fault," Syed protests.

This is why I avoid hiring telepaths.

10-minute break. 10:00 a.m.

"So SUE me if I was giving off negative mental vibes. I just got in from Syria and I have the biggest headache of all time." Salvo goes to the mini-fridge and takes out another can of Diet Coke; it's his third so far this morning. Earlier, he made it clear to me that the availability of Diet Coke was a prerequisite for his attendance today; he's addicted to the stuff. He opens the can and drains half of it.

"I saw the 'airstrikes' on the news," I mention. "That was nice work."

"I was supposed to get back in last night, but got held up in customs. *Again.*" Salvo's civilian name is Syed Kassam. His powers include perfect recall and the ability to generate massive explosions that flatten everything up to a ten-mile radius around his own body. Also, he speaks five languages. Most of the work Salvo does for the Legion of Six at the request of the United States government and other democratic world leaders involves infiltrating hostile organizations around the world, walking in, and reducing their bases to smoking heaps of rubble.

Unfortunately, the TSA is under the impression that the unmarried, childless, well-travelled engineering professor Syed Kassam is a terrorist, so Syed is always being detained in airports until one of the Legion of Six's liaison agents in the Defense Department is dispatched to bail him out. Also unfortunately, creating explosions is very dehydrating and gives Salvo headaches.

There aren't a lot of sane people that would want Salvo's job, and I don't know how he puts up with some of the crap he does, but . . . I admit I envy the man a little. I do miss my days in the field, especially back when it was just the original Legion of Six. Whether it was the Armageddon Virus, or the evil machinations of the Tenebrous Society, or stolen nuclear warheads, the job was different every day. Each member of our team was needed. Given my ability to communicate instantly with anyone via astral projection, it was always up to me to relay crucial information and to coordinate the Legionnaires, no matter where on earth or in spacetime we were. Once, while wounded and imprisoned by the agents of the Malix Syndicate, I was nevertheless able to send the override codes of their supercomputer to Mr. Phenomenon in time for him and Desert Fox to stop the Decimator from destabilizing the Earth's crust from his undersea base of operations. One of our finest moments, if I do say so myself.

Nowadays . . . well, nowadays the rest of the original six Legionnaires are retired, dead, or in the case of Sergeant Freedom, in cryogenic stasis. My powers haven't faded with age, but no one needs them anymore, not with cellphones and GPS and the Internet. I suppose I am due to retire . . . but I'm just not ready to quit the Legion. Honestly, I'm not sure I ever will be. It may sound cheesy, perhaps even a few shades close to pathetic, but defending the world from evildoers has been my entire life and I wouldn't know what to do with myself otherwise.

Interview #3 - 10:12 a.m.

"I WORK ALONE," growls Raymond Scott, known as Night Strider. He remains standing and his eyes burn like embers behind the black hood and mask obscuring his face. "I have genetic, cybernetic, and supernatural enhancements that endow me with unparalleled strength, speed, reflexes, intelligence, and invulnerability. I'm extraordinarily wealthy as a result of having inherited the three-hundred-year-old riches of the Brotherhood of Shadows, which created me to be their instrument of conquest, but which I am now sworn to destroy."

"Okay." I make some notes. "So . . . why are you interviewing with us?"

"There may be occasions for me to request the aid of allies. I expect there are several among you who would gladly join my quest of vengeance against my archenemy Duke Bale, and his Gathering Horde."

Oh, he's one of *those*. Eternal Vengeance types. I glance at my fellow panel members before turning back to our interviewee. "We'll be in touch," I tell him.

Night Strider sweeps from the room with a heavy rustle of his dark cloak.

"Diva," mutters Helena. "Enough of those in this line of work."

I have to agree. There are leagues out there (*cough*, Alpha Squad) that are big on promoting their angsty, Lone Ranger A-listers, but the Legion is more of a teamwork kind of place. In this day and age, open collaboration is where it's at. One superhuman just can't handle the variety of apocalyptic threats anymore.

"I'm going to pop out for a sec," says Camille. "Be right back." There's a disturbance in the air as she teleports out, leaving her chair empty. A minute later, she's back, looking relieved. She pulls off her gauntleted gloves and tucks a stray strand of hair back under her cowl. "Sorry 'bout that. Ryan's still asleep, thank good-ness. He's going through this cranky phase where he's fighting naps."

Helena Kim and Camille Frank both possess the power of tele-portation, so they've arranged to share the identity of the Spook. They're wearing identical silver costumes and masks. Camille's blonde hair is dyed black to match Helena's, and Helena's boots have two inches of lift to match Camille's height. Still, up close, it's not that hard to tell them apart. Luckily, most villains don't get to study the Spook up close for long. Helena is a former assassin, skilled in all forms of combat. Camille can project illusions into people's minds and alter their memories. When she's on duty, she manipulates the minds of opponents to make them believe they're being soundly beaten by Helena, and they obligingly throw themselves to the ground unconscious, so the single-identity ruse works out fine. See, teamwork.

Interview #4 - 10:25 a.m.

ZOE SALINAS SITS FORWARD in the seat in straight-backed expectation. She looks like she's about to jump up and hit a buzzer, like a contestant in a quiz show. Her shiny red-and-tan costume looks brand-new, and probably uncomfortable.

"What are your powers, Zoe?" I ask.

"I can fly," she says.

"Anything else?"

"No . . . just flying. I'm fast, though." Zoe looks a bit uncertain now. "And I'm athletic? I play a lot of sports. I could definitely learn to fight; I'm already taking lessons. And, um, I have straight A's in school?"

"Why do you want a career in the superhuman forces?"

Zoe briefly lowers her eyes, then looks back up with a tentative grin. "Doesn't everyone with special powers want to be a hero? I mean, okay, *some* people want to be villains, but *come on.*" She gestures vaguely but enthusiastically around herself. "I mean, this is the Legion House! The original secret hideout of Mr.

Phenomenon and his allies: Snakeman, Sergeant Freedom, Desert Fox, The Brain, and *you*, Nexus. How cool is *that*? You guys proved that a single person with superhuman powers could make a difference in the world." She hunches her shoulders up around her ears. "I just want to, you know, be part of that."

Helena studies the candidate's file. "Whether you get onto the team or not, I'm going to suggest you don't use the name Sparrow Girl. Go with the Sparrow, or Silver Sparrow—something without the word 'girl' in it. Take it from me, it doesn't matter if you can kill a man with your pinky finger, people won't take a 'girl' name as seriously, and it'll only last a few short years before you have to rebrand yourself." Helena's speaking from experience; she was Spookgirl once.

"That goes for anything with 'Miss' or 'She' in it as well," adds Camille, who started out as Miss Astounding years before she joined up with Helena.

"Oh," Zoe says, looking down. "I hadn't thought of that."

Interview #5 - 11:05 a.m.

THE FIFTH AND FINAL CANDIDATE, Jason Sacks, is an exceedingly pale, thin-faced young man who, contrary to instructions sent prior to the interview, is not in costume. The kid looks like he was grown in a tank under fluorescent lights. He sits down in the chair and laces his fingers together. "Allow me to explain what I can offer to your organization. As you will already know if you've done your research, I am a cyborg genius with the ability to interface directly with any piece of computer hardware and to control and manipulate digital data with my mind."

I flip through the five-page resumé before me. "It also says here you earned two doctorates by the age of sixteen, Jason."

"I prefer to be called Dr. Omniscience," Jason says.

Syed squints at the doctor. "After such a lucrative career in financial derivatives, what makes you now want to be a Legionnaire?"

"You mistake my intentions," says Dr. Omniscience. "I have no interest in racing around in some garish costume to serve hapless governments or save helpless masses. If I wished to, I could bring down the stock exchanges of the world while having breakfast. I could crash the Internet by lunchtime, or launch the entire nuclear arsenal of the planet out of boredom. I suggest you make me a member of the Legion of Six to ensure I remain a friend and not an enemy."

Camille's eyes narrow skeptically. "You're suggesting we ought to make you a hero just so you don't become a villain?"

"Oh, the old 'Hero versus Villain' narrative. *Please.* We're in the new economy of superhuman talents. I'm a *free agent.*" Dr. Omniscience offers a faint smile and waves a hand across the table at us. "You, on the other hand, are behind on the times and have much catching up to do. Case in point: why are you still called the Legion of Six if you now have eighty-three members?"

"It's historical," I point out. "It shows respect for our founders."

"Including you, Nexus?" Dr. Omniscience's voice is coolly curious. "You were the sixth, the youngest, of the Legionnaires. Would you say that the league still respects *all* things that have ceased to be relevant?"

"I'm not liking your tone, kid," says Syed before I can respond. "That arrogant attitude is not the way to get in with us, super-genius or not."

"If you're planning to become a supervillain, what's to stop us

from preventatively taking you out right now?" Helena cracks her
knuckles.

Dr. Omniscience rolls his eyes. "This isn't my real body. It's an
avatar."

"Of course it is." I award him points on my interviewee evalua-
tion form under *Planning & Initiative* and dock as many from *Inter-
personal Skills.*

Group Interview Round - 11:45 a.m.

LIMINAL HAS GONE HOME, and Night Strider took off without notice,
so that leaves Strikeforce, Sparrow Girl, and Dr. Omniscience to
complete the second, more interactive half of the interview in the
Threat Chamber.

Salvo, the Spook, and I stand by the wall of one-way glass,
looking out over the aircraft-hanger-sized training room. The
three candidates appear through an entry on one side of the
Threat Chamber. On the other side, a massive steel door lifts to
reveal a fifteen-foot-tall four-armed robot with laser eyes, and
cannons mounted on its shoulders. It proceeds to attempt to
stomp, smash, and blast the three interviewees into smears.

The Threat Chamber vibrates with the fighting but fortu-
nately, the observation deck is soundproofed against the noise. As
they watch the battle below, Camille asks Helena, "How's Andrew
doing these days?"

"Much better. The physio's really helped; he can pretty much
walk on his own now." Helena's fiancé, Andrew Wickham, better
known as the Blue Blaze, was killed by Direwolf last year but
brought back to life by the Genesis Crystal. The job share with

Camille has allowed Helena to take the time off from her Legion of Six duties to help nurse Andrew's reconstructed body back to health. Since everyone knows that the Spook is still engaged to Blue Blaze, Camille, for her part, keeps her non-superhuman wife, Stacey, and their son, Ryan, a secret.

Strikeforce releases an energy beam that blows off one of the robot's arms. Sparrow Girl flies around the machine's giant head, confusing it as she dodges laser blasts. Dr. Omniscience is standing off to the side with his arms crossed.

"What's wrong, Tod?" Helena has noticed my silence. "You're not upset about what that kid said, are you? You know cyborg super-geniuses; they're always trying to get under your skin. You have a very important job here, you know that."

"Sure, I know." But I'd be lying if I claimed it hadn't gotten to me, what that brainiac said. He's right; times change. Some of us can't change with it.

Strikeforce blasts off another of the robot's arms. It goes hurtling past Sparrow Girl, who whizzes through the air wielding a metal pole. With a shout muted behind glass, she spears out the laser eyes in a crackle of spraying sparks.

Suddenly, the robot stops moving, frozen in mid-crushing motion. It powers down, cannons folding into its shoulders, remaining arms falling to the sides of its metallic torso. The Threat Chamber goes dark and the overhead lights in the observation room flicker for a few seconds before the backup generators kick in.

We stare down into the suddenly still training room, where Dr. Omniscience is standing with his hand inside an open access panel.

"Well, I guess he aces the interview, the little prick," says Camille.

Decision Time - 12:50 p.m.

THE CANDIDATES HAVE BEEN HELPING themselves to the catered sandwiches in the lounge room outside of the Threat Chamber while we hold our deliberations. It's a lengthy discussion. In the end, Helena says, "I support your choice, Tod."

"Me too," says Camille.

I look to Syed. He rubs the back of his neck and nods. "There's a reason why you're league recruiter," he grumbles, though he gives me a weary smile. "Sometimes a pair of rose-coloured glasses is what keeps it from getting too dark."

"That's deep, Salvo," Helena says.

Camille is looking at the clock. "I have to get back before Ryan wakes up."

"Thank you all for taking the time out of your busy schedules to be part of the interview panel," I tell them. I know that coming here isn't an urgent priority like answering a call from the CIA, or stopping Necromage from gassing the city again, but for the first time, I wouldn't trade my spot for any of theirs. Helena's right. This *is* an important job. Remembering that . . . hell, I feel like Nexus again.

Both halves of the Spook wink out of the room, causing twin concussive vibrations in the air. Syed's cell phone rings. He takes the call, speaking first in animated Russian, then Arabic, before hanging up. "I have to be on another red-eye flight tonight, so I'll leave you to do the honours with the candidates." He packs two cans of Diet Coke into his jacket. "Later, Nexus." Salvo disappears out the door.

As I put the cans in the recycling bin and gather up the

discarded papers and folders from the table, I'm grinning. Sure I still miss the old days, being young and in the field, fighting supervillains or crises, but this is where I'm needed now. This is the new way that I can be the connection, the fulcrum, of the Legion of Six: as a bridge between the values of the past and the needs of the future.

And then I catch a reflected glimpse of myself in the darkened glass over the Threat Chamber, and I have to say: I still think the metallic stripes look cool.

With a smug sense of once-familiar satisfaction, I astral project into the lounge downstairs, asking Zoe Salinas to come up to the room. She jumps at the sight of my miniature image hovering in the air in front of her, then half-runs, half-flies up the stairs. I adjust my costume and pull in my gut.

Sometimes you need a little idealism in this line of work.

"Sparrow." I extend my hand as Zoe Salinas bursts into the room, wide-eyed and breathless. "Welcome to the Legion of Six."

GOOD INTENTIONS

By Christopher Ruocchio

The sky above Sadal Suud shone with a blue so pure and perfect it might have rivalled the skies of Earth in its youth, and even approaching sundown, the day was hot. Valka sat in the rear of the wagon and watched the drover urge his oxen on. *Oxen.* These Imperial primitives used *oxen* to pull their carts. When groundcars were available! And fliers! She had seen fliers in the starport, had she not? Were it not for their idiotic Chantry and its dogmatic stranglehold on technology, she might have made it to the dig site at Menhir Dur in a matter of hours. But no. She was condemned to sweat her way through the invasive jungle and the native fungal forests for *three days* before their caravan reached the foot of the Kalpeny Mountains.

It could be worse, she told herself. They might have forced the native to pull the cart.

Valka could hear the dull smack of its heavy footsteps through the wagon's canvas walls and feel the way the ground trembled beneath its trunk-like feet. As it marched, its alien song rose and fell, reminding the foreign xenologist of recordings she had heard of ancient whale song. Listening with shuttered eyes, Valka wondered what the creature was singing of, and if any more of its kind were near enough to hear. She liked to think it sang of home, of the ancient folklore of its people—of the freedom it did not have.

"Wayshrine's not far off, ma'am and sirs!" said Coram, the drover. He looked back over his shoulder and doffed his wide straw hat, smiling his gap-toothed smile. "Figured we should stop there for the night—sun going down and all—less of course his reverence here has any objections."

Valka spared the Chantry priest beside her a passing glance. Indrassus was the only other man in the carriage not native to the planet. *Not born here,* Valka corrected herself. No human being was native. Neither were the birds she heard singing in the trees, nor the trees themselves. The whole green jungle was an assault on Sadal Suud's native lifeforms: the fungal forests, flying polyps, and the various sponge-like creatures that inhabited the fleshy under-brush—and upon the native Giants most of all.

Despite the heat of the day, the aging priest wore a black wool cassock slashed with white. A medallion fashioned in the form of a copper sun hung about his neck, and copper rings decorated his gnarled fingers. He smiled, turning from Coram to Valka. "Of course, you're welcome to stay!" he said, voice nearly as deep as the keening of the alien marching alongside the covered wain. His dark eyes took in the half-dozen other men in the compartment: labourers meant for the construction of the wayshrine whose sanctum marked the start of the pilgrim road over the mountains. "You're sure we can't persuade you to stay a day or two with us, Doctor Onderra?"

Valka could hardly believe the holy fool had asked the question. "'Tis better if I were gone in the morning, I think. Your slave disagrees with me."

"Dim?" Indrassus asked, bushy brows rising. "He keeps to himself, but I'll see he leaves you alone if he frightens you."

"He does not *frighten* me," Valka replied. "Forgive me, galactic standard is not my first language. I mean that *slavery* disagrees with me." She turned away—giving the old fool her shoulder— and shut her eyes. Images of the Menhir Dur displayed themselves in her perfect memory. The locals and the idiot priests all said the native Giants had raised the towers, had set them in a chain along the Kalpeny Mountains to better reach the stars . . .

Valka knew better.

The towers of the Menhir Dur were far older, built by hands, shaped by minds the Empire and its Holy Terran Chantry pretended did not exist—the same hands that had raised similar ruins across the galaxy. Not for the first time, Valka wondered why Indrassus and his faith had not simply torn the towers down. It would be just like his kind to disappear an inconvenient truth: that mankind was not the first species to spread among the stars.

She must have dozed in the heat, for the wagon had stopped without Valka's ever being fully aware of it. The sound of bare feet came slapping from outside, along with the thudding of wood and plastic. Without warning, someone threw back the flaps to the rear compartment and admitted the waning sun—and there was a bright, smiling face beaming through the rear door.

"We're there!" said Malky, Coram's boy.

The men all started to move, and Indrassus said, "Let the lady go first." He raised a hand to bar his labourers from disembarking. "She may not understand our ways, but she is our guest." He flashed Valka a curious look, and for a moment, he seemed no more than an old man, smiling and grandfatherly.

Valka forced down a scowl.

Malky had folded the stepladder down and was standing with the canvas flap held fast in one brown hand. "Hope the ride wasn't too bumpy, miss," he said with a smile. He couldn't have been more than six or seven standard years of age. Valka didn't doubt that a life led at the bottom of this Imperial mud-hole would turn this happy child into a toothless, sun-spotted ruin like his father. The Empire cared so little for its people, its *subjects*.

And yet, the boy was smiling up at her with eyes wide and shining. She supposed she *was* a foreigner, a Tavrosi witch. Probably the boy had never seen an offworlder before, not counting Chanter Indrassus.

"'Twas lovely, thank you," she said, remembering to smile back as she donned the white, wide-brimmed hat she'd bought in the starport. Unsure where to go next, she turned on the spot, taking in the out-of-place trees and the grey and red caps of the mighty fungi that towered over them. Up ahead, the half-finished wayshrine and the whitewashed walls of the caravansary beside it squatted on a horn overlooking the road. And beyond? Level upon level, terrace upon overgrown terrace rose the first foothills of the Kalpeny Mountains, green where the human jungle ended and red-grey where the fungal cloud forest began. When she craned her neck, Valka thought she could make out the black shape of the first tower of the Menhir Dur atop the nearest peak: a lonely finger thrust resolute against the sky.

Moving toward the buildings, she passed the mighty sledge the native had dragged up from the city behind the wagons. It was laden with new stone and construction equipment for the chapel dome, secured with bright-yellow bands. She almost missed it at first glance, so like the mushroom trees it was in colour and texture—and in height. But there it was, standing just clear of the sledge, swaying gently in the sun. One of the flying polyps drifted near its crown, a membranous, insubstantial thing . . . like a jellyfish.

The Giant.

Thirty feet tall it stood, its mottled hide more clay than flesh, spongy like the substance of the native flora. It stood upon legs vast as tree trunks, its two feet round and flat and fringed with countless toes like roots. Its great arms trailed the ground like an ape's, though they terminated not in anything resembling hands, but in a fibrous tangle of feelers more vegetable than animal.

Something deep in Valka—some animal instinct—urged her to stop ten yards from the creature, well outside the reach of those mighty arms. Nothing should be so big. Nothing. No land creature of Old Earth ever grew to such a size, and to be faced with one beneath the light of day put a horror and a wonder in her beyond words, for here was something really, truly *alien*, and the alienness of it sang in her.

This was what she lived for. She was a xenologist, after all, and though she studied the ancient, extinct, and forbidden creatures who had built Sadal Suud's black towers and sites like it across the galaxy, meeting any new, strange creature was her privilege and joy.

They said the Giants were immortal, as old as the bones of the mountains in which they lived. Valka wondered how old this particular creature was, whether it had been born when mankind was yet in its grubby infancy in the forests of Old Earth. Had it watched across the light-years from beneath these silent trees as humanity grew and spread across the stars? Had it counted the drive glows of starships and the flares of repulsors and rocketry as man first arrived in-system, thinking them no more than falling stars? How many men were born and died while this alien walked the hills of its native mountains and lived its life free of man? How many kings and empires perished?

And now, it pulled a sledge.

"*Anaryoch*," she swore in her native tongue, and glared at Indrassus from beneath the brim of her hat as he passed. *Barbarians.*

"Dim!" Indrassus exclaimed. "Get these blocks unloaded and up to the chapel, double-quick!" He clapped his hands above his head, trying to attract the Giant's attention. "Come along now! That's enough lying about!"

Slowly—as though it were just a tree bending in the wind—the Giant turned its too-small head to face the priest. Indrassus halted his advance, apparently afraid himself to come too near the native Giant. Valka felt a chill steal over her, even as hot as it was. The Giant's face was no face at all. A single black hole—like a toothless, gaping mouth—stared down at them, filling the creature's entire head like shadows beneath an empty hood. It had no features to speak of, no ears or nose or mouth. Valka was not even certain the thing had eyes.

A low keening sound filled the air, so low and deep that Valka more felt than heard it.

"I said *move!*" the chanter shouted, gesticulating at the sledge and the stones piled on it. Valka thought she saw a flash of silver in the man's hand, and at once the Giant's song became a cry, and the enormous xenobite tumbled to its knees like a mountain falling.

"What did you do to it?" she demanded, dropping her bags on the spot. She started hurrying forward, pressing her hat down with one hand. "Stop!"

Indrassus brushed her off, not taking his eyes from the Giant.

"On your feet!" he said. The Giant, Dim, made a low groaning noise as it stood. As it flexed, Valka saw cracks widen in the caked surface of its mighty thighs, as if its skin were dirt gone too long in want of rain. Then she saw the restraints. Metal shafts festooned the Giant's back and legs and shoulders, studding the alien flesh like harpoons.

Valka understood then, all too clearly, what the priest had done. The Giants had no bones, for no bones could support a creature of such mass and height in Sadal Suud's heavy gravity. Their very flesh kept the Giants standing tall, each layer of cells stacked upon the next like the substance of the surrounding mushroom trees, like clay. And like clay, the priest had *baked* it. The harpoons were not harpoons at all, but heating elements thrust deep into the sponge-like flesh that baked that flesh to stone.

Looking on, Valka could not even find words to curse the old man. She curled her shaking hands into fists, but if Indrassus felt her fury, he said nothing. The Giant took up its chains and began dragging the sledge up the last slope toward the half-finished dome. As it moved, bits of stony flesh chipped and flaked away from the scabrous patches the harpoons had made on shoulders and thighs.

"Are you insane?" Valka asked, voice barely more than a whisper. Checking herself, she took in a deep breath and said, more forcefully, "You're torturing it!"

The priest turned to look back at her, his heavy brows furrowed. "I thought you'd gone inside, doctor." Incredibly, he *smiled,* as if she'd caught him at little more than an afternoon stroll. "Don't worry about Dim. He's a hardy sort. His kind regenerate with remarkable speed, you'll see. In an hour or so, he'll be right as rain. It's no worse than striking a dog, I assure you."

"Why would you ever strike a dog?" Valka's voice had gone almost shrill, twanging with the strain of her Tavrosi accent. She could hardly believe what she was hearing.

The barbarian blinked. Valka could tell that he had failed to comprehend her question. In a voice utterly befuddled, he answered her, saying, "To teach it not to bite." Before she could respond, one of the priest's labourers called from up the hill, and Indrassus said, "Forgive me, I must go. The drover's boy can show you to your room. Malky!"

The boy appeared as if from nowhere. "Here, sir!"

"Fetch the doctor's bags and show her to her room, there's a good lad!" Smiling, he ruffled the boy's dark hair and prodded him in the direction of the caravansary. He left without another word, trudging up the slope toward the unfinished sanctum as if nothing at all had happened.

NIGHT WAS HARDLY COOLER than day, and after little more than an hour, the linens the novices had given Valka for her pallet in the caravan house were soaked with sweat. Why had she even bothered to wash? An electric fan whirred overhead, its power drawn from the unsightly solar cells the barbarians had clear-cut three acres of jungle to install. How was anyone to sleep in such a climate, or among such people?

Not knowing what to do after the incident in the yard, Valka had taken the evening meal in her room, citing a desire to review her notes. That had not been a lie, she *had* reviewed what small literature she had on the Menhir Dur and the excavations previous xenologists had carried out about the so-called Marching Towers. There wasn't much. So little had been smuggled out from behind the Imperial curtain. The Sollan Empire forbade recordings of the ruins—phototypes and holographs and so on—and anyone leaving the planet was subject to search and seizure by customs. Those caught with contraband were handed over to the Orbital Defense Force or—worse—to the Terran Chantry and their Inquisition.

Lying in her bed, Valka massaged the bony nodule at the base of her skull where the implant jack lay capped beneath her red-black hair. It appeared no more than a mole, even to deep scans, for the machinery in her head was subtle and as organic as the rest of her body. Valka was of Tavros, and in Tavros it was neither crime nor sin to mingle flesh and machine. She could access and interface with other machines, even the comparably simple ones permitted within Imperial borders . . . and her memory was perfect. She forgot nothing, and so could carry away images and impressions—everything she saw and experienced on Sadal Suud —and share it with the scholars at home, and there was nothing the Chantry could do to stop her.

Except to kill her, of course. And they *would* kill her . . . if they discovered what she was.

But she was leaving in the morning. Indrassus and his ilk were staying behind to oversee construction on the wayshrine, and she, Coram, and Malky would continue on to the first of the Menhir Dur on the slopes of the mountain above. She would not have to speak with the chanter again . . . which was just as well. She wanted to strangle the man.

Long she lay awake, watching her reflection in the window glass. She disliked the look in her narrow, golden eyes, the anger and tiredness of them, and the way her sharp jaw clenched, thinking of the way the Giant cried out when it was burned. She massaged her left arm—the one that bore the fractal tattoo of her clan, striped and spiralling like the rippling pattern of good steel.

It wasn't right that she should leave without helping the native . . . but what could she do? She could hardly rip the harpoons out of the Giant with her bare hands, nor could she hope to get close enough to Indrassus as he slept to smash his evil remote. Besides, for all she knew, the priest had a spare squirrelled away in his luggage. And whatever she did, suspicion would surely fall upon her shoulders. She was the outsider, the witch from Tavros, and though the Imperials would have no proof, they would not need it.

There was nothing she could do.

Unless . . .

ALL WAS STILL beneath the fungal trees. Not even the air moved, though the jungle sang, and the native forest, too: battling choruses of birds and bugs and things that were like neither, but belonged. Sadal Suud was a world at war, and those night sounds were the sounds of battle as the invading jungle crushed the native flora and mankind crushed the Giants.

Valka thought she could hear the Giant's breathing, and she crouched behind the sledge to brush the hair from her eyes. If the xenobite slept at all, it did so standing, and swayed with its arms at its side. How long Valka crouched there, she could not guess— though her implants might have told her. They were alone, human and Giant.

The chanter's remote had to communicate via radio with the harpoons, which meant Valka should be able to detect the receivers and interfere with them. Maybe she could lock Indrassus out, just long enough to give the creature time to escape into the mountains, to find its own kind and remove the horrific restraints from its body. Maybe she could make it look like an error—a simple glitch.

She could *hear* the receivers in the probes studding the Giant's flesh. Or . . . not *hear*, precisely, but it was like hearing. The implants in her head bled into her sensory cortex in such a way that using her neural lace felt only like an extension of her senses as she interacted with the planet's limited datasphere. The ice layers securing the probes were surprisingly amateur—but then, she supposed that with so many machines banned across the Imperium the few that remained needed little security. There wasn't much to secure, and less to secure it *from*.

To a Tavrosi like Valka, it was a small matter to access the receivers and reset the permissions that tethered them to the chanter's remote.

She felt the success like a tingling in the tips of her fingers.

Quietly and with painstaking slowness, she moved out from the shadow of the sledge, hands extended like those of someone trying to placate a crouching tiger. "Hey!" she hissed, speaking Standard, since it seemed the creature understood a measure of the Imperial tongue. "Hey!" She waved her hands, desperate to attract the creature's attention.

It turned only slowly, the black hole of its face peering down at her like the mouth of some terrible, bottomless pit. Though it loomed above her, she was gripped by the sudden terror that she might fall *upwards* into those hideous depths. Valka suppressed a shudder.

A low, warbling cry filled all the air. No louder than the murmurous haunt of flies at first, but it mounted until Valka felt as though she stood beneath the head of some mighty drum. What alien words might lay hid in that inhuman song, Valka never learned.

"You're free!" she said, and pointed at one of the spears protruding from the Giant's leg, just above the knee. When the xenobite did not move, she repeated herself, gesturing more emphatically. She had to make it understand! Realizing the creature might understand but that it might not *believe,* she added, "I can remove them, if you'll let me." She mimed the action. "Take them out!" Still the Giant did not move. Valka glanced back at the lime-washed walls of the caravansary, half-expecting to see Indrassus storming across the yard with his men in tow. "Please," she hissed, and took a brave step forward. "Let me help you!"

Like a mountain falling, the Giant knelt. It braced itself with one overlong arm, its fibrous fingers spreading like the roots of a tree. Her own fingers trembling, Valka reached up and touched the Giant's leg. She'd imagined the alien would feel rough and stony, but the flesh gave beneath her fingers like wet plaster, and she left depressions—fingerprints—on its soft hide. Nearly a foot of damp metal emerged from the flesh above her head. She seized the spike in both hands and pulled.

The Giant twitched beneath her ministrations and flinched away, but the shaft came free with only minimal resistance, leaving a hole about half as wide as her forearm. Even as she watched, the waxy flesh flowed shut,ntil it seemed there had never been a wound at all. She grimaced, remembering what Indrassus had said about the Giants' regenerative powers. Thinking of Indrassus set her teeth on edge, and she said, "You try it."

The Giant reached up with cord-like fingers, fronds coiling about half a dozen of the shafts in its left shoulder. With a low bellow, it yanked on the probes and tugged them free before crushing the lot of them in its fist. It found another. Then another.

With each success the Giant moved more quickly, and at last it stood again. It seemed to grow taller and flexed its mighty arms. Imagining the look on Indrassus's face when he discovered the ruined probes in the morning, Valka might have laughed for joy.

"Run!" she whispered, pointing toward the tree line. "You have to run!" She could see it all so clearly: the Giant's flight through the forest, its reunion with its people where they yet dwelt on reservations high in the vales of the Kalpeny Mountains. She could not give it back its world, but she had given it something.

"What are you doing?"

Valka felt her every muscle tense as she turned, but it was only the boy, Malky. From his rumpled nightshirt and tangled hair, Valka guessed that he'd just rolled out of bed. She did her best to smile. "I couldn't sleep. 'Twas just out to catch a bit of the night air, Malky. You go back to sleep now."

Half-asleep as he was, the boy was not so stupid as that. He rubbed his eyes and squinted up at her and the Giant behind her. "But what are you *doing?*" he asked again, coming closer. "Papa says we shouldn't bother Dim!"

"Just go back to sleep," Valka said. The boy had caught her in the act. What was she going to do? What *could* she do?

It was no use. The whites of the boy's eyes stood sharply out in the fungal gloom. "His bolts are out! Did you take them out?" He half-stumbled back. "You can't do that!"

"Malky!"

But the boy was gone. He turned and scurried back across the yard toward the caravansary. Throwing all caution to the winds, Valka shouted after him. "Malky, come back!"

Behind her, the Giant bellowed, and the noise of it startled a flock of terranic birds from their nightly perch atop one of the smaller mushroom trees. All at once, the Giant leaped over her, bounding ape-like after the boy.

Valka didn't even have time to cry out. To warn him.

She had a brief impression of the boy as a pale wisp against the night, like the flame of some brief candle. Then the Giant fell upon him and snuffed him out with a fist as big around as a tree.

Valka did scream then.

She took off running toward the bathhouse that stood apart from the main caravan house. Malky must have awakened in the night to use it, and had paid for that innocent impulse with his life. She had some vague thought of finding shelter in the squat, flat-roofed building. She didn't know what to do. She wasn't a soldier anymore, and at any rate, had never seen action on the ground, and certainly never against something so huge and so evidently lethal as the Giant.

And Malky was dead—must be dead.

Why? Why had the Giant done that? It didn't make any sense. The boy was innocent.

Why hadn't it just *run away?*

She heard shouts behind her and pressed herself against the wall of the bathhouse, peered back around the corner toward the chaos she had caused. Two of the labourers burst out of the caravansary with hunting rifles. When they saw what they were up against, they retreated just as fast, cursing to scorch the ears of the foulest spacer. The Giant drew itself up to its full height and bellowed once again. One of the workers fired on the Giant, but if his shot was true, it did nothing to harm the massive xenobite. While Valka watched, the creature tore through the corner of the caravansary, and the sweep of its arm was like a tree falling. Masonry crumbled like old plaster.

In the distance, someone screamed. Another gunshot split the night.

It was supposed to just . . . *disappear* into the forest. It was supposed to *flee*. But the Giant seized one of the workmen by the ankle and hurled him clean over the wayshrine's unfinished dome. Where he landed, Valka never learned.

"Dim!" a deep voice rang. "Stop this at once!"

Indrassus had appeared in the arched door to the caravan house. Valka saw the flash of something silver in his hand by the light of stars, and for a moment—even still—she felt the warm flush of satisfaction. It was only too bad that at this distance she would not see the colour drain from the priest's dark face.

The Giant wheeled on its master. Its *former* master.

A shout of violet light split the darkness like a wedge. The shot took the Giant where ribs ought to be even as it lurched toward Indrassus. And only then did Valka realize . . . the silver instrument in the priest's hand was not the remote. It was a plasma burner.

The priest fired again, plasma fire burning hotter than the surface of Sadal Suud's binary suns. The Giant let out a strange, ululating cry and toppled as flames engulfed one of its legs.

When she was a girl, Valka had seen an old courthouse demolished. She had never forgotten the way the grey pillars of its façade—which had seemed so immutable, so permanent to her young eyes—had crumbled when the wrecking ball struck. The Giant's leg was the same, and with a dreadful crunching, splintered just below the knee where the damp flesh turned to stone.

The Giant fell with a cry of pain and a noise like the ending of the world.

THEY SAID the Giants were immortal, as old as the bones of the mountains in which they lived . . . but mountains are worn down in time. By wind. By water.

This one died by fire.

It was a long time dying.

Indrassus shot the Giant a dozen more times, and when the flames all died, the priest ordered his labourers to hammer the body into pieces and to load the pieces on the sledge. Indrassus said they'd have to take the pieces to a kiln when they returned to the city, for even broken, a single living cell was sufficient to regenerate the whole Giant in time. When she'd heard that, Valka had discreetly snatched a fragment of it. She still held it in her hand, sharp edges cutting into the flesh of her palm. Despite the heat of the night and the burning, she clutched the blanket tight about her shoulders.

"I don't know how it happened," she heard herself say. "I was in the bathhouse when I heard it, I . . ." She trailed off, unable to look Malky's father in the eye. Coram's sun-spotted face was empty. Of colour. Of feeling. Of everything. She had seen that emptiness a moment earlier and—seeing it—could not bear to see it again. She clenched her fist over the bit of dead clay until she thought she might bleed. "I'm sorry."

To her astonishment, Indrassus spoke. "It's all right, doctor," he said, not unkindly. "The restraints must have failed . . . the poor boy." He reached out and put a comforting hand on her shoulder, peering down into her face. "If you'd been outside, you'd have been killed, too."

Valka swallowed and looked down at her feet. She could say nothing. They had thought she was apologizing for being unable to save the boy—not that she was apologizing for his death. She shut her eyes, but it did no good. Her memory was perfect, and whenever she closed her eyes, she saw Malky's pale outline crushed beneath the Giant's bulk. She'd only been trying to help, to do the right thing and save the Giant from its enslavement . . . and now it was dead.

And Malky was dead. And one of the workmen.

She clutched her blanket tighter.

She wished she could forget like normal people, forget the image of the boy stamped out by the Giant. She *could* delete the memory, if she wanted, cut out the images wholesale.

But the human mind is a tricky thing, plastic and changeable. If she *did* remove the memory, she would not know why it was she cried, and *that* would have been so much worse.

She clenched the little piece of the Giant tighter in her hand, afraid to keep it, afraid to toss it on the sledge with the rest. Was it dead? There was no way to be sure that some spark of life did not yet remain in the alien clay. It was not impossible to imagine the inert lump growing once again, softened in some pool or by rain. Was it a seed she held? Part and particle of the creature—the killer —that had died because she freed it from its bonds? Would the Giant that grew from such a seed remember its former life? Remember the torment and the anger of its imprisonment?

She listened to Indrassus and the men rattle on, reassuring her and comforting Coram as they continued the work of cleaning. Not a one suspected her hand in what had happened—and why should they? They were humble Imperial peasants and knew little of the technologies in play. Even Indrassus was only a country preacher, not one of the Chantry witch-finders who made a career of hunting for thinking machines. In time, she stood.

"I need to sleep," she said, leaving them all by the sledge and the bathhouse as she crossed back to the caravansary. One more day. One more day and she'd be free of them.

Valka stopped for a moment halfway between the men and the door. Unseen beneath the blanket, she opened her fingers.

The shard of the stone Giant tumbled to the earth at her feet.

Maybe they would find it.

Maybe they would not.

"SHHHH ..."

By David Brin

Nobody speaks much of the Talent, anymore—that aspect of our nature we were once asked to give up for the sake of pity. We gave it up, something precious and rare, for the sake of the Lentili.

Or did we?

No one doubts the Lentili merited such a sacrifice. They have done so much for humankind, after all. Had we never met them, would we or our Earth have survived mankind's childish greed and temper for much longer? I know this—I would never have been able to put off writing my memoir so long, procrastinating for two centuries of augmented life span, were it not for the medical technologies donated by our benefactors.

Ah, but Time is inexorable, or so the Lentili philosophers tell us. So now, I'll pour my testimony into Write-only Memory, that bank that takes only deposits, never withdrawals. Someday, there will be no men or women still corporeal whose vivid neuronal recollection recalls that time of excitement, when our first starprobes brought back word of contact. But for now, I remember.

Contact—a word so sweet, yet chilling, promising an end to loneliness and a beginning of . . . what?

Oh, such fears we had. The high hopes! Each pundit had his or her own theory, of course. This would end the miserable, solipsistic isolation of mankind, some predicted. Others said this would be our end entire.

Initial reports arrived from our contact team. They sounded so optimistic, so wonderful. Too wonderful, we thought, to be true!

As it turned out, they understated the case. In dazed wonderment, we came to realize that the Universe might actually be sane, after all! How else could there ever come about beings such as the Lentili?

Oh, there were many ancient, wise races in the Galactic Commonweal, advanced, philosophical species who had no more interest in swooping down to seize our grubby little world than a professor might wish to steal a small boy's ball. All of a sudden, all our worst fears seemed so silly. Of course, we would remain awkward newcomers for ages, but starfaring had transformed us overnight and forever from the status of clever animals into citizens.

Our appointed advisers in this process would be the kind, gregarious Lentili, so beautiful and gentle and wise. Could we ask for any better proof that the Universe was kind?

They were on their way, great Lentili starships, escorting two crude Earth Survey vessels they could just as easily have swallowed and brought here in a fraction of the time. But there was no hurry, and the Lentili were sensitive to matters of honour.

Honour can be costly, though. We learned this when the *Margaret Mead*, containing half our contact team, exploded halfway home to Sol. In the midst of this shock, the widely respected European president—newly elected chairman of the Interim Council of State Leaders—went on the air to address the world.

Platitudes and paeans can be clichés, but that is not lamentable. Originality is not useful to those freshly numbed with grief. So, President Triddens spoke of our lost emissaries in words used oft to eulogize heroes, yet seldom so aptly.

But then there came an unexpected coda. He said something that took the world by surprise.

Officially, no copies of his address exist any longer. And yet, while it is seldom spoken of, has any speech ever had more far-reaching effects? It endures in secret tapes all over the Solar System. Here is how Triddens revealed his shocking news:

"Fellow citizens and people of the world, I must now talk to you about something I learned only hours before hearing about the loss of the *Margaret Mead*. It is my duty to tell you that the Lentili, these gentle, fine beings who will so soon be our guests on this planet, are not quite as perfect as they seem. In fact, they have a serious, tragic flaw.

"Just before she died aboard the *Margaret Mead*, the eminent psychologist-sociologist Dr. Ruth Rishke sent me a most disturbing document. After two days of sleepless agonizing over what to do, I've decided to share this information with the entire human race. For if anything is to be done about Dr. Rishke's disturbing conclusions, it must be now, before the Lentili arrive.

"First off, I don't want to disturb you all unduly. We are in no danger from our approaching guests. Quite the contrary. Had they wished us harm, resistance would have been utterly useless, but all evidence shows them to be benevolent. Indeed, we are offered all of the secrets of an ancient, wise culture, and solutions to many of the troubles that have vexed us for ages.

"But I must report to you that there is a danger, nevertheless. The danger is not to us, but to our benefactors!

"You see, for all of their advancement, the Lentili appear to be *deficient* in an unexpected way. Before her untimely death, Dr. Rishke was quite concerned.

"Apparently, we humans have a certain talent, one which seems to be completely absent from the Lentili. One which they appear barely capable of even comprehending. At first, when she referred to it, they did not seem to understand what she was talking about. When her persistent efforts resulted in a few of them finally catching on, Professor Rishke said, and I quote, 'I was appalled at the consequences to those poor Lentili,' unquote."

———

HOW WELL I remember the expression on President Tridden's face. His sympathy for the plight of these poor creatures was apparent. We had all come to admire the Lentili so, over the recent weeks. Tall and gangling, with faces that seemed almost droopy with kindness and gentle humour—they looked so harmless, so incapable of doing harm.

They also seemed so omnipotent! Terrifically strong and coordinated, they lived, as corporeal individuals, for thousands of years before going on to join their Universal Mind. Skills a man might spend a lifetime perfecting were the study of a lazy vacation to a Lentili. Their accomplishments, both as a race and as individuals, were awesome.

The Lentili spoke kindly of the arts and achievements of mankind, of course, never qualifying their praise as some of us would have, allowing for the fact that these were, after all, the simple works of children. And yet, how could we avoid inserting those burning qualifiers ourselves?

Humanity's overweening pride had come near to wrecking our beloved world. Even by the time we launched two crude starships, the Earth was still a fractious, nervous place. So, our newly discovered humility went down as medicine that did not taste anywhere near as bad as we'd feared. Despite a few dissenting voices, our people were determined to become good students, to be grateful, hard-working pupils.

So, imagine our surprise! How could the President be saying this to us? How could such creatures as the Lentili be flawed?

Such was President Tridden's great authority, however, and such was the renown of the famed professor Rishke, that we had no choice but to take their word for it, and be amazed! We leaned forward toward our sets and concentrated as few ever have in times of peace.

"PROFESSOR RISHKE SENT her information directly to me," the President went on. "And now, I pass the buck to all of you. For it is up to all of humanity to decide what we are to do.

"At the very start of our long relationship with a kind, decent race—one whose interest in our welfare is indisputable—we find we actually have it within our power to wreak untold psychic harm upon the Lentili. The Lentili have a mental block, something like an odd inferiority complex, and it concerns something so mundane to us that few human beings ever bother even thinking about it, past the age of ten! It certainly isn't our fault. And yet, we can hurt our new friends terribly if we are crass or rudely force them to see what they would rather not see. We are duty-bound to try to minimize that harm as best we can.

"Therefore, I have decided to ask you all to join me in making a grand sacrifice.

"Over the coming weeks, as we prepare to receive our visitors, our guests and future guides, we must expunge all references to this human talent from our literature, from our language, from our outward lives!

"To begin with, I have already given orders to various governmental agencies using my emergency powers. Commencing this hour, the indexes of the Library of Congress are being destroyed. No books will actually be burned, but in the laborious process of reconstruction, the new indexes will exclude all reference to this human ability that so disturbs our new friends.

"All of you can do the same, in your towns and villages and homes. We must not, of course, destroy our heritage. But we can at least make an effort to mask this thing, so that when the Lentili arrive, we can hope to spare them avoidable pain."

OH, the sadness in his eyes. The human wisdom of President Tridden as he spoke these words. I can tell you now what so many of us were feeling, then. We felt dread. We felt fear. But most of all, we felt pride. Yes, pride that we humans, too, could bring forth nobility and charity to those in need. We were determined, listening to this great man, that we would follow his example. Yes, we would do this great thing, and begin our relationship with our mentors nobly, in an act of self-sacrifice and pity.

Only a few of us had begun to worry about *how* to do this. But then, the President went on.

"OF COURSE, we all know human nature. Part of the work we did in becoming civilized enough to be allowed to join the Galactic Commonweal involved the way we learned to despise secrecy. We've become a race of eccentric individualists and are proud of that fact. How can we, then, hide forever the existence of a human talent? It just wouldn't be possible, even if everyone agreed to do so, even if we found and eradicated every record.

"And there will certainly be those humans who do not cooperate in this undertaking, those who, rightly or wrongly, disagree with me that our benefactors are in danger, or that we should care or bother to try to spare them pain.

"Certainly, despite all our efforts, there will be many retained copies of this very broadcast!

"But there is hope. For, according to Dr. Rishke's analysis, this will not matter! Not so long as the majority of us make a good effort. And so long as we agree in advance upon the right cover story. Any clues, evidence, or testimony remaining will then be largely overlooked by the poor Lentili. For subconsciously, they will be our collaborators in suppressing this threat to their collective mental equilibrium. So long as the talent is not flaunted too blatantly, Dr. Rishke was convinced the Lentili will simply ignore it.

"This, then, will be our cover story.

"It shall be recorded that on this day, in this year, Joseph Triddens, President of North Europe, Chairman of the Interim Council of Terra, went stark, raving mad."

WAS THERE A HINT OF A SMILE? Just a flicker of one, as Tridden said those words? I have debated it with myself a thousand times, watching my own secret tape of that broadcast. In truth, I cannot say, nor can anybody, what fleeting thread of whimsy might have woven through the man's earnest appeal.

Certainly, the Earth seemed to *wobble*, at that moment, with the gravitational torque applied by six billion human jaws, all dropping open at the same time in stunned surprise.

"Yes, people of the world. That is the only way. Tonight, millions of you will do as I ask. You will go forth and meddle, alter records, change archives. It won't matter that you will not be entirely successful, for the resulting confusion can be used as an excuse when the Lentili wonder why we talk so little about certain things.

"And next month, next year, on into history, tonight's temporary hysteria will all be blamed on me.

"*There is no such talent* . . . no human attribute that makes Lentili inherently jealous, that makes them feel painful pangs of inferiority.

"That will be our cover story! It doesn't exist! It was all a myth perpetrated by a single man, a neurotic human leader driven over the edge by the approaching end to his days of petty power, a man who seized the airwaves in one last, futile spasm and sent a few millions into the streets for a day or two of relatively harmless tape-shredding, index-burning, and other silly, repairable acts of sabotage.

"This is what you must do, my fellow citizens and people of the world. You must expunge all official mention of this talent, out of kindness to our approaching mentors. And then you must say that all of this was the product of one deranged man:

"Me."

AT THIS POINT, I know he *did* smile. By now, half the world was convinced that he was insane. The other half would have died for him then and there.

"I WILL TRY to delay my resignation long enough to see the task well underway. Already, at this moment, political battles are being waged, physicians consulted, Constitutional procedures set in motion. Perhaps I only have a little longer to talk to you, so I will be succinct.

"It occurs to me that I have been too vague in one respect. The talent I am referring to, about which I cannot be overly specific, is one that is common to human beings, though apparently incredibly rare out in the Galactic Commonweal. So far, we have developed it hardly at all. In fact, it has seemed of so little importance that all but a few of us take it completely for granted, thinking of it no more than in passing, throughout our lives.

"And yet, it is something that—"

HE STOPPED SPEAKING QUITE SUDDENLY, and, reflected in his eyes, we could all track the approach of those intent on bringing an end to his monopoly of the airwaves. President Triddens had time only to bring one finger to his lips, in that age-old sign of secrecy and shared silence. Then, abruptly, the broadcast ended in that famous burst of static that held an entire world hypnotized for endless minutes until, at last, the screens were filled again with the

breathless upper torsos and heads of government officials and
newscasters, blinking rapidly as they told us what half of us
already knew—that the President was not well.

The rest of us—the other half—did not wait to hear the diag-
noses of all the learned doctors. We were already tearing the
indexes out of our encyclopedias or striding out the door with
axes in our hands, heading toward our local libraries with evil
intent upon—not the books—but the sorting catalogues.

Among those who had technical skill, thousands set to work
creating computer viruses . . . the dawn of the Search Crisis, when
even the legendary find-efficiency of Google and Yahoo and Baidu
and Coriboa suddenly collapsed.

At the moment, it hardly seemed to matter that Triddens never
got around to telling us exactly what it was we were trying to hide!
Cause a muddle. we thought. Help disguise this thing of ours that
can hurt our friendly guests.

Do something noble, while we are still in command of our
own destinies . . .

THAT NIGHT'S hysteria came in a surge of passion, a Dionysian
frenzy that did little actual harm in the long run—little that could
not be repaired fairly easily, that is. It ended almost as quickly as it
began, in embarrassment and a sheepish return to normality.

Yes, the psychiatrists announced. The President was mad.

When the *Gregory Bateson* arrived, and Dr. Rishke's colleagues
were interviewed, all of them swore that she could never have sent
such a report home. It just wasn't possible!

Rumours ran rampant. There was no solid evidence to support
speculation that Triddens himself ordered the destruction of the

Margaret Mead, a crime too horrible to credit even a lunatic. Anyway, it was decided not to rake those ashes. The man was now where he could do nobody any harm anymore.

Soon, we were into the glorious days of the Arrival. Lentili were being interviewed on every channel. And in their charming ways, their humour and their obvious love for us, we realized that what we had really needed, all along, were these wonderful, wise, older brothers and sisters to help ease away the pain of our awkward, adolescent millennia. The earnest work of growing up had finally begun.

TODAY PEOPLE seldom speak of President Triddens, or of the strange hoax he tried to pull. Oh, there will always be the Kooks, of course. Artists, writers, innovators of all kinds are forever coming forth and "announcing" that they have "found the Triddens Talent." Often, these are the silly ones, the half-mad, those at the fringes whom we all tolerate in much the same way the Lentili must love and tolerate us.

But then, on other occasions the discoveries are bona fide accomplishments. How often has the public watched some brilliant new performer, or stared at some startling piece of art, or listened to new music or some bold concept, and experienced momentary uncertainty, wondering, *Could this be what Triddens spoke of? Might this prove him to have been right, after all?*

Inevitably, it is the Lentili who are the test. How they react tells us.

As yet, none of the fruits of our new renaissance seem to have caused them much discomfort or any sign of hysterical rejection. They say they are surprised by our behaviour . . . it seems that most neophyte species, most "freshman" members of the Commonweal, go through long periods of humility and self-doubt, giving themselves over excessively to slavish mimicry of their seniors. The Lentili say they are impressed by our independence of spirit and our innovation. Still, they show no sign of having yet been intimidated by some mysterious latent human talent, suddenly brought to flower.

But that doesn't stop people from looking.

WE SPEAK OF TRIDDENS, when we speak of him at all, with embarrassment. He died in an institution, and his name is now used as a euphemism for passing through a wormhole, for going off the deep end.

And yet...

And yet, sometimes I wonder. A small minority still believe in him. They are the ones who thank our mentors politely, and yet *patronizingly*, with a serene sort of smugness that seems so out of proportion, so inappropriate, given our relative positions on the ladder of life. They are the ones who somehow seem impervious to the quaking intimidation that strikes most of the rest of humanity, now and again, despite the best efforts of the Lentili to make us feel loved and at home.

Is it an accident, I wonder, that every time a human team is sent to negotiate with the Commonweal on some matter, always a few Triddenites are named among the emissaries? Is it a coincidence that they prove the toughest, most capable of our diplomats?

They search—these believers in a mad president—never satisfied, always seeking out that secret, undeveloped niche in the human repertoire, the fabled talent that will make us special even in this intimidating, overpowering Universe. Spurning the indexes they call useless, they pore through the source material of our past, and explore the filmy fringes of what we know or can comprehend. Neither time nor the blinding brilliance of our mentors seem to matter to the Triddenites.

Perhaps they are lingering symptoms of the underlying craziness of humankind.

THE LENTILI WALK among us like gods.

We, in turn, have learned some of what we taught dogs and horses. We've supped from the same bowl as we once served up to our cousins, the lesser apes: the bowl of humility.

There is no doubt that humans were arrogant when we imagined we stood at the pinnacle of creation. Even when we worshipped a deity, we nearly always placed Him at safe remove, exalting Him out of the mundane world altogether, which was in effect the same thing as naming ourselves paramount on Earth.

Now, humbled, we earnestly study and devote ourselves to making our species worthy of a civilization whose peaks we can only dimly perceive.

No question but that we are better people now than those savages were, our ancestors. We are smarter, kinder, more loving. And, against all expectation, we are also more creative, as well.

I have a theory to explain the latter—a theory I keep to myself. But it is why, once a year, I risk being labelled a Kook by attending a memorial service by the side of a small grave in Bruges Cemetery. And while most of those present speak of honour, and pity, and the martyrdom of a decent man, I pay homage instead to one who perhaps *saw where his people were headed*, and the danger that awaited them.

I honour one who found a way to arm us . . . and changed that future.

And yes, he was a martyr. But of all the solaces to accompany him into his imprisonment, I can think of none better than the one Triddens took with him.

That smile . . .

THEY WALK amongst us like gods. But we have our revenge.

For the Lentili know Triddens must have been mad. They know there is no secret talent. We are not sheltering them from some bright truth, hiding something from them out of pity and out of love.

They *know* it.

And yet, every now and then, I have seen it. I have seen it . . . seen it in their deep, expressive eyes each time something new from our renaissance surprises them, oh, so briefly.

I have seen that glimmer of wonder. Of worry. That momentary doubt.

That is when I pity the poor, deprived creatures.

Oh, thank God, I can pity them.

THE GREATEST OF THESE IS HOPE

By D.J. Butler

Shepherd: And now abideth faith, hope, charity, these three.

The Ecumene Shepherd stood at the front of the long Ecumene Community Hall, atop the short minbar tower. His avatar had a thick grey bar across the top of its block-like head, which Izzy thought must be a skullcap, and wore black. The avatar's mouth was a flat, serious line.

All the avatars had block-like heads, including Izzy's. That was just how avatars looked. The blocky head of Izzy's avatar was a sunset gold, with curlicues meant to approximate the look of her real, wildly curly, hair.

Shepherd: And sometimes . . . the greatest of these is hope.

Behind the Shepherd rose a dark-blue panel spangled with silver and gold dots. The dots slowly revolved around a central point, slightly to the side of one of the fainter stars. This was an

image of the night sky, but not any night sky Izzy had ever seen—
it was the night sky of Earth. Mom and Dad hadn't ever seen it,
either—Izzy's family was four generations off-Earth.

But that revolving night sky of Earth was one of the symbols of
the Ecumene.

Rowland-Beta, sometimes called Elizabeth's World, had its
own night sky, with a dense skein of stars that came and went and
thick smeared bands of various colours and large patches of void.
Izzy liked to sit on the broad, flat space on top of the kelp-
processing tanks with Mom, Dad, and Bear, turn off their station's
lights, and watch that sky. There wasn't another station in sight of
them in any direction, so with the lights turned off, the night
became glorious.

Everyone on Elizabeth's World lived this remotely. That was
why the Ecumene Community Hall was virtual, located in a
walled-off section of the Sphere where many of the controls were
disabled, to prevent vandalism. During sermons, like this one,
communication abilities were limited, to avoid disruptions.

The Ecumene and the government had controlled spaces in
the Sphere. Outside those controlled spaces, the Sphere was
where children met and played.

"Burp!" Bear yelled, but no one in the Sphere could hear him.

The Shepherd interrupted a description of Eli and his
favourite activities—which conspicuously left out his love of
griefing in the Sphere and all the dirty jokes he'd learned from his
older brother, Tim—to quote scripture again.

*Shepherd: Call on Him in fear and hope. Lo! The mercy of the Infinite is
nigh unto the good.*

Viv (group PM): I miss Eli.

The other participants in the funeral couldn't see the group chat, which made it much more discreet than a whispered conversation. Izzy snaked a hand to her keypad and quietly typed a response.

Izzy (group PM): I do, too.

Izzy had never met either Viv or Eli, or the fourth member of their group, Ahmad, in physical space. Their families all operated stations thousands of kilometres apart, but the children met in the Sphere to heap up mountains, go into the cubes to mine Unobtainium and Handwavium, which allowed them to build fantastical devices in the Sphere, and fight Stalkers. Rowland-Beta itself had no mountains, and indeed virtually no dry land, no rare elements, and, of course, no Stalkers. Most of the planet's devices were tools used in cultivating and processing kelp.

Now Viv sat on a virtual pew two rows ahead of Izzy and to the right. Ahmad sat somewhere behind the girls. Izzy knew that because Ahmad had told her; her avatar was frozen in place during this part of the service and couldn't turn its head.

Eli lay in the coffin in front of the Shepherd.

"Juice!" Bear yelled. The only juice he knew was a sweet distillate from kelp.

The station shook. Not the Community Hall, which was virtual, but Izzy's family's station. Over the Shepherd's muscular voice, she heard large waves slapping against the side of the station's tanks. She heard Dad curse and slip out of his Sphere-helm, then run to the station's control room.

His avatar remained poised and solemn, sitting on the other side of Mom. For the funeral, the family's avatars all wore black.

Ahmad (group PM): Did you guys feel that?

Izzy (group PM): Whoa.

The tremors had been getting more frequent, and bigger. Since virtually everyone on Elizabeth's World lived on floating stations, the tremors manifested as waves. It was a tremor that had killed Eli, apparently; a tsunami had swept him from his family's station, and he had drowned in the kelp.

At least, that's what Viv had heard from her parents. Izzy's parents had said nothing, but had forbidden Izzy and Bear to go outside alone. Bear, who could barely talk, really shouldn't be outside alone anyway, but Izzy was eleven years old, and the sudden restriction on her liberty chafed, however sensible it was.

But how big must a tremor be to throw waves against Izzy's station and also Ahmad's? Or could there be two tremors at the same time?

Either possibility seemed ominous.

Shepherd: Let us say the prayer for the dead together. Be exalted and sanctified His great name in the world He created . . .

The communication controls relaxed, and members of the congregation recited along. Izzy's text scroll filled with multiple versions of the prayer, some misspelled, some using variant words, and a few in different languages. She copied and pasted the prayer herself, mechanically, one line at a time, from an open file.

Viv (group PM): This really makes me want to go griefing. Just find a building somewhere and trash it. A whole village. A castle.

Izzy (group PM): You can't grief in here.

Viv (group PM): Duh. Meet me at ZL 1200?

ZL 1200 was a time, midday at the zero-longitude line of Elizabeth's World. The place of the meeting would be the same place they always met.

Izzy (group PM): I'm in. Ahmad?

Ahmad said nothing. Izzy couldn't look for his avatar or the avatars of his two mothers. Instead, she checked the scroll and realized that none of Ahmad's family were saying the prayer for the dead.

Viv (group PM): He's just glitching. I bet he meets us.

WHEN IZZY ARRIVED at Mount Mountain, Viv was waiting. Her avatar had orange hair and literal cherries on its creamy cheeks. Ahmad was nowhere in sight.

None of the children had ever seen a mountain in real life, because Elizabeth's World had no mountains. Ahmad claimed he had once stood on an island, but Izzy was skeptical. So, when they had decided to build a meeting place in the Sphere, it had seemed natural to make it the most earthy, the most mountainous, the most kelp-free place they could possibly contrive. Mount Mountain was a forest of steep, needle-like spires, thick with vegetation. The others told Izzy it also echoed with the cries of the seventeen species of birds they had created and given homes on Mount

Mountain, but Izzy had an old Sphere-helm, with limited audio capability. The resolution was so bad it made voices, birdsong, and avalanches all sound the same, so she just left the audio off.

Bear liked to listen to the audio when he was in the Sphere, and would yell "burp!" every time he heard any sort of Sphere-sound. Apparently, that was what it all sounded like to him.

Izzy: No news from Ahmad?

Viv: Nothing. I've been looking at the map, and there's a river valley about two hundred klicks from here, full of defenceless villages and herds of cattle. Easy pickings.

Izzy: Maybe we should wait for Ahmad?

Viv: Not too long.

While they waited, Izzy walked in circles, looking for her friend. Viv stepped to the edge of Mount Mountain and began work on another peak.

Viv: I'm going to name this one Eli Hill.

Izzy: Good idea.

Izzy helped. They were experienced builders, and the mountain didn't take long. When they had finished, and filled its cliffs with nests full of an eighteenth species of bird that Izzy named Eleazarids, also after Eli, Ahmad still hadn't shown up.

They gave up on him and went griefing.

Running to the location Viv had chosen took about fifteen

minutes. The avatars in the river valley were all in sleep mode, or just walking in circles. A few NPCs resisted, but they were weak. With their wide silver swords, Viv and Izzy smashed fences, cut holes in the walls of houses, and massacred herds of cattle and sheep. Every time she came across a chicken, Izzy picked it up and hurled it onto the nearest rooftop. The two girls carried out their mayhem with eggs and chickens raining from the sky.

When they had carved a path across the cluster of villages and were turning to cut through again, they met another avatar. It stood in their path, flickering as if the user's connection was weak.

Viv: Ahmad?

But it was Eli's avatar. Sandy brown hair, dots for freckles, a permanent grin.

Had Eli looked like that in real life?

Izzy: Viv . . .

Viv attacked. Her blocky avatar blocked Izzy's view, but around the bobbing rectangular head, Izzy caught glimpses of Eli's digital body, marked by star after star as it took blow after blow, until virtual Eli fell to the virtual ground and his flickering eyes were replaced by flickering Xs.

Izzy: Viv!

Viv abruptly vanished.

Izzy stood looking at the avatar until she felt her station rocked by three big waves in quick succession. "Izzy!" she heard Dad yell.

"The coupling with the processor is broken! I need the welding gear and the rappelling harness!"

She disconnected.

———

IZZY TOLD Mom about seeing Eli, and Mom gave her a hug.

She didn't get on the Sphere for a few days, and no one suggested she should. There was plenty for her to do, helping Dad fix the processing-tank coupling, and then fix it again when another wave broke the weld.

Dad looked a lot at the horizon as they worked. There were dark circles under both his eyes and a patchy beard starting to sprout on his jaw.

An ethernote from Ahmad reassured both her and Viv that he was alive, his family's station had just lost power for a while, but she and Viv both answered so briefly they were almost curt.

A guest came to dinner, and Izzy was surprised to see that she recognized him: it was the Ecumene Shepherd. She'd never seen him in the physical world, but she recognized him by his similarity to his avatar. He was dressed in a black cloak and tunic, and where the avatar had a thick grey band across the top of its head, the Shepherd had eyebrows thicker than his thumbs, running in a single bar from ear to ear at the base of a deeply wrinkled forehead.

Not a skullcap, after all.

The Shepherd smiled a lot and had kind eyes.

Izzy's parents seemed to expect him, but no one had given Izzy any warning, and no one explained why there was an Ecumene Shepherd on the station for the first time ever.

The small talk the adults made over dinner was elliptical. Their voices were subdued.

"Any sign of the wormhole re-opening?" . . . "PlanSec doesn't have any evacuation capacity, that's not what they were made to do!" . . . "Not enough metal to build that colony ship Patel was talking about, I heard." . . . "We could put something in orbit, but it wouldn't hold everyone." . . . "The tremors are getting worse. Forget about plate shifts; if the planet goes, being in orbit won't be safe enough."

Did they think she was too young to understand? Or were they trusting her enough to show her their own fears? Izzy's stomach hurt.

Mom smiled at her and held her hand.

Over steamed kelp-noodles and chunks of fried eel, the Shepherd turned to Izzy. "I hear you saw your friend, Eli."

"The Sphere was glitching, that's all. I'm not stupid. Eli's dead."

Dad chuckled grimly and looked out the window.

Bear yelled, "Burp!" He wasn't wearing his Sphere-helm, so maybe he just recognized the word *sphere* and gave his usual war-cry.

The Shepherd nodded. "Only, your mother ethered the Sphere techs, and they can't find a record of the glitch."

Izzy felt very small. "Did you come out here to call me a liar?"

The Shepherd shook his head, eyebrows furrowing. "Your friend Viv saw it, too. I believe you both."

Izzy shrugged, chewing a mouthful of kelp. It had a mild, salty taste, under a chutney of hydroponically grown tomatoes. "Then the techs missed the evidence of the glitch."

The Shepherd nodded. "Or maybe what you saw was something else."

"A ghost?"

"The line between a ghost and an angel can be very fine."

Izzy put down her fork and knife. "If Eli came back as an angel, worse luck for him. And for Viv, who chopped the angel to bits."

"If Eli came back as an angel, maybe he was sent to help us. For instance, maybe he came to bring you feelings of peace and comfort."

"And we killed him." Izzy picked up her knife and fork and took another bite of food. "But it was just a glitch."

The station shook once during dinner, throwing a bowl of legumes across the floor, and twice after. When Mom flew Roo out to deliver the Shepherd to his flyer, Izzy stood in an observation bay with Dad and watched.

Roo was the utility vehicle that Mom and Dad used to reach remote combines or, occasionally, shuttle to other stations. It was a small flyer, shaped like an eggplant, with a pocket containing four seats. Roo was also the name of the AI that flew the utility vehicle. Mom landed Roo alongside the Shepherd's flyer, riding at anchor, and tethered the vehicles together. Then the pocket opened and the Shepherd stepped across into his own craft.

Dad snorted and walked away.

Izzy watched until Mom and Roo had returned to the station's dock and the Shepherd had disappeared over the southern horizon.

Where was her friend Eli?

———

"DAD," Izzy asked, "is the planet going to blow up?"

She asked it when Bear wasn't around. He was too young to worry about this sort of thing.

Dad looked up from the processing unit he was tinkering with and wiped sweat from his eyes, smearing grease on both his cheeks in doing so. "Look, all this god stuff . . . you don't have to believe it."

"That's not what I was saying." Izzy handed her father a spanner.

"I figure the real meaning of it is, live your life from moment to moment as if the whole world could end. Because you could die, from moment to moment, and then your world would be over. So, live as if you were about to be judged at all times."

"By a god?"

"Or by people. Because you might have a heart attack, or a stroke." Dad sighed. "Or you might get knocked off your station by a bad wave and drown in the kelp."

Like Eli had. "Dad, is Rowland-Beta going to blow up?"

"Someday. Maybe tomorrow. Maybe in a million years, maybe in a billion."

"So, there's no hope for any of us."

Dad gripped a bolt with the spanner and grunted while he forced it to turn. The dented protective plate popped off, and he set it aside. "In the long run, as individuals?" He considered. "We all die. But the species gets better. There's always hope for our children."

"And for us? On Elizabeth's World?"

"Smart people are working on it." Dad grinned, but his eyes were flat. "There's always hope."

Izzy took a deep breath. "There sure are a lot of tremors."

"There sure are." Dad picked up the replacement plate and snuggled it into place.

"BE CAREFUL OF A BIG WAVE, MIRIAM."

"I know you'll protect us."

Dad watched, sitting on a catwalk above the rest of the family. Mom sang over three short candles, one red, one white, and one black. Even unlit, the candles smelled of citrus and spice.

"One light is the Bridegroom," Mom sang, as she lit the first candle. "Sing it with me, one light is the Bridegroom."

"One light is the Bridegroom," Izzy and Bear sang together.

"One light is the Bride." Mom lit the second.

"One light is the Bride."

"And the third light is Secret Wisdom, watching over them both."

"The third light is Secret Wisdom."

"Secret Wisdom watches over us now," Mom said. "She gives us what we need. What do you need, Bear?"

"Juice!"

At least he hadn't said "burp."

"And what do you need, Izzy?"

Izzy hesitated. "I want the tremors to stop. Or I want us all to get away from them."

Mom looked thoughtful and was silent for a time. "And what does Eli need?"

"Juice!" Bear offered again.

What *did* Eli need? What would Izzy need, if she and Eli traded places? "Maybe he misses his friends."

"Let's pray for those things." Mom smiled. "For the tremors to stop, and for Eli not to miss his friends anymore."

"Juice!"

"And for juice."

Mom and Izzy and Bear joined hands and prayed without words for a long time.

Waves rocked the station violently that night, and tore up kilo-metres of kelp, but not until the entire family was inside and safe.

In the middle of the night, Izzy awoke to the sound of foot-steps. The station rocked, and she saw Dad's shadow, pacing past the opening to her sleeping pod.

IZZY RETURNED TO THE SPHERE. She met Ahmad and Viv to add more to Mount Mountain, and to repair some damage that had been done by griefers in their unusually long absence. Eli Hill, standing at the edge of Mount Mountain, had been gnawed by hostile pickaxes down to a nub.

While they rebuilt, they had to fight off Stalkers. The Stalkers were pink, simple-faced marauders. They were operated by central processing, rather than by a live user, and all they did was march toward an active user's avatar and attack it when they arrived. Their attacks were clumsy, and they were usually unarmed, so experienced players killed Stalkers by the thousand.

Izzy and her friends killed several hundred while repairing Eli Hill, and then dug a moat around Mount Mountain to protect it. They dug the moat down to the substratum, then obliterated the stairs by which they'd descended into the moat, and then used all their combined Unobtainium to make an invisible bridge at an agreed spot.

In the century and more since humans had left Earth, they had never yet encountered an *intelligent* species from another planet. Plants and animals, yes, but nothing that could communicate, or, apparently, think.

Everything that had evolved off planet Earth was either a cow or a Stalker, was how Izzy had restated this fact to her Sphere-tutor, Ms. Wilson. Eventually, she had been able to make Ms. Wilson understand what she meant.

After the others had to go (the sun set earlier in their longitudes), Izzy stayed, replacing nests, layering on additional tiers of shrubbery, and widening the protective ditch even further. While she was hacking away at the edge of the moat, she found a trail she had never seen before.

Out of curiosity, or hoping it might lead to a new source of Unobtainium to replace what they'd used, she followed it.

At the end of the path, though, and not very far from Mount Mountain, was a structure. It was long, black, and rectangular. Izzy couldn't tell at first glance what it might be made of, but it hung suspended in mid-air.

Izzy knew of no way to hang a structure above the ground in the Sphere. Surely this oddity must conceal a source of a rare material.

On the structure's underside were red markings in a square around an opening. The structure was low enough to the ground that Izzy could walk underneath it, and then jump up into it.

Inside the structure was a room, and a small console, like a table. Standing on the other side of the console was her friend Eli.

Eli: You have sufficient breathable atmosphere?

The avatar wasn't flickering anymore, but it shifted left and right, as if the user were new to the game's controls.

Eli: You have enough food?

Izzy put her fingers to her keypad.

Izzy: Here? In the Sphere? I don't need food. I was looking for some-
where to mine Unobtainium.

Eli took a few moments to respond.

Eli: Not in this simulation. On the planet.

Izzy: There is air, and plenty of food and water.

Eli: Why are you all frightened?

Eli didn't sound lonely. Izzy didn't like the questions he was
asking, but they weren't the questions of a lonely person.

Was the Shepherd right? Could this be the ghost of Eli, or
his . . . angel?

Izzy: Are you frightened?

Avatars couldn't change expression, so Eli stared without
responding for a few moments.

Eli: I am safe.

Was Eli safe because he was dead, and not exposed to the
tremors and the waves they caused?

Izzy: Do you have air, and food, and water?

Eli: My vessel has more than enough.

What kind of vessel sailed through the lands of the dead?

Izzy: Is it cold where you are?

Eli: It is very cold.

Eli moved forward, edging around the table. Out of reflex, Izzy pulled her avatar back, and promptly fell down through the hole in the floor. As she tumbled to the ground in the Sphere, Izzy felt her chair in the station topple sideways and heard Mom shout.

Izzy cut her connection before she hit the ground.

THE SHEPHERD RETURNED to the family station two days later, and this time Izzy's parents looked surprised. Mom took Bear and hid, somewhere down in the engine rooms where Izzy couldn't see them.

Dad took Izzy out in Roo to meet the Shepherd and the man who had come with him.

"Roo," Dad said. "Land alongside the open hatch of that flyer."

"Acknowledged." Roo followed Dad's instruction, and Dad tethered the two vehicles together with Roo's magnetic arms.

In the Shepherd's open hatch stood both the Shepherd and a man in a plain blue suit, with his name on a black tag on his chest. They wore safety harnesses, anchored to the flyer; Izzy and her father were belted into Roo's seats. The man in the blue suit wore a large pistol, strapped to the outside of his right leg in a glossy black holster. Izzy tried not to stare.

The starry symbol of the Ecumene, painted and static, surrounded the opening.

"Sure, my daughter is happy to talk to PlanSec," Dad said. "Just as soon as you tell me why."

The newcomer didn't smile. "We haven't been able to communicate with the Galactic Main since the wormhole collapsed, Mr. Reiter."

Dad laughed. "You think Izzy can help you with that?"

"Hear him out," the Shepherd said.

"What is PlanSec?" Izzy asked. It had something to do with the government of Elizabeth's World, but she wasn't sure what.

"Planetary Security." The Shepherd smiled at her. "You don't hear from them often because Elizabeth's World is such a safe place."

As he spoke, a wave threw both vehicles into the air and spun them 180 degrees. The Shepherd cried out, but no one fell into the water. Dad looked up at the station, hulking above them with its various pods, platforms, and connecting catwalks.

"Go on," Dad said.

The motion of the vehicles had thrown Dad's jacket open, and Izzy now saw that he, too, was carrying a pistol. She's seen it for years in the locked emergency compartment, and he'd taught her to use it, shooting at birds and at floating objects, but she'd never seen her father carry it to a meeting with another person.

She fixed her eyes on the Shepherd and his companion.

"We've detected a tight-beam transmission from off-world," the PlanSec man said. "It was aimed at this station."

"Nothing else out here for thousands of kilometres," Dad said. "But I didn't receive any transmission. I didn't even detect one."

"It wasn't in one of our standard frequencies," the PlanSec man said. "We only caught a small part of the transmission, but the data looked like Sphere-code."

"Izzy plays in the Sphere." Dad's voice sounded tense. "So does Bear. That's Barak, my son. I believe he knows two words. Are you saying my kids are communicating with the Galactic Main? My wife and I attend an Ecumene service, from time to time . . . does that mean we might be receiving messages?"

Dad's hand shifted perceptibly closer to his pistol.

"I'm saying we want to ask," the PlanSec man said.

He, too, moved his hand to his belt, not far from his weapon.

"I'll talk to them." Izzy nodded at the PlanSec man. "I'll talk to you."

The Shepherd knelt, bobbing up and down slightly in her view as the two vehicles moved on waves not quite in sync. His safety harness pulled his tunic as he did so, exposing soft brown belly. "I know you saw someone surprising in the Sphere."

"Your dead friend," the PlanSec man added.

Izzy felt the skin at the back of her neck prickle. "Is that what this is about?"

"Maybe," the PlanSec man said. "Did you talk to your dead friend?"

Izzy nodded slowly. "He talked about breathable air. And he said it was cold where he was, and he wanted to know if I had food."

"Food?" PlanSec asked.

Izzy nodded again. "I think maybe he was hungry."

"Anything else?" PlanSec asked. "Any talk of rescue? Discussion of planetary stabilization? Coordinates for other habitable planets? Any mention of the Governor, or Planetary Security, or the Ecumene?"

Izzy shook her head to all the questions.

"I don't think Eli knows anything about those things," she said. "Eli liked griefing and dirty jokes."

Dad snorted.

The PlanSec man took a deep breath, exhaled, and shook his head. Izzy kept her eyes on his pistol until he had disappeared into the vehicle, and then stared at the vehicle until it had crossed the horizon.

She didn't stop trembling for three hours.

VIV SENT HER ETHERNOTES: *Come join us at the Sphere. Mount Mountain feels empty without you. Ahmad is a terrible griefer, he wants to fill up his inventory instead of just smashing stuff. Come baaaaaack!*

Ahmad ethered her, too: *Hey, where are you? I like Eli Hill, good job with the new bird species! Why does Viv like breaking everything to bits, when we can take it and use it ourselves?*

Izzy didn't answer.

She didn't get any ethernotes from Eli.

The waves got bigger and more frequent. Dad stopped sleeping. Mom lit more candles.

"JUICE!" Bear said.

It was the middle of the night and he woke Izzy up. She rubbed her eyes and stared through the transparent ceiling of her sleeping pod. A brilliant crimson band crept overhead, punctuated by distant stars here and there.

"Juice!" Bear said again. Then he added, "Eli!"

"Go to bed," she told him. "It's late."

Bear reached under her light coverlet and grabbed Izzy by one foot. "Eli!" he said again.

The name brought Izzy fully awake. She'd never heard Bear say Eli's name before.

Where would he have heard it? At Eli's funeral? But that had been in the Community Hall, and Bear imitated all the low-res noise he heard in the Sphere as "burp." From Izzy's own lips, in some casual discussion of what she did in the Sphere? From Mom or Dad?

It didn't matter. "Go to sleep."

She rolled over and tried to find sleepiness again.

"Burp!" Bear said, and then she heard his feet padding away across the station.

Izzy was just beginning to drift off when it occurred to her that Bear had left her dormitory and walked *away from* his own sleeping pod.

"Bear?" She leaped from her bed.

She ran down the hall. Dad lay crumpled against a control console, snoring erratically. Beside him, on the console, stood an open bottle of kelp-liquor, half empty, and his pistol. She wanted to stop, to hide the gun and the bottle, but she was afraid Bear might be headed for the outside.

The door to her parents' sleeping pod was shut. All over the station, lights were off, and the celestial glow shone down through the transparent ceiling, lighting her path.

The one light that was on shone in the ladderway leading down to Roo's port. Izzy stuck to the balls of her feet but ran faster.

"Coordinates acknowledged," she heard Roo say.

What coordinates could Bear give Roo? Burp-juice-burp-Eli? Izzy threw herself down the shaft of the ladderway, sliding down the ladder's rails rather than climbing down its rungs. She landed heavily and off-balance, just in time to see Roo's pocket begin to close.

Izzy lurched to her feet and threw herself down the dock, falling down the short stairs and into the pocket just as the transparent shell of the pocket shut.

Bear sat in the pilot's seat, his hands on the steering controls.

"Bear, what are you doing?" Izzy smiled at her little brother, trying to make light of the moment. "Roo, open the pocket."

"Please fasten all safety restraints," Roo said. "Launching in ten seconds."

"Roo, override!" Izzy said. "Roo, stop!"

"Nine," Roo answered, "eight . . ."

Izzy quickly shoved Bear into the pocket's second seat and buckled him in, and had just enough time to dive into the pilot's chair and fasten her own harness before Roo left the dock.

———

Roo's acceleration to maximum speed was so gradual that Izzy scarcely noticed it. But by the time she gave up trying to find a manual override or activate the comms, which absolutely refused to cooperate, the utility craft was skimming above the water at 300 kilometres per hour.

The waves were enormous. Looking over her shoulder, she saw the station heaving up and down so violently it seemed about to flip upside-down.

"Roo, go back!" she said to the vehicle.

"Where are we going?" she asked it.

"I'm going to tell my dad!"

Roo ignored her.

Bear promptly fell asleep.

In less than an hour—travelling always due west, Izzy could tell by watching the moving crimson band overhead—lights appeared ahead, just above the water. She had studied the charts, and she knew that there was no station here. What, then? Some craft in transit, or some bioluminescent sea dweller, come up to the surface for air?

But the lights were stationary, and the colour was a deep red, not the blue or white she usually saw in eels and crustaceans. And as Roo drew closer, she saw that the red lights were embedded in the underside of a long black cylinder. It was enormous, ten times longer than the station was across, and smooth and black, and it hovered above the water without any visible means.

Izzy felt as if her heart had stopped beating.

Encircled by red lights, on the underside of the cylinder, was an opening. Roo decelerated, positioned itself beneath the opening, and then rose vertically into the cylinder. Within the cylinder was darkness.

"Initiate docking procedure," Roo said.

"Where is this?" Izzy asked.

"This is Eli's house."

THE POCKET'S transparent shell opened, and there was a black staircase, leading up.

Should she leave Bear, or bring him with her? Neither seemed safe, but she picked Bear up and slung him over her shoulder. It seemed like a way to honour his part in bringing her here.

At the top of the stairs, she found herself in a room.

The only thing in the room other than herself and Bear was a console.

Bear woke up, and she set him down. "Juice," he observed.

"Juice," Izzy agreed.

An opening appeared in the wall, and a being came out. It slid forward slowly, moving by rolling a hedge of muscular tentacles beneath itself, and came to stand on the other side of the console.

Izzy had been here before.

"Eli," she said. "This is Eli's house."

The being was slightly shorter than Dad, and broader, and covered with wrinkled yellow skin. It had a skirt of tentacles ringing its upper body as well as the mass of tentacles beneath it, and something that looked like a face in between. Its eyes were large and unblinking, and its mouth was a birdlike beak.

The being stood still for a few moments, then reached forward and touched the console. A synthesized voice poured out, low-resolution and deep,.but understandable.

"Izzy. I have peaceful intentions toward you. I have peaceful intentions toward your family. I have peaceful intentions toward your whole people. I am like you. I live in isolation. You farm kelp. I mine cosmic dust. I watched you. Your planet is dying. You are cut off from your other planets. I tried to reach your people's communications. I failed. Then I connected with your simulation. I have capacity in my vessel to hold the entire human population of this planet. I am here to help."

"Burp!" Bear hollered.

Izzy's heart beat so fast she could barely breathe. "What's your name?"

The being touched its console repeatedly, with both upper and lower tentacles. The motions reminded Izzy of typing.

"My name is hard to say," the voice said. "Please call me Eli."

"Eli." Bear nodded, and hugged Izzy's leg.

Somehow, Izzy managed not to cry.

Eli-the-Dust-Miner touched the console again. "And this is my family."

Another opening appeared in the wall. From it emerged three

beings that resembled Eli-the-Dust-Miner. One was his size, and faintly green. The other two were smaller, closer to Bear's height, and bright-pink.

Bear rushed three steps forward, stopped, then shook a fist in the air. "Juice!" he said. "Burp! Eli!"

One of the pink creatures clung to its green parent, but the other came to meet Bear halfway, upper tentacles trembling with excitement. It made a noise that sounded like squealing.

"May I use the comms in Roo?" Izzy asked. "In my vessel? I want to contact my parents."

"Yes," Eli-the-Dust-Miner's synthesized voice said. "Tell them we are coming."

Izzy nodded. "I'll tell them there is hope."

A THING OF BEAUTY

By Dr. Charles E. Gannon

"The children have become an unacceptably dangerous liability. Don't you agree, Director Simovic?"

"Perhaps, Ms. Hoon. But how would you propose to resolve the problem?"

"Director, it is generally company policy to . . . liquidate assets whose valuations are subpar and declining."

Elnessa Clare managed not to fumble the wet, sloppy clay she was adding to the frieze, despite being triply stunned by the calm exchange between her corporate patrons. The first of the three shocks was her immediate reaction to the topic: *Liquidate the children? My children? Well, they're not mine—not anymore—but just last year they would have been mine, when I was still the transitional foster parent for company orphans. How could anyone—even these bloodless suits—talk about "liquidating the children?"*

The second shock was that these two bloodless suits were discussing this while Elnessa was in the room, and only twenty feet away, at that. But then again, why be surprised? Their company, the Indi Group, was simply an extension of the mega-corporate giant CoDevCo and evinced all its parent's tendencies toward callousness and exploitation. It also possessed the same canny ability to generate profits, often by ruthlessly factoring human losses into their spreadsheets just like any other actuarial number.

The third shock was that Elnessa could hear Simovic and Hoon at all, let alone make out the words. Because of the xenovirus which had hit her shortly after arriving on Kitts—officially, Epsilon Indi 2 K—Elnessa had suffered losses in mobility and sensory acuity. But every once in a while, she experienced an equally troublesome inversion of these handicaps: unprecedented (albeit transient) sensory amplification. Six months ago, she had had to endure a hyperactive set of taste buds. All but the blandest of foods had made her retch. And now, over the past four days, her steady hearing loss had abruptly reversed, particularly in the higher ranges. Elnessa had acquired a new-found empathy for dogs, and could now pick out conversations from uncommonly far off, whereas only a week ago, she had been trying to learn lip-reading.

She realized she had stopped working; had, in fact, frozen motionless. And Simovic and Hoon had fallen silent, were possibly watching her, wondering if she had—impossibly—heard them. Elnessa raised her hand haltingly, then paused again, hefting the clay. Then she shook her head, plopped it back, and began rolling it to work the water out. Meanwhile, she continued to listen carefully, hoping they had believed her depiction of "distracted aesthetic uncertainty."

Simovic's voice resumed a beat later. "So, Ms. Hoon, do you have any suggestions for the most profitable method of divesting ourselves of these young—er, high-risk commodities?"

"Director, at some point, the attempt to find a profitable method of divestiture can itself become a prime example of the law of diminishing returns. Sometimes a commodity becomes so valueless that the simplest and least costly method of liquidating it is best."

Elnessa reminded herself to keep breathing. The good news was that Simovic and Hoon had believed her performance as "the Oblivious Artist," contemplating the frieze before her. The bad news was that the discussion at hand had already moved from, "Should we get rid of the children?" to "How do we go about doing so?"

Simovic carried the inquiry further. "So we just abandon the asset in place?"

"Director, I would suggest junking the asset at a considerable distance from the main colony, and even the outlying settlements. I suggest using an infrequently visited part of the planet. No reason we should risk being seen and reported for disposing of unwanted material off-site."

Elnessa was now acclimated enough to the horrific conversation that she could actually work and listen at the same time. She straightened, began layering in thin strips of micro-fibre pseudo-clay that would hold and provide a reflective receptacle for the backlit acrylic inserts with which she would finish the high-relief centre panels of the mixed-media frieze. With one eye on Simovic's and Hoon's reflections in the inert monitor of her combination laser-level and grid-plotter, Elnessa smoothed and sculpted the materials while straining her ears after every word.

Simovic chuckled: the sound was more patronizing than mirthful. "Ms. Hoon, sometimes the direct approach to seemingly low-value divestiture is not the best alternative—particularly if one has had the opportunity to plan in advance."

Hoon's shoulders squared defiantly. "What advanced planning are you referring to, sir?"

"Well, in fairness, it's nothing that you could have been aware of. Suffice it to say that with the appearance of this—ah, unregistered vessel—in main orbit, the asset in question may not be wholly valueless."

Hoon sounded skeptical. "And just why would a bunch of Grey World orphans be of interest to—to whoever it is that's hovering just outside Kitts's own orbital track?"

Elnessa watched Simovic lean far back in his absurdly oversized chair and steeple his fingers. His smile had mutated from smug through shrewd and into predatory. "Come now, Ms. Hoon; surely you can think of at least a dozen reasons why unrecorded corporate wards would be items of interest to any number of parties."

Hoon's defiant frown slowly evolved into a smile—at about the same pace that Elnessa felt her blood turn into ice. People, particularly kids, who were "unrecorded"—who lacked birth certificates and national identicodes—were rare, and therefore inherently valuable, black-market commodities. And there wasn't a single use for such commodities that was anything less than hideously illegal and immoral.

"And why," Hoon asked in what sounded like a purr, "are you so sure that our mysterious visitors will be interested in such a trade good?"

"That," Simovic answered with a self-satisfied sigh, as expansive and deep as had he just finished a very filling meal, "will become obvious within the next twenty-four hours."

Elnessa blinked and doubled the speed at which she was putting the finishing touches on the clay components surrounding the central space she had left open for what she had silently labelled The Brazen City. She had to complete the frieze soon, and in particular, she had to finish on time today, because she needed to make an early visit to her dead-drop site.

She had to make sure that her contact, Reuben, came to debrief her. As early as possible.

SITTING ON THE SPONGY, close-mowed *kitturf* that seemed half-lichen, half crabgrass, Elnessa surveyed the small patch of ground that served as the colony's park, promenade, and grey market. She watched as Reuben led the newest batch of fresh-faced PDPs—Parentless Displaced Persons—to the sparsely appointed playground at the other end of the public square. Although the orange-yellow disk of Epsilon Indi had almost dipped behind the horizon, the amber-white gas-giant Lee was in gibbous domination of the darkling sky. If one looked closely, the resulting double illumination created faint secondary shadows, with the stronger ones (generated by the system's primary) rapidly losing ground to those created by the weak but steadily reflected light of Kitt's parent-world.

Elnessa smiled as several of the younger children lagged behind, mesmerized by the ghostly effect. Reuben cycled back to the end of the group, gently urged the stragglers to keep up, evidently throwing down the claim that he could reach the playground first. Cries of glee provided the soundtrack for the impromptu footrace to a dilapidated jungle-gym.

Nice kids, thought Elnessa. And they almost always were, despite the hellholes that invariably spat them out. Usually, their parents or parent had died on a Grey World, still indebted to the company store or transit office, and—presto—the kids became the wards of the corporation. Which grudgingly fed them and clothed them as generically as the parents it had killed—unintentionally, of course. But once wearing a megacorporate yoke that shackled them to the company store, a great many desperate employees discovered that they had to work in increasingly risky and brutal jobs to defray the debts that accumulated faster than the pay.

Elnessa scowled. The corporations were nothing if not ruthlessly efficient, even in the smallest of matters. Here it was, only two days past the collectively observed year-end holidays, and the physical-plant flunkies were already making the rounds, taking down the ornaments that ringed the periphery of the park. Elnessa watched the strings of white and red lights wink out, one after the other, just before they were re-coiled into storage spools by the coveralled workers. *'Tis the season to be stingy*, she thought. *After all, what is the value in prolonging the modest, celebratory mood of the community when the company could burn a few less kilowatt-hours? And all for the sake of something as intangible as* joy? *Bah, humbug.*

She emerged from her bitter reverie, discovered that she was still watching the kids, unconsciously drinking in their innocence like an antitoxin. A moment later, Reuben drifted away from his charges, began approaching her obliquely.

She spared a quick glance at the younger man as he strolled across the spongy *kitturf,* then she looked back to watch the kids playing. One of them standing at the edge of the playground looked to be the oldest, but he certainly wasn't the biggest. He was a little short for his age, thin, standing quite still, milk-chocolate skin, dark brown eyes, and very straight black hair.

"El," Reuben said.

She looked up, almost surprised: he had not meandered toward her as he should have. "Hi, Reuben. Have a seat."

"Okay. Jus' for a second, though." He flopped down on the ground. A slightly musky smell—the one given off by quickly compressed *kitturf*—rose up around them. "So what's up, Mata Hari?"

Elnessa snorted, stared down at herself. "Oh yes, I'm one spry, sultry sex-pot; that's me."

Reuben—a good kid, but very new at coordinating the activities of Kitts's illegal (hence, underground) union—seemed uncertain how to respond. "El . . . Elnessa, you're really not . . . not so—"

"Christ, Reuben, I'm not fishing for a compliment, okay? Thanks to this delightful xenovirus, my leg is almost shot, my muscle tone is going, and I stand zero percent chance of becoming a tantric mistress of the Kama Sutra. I know all that. And I know you didn't mean to get yourself into this conversational mess, so let me help you escape it: I, your inside agent—'Mata Handicapped'—heard some nasty chatter today between the big cheeses. Concerning your new PDPs."

Reuben first looked relieved and thankful when Elnessa put aside the unfortunate reference to Mata Hari, but frowned as she concluded. "So, tell me the news."

Elnessa did.

Reuben blew out his cheeks, stared at the patchwork façade of the stacked modular uniroom workers' quarters. "The suits are monsters," he said. But he didn't seem surprised.

Elnessa narrowed her eyes. "Give," she said.

"Give what?"

"Come on, Reuben, you're going to have to feign innocent ignorance a lot more convincingly than that if you don't want the suits sniffing you out and introducing you to a sparring partner while you're strapped into a chair."

Reuben turned very white. "I'll work on the act, okay?"

"Don't do it to please me, Reuben. Do it to save yourself. Now, what have you heard?"

Reuben frowned. "Well, it's not what we heard; it's who was talking. And how much."

"What do you mean?"

"Coded government traffic spiked big-time today. Bigger than during inter-Bloc naval exercises."

"What? You monitor military channels?"

Reuben looked sidelong at her. "You think the Megas are above calling in troops to keep us working?"

"Their private security forces, no. But not the Blocs'. That's your old-school union dinosaurs talking, Reuben. Nations and corporations have been at each others' jugulars for almost twenty years now, with the nations supporting the unions ninety percent of the time."

"Yeah, well, the *industrial* megacorporations haven't become hostile toward the nations." He leaned his index finger across his middle finger. "The Industrials and nations are like that. More than ever."

Elnessa shrugged. "Sure. I can't argue that. But when was the last time the Industrials made a move that even *looked* like a prelude to strike-breaking?"

"Well, in China—"

"Don't get cute, Reuben. We're not talking about Beijing's 'companies,' here. They're not genuine corporate entities any more than their army is. They just get their orders from different people. Sometimes. But in the other Blocs—"

"Okay, okay, I get your point. But regardless of that, it's still SOP for our membership on the other moons, like Tigua, to monitor all spaceside commo, even the coded stuff. Increased

activity is positively correlated with impending operations, whatever those operations might happen to be."

"Makes sense. So, what's the best guess about the cause of the
chatter? War?"

"Maybe, but the command staffs of all the Blocs seem
agitated."

"Well, they would be if they were on the brink of war."

"Yeah, but they'd be agitated at each other. Instead, the various
Bloc naval commands were burning up the lascom beams communicating *with* each other. If anything, the different militaries seem
to be cooperating more, not less."

"So, what's your hypothesis?"

"Well, the only thing that would worry all the Blocs and push
them together would be something from—well, from outside their
respective command structures."

Elnessa stared at him. "Meaning what?"

"Meaning—maybe—that unidentified ship Simovic was
talking about is not part of anyone's navy."

"So, whose do you think it is?"

"Look, El, we just don't have any guesses about that. Maybe
some military ship mutinied. Maybe the megacorporations have
built their own warship, are throwing their weight around."

"Then why does Simovic think he can sell orphans to—?"

"Okay, so maybe it's a ship the megas have slipped into the
hands of some of the local raiders you hear rumours about. *They*
might have an interest in kids without records."

Elnessa nodded; that seemed reasonable—and gruesome—
enough. But even so—

"El," Reuben said after a moment, "have you changed your
mind yet?"

"About what?"

"C'mon El, don't make this harder than it is. Will you take a—a package inside corporate headquarters?"

Elnessa shrugged, looked away. She heard Reuben lay something down on the *kitturf* beside her.

"What is that?" she asked, not needing to look.

"You don't need to know, El. Any more than you already do. That way you're not implicated if you're caught."

She turned back to look at him, ignoring the plain brown paper package on the ground between them. "Hell, you're not very good at this are you, Reuben? If anything in that package is selected for inspection when I go in, then I've got to have a plausible explanation ready, don't I? So I'm going to need to know what each object is, so I know how best to hide it, or how to explain it away if they take special notice of it. Right?"

Now it was Reuben's turn to look away. "Yeah, I guess so. I just don't want you to get—"

"Reuben, don't you stare away when the topics get tough: that's the most important time to stay eye-to-eye. Yes, I've been reluctant about doing anything more than listening and reporting. Which, admittedly, has worked out just the way you and your advisers back on Tigua thought. Since the suits have decided I'm nothing more than an unassuming, crippled artist-lady, I'm an operational non-entity to them, well beneath the notice of their security elements. So, it's been easy enough to be your ears inside the lion's den. But now, with them talking about the kids that way—well, I'll take the next step. I guess I have to. But I don't know anything about—"

"El, we only want you to bring the materials inside. You can leave it anyplace you want. Just tell us where you've left it when you come out. We'll take care of everything else."

Elnessa felt relief at not having to do the real dirty work and, in the same instant, felt like both a hypocrite and a coward. *So if I'm in on this plan, then why* shouldn't *I take risks equal to—?*

"El, there's something else."

Reuben's tone had changed, seemed to have become even younger, and more uncertain, somehow. She looked back up at him.

"Please, El: don't stare at the kids. Not so much, or so long. It makes them—well, uncomfortable."

El looked away, felt her chest tighten, forced that to stop— because if she didn't, she feared she might cry. "I can't help it, Reuben. They should have been mine."

"I know. But the youngest is five and . . . well, you scare them."

She wanted to ask, *Scare them? Why?* But she knew: of course she scared them. Her face was framed by the strange and shocking streaks of silver-grey hair that the first set of transient ischemic attacks had left behind. Since then, she had started hobbling along unevenly with the aid of a cane. There was an ever-changing array of intermittent facial and body tics. And of course, there was her riveted attention upon them whenever they came into view, yearning after what she had lost and now could never have again. She lowered her head. "I'll stay away."

Reuben almost whined his objection. "Look, you don't have to stay away."

"Yes. I do. If I'm there, I'll slip into fixating on them. Never had kids of my own, you know." It had been an utterly meaningless addition: of course Reuben knew that.

And the tone of his response indicated that he understood the statement for what it was: an unintentional plea for sympathy and understanding. "Yes, El—I know." The silence that followed was not at all comfortable. "So, um . . . so maybe I should start explaining what's in the package?"

"Might as well," Elnessa said, looking up. And what she saw made her smile.

Reuben followed her steady gaze over his shoulder. The little boy with quiet eyes and shiny black hair was only two metres behind him. Waiting.

"Hi," Reuben said with a quick smile.

"Hi," the boy answered without looking at Reuben.

He started to rise: "Waiting for me? I'll be there in a—"

"No, I'm waiting for her."

"*Her?*"

Elnessa felt a hot pulse of annoyance: *You don't need to sound surprised that someone might actually want to talk to me, Reuben.*

Who asked the child, "Why her?"

Oh, you're just flattering me no end, now, Mr. Empathy.

Elnessa could see the boy labouring—mightily—to keep his face blank. Why? To conceal his dismay, possibly disgust, at Reuben's thoughtlessly rude inquiry? "I'd like to talk to her. If you don't mind."

"Well, she and I—"

Elnessa interrupted. "We can finish this later, Reuben. Come by about seven, okay?"

"Uh, yeah . . . seven o'clock. In private is better, anyway—for what we have to discuss, I mean."

Elnessa nodded tightly, amazed that Reuben's idiot, injudicious utterances had not already undone him and the rest of the unofficial union.

The boy with the big, watching eyes moved into the space Reuben vacated. "Hi," he said again.

"Hi," Elnessa replied. "What's your name?"

"I'm Vas."

"'Vas?'"

He smiled a little. "It's short for Srinivasan. But most people can't say that too well. Anyhow, I like Vas better. What's your name?"

"I'm El."

He cocked his head. "Just 'El?'"

"Well, my real name is 'Elnessa,' but people have a hard time remembering that, too. They keep calling me Elaine or Ellen or Elise . . . or Bob."

Vas stared, then laughed. "You're funny."

"I'm glad you think so, Vas. And I'm very glad to meet you."

"I'm glad to meet you, too. I've been wondering: what do you do? I mean, for a living?"

"Well, I started out as an artist, but that was back before I came to settle in the Indis."

"But aren't you still an artist? At least some of the time?"

Elnessa started. "Why do you ask?"

Vas looked down at her hands and pointed. "They're stained a lot, almost every time I see you. Or they're caked with dirt or clay, I can't tell which. And you look at things very carefully, for a long time. Like you're measuring them—or feeling them—with your eyes."

Clever boy: he sees far more than he mentions. He could teach Reuben a thing or two. Elnessa smiled. "You look at things a long time, too. I've noticed."

"Yeah, but that's just because I'm really careful. I have to be." Before Elnessa could ask him why he needed to be careful, Vas had pressed on. "What kind of artist are you?"

"I used to create all sorts of art. I still did some pieces on the side when I first arrived on Kitts. Old-style paintings, 3-D comp-gens, I even dabbled a little in holos."

"What happened?"

She shrugged and looked down at her body. "A xenovirus."

"You mean a disease that was already here?"

"Well, sort of. Not really a disease. It's just that . . . well, most of the life on this planet—er, 'moon'—just ignores life from Earth because it's too dissimilar. Even though the life here is built from the same basic stuff—"

Vas nodded. "Carbon. Water."

"—yes." *Darn, he's sharp.* "But sometimes, the local microbes go after our cells, anyway. Or sometimes, the weaker unicellar organisms from Kitts decide to use our bodies as hiding places from the stronger ones that eat them. It's bad enough when those hiding microorganisms build up in our system, but sometimes, while doing so, they block or consume the few parts of us that they can use. And that's not good for us."

Vas nodded solemnly. "Your xenovirus blocks parts of your nervous system, doesn't it?"

He is very, very sharp indeed. "How did you know that?"

Vas shrugged. "Because you don't act sick so much as—well, just not able to control yourself as well as other people. And if the microbes were really, uh, consuming your nerves, I just kind of guessed that you wouldn't still . . . well, still be alive."

And how right all your guesses are, my bright little Srinivasan. Despite the concise recitation of her medical woes, Elnessa only felt joy when she was looking into the warm brown eyes of this child. "You know, Vas, I'll bet you could be a doctor someday."

He shrugged, looked away, then back at her. "Will we get it too?" Seeing her momentary incomprehension, Vas added, "The disease, I mean."

She had been slow to understand his question because she assumed that everyone—even kids—were informed upon arrival that, thanks to the new pre-planetfall vaccinations and six-month boosters, there hadn't been any infections since the first wave of settlers. "No," she said with a firm shake of her head. "You're safe. It only got the first colonists who settled here. And only some of us."

"Why did it only get some of you? And how did they cure it?"

Elnessa took care to compose herself before she answered. "Well, you see, Vas, when the Indi Group got permission to settle Kitts, they started with a really diverse group of people. At first, it just seemed that they were taking whoever was willing to come here, probably because they couldn't be picky. But it turned out that the mix of colonists was actually carefully selected, and was made up of an equal number of persons from every major human genotype. When we asked why they had done that, the company explained that they wanted to create a truly 'blended' colony. We still thought they were just trying to make up a nice-sounding story to cover up the fact that they were willing to sign on anyone who was willing to travel here. Of course, they *were* building a carefully mixed community, but not because they were trying to create social diversity." She watched to see if Vas had understood all the terms she had used. His brows remained unfurrowed, signifying easy and complete comprehension.

Elnessa went on. "In fact, Vas, we were guinea pigs, and they had to have a reasonable sample size of every strain and subspecies of us guinea pigs."

Now a frown bent Vas's brow. "I don't understand."

Elnessa had her mouth open to explain and then halted: *he's only a kid, El, even if he* is *a very, very smart one. Kids worry, have nightmares, particularly if you say something that makes them realize that the world is less safe than they think it is. I really don't have the right—*

"Look," Vas said very matter-of-factly, his eyes still calm but also resolute, "I grew up on Hard Nut, in the Lacaille 8760 system. Life is—hard—there. I lost my Mom, then my Dad, and my Tito Thabo, all in the last few years. So whatever your bosses did, you can tell me. I can take it."

Elnessa blinked, then sighed and folded her hands. "Vas, the Indi Group wanted to discover if any given genotype of *Homo sapiens* had a particular advantage or disadvantage in this environment. Not that there's any evidence for such a theory. But that's the way they think. Racial 'groups' do have unique diseases; ethnic groups can carry 'predominant genetic patterns' for certain developmental abnormalities. So they decided it would be best to test people from each genetic hiring pool to see if any of them had special advantages or challenges in Kitts's biosphere."

"And was there any difference among the groups?"

"No. And when other megacorporations run the same tests in other biospheres, they never find any differences there, either. But that doesn't mean there aren't biological dangers. Here on Kitts, as elsewhere, it turned out that the local xenobugs were all equal-opportunity pathogens."

"'Equal opportunity?'"

"Yes. That's just a silly way of saying that the xenobugs didn't care about our race, or colour, or sex. And I was one of the twenty-four colonists that the xenovirus decided to infest. After the xeno-biot surveys declared the biosphere 'safe,' that is."

"So how did the surveys miss detecting these, uh . . . these xenobugs?"

"Vas, to be fair, the real question should be, 'How could the surveys be expected to *find* the bugs?' Computer modelling, lab-testing on human-equivalents: those tools are crude and imperfect. And biosensors? A sensor only knows to look for something that has been identified for it already. The sad truth, Vas, is that you don't really get a good, reliable assessment of what will happen to a human body in a new biosphere until a couple of hundred of those bodies have lived there for a while."

She tapped her chest. "So we were the canaries in this coal mine. And those of us who became sick were immediately sequestered for study, which is how they learned which genetic markers put humans at highest risk, and then which vaccines or prophylaxes offered the best protection. And after that, I guess you could say my real work here was done."

"But you still work."

"Oh, they give me make-work because it was part of my agreement. I can have a job for as long as I like, and they'll provide for me; that's what they promised. But if I leave my employment here, I can't afford the shift-ticket to another system. And they'll also stop giving me the experimental xenoviral suppression cocktails, which are what have probably kept me alive this long. Since each new concoction eventually loses its efficacy, they've been willing to keep me around as a guinea pig, because I'm still a useful 'research platform.' But once they feel they've taken that research as far as they need to—"

"I thought you said they made a commitment to provide for you as long as you were their employee. Doesn't that include medical care?"

"Yes, but routine medical care does not mean that they have to keep a dead-end research program active just to give me the chance to live another year, and then another, and then another. If they stop, then they'll be responsible for providing for my minimum needs. Until I no longer need anything at all."

As she ended her description, Vas was looking up at Elnessa with the same quiet, attentive expression that had been on his face the first time she saw him. But now there was the hint of some emotional battle going on behind it. It almost looked as if he might cry—

—but then Vas leaned toward El and caught her in a firm, unyielding hug. El looked down at his crown of shiny hair, and then put her arms gently, carefully, around him.

ELNESSA RESISTED the urge to close her eyes as Wehns Shoniber, the big Micronesian leader of Simovic's personal security detail, started rummaging about in her road kit: a carpenter's toolbox converted into an artist's travelling studio.

"Hey, El," Wehns wondered, still staring down into the battered red box, "what's this?"

"Battery," Elnessa said, trying very hard to keep her response from becoming a sharp, anxious chirp.

"El, you know I can't let you take that in."

"Well, then how am I going to power the lights in the high-relief panels?" she replied. "I got Mr. Simovic's permission before I started the project that some of it could be illuminated."

"Well, I'm sure you did, El, but he didn't authorize an independent power source. I'm sure of that. Security protocols, you know."

El shrugged as if only mildly disturbed, thought: *oh, I know, Wehns, I know. In fact, this was exactly what I was afraid would happen. As I told Reuben last night.*

Wehns continued riffling through the rest of her gear, inspecting each of the picks, carvers, and files. He stared uncomprehending at an impress set for creating intaglio patterns, and asked, as he did every day, "Anything toxic, explosive, flammable, dangerous?"

"Not unless you're allergic to clay or acrylics."

Wehns smiled, scratched one of the clay bricks with a fingernail. "Sorry. Gotta ask."

"Why? Can't the big, bad megacorporation afford a couple of
chemical sniffers?"

"No, not yet. But it's just a matter of time, now that the bigwigs
are here to stay."

"Bigwigs?"

"Sure," Wehns nodded. Then in a lower voice, so his assistants
couldn't hear, added, "You know: Simovic and Hoon. He's got an
insane amount of autonomy—which came over with him when he
promoted up out of the Colonial Development Combine into his
post here."

"And Hoon?"

Wehns' face went blank. "She's as cutthroat as they come.
Jumped from field rep to junior director in only six years."

"Don't like her much?"

"Don't much care. She doesn't notice me; I'm just muscle. And
frankly, that's the way I like it. Don't want to be noticed. Just want
to do my job."

Elnessa looked down at Wehns's broad back as he neared the
completion of his daily search through her kit. Amiable Wehns
Shoniber was proof that you couldn't hate all the people who
worked for a megacorporation. It was not the homogeneous
conclave of demons and sociopaths that the worst anti-corporate
radicals tried to claim. In reality, any given mega only had a
smattering of those truly misanthropic monsters, but most of
them were in charge, leading a vast organization of average folks
who only wanted to work, get ahead, and not worry too much in
the process. She sighed: *for evil to triumph, all that's needed is for
good men to stand by and do nothing. Or for people to be too lazy to
care.*

"Hey, what's this?" Wehns had produced something that looked like the guts of a remote-control handset.

"IR receiver, so you can operate the frieze's lights by remote control from anywhere in the room."

"Aw, El," Wehns muttered, shaking his head in regret, "I'm sorry, but that one's off-limits, too."

"What? Why?"

"Because some nut-job might try to use it as a remote receiver for—something else. Or as a timer, because they all have internal time-chips."

Elnessa quirked an eyebrow. "A remote receiver or timer for what?"

Wehns looked abashed. "You know. Something—dangerous."

"You mean, like a piece of art?" Elnessa didn't think she'd be able to shame Wehns into looking the other way on this violation, but it was worth a try.

If Wehns blushed, she couldn't tell. His tropic-dark skin hid all such emotional responses. But his voice sounded regretful, apologetic. "El, look, you're okay—everyone knows *that*—"

Yeah, sure. Because I'm a nice little cripple lady . . .

"—but rules are rules. I'm sorry, I'm going to have to hold these for you. You can get them back when you leave today." With a nod that punctuated the end of both his search and their discussion, Wehns carried the offending items away to his secure lockbox. As he withdrew, he caught the eye of his senior assistant and tilted his head toward Simovic's office. The assistant turned and, with a smile that was as much a part of his equipment as his outdated taser, motioned that Elnessa was free to go into Simovic's *sanctum sanctorum*.

With a sigh, she followed his gesture and dragged her battered red box into the expansive Bauhaus-meets-Rococo gauche opulence in which Simovic held court, limping as she went. With the power supply and timer/actuator gone, Reuben's plan for sending a loud—and destructive—after-hours message to their megacorporate masters was pretty much busted before it had begun. She began hobbling toward the raised walkway that ran the length of the mostly finished frieze. Behind her, the door detail resumed their argument about whether today—New Year's Day, 2120—commenced the last year of the Teens decade, or the first of the Twenties.

"Ms. Clare." It was Simovic. Whom she had no desire to talk with. Or to look at. Or to share a common species with. And besides, she was supposed to be half deaf, now. So, without giving any sign that she had heard, Elnessa continued to make her slow, painful progress toward the work-ramp.

Simovic's voice was louder—so much louder, that she would have had to have been stone deaf to miss it. "Ms. Clare!"

Elnessa turned with what she hoped was a look of surprise and ingratiating eagerness. "Yes, Mr. Simovic?"

"Your project: how is it coming?"

"Should be finished tomorrow, Mr. Simovic. Although I hardly think of it as 'my project.'"

"Oh? Why not?"

"Well, sir, it's you who commissioned it."

"Yes, but the concept—and the handiwork—is yours, Ms. Clare. I trust you'll explain its content to both of us," he gestured diffidently toward Ms. Hoon, "when you are finished?"

"Of course, Mr. Simovic. Although it's neither abstract nor highly stylized. I think you'll see right away that—"

"Yes, yes: that's wonderful, Ms. Clare, wonderful. Just make sure that it radiates the humanitarian side of the Indi Group, would you?"

Oh, yes, I'll be sure to represent the way it exploits workers and gives us just enough pay to struggle on from one day to the next. I'll depict how, after the xenovirus incapacitated me, you made me your corporate nanny, and then, when I couldn't do that any longer, you met your minimum employment requirement by commissioning this frieze. Dirt pay for me, but a tax dodge for you, and a great PR op to demonstrate how the Indi Group encourages the remaining abilities of even its most severely handicapped employees. But Elnessa's only reply was, "I'll explain the frieze to you when I've completed it, Mr. Simovic."

"Excellent!" Simovic actually clapped his hands once in histrionic gratification and pleasure, nodded his thanks, and then drew closer to Hoon. For a moment, their voices were too low to hear, but then, evidently reassured by Elnessa's near-deafness, they resumed the discussion her entrance had interrupted.

"So you see," Simovic said in the voice of a smug tutor, "our visitors—I should say, our new clients—have good reason to be interested in our commodity."

"And our cooperation, along with it."

"Well, this goes without saying, Ms. Hoon. But the children will be out of our hands and out of our files as soon as they take possession."

"Exactly when and where will that occur?"

"We are uncertain, Ms. Hoon. But we do know this: the commodity must be delivered to the client in pristine condition. The client's, ah, research program would be ruined by any damage to the goods."

Research? On the children? On Vas?

"'Research'?" Hoon echoed. "With respect, sir, all these euphemisms are getting a bit ridiculous."

"How do you mean?"

"I mean that our new customers certainly aren't scientists, sir.

Corporate wards without identicodes are not going to be interred in laboratories. They're bound for raider ships, brothels, snuff producers, maybe a few rich pederasts, but not—"

El thought she was about to lose her breakfast, and then something calming yet more chilling insinuated itself into Simovic's even-toned interruption: "Oh, no, Ms. Hoon. You really don't understand, after all. These wards *are* going to a lab, which is why their utter lack of a traceable background makes them so optimal for this particular trade. Because it is imperative for both us and our clients that they receive humans who, insofar as the nations know, never existed."

Hoon was quiet for a moment. "Director Simovic, I find your change of label somewhat . . . confusing. Why are you referring to our commodity as 'humans,' now, instead of 'children?'"

"Because that is our client's primary interest in our commodity. It is not so much because they are children—although it has been intimated that this is the ideal age group for their researches—but because they are healthy, paperless specimens of *Homo sapiens*."

In the pause that ensued, Elnessa lifted a long, slightly convex, copper sheet from the floor, and, with a couple of touches of an exothermic chemical welder, affixed it to the naked wall of the room.

Hoon's voice sounded raspy, as if her throat had suddenly become dry. "Sir . . . I don't understand. The client wants them just because they're humans?"

Lifting a thin layer of protective gauze from the copper sheet, Elnessa unveiled what would soon occupy the top third of the frieze's centre: a cityscape cluttered by the various architectures of antiquity. She also reminded herself to breathe, despite what she was hearing.

"Oh, I think you are starting to understand after all, Ms. Hoon.

Rest assured; this exchange is not being conducted without adequate planning. Indeed, we had contingency directives sent out to us from Earth more than half a year ago, shortly after the Parthenon Dialogues became public knowledge."

Elnessa removed six sizable blocks of clay from her studio box and compared them to the virtual assembly plan on her grid-plotter. She then unsheathed her matte knife and carefully shaved an inch from the rear of the five smaller blocks.

Hoon had paused again, but not for as long. "Are you telling me that the contingency plans governing this, this—exchange— were crafted in response to the Parthenon Dialogues?"

Simovic considered his protégé over steepled fingers. "Let us rather say that the revelations of the Parthenon Dialogues prompted some of CoDevCo's more speculative thinkers to provide us with guidelines to handle a situation such as this one."

Even in the grid-plotter's illuminated screen, Elnessa could make out the profound scowl of doubt on Hoon's face. "But the evidence presented at Parthenon only proved past events: that— ages and ages ago—this area of space had been visited by aliens—"

"'Exosapients,'" Simovic corrected.

"'Exosapients,'" Hoon parroted peevishly, "but there was no evidence of a more recent presence."

Simovic smiled, smug and satisfied. "Yes, that's the story that was released to the public."

Elnessa forced herself to keep working. That made it easier not to imagine little Vas spread-eagled on an operating table, surrounded by hideous extraterrestrial vivisectionists. She mentally slapped herself, and mounted the five modified clay blocks on studs protruding from the copper plate. She stood back, admiring the effect: the blocks now seemed to be the stony slabs of an ancient fortress wall that curved out from the faintly raised copper cityscape directly over it—a metropolis which, by virtue of the oblique perspective, now seemed to be sheltered behind the wall.

Hoon had recovered enough to continue. "And so the full truth of the Parthenon Dialogues was—?"

"—was not shared in detail outside the meeting itself. However, let us say that while the evidence certainly established that exosapients did exist twenty thousand years ago on Delta Pavonis Three, it did *not* go on to assert that there were none left in existence."

"So you suspect that actual contact has been made in the recent—?"

"No, there's been no contact that we know of or suspect." Simovic smiled. "Not until now, that is."

"So you really think that the unidentified ship up there is, is—?"

"Ms. Hoon, the persons we are currently negotiating with are not human, of that you may rest assured. The communication challenges have been proof-positive of that."

Elnessa felt as though she might swallow her tongue, but instead, she picked up the last, and the largest, of the six clay blocks she had brought with her. She carefully carved the top to resemble a peak-roofed gallery at the pinnacle of a watchtower. Then she bored a small tube up through the centre of the block, making sure that it was wide enough to fit the wires for its small beacon light.

Hoon hadn't stopped. "So how did these, er, exosapients know to contact us and that we'd have these particular 'items' that they needed?"

"An excellent question, but those kinds of details are not even shared with regional managers, Ms. Hoon. However, I conjecture that there must have been some prior contact between our chief executives and some representatives of theirs."

"And you suspect this because—?"

"Because they arrived knowing and inquiring about the commodity we have in our possession. And because they knew our communications protocols, our location here instead of on Tigua, and a reasonable amount of our language. Although that latter knowledge has been decidedly imperfect."

Elnessa ran the wiring leads up through the tube in the watchtower: the slim copper alligator clips poked their noses out the top of the hole. Deciding to finish the sculpting and wiring later, she mounted the watchtower on its own copper stud, thereby completing the wall around the Brazen City. Then she ran the other end of the leads to a junction box mounted on the bottom of the copper plate, just beneath and behind the lower edge of the frieze. She then covered the wires—and the lower half of the copper plate—with strips of clay that she started sculpting into a semblance of furrowed farmland. Beneath those, she left just enough room for the band of blue-white acrylic that lay ready at hand: a stylized river, frozen in mid-tumult.

Hoon still hadn't stopped. "So what we're doing now is—"

"—is working out the particulars of the exchange, while we wait for Tigua to send us word on the outcome of the official first contact."

"Which we expect to be—unsuccessful."

Simovic shrugged. "It is most unlikely that Bloc-controlled Tigua will concede to our clients' military superiority—"

You mean, will refuse to surrender without a fight—

"—whereas *we* have already assured them of our complete and immediate cooperation."

You mean, traitorous collaboration offered up to them on a silver platter.

Hoon was smiling now. "How very convenient. For us."

"Yes, rather a nice reward for patiently enduring the pomposity of the nation-states, don't you think? Always nattering on about social contracts, and consent of the governed, and the greatest good for the greatest number. I can hardly believe they don't laugh themselves to death as they spout all that antediluvian rubbish."

Hoon's contempt for these same concepts was obviously so great that it exceeded polite articulation: she merely expelled a derisive snort. Then she added, "Well, good riddance to Bloc sanctions and antitrust restrictions."

Elnessa delicately swept her wire brush up, up, up, all along the first furrowed row of clay she had set before the city walls, imparting to it an impression of young wheat or corn, just as it sprang from the ground toward the sun. And as she did so, she listened to the unfolding plans for the cool, calculated, and above all profitable, betrayal of her species.

ONCE AGAIN RESPONDING to the gum wrapper Elnessa had inserted into the dead-drop crevice, Reuben approached her hurriedly. He had his mouth open to ask something—

Elnessa preempted him. "Have you heard?"

"You mean, about the aliens?"

"Exosapients," Elnessa corrected him.

"Whatever. Yeah, I heard. It's got to be the worst-kept secret there's ever been. No one seems to be able to shut up about it, even in the military. The word has been leaking out of navy comshacks, out of the commercial transmission offices, everywhere."

"And you know they're planning on coming here, evidently?"

Reuben frowned. "Well, amidst all the rest of the panic talk, I've heard that rumour, too. But the evidence for it seems pretty vague, pretty much hearsay."

"Well, it's not. These exosapients are apparently Indi Group's newest preferred customers. And they want the kids. For research."

She thought Reuben would goggle. But like her, his capacity for shock was almost exhausted. All Reuben did was shrug. "Figures. Which makes our mission all the more imperative." His expression became eager, more focused. "So, how did it go when you went in today? Is everything there, ready and waiting?"

Elnessa shook her head. "I got the payload in, but nothing else."

Reuben's jaw dropped open. "What do you mean?"

"I mean that they wouldn't let me take anything electronic into the office: no independent power supply, and no remote activators of any kind. Like I told you. But even so, I think I've found a way to—"

But Reuben was shaking his head. "No, El. It's finished. Our guy on the inside is strip-searched every day: they've got all the usual means of access covered. Without power and a way to trigger the device, it's no good."

"I understand your problem. But actually, there's a pretty simple alternative: you can—"

Reuben stood abruptly. "No, El: I don't want to know. The less I know, the less I can tell if they eventually root up some pieces of this plot and then try to discover who was involved. I've got—*we've* got—to forget about this. Right now. As if it never happened."

Elnessa looked up at him. "I'm not sure I can forget it, Reuben. Particularly not with what's at stake, now."

Reuben looked at her. "Don't make trouble, El. And don't make me warn you about coming near the kids again. Vas told me."

"Told you what?"

"That you made him dinner last night, let him stay until it was way too late—"

"Feeling guilty you didn't even notice he was missing, 'Daddy'?'" The moment she said it, Elnessa was sorry: no one knew better than she how hard it was to keep track of almost a dozen kids between the ages of five and thirteen. "Look, Reuben; I'm sorry. I shouldn't have—"

"El, just—just leave it alone. Leave it all alone. And I mean both the mission and Vas. And that's an order." His utterance of the word "order" was, laughably, a half-whining appeal, rather than a command.

"Sure," El answered. "Whatever."

Reuben turned and walked stiffly into the deepening gloom. About ten metres away, he reached down into a cluster of bushes and gently extracted its hidden occupant—Vas—before resuming his steady march away from Elnessa. Vas looked back, eyes troubled. He waved and was gone.

Elnessa waved, sighed, wiped her eyes, and went home in the dark.

IT WAS only midmorning of January 2, 2120, when Elnessa stepped back to examine the frieze, in all its finished glory. All that remained now was to put in the prism-projecting Cheops eye, just over the watchtower light, and complete the light fixture itself.

Behind her, Simovic and Hoon continued their plotting, as though they had been at it ever since she had left yesterday. And who knew? Maybe they had.

Hoon continued with her seemingly inexhaustible list of questions. "Our personnel—the ones who will gather the children, and the ones who will convey them to the rendezvous point—do any of them, well . . . know what's really going on?"

Simovic shook his head. "No. They have the necessary timetable, coordinates, and orders, but no knowledge of who our clients are or why we are engaging in this trade."

"Which is scheduled for when?"

Simovic looked at the digital timecode embedded in the ticker bar of his media-monitoring flatscreen. "Two hours."

"Short notice," Hoon commented.

"True. But it's really quite logical. Even if our new customers trusted us—which they have no reason to do at this point—they have no way of knowing if our communications are secure. Maybe Bloc naval forces have hacked our cipher, know when and where to expect our clients, and will set up an ambush. No, our clients' prudence is a good sign. It means they are not rash, and, after all, we will need these new partners to be very discreet indeed."

Elnessa looked over toward the two of them. "Mr. Simovic," she called.

"Yes, Ms. Clare?"

"Could you please have your security people pull the fuse for the power conduits all along this wall?"

"Why?"

"Well, I need to finish wiring the lights."

"Can't you leave the power on while you do it?"

"Only if I want to take the risk of electrocuting myself."

Elnessa noted Simovic's hesitation. It didn't arise from any

sense of suspicion—that was manifestly clear—but rather from
the inconvenience of her request. Her safety was almost beneath
his concern, especially at this particular moment. However, he
ultimately signalled his annoyed acquiescence to the guard at the
rear of the room, who left to comply with the request.

A moment later, the lights glaring down upon the frieze, along
with the rest of the devices which drew their power from outlets
along that wall, shut down.

Elnessa nodded her thanks and limped over to the watchtower,
the Cheops eye in hand. She emplaced the round, vaguely
Pharaohic piece of multi-hued crystal just above the pointed roof
of the watchtower.

Then, picking up the bulb that was to be the watchtower's
lamp, she set it down on the section of the clay "wall" next to the
tower, and inspected the two small alligator clips grinning toothily
up at her from just beneath the rim of the passage she had bored
lengthwise in the tower. She stuck her finger in between the leads,
widening the hole slightly, and then buried the two clips side by
side into the dense matter surrounding them.

She went to check the switch that provided the manual control
for all the lights in the frieze. It was, as she had left it, in the "off"
position.

She turned to face Simovic. "It is finished," she announced.

"Hmmmm . . . what?"

"I said, 'It is finished.' Can you please have the power restored
to this wall?"

Simovic and Hoon looked up: he surprised, she bored and
impatient. He nodded for the guard to go restore the power, and
then stood straighter, scanning the length of the frieze. Elnessa
detected surprise and gratification: despite the fact that she had
spent the last two months crafting it literally under his nose, he

had never truly examined it until now. Simovic cleared his throat. "That is really . . . "

" . . . really quite good," Hoon finished, with an approving nod-and-pout, and a tone of voice that sounded like a grudging concession. Then she was turning back to her documents and data-feeds.

"But you have not seen it all," Elnessa said.

Hoon looked back up, Simovic smiled faintly. "No?" he asked.

"No. Several elements light up and can be set to show different times of the day. The sun light is here, and small spotlights are embedded here and here to make the city roofs gleam during the day mode. These other lights—inside the blue acrylic—make the water seem to ripple and churn."

"And at night?"

Elnessa turned on the switch. "The city's watchtower burns a faint, but steady amber, guiding lost travellers to shelter on dark nights and in dark times. And all the while, the great prismatic eye of Cheops judges the worthiness of those within the city, and without."

Simovic seemed to suppress a flinch at the mention of *judgment*. Elnessa wondered if perhaps he had enough vestigial soul left in him to feel a faint pulse of guilt. Hoon simply frowned, as though slightly suspicious that they had funded the creation of radical art. She asked, "And just what do you call this piece of art? And why doesn't the tower's light work?"

Elnessa smiled. "I call this frieze *Jericho Falls Outward*. Or, if you prefer a less metaphorical title, you can call it, *I Will Not Let You Assholes Kill My Children*."

Simovic did flinch now. Hoon's head snapped back as if she had been struck—and then her eyes went wide with comprehension. She turned toward one of the guards, mouth open to scream a command—just as Elnessa finished her silent count to ten.

As Elnessa reached "ten," the current from the wall had spent that many seconds both illuminating the lights of the frieze and coursing through the alligator clips that were buried in the side of the hole Elnessa had bored through the length of the watchtower. However, the electricity directed into that substance was neither wasted nor idle.

Concealed inside the block of clay, down where the leads were embedded, was a core comprised of an identically coloured, but somewhat denser, malleable material. With every passing second, the complex nanytes which pervaded that substance had been changing their chemical composition and aligning to follow (and thereby offer less resistance to) the electric current. However, unlike the aligning of atoms in an electromagnet, when the nanytes of this complex compound were all finally aligned, they began to work like a battery—which rapidly soared toward overload.

As Elnessa Clare realized that her ten-count had come and gone, she thought about continuing on to "eleven," and felt a pulse of worry shoot through her. According to Reuben, the substance that had been embedded at the core of each of the clay blocks—Selftex —could only absorb ten seconds of standard outlet current from the watchtower's diverted leads. But then Elnessa realized that this one extra second was a gift, time with which she could recall Vas's steady, warm brown eyes—

THE SELFTEX—A recent, self-actuating evolution of the plastic explosive Semtex—had been developed to do away with the need for blasting caps or other explosive initiators. Hooked up to a low electric current, it gave miners and construction workers a long, precise interval in which to evacuate a blast site. However, when the current was as powerful as that running through a standard electrical outlet—

FROM ALMOST TWO KILOMETRES AWAY, Vas not only heard, but felt, the blast. A few nearby windows shattered, people stared around wildly, a few—probably the ones who had heard the rumours of approaching exosapients—looked skyward.

But Vas straightened and looked toward the roiling mass of thick black smoke rising up over the Indi Group's corporate headquarters like a fist of angry defiance. And, through his tears, he smiled. That was the work of El, his El. He had heard Reuben's injudicious radio talk, had seen some incoming messages foolishly left unpurged from the house computer, and so knew that El had been helping to resist the Indi Group—and as of yesterday, was the only one still actively doing so.

Vas looked over toward the headquarters again, wondered about the frieze Elnessa had spoken of working on for so long, yearned to have seen it. He knew that, since she had crafted it, the frieze had been, without doubt, a thing of beauty—every bit as much as she herself had been. Then he stared up at the crest of the ugly black plume that marked its destruction, and reflected: this was her gift to him, to all the children.

And therefore, it, too, was a thing of beauty.

HOME IS WHERE THE HEART IS

By David Weber

The first hint something might be wrong was that I was flying through the air. The second came a second or so later, when I landed face-first on the asphalt.

The third came when I sat up shakily . . . and realized I didn't have a clue who I was.

I shoved myself into a sitting position and looked around. It was dark, the alley illuminated only by the fringe wash of the streetlamp just beyond its mouth. It smelled of garbage—not surprisingly, given the dumpsters on either side of me and the back door of the Chinese restaurant opposite me. And it was raining.

Of course.

I sat on the wet pavement, feeling cold water soak through my trousers and run down into my eyes, and waited for the world to stop spinning beneath me. It took a while, but eventually a sense of stability oozed back into me and I used one of those convenient dumpsters to pull myself to my feet.

The icy rain fell a little harder. I swiped water from my face with the palm of my hand and poked at the strange blankness deep inside where memories of self were supposed to live. Nothing. Just . . . nothing at all. There was plenty of other information, like a pavement with a single me-shaped brick missing in the middle of it. I knew the name of the city, who was president, the date, what day it was—Wednesday, as a matter of fact—but not who I was.

I looked down at myself in the feeble light and was . . . unimpressed by what I found. I wore a pair of ratty running shoes with mismatched laces, my cargo pants had seen much better days, and my T-shirt had a hole under the left armpit. I checked my pockets and found exactly twenty-seven cents and a mostly empty butane lighter. No keys, no wallet, and—obviously—no helpful ID that might have told me who I was.

I wasn't surprised when my rubbing hand discovered well-grown stubble on my cheeks. I might not know who I was, but it was depressingly clear *what* I was, in at least one sense.

I poked at that blank spot again, harder, and wondered why I didn't feel more panicked. Worried as hell, yeah. Even more confused. Perplexed, check. But not really panicked, which I supposed said something about the personality of whoever it was I couldn't remember.

I sighed, swiped more rainwater from my face, and headed for the alley mouth. I might not know where "home" was—assuming I had one—but getting out of the unpleasantly cold rain seemed like a reasonable first objective.

"HEY, Laz! Got somebody here who needs some yardwork done. Interested?"

"Yeah—sure."

I turned from the sink full of dirty dishes I'd been washing as Samantha Dellinger waved a message slip at me from the kitchen door.

She and her husband, George, ran the Tannerman Shelter, where I'd been living for the last five weeks. "Call me Sam" was short, stout, plain-faced, and grey-haired, and like anyone else who'd ever been one of their "guests," I thought she was the most beautiful woman in the world. She and George had not only gotten me out of the rain that first night, they'd fed me, and they'd gotten me to the clinic the next day, as well.

The clinic docs were surprisingly good, but there wasn't much they could do. They'd seen a lot of memory loss, but not like mine. No obvious drug use, no physical trauma, no . . . anything that could point to its cause.

Without any ID, there was no way to figure out who I might have been, which obviously ruled out any sort of detailed medical history, even if the clinic had possessed the resources to hunt one down. And the fact that I was apparently in perfect health, aside from my memory loss—not even a filled tooth—understandably put me a little lower on public health's emergency medical services queue.

No ID also ruled out most steady sources of work, too. George and Sam found me things to do around the shelter to earn my keep, and after a week or so, they'd put me on their "A" list. Lots of people who needed temporary workers knew the Dellingers and trusted them if they recommended someone. A lot of those "someones" were undocumented, although few of them were quite as undocumented as *I* was. But George and Sam were picky about who they put on the A List. Employers who turned to the two of them for recommendations knew they'd get hard workers who didn't steal, and a lot of those employers were known to throw in free meals.

"Yardwork, you said?" I asked, drying my hands on my apron before I took it off and hung it by the sink.

"Yeah." Sam handed me the message slip once my hands were dry. "Out on the west side. The Number Seven bus'll get you there. He says he'll spring for lunch, too, so at least *we* won't have to feed you this afternoon!"

She chuckled, but she had a point, and I grinned.

"He may change his mind after he sees me," I replied. I stood five inches over six feet, and my appetite was as healthy as the rest of me. I went through a lot of their groceries.

"I warned him—I warned him!" She shook her head, and I glanced at the slip to memorize the name and address. For someone with amnesia, I had a damned good memory for things like that.

"Ninazu?" I said, looking at her. "Odd name."

"Odder than 'Lazarus Boyd'?" she challenged with a grin, and I snorted. Among the many things I couldn't remember was when I'd seen a production of the musical *Damn Yankees*, but I did remember how much I'd always loved the character Joe Boyd. As for Lazarus, well . . .

"This is the first time he's called us," she said, "but he got the number from Jolene Sampson."

"Hey, if he's okay with Jolene, he's okay with me," I told her with a grin of my own.

"Bus fare?" she asked.

"Got it," I reassured her, patting my pants pocket. There were actually almost fifty bucks in that pocket at the moment. Which is why it was carefully safety-pinned shut.

"Good. Don't be late for supper—one of your favourites!" She rolled her eyes. "Refried beans and hotdogs."

The shelter served that menu a lot. It was cheap, and it could be thrown together in job lots by relatively unskilled labour . . . such as myself. It helped that I really did like it, but four or five times a week did get a little old sometimes.

"I'll be here," I told her. It wasn't like I had much of anywhere else to go, after all.

"Good," she repeated, and leaned closer for me to give her a peck on the cheek before I headed for the bus stop. That cheek only got offered to her genuine favourites, and a wave of warmth washed over the cold emptiness deep inside me.

———

I WAS GLAD, as I climbed the steps of the townhouse, that I'd at least had the opportunity to replace my original wardrobe. I was still in running shoes and cargo pants, but like my T-shirt, they were both new, purchased with the first cash I'd earned on one of the Sam-and-George jobs. Given the affluence of the neighbourhood, that was probably a good thing.

I pressed the doorbell button and listened to the sound of musical chimes, receding into the depths beyond the green-painted front door. Several seconds passed, and then a smallish fellow—he was almost a foot shorter than I—in a three-piece suit, minus the jacket, opened the door.

"Mister Ninazu?" I said. "My name's Boyd. Sam and George Dellinger sent me. I understand you need some yardwork?"

"Yes!" He beamed at me. "Yes, I do, actually. Although 'yard-work' may be a bit of an understatement."

"Excuse me?"

I looked around the small yard between the townhouse and the edge of the large residential square's sidewalk. The west side was the expensive side of town, and it looked it. Every yard I could see was immaculately landscaped.

"Oh!" Ninazu chuckled. "It's not the *front* yard, Mister Boyd. It's the back." He rolled his eyes. "Come on—I'll show you."

He stood back, waving me into the house, and I took off my Red Sox cap and followed him through the vestibule and down a central hallway to the back door. He opened it as we got there, and waved.

"*That's* what I need taken care of," he said.

The backyard was much deeper than the front yard. It looked as if Ninazu or one of the previous owners had bought the back-yard space of both of his townhouse's neighbours, as well. Or possibly they all shared it. At any rate, the triple-sized yard was centred on a brick gazebo with a somewhat listless fountain in front of it. Fountain and gazebo alike were surrounded by a sprawl of tangled rosebushes that obviously hadn't been pruned in a while, and drifts of dry leaves were knee-deep in places.

"I need all the leaves cleared," Ninazu said. "I understand there are actually flowerbeds under them somewhere, too, and if you can find them, I'll need them cleared, spaded, and replanted. You can see what kind of shape the roses are in, and I'll need them pruned back hard. And, assuming you're game for it after all of that, I need the gazebo's trim cleaned and painted. If you happen across the plumbing for the fountain during your excavations, I probably need to get it looked at, too."

"As I said," he smiled up at me, "'yardwork' may have been just a little misleading, Mister Boyd."

"Yeah, I can see that." I smiled back, and not just in answer to his expression. This looked like at least three days' work—maybe four—even for me.

"Would . . . twenty dollars an hour seem reasonable?" he asked.

"That'd be fine," I said, happily putting aside any temptation to haggle. That was the next best thing to six bucks an hour above the going rate for yardwork by *documented* workers, which I wasn't.

"Good! Tools're in the shed." He pointed at a small storage building built out from the side of the townhouse's rear porch. "If there's something you need that's not there, let me know. I'll be working out of the house today myself."

"Sounds fine," I said, and he took the key to the storage building's padlock from a ring in his pocket and handed it to me.

I'D HAD FAR LESS pleasant jobs in the brief lifetime I could actually remember. It was July, but the temperature was unseasonably cool, and the Japanese Maples that had produced the deeply piled leaves also produced a welcome shade. The work wasn't what anyone could call mentally challenging, but I'd discovered that I liked working with my hands, and the perfume of blooming roses and the smell of freshly turned earth, once I found the buried flowerbeds, filled my nose.

I didn't know what Ninazu did for a living. I'd originally guessed banker or lawyer, and I might have been right. He could have been a financial adviser, though. Whatever his profession, he saw a fairly steady stream of clients, and he apparently liked fresh air. The townhouse's third floor was only half as deep as the two lower ones, and the top of the second floor was a roofed-over elevated terrace. That was where he ended up with most of the people he saw that day, and he looked down and waved to me a couple of times.

I didn't think he was keeping an eye on me to be sure I was earning my twenty bucks an hour. I think he was just being. friendly. And even if he was monitoring my progress, I was fine with that. I believed in an honest day's work for an honest dollar, and he was paying me well, under the circumstances.

He kept his promise about feeding me lunch, too. Didn't even have to go find it somewhere; he had deli subs delivered and even sat on the rear porch with me, eating a sandwich of his own, while I ate. Like I say—nice guy. Friendly.

I didn't finish all the yardwork that day, but he was obviously pleased with what I had gotten done.

"This is really nice, Lazarus," he said to me, looking around the mostly cleared yard as darkness flowed into the sky. "Should I assume you'll be interested in doing the painting, as well?"

"For sure." I nodded. "And if you can get me a couple of pipe wrenches and a few bucks for supplies, I think I can get that fountain flowing for you the way it ought to, too. Looks like about an eight-foot section of rusted-out pipe needs to be replaced. Probably need new couplings as well as the pipe."

"If you can take care of that, too, that'd be great," he said enthusiastically.

"Here's what I think we'd need." I handed him the paper bag my sandwich had come in, with the jotted notes about the pipe and fittings. "If you want to order them, probably be simplest to have them delivered. I'm afraid I left my car in my other pants—" I chuckled "— so I can't pick them up for us!"

"I'll take care of it." He nodded. "See you tomorrow, then. Nine o'clock?"

"I'll be here."

"Good. Here you are."

He handed me three fifties.

"Mister Ninazu, I was only here about six hours," I said.

"Don't have any twenties," he told me with a twinkle. "Besides, you got a hell of a lot done today, Lazarus."

"Well . . . thank you!"

I un-pinned my pocket and slid the folded bills into it.

"Tomorrow, then," he said, and I nodded.

"Tomorrow," I replied, and headed for the bus stop.

I WAS BACK thirty minutes early the next day, and I was hesitant about ringing the bell at eight-thirty. But I was also hesitant about sitting on the front steps in that neighbourhood. So, I went ahead and rang the doorbell, and he opened it as quickly as he had the day before. He was *much* more casually dressed today, I noticed— he'd left off his vest—and he gave me a welcoming smile.

"Sorry I'm early," I apologized. "Bus schedule."

"Not a problem," he assured me, and led me through the town-house to the backyard once more.

I put in another solid day of it, and I did have the fountain splashing merrily away by the time I was done. I hadn't quite gotten around to painting the gazebo, but I was regretfully aware that I would definitely finish up the next day. This job had been one of the most pleasant in my admittedly short memory. Not only was the pay excellent, but I'd discovered that I liked Ninazu.

"This is really good, Lazarus," he said, inspecting the results of my labour as evening rolled closer. "You do good work."

"I try," I said.

He cocked his head, looking up at me, and his expression was thoughtful.

"I have to say, you're not quite what most people think of when they hire someone from a shelter for yardwork," he said. "I hope that doesn't offend you."

"It doesn't offend me." I shook my head. "You might be surprised by some of the other folks in the Dellingers' shelter, though. One of them used to be a surgeon, before he lost his licence to practice. And there's another guy who taught literature over at the College." I shrugged. "They're good people, the Dellingers. They believe in second chances . . . and they know folks fall off the grid for a lot of reasons."

"And yours?" he asked almost gently.

"Mine's a little . . . out of the ordinary." I shrugged again. "Probably, anyway. I don't really know what happened to me."

"All right, *that* one needs a little explanation, I think!" He shook his head with a smile. "You don't know?"

"Actually, it's more a matter of not *remembering*."

Bitterness edged my tone, and his smile disappeared.

"I didn't mean to step on any sore toes," he said. "I'm sorry, Lazarus."

"Oh, it's not anything you said!" I assured him, and then, to my surprise, I found myself telling him the story of my life . . . such as there was and what I remembered of it.

"Oh ho," he said softly when I'd finished. "Maybe there's a reason Ms. Dellinger recommended you to me when I called in."

"She knew I needed the work."

"Besides that, I mean."

He folded his arms and regarded me with a very thoughtful expression.

"Such as?" I asked.

He didn't say anything for several seconds. Then he gave himself a little shake and unfolded his arms.

"You aren't the sort of client I usually see, Lazarus," he said in a much more serious tone. "In fact, under normal circumstances, I probably wouldn't think of you as a potential client, at all. But I'm tempted to make an exception."

"Exception?" I cocked my head at him. "Mister Ninazu, I don't know what you do, but I doubt a shelter guy could afford to pay you for it, whatever it is!"

"You'd be surprised," he said with an odd smile. "No, Lazarus. The problem isn't that you couldn't pay me. It's that I wouldn't normally offer to pay *you*."

"Excuse me?"

"Sit down," he invited, settling onto the porch's top step.

I looked at him for a moment, then sat.

"What I do," he said then, "is to provide . . . services. All sorts of services. I can guarantee my clients anything they need."

"Oh?" I smiled crookedly. "Including lost memories?"

"I should've said *almost* anything they need," he replied with a slightly apologetic smile.

"Not surprised." I shrugged. "But, like I say, I don't see how I could pay you for anything, much less 'anything I need.'"

"You're wrong." He shook his head. "You can. The question is whether or not you'd want to." He leaned back. "Assume that I could give you anything—literally anything in the world—except your memory. What would you want?"

"What anyone would, I guess." I shifted on the step. "Money—enough to be comfortable, at least. More than that, if I could get it!" I grinned quickly. "Somebody to care about, and to care about me. Kids, probably. And maybe the chance to pay back some of the good things people have done for me. People like Sam and George. Heck, people like *you!*"

"Somehow I'm not surprised to hear that. Especially that part about 'paying back.'"

He looked at me with that same thoughtful expression for a long time—two or three minutes, at least—then shrugged.

"Okay. Suppose I told you I could guarantee you the chance to build new memories in a life in which you'd be wealthy, have the same excellent health you appear to have right now, live to a ripe old age, have the opportunity to find a woman who loved you, have kids *and* grandkids. What would you pay for that, Lazarus?"

I started to laugh it off, but his eyes were level and his tone was very serious.

"For all that?" I looked back at him. "Just about anything, I guess."

"Would you be willing to sell your soul for it?"

For a moment, the question completely failed to register. I mean, he'd asked it in a completely serious tone, as if it were actually a rational inquiry. But then it did.

"Sure!" I said with a laugh. "Why not? Where do I sign?"

"Not so fast," he said. "It's a serious transaction, you know. One with which you might call long-term repercussions."

"I can see that," I replied, still grinning. "Assuming I believed in souls, and I'm not sure I do, 'long-term' is probably a pretty good way to describe it."

"Absolutely. So, seriously, would you pay that much?"

"And you seemed like such a sane, rational person."

I shook my head, and he smiled oddly in the gathering twilight.

"'Rational' is an overused adjective," he said.

"What do you mean?"

"This," he said simply, and his brown eyes turned suddenly a deep, dark red and *glowed*.

"Whoa!"

I twitched back in astonishment. I suppose I should have been scared shitless, too, but I wasn't. Probably because he'd seemed so normal over the last couple of days. And maybe because of how much I liked him.

"I notice you aren't running for the hills," he observed after a moment.

"Not yet, anyway," I said a bit cautiously, and he chuckled. Then the glow vanished, and his eyes turned brown again, as if he'd thrown a switch.

"Who *are* you—really?" I asked.

"Ninazu will do," he told me. "That actually was my name, once upon a time. But in answer to what I think you were really asking, I'm the fellow who can buy your soul by giving you everything I described above. All of it, Lazarus."

"For my soul?"

"Yep." He leaned back against the back steps' banister. "That's it."

"And what, exactly, *is* a soul?" I asked. "People throw that word around a lot. What does it actually mean, though?"

"I'm not surprised you're a little puzzled about that. Once upon a time, it was something everyone had—and recognized, for that matter. But today? The twenty-first century?" He shook his head. "Not very rich hunting grounds for properly nourished souls, I'm afraid. It's like most people've forgotten they still have one." He sounded remarkably rational, I thought. "But, in answer to your question, souls are what make mortals who they are. Good, bad, indifferent—it all goes back to the soul, in the end. Like I say, under normal circumstances, I wouldn't be in a position to make you an offer for yours, but since you don't even remember who you were before, or what you might have done, yours is in what you might call a pristine state. And I like you. So, I'm willing to make an offer for it."

"And what happens to it after I die?"

"I collect it," he said simply. "I cart you off to the hereafter."

"To Hell?"

"In a manner of speaking. I don't think it'd be exactly what you're thinking just now, though. Oh, it wouldn't be *Heaven*, but in my personal—and possibly somewhat prejudiced—opinion, Heaven isn't all it's cracked up to be, either."

"You do realize this has to be one of the most . . . bizarre conversations ever, right?" I asked.

"Oh, trust me! I've had quite a few like it over the years. Not *quite* like this one, perhaps, now that I think about it. I mean, it's not very often a pristine soul as old as yours comes along."

"I guess not."

I frowned at him, and rather to my astonishment, I discovered I was actually taking this entire weird conversation seriously. And that I wasn't panicking. For that matter, I wasn't automatically writing it off, either!

"So, let me get this straight. No eternity of torment?"

"No," he said. "Although, I have to confess, you would spend eternity in *Hell*, you understand." He shrugged. "That part's not negotiable, I'm afraid. But Hell doesn't have to be all that horrible. And at least this way, you could make some good memories along the way."

"That might be nice," I said a bit wistfully.

"I understand this has all come at you rather . . . unexpectedly,"

he said. "And the last thing you should do is rush into an agreement like this one. So, I think what you need to do is go home and
think about it. We're not quite done with the yardwork," he smiled
briefly, mischievously, "so there's a perfectly good reason for you to
come back tomorrow, whatever you decide. And no hard feelings
from my side, either way. Like I say, I like you, and I'm not on a
quota system or anything like that. For that matter, I may not be
the most unprejudiced judge of how bad or good things are in
Hell, and you should probably bear that in mind, too. So, what say
you go catch that bus and then come back tomorrow morning and
give me your answer? Or not come back at all, which would be an
answer of its own, I suppose."

"I'll . . . think about it," I told him, and realized even as I spoke
that I really would. Which was, in many ways, the strangest thing
of all, I suppose.

———————

I DID THINK about it that night—after refried beans and hotdogs,
yet again. I thought about it long, I thought about it hard, and to
my ongoing surprise, I thought about it *seriously*. Thought about it
as if it were a real decision. There were moments when I was
tempted not to. When I was tempted to think of Ninazu as an
especially personable lunatic. But then I remembered those
glowing red eyes, and how earnestly he'd urged me to consider the
consequences of his offer.

I have to say that it was that urge to consider carefully that
struck me as the oddest part of the entire thing . . . after discov-
ering that Heaven and Hell really existed, that was. Nothing in
existing popular entertainment of which I was aware—and that I
remembered—suggested that a . . . purchasing agent for Hell

should be such an apparently nice guy or urge his prospective buyers to consider the price so carefully. I supposed that someone in his position would probably be capable of pretending to be a real prince, and if he'd been around as long as he seemed to be implying, he'd certainly had plenty of time to perfect his act. Yet, somehow, I didn't think he was pretending. He might be crazy, but he wasn't pretending to be something he didn't truly think he was.

And then there were those eyes . . .

"ALL RIGHT," I said the next morning. "I've thought about it. And I've come to the conclusion that you probably are who—what— you say you are. Or that you certainly believe you are, anyway."

"And that I can give you what I've promised to give you?"

"Yeah. Or, again, that you honestly *believe* you can, at least. Which means you really are interested in buying my soul and taking it off to Hell for the rest of eternity. You said I wouldn't have to worry about all that 'eternal torment' stuff. You wouldn't be telling me that because what would actually happen would be something more like Screwtape?"

"Oh, Screwtape!" Ninazu laughed in delight. "I *loved* that book! But, no. No one is planning on *devouring* your soul, Lazarus." He shook his head. "I can see where some people would consider being separated from God for all eternity a horrible punishment in its own right, but that's about as bad as it would get. And, let's face it, there are plenty of people alive right this minute who have *already* separated themselves from God without so much as a passing qualm."

I nodded a bit glumly. I'd certainly seen evidence enough of that in the few short weeks of my own memories. Then there were people like Sam and George, though. I couldn't imagine the two of them ever separating themselves from God! They never threw Him into people's teeth, but they didn't have to.

"Okay," I said after another long, thoughtful moment. "Okay. I'll do it."

"You're sure about that?" He regarded me steadily. "This isn't the sort of deal you can change your mind about, Lazarus. And any buyer's remorse is going to last a *long* time."

"Kind of figured that." I chuckled, just a bit nervously. "But, yeah, I'm sure. Of course, it could still turn out I'm almost as big a lunatic for taking you seriously as you are for believing you can deliver on this. I don't think I am, though. So, where's the contract? And what do we sign it in? Blood?"

"Nothing like that." Unlike mine, his chuckle didn't sound at all nervous. "I'm afraid asbestos contracts and signing in blood are myths, Lazarus. No, this is a handshake deal. I'm assuming you're an honest man who intends to observe its conditions. And I assure you that we've got all the . . . 'enforcement authority' we'll ever need."

"Figured you might." My mouth felt a little dry, but I extended my right hand. "Shake on it?"

"Exactly."

His hand was much smaller than mine, but his grip was strong. And, now that I thought about it, unnaturally warm somehow.

I sat, still gripping his hand and looking into his eyes, for two or three breaths, then released it.

"I don't feel any different," I said.

"Really?" He looked amused. "It doesn't work that way. You *aren't* any different."

"So how does this suddenly wealthy thing work? Do I turn up tomorrow at my luxurious office downtown?"

"It doesn't work *that* way, either, unless you want it to." He shrugged. "We *could* do it that way, you understand, but I'd advise against it."

"Really?" My eyebrows rose. "Why? Sounds like the simplest way to go about it."

"From your perspective, maybe." He laughed. "From the perspective of everybody else in the world, it could be just a *little* complicated. We'd have to rearrange a lot of people's lives, and some of them would probably get hurt along the way. From what I know of you, I don't think you'd want that. Besides, it's less *satisfying* that way."

"Satisfying? Being instantly rich isn't 'satisfying'?"

That was the question I asked, although the one I wanted to ask was why an agent of Hell might be concerned about anyone's getting "hurt along the way." Unless he meant he thought *I'd* feel guilty about that. Which, thinking about it, I probably would have. Still, an . . . odd thing for a minion of Hell to be thinking about.

"Of course, it's less satisfying! Oh, it probably has its good points, and if that's how you insist on doing it, we can. But think about it first. Would you rather just suddenly be as rich as Bezos or Gates? Or would you rather build your own empire along the way to getting there?"

"How much real 'building' can there be with Hell in my corner?"

"Quite a lot, really. Don't worry!" He raised an extended forefinger as I started to open my mouth. "We'll always be there as a fallback if you need us. But based on what I've come to know of you, here's the way I think will give you the most satisfaction, Lazarus."

He reached into his jacket—he was wearing the entire suit this morning—and extracted a long, elegant coat wallet, made of supple black leather and adorned with the monogram *L. Boyd* in gracefully flowing golden letters. I took it from him, and the instant it touched my hand, it became a worn, cheap, *brown* billfold with the same monogram stamped in block letters in flaking silver.

An icicle ran delicately down my spine as that transformation confirmed that whatever else he might be, he wasn't a simple lunatic. On the other hand—

"And this is . . . what, exactly?" I asked.

"Look inside," he suggested.

I opened it to the card slots, and my eyes narrowed as I found a worn driver's licence in my name. There was a Social Security card, also in the name of "Lazarus Boyd," to keep it company, along with a Blue Cross insurance card and a couple of credit cards. Then I opened it completely and found a fairly thick stack of bills. I spread the compartment wider and realized they were all worn fifties and twenties.

"Seems a little scruffy and thin on the ground for fortune building," I said with a slow smile, and Ninazu chuckled.

"Looks can be deceiving, my friend!" he said. "As in your own case, for example. First, there's documentation on record to back up all of that identification. You have a past, now, and it's guaranteed to stand up to any scrutiny. You'll 'remember' all of it when you wake up tomorrow morning, and there are even people who'll remember you from school, although, alas, none of them were very close friends of yours."

He smiled briefly, and I nodded.

"Second, you can never lose that billfold. It will stay with you, and its appearance will change to suit your status, however that status changes. Pickpockets won't be able to steal it, you won't be able to lose it, and no one can ever take it from you against your will."

"That sounds useful," I acknowledged.

"Third, you now have two credit card accounts, although there isn't a huge balance in either of them at the moment. Back in the good old days, it wouldn't have been a problem to stuff them full of cash, but it's a little trickier these days with all of the computerization and digital bookkeeping. Besides, I think you'll have more fun the other way."

"What other way?"

"Why, paying cash!"

"There can't be more than—what? A thousand bucks in here?"

A thousand dollars was, in fact, way more cash than I remembered ever having seen, of course. That wasn't exactly my point, though.

"Around twenty-five hundred, actually. In used, nonsequential bills. That's your seed money."

"Twenty-five hundred dollars to build my empire?" I snorted. "There's got to be a catch. Right?"

"Of course!" He chuckled. "Take it out."

I did. The stack of bills between my thumb and forefinger was thicker than it had looked in the wallet, but it was still only twenty-five hundred dollars, and I looked at him, one eyebrow raised.

"I said take it out," he said.

I opened my mouth to reply, then paused as he pointed at the wallet in my other hand. I looked down, and my eyes widened. It was still full of money.

"That wallet will *always* contain exactly two thousand, four hundred, and ninety dollars," he told me. "You can empty it as many times as you want, and it will still contain that amount— always in used, nonsequential, absolutely genuine, US dollars. Well, there *is* an inflation clause built in. It will always contain the equivalent of that amount in 2021 dollars, so it's probably a good thing it's a coat wallet, once it's all grown up again. I imagine sitting on something that thick could get uncomfortable in a decade or two."

My jaw dropped slightly, and he laughed again, harder.

"If it gets *too* thick, we can always adjust the bills' denominations. Oh, and here's this."

He reached into his jacket again and extracted an iPhone.

"The security code is your birthday. Congratulations, by the way; you turned thirty today. You can't lose it, either, and it contains all of the access codes for your Internet subscription, your web sites, your credit cards—with Wi-Fi, of course. There's also a rather lengthy memo file saved on here. It contains the names of stocks and purchase dates over the next, oh, five years or so. Between that info and the wallet, you should have everything you need to build yourself a healthy little portfolio. I think of it as your grubstake. After that, you'll be on your own. Like I say, knowing you, I expect half—more probably two thirds—of the fun to come from making your own decisions down the road. On the other hand, you'll find me in your contacts list. If you decide you'd rather take a shortcut after all, drop me a text."

I slid the billfold into my back pocket, then took the phone— which, predictably, was suddenly in a cheaper, scratched case— and slid it into another pocket.

He was probably right, I realized as I put the phone away. Oh, I'd be "cheating" a little bit—quite a lot, actually—at least to start. But after that, after I had a certain level of security, the wherewithal to back my own decisions . . . that would be when it became truly enjoyable for me.

"You said something about meeting someone who loved me?"

I kept my tone casual, but even as I did, I realized that was important to me. Way *more* important than getting filthy rich, in fact.

"Lazarus, I probably won't even have to cheat for you on that front. You're the sort of person people find it easy to love. Trust me. Just be yourself. You're a pretty good judge of character, anyway, and this little agreement isn't going to hurt that one bit. Just . . . think about the people you meet. Don't jump until you've looked. I don't think you want me to 'make' someone fall in love with you any more than you'd want me to just hand you the keys to the penthouse suite at Amazon. You're not that kind of guy, and you believe in free will—maybe sometimes a little too much. So, no, I'm not going to throw anyone into your arms unless she wants to be there. But I will confidently predict that someone—the right someone—will *want* to be there. And I *will* guarantee that, just like you, she'll live a long, long life in good health, and that the two of you will have a stack of kids to love. Deal?"

"Deal," I said firmly, reaching out to shake his hand again.

"Good." He gripped my hand. "And if everything goes the way I confidently expect it to, this is the last time we'll be speaking to each other until, well—"

He shrugged, and I smiled.

"In that case, until then," I said.

―――――

"I WAS WONDERING when you'd be along," I said, leaning back in my chair as my visitor stepped through the study door. "I figured it couldn't be too much longer. Especially after Emily died."

"No. No, it couldn't have been much longer," Mister Ninazu agreed. "I thought you wouldn't want to wait too long after that."

"Know me pretty well, don't you?"

I stood and reached out to shake his hand as he crossed to the enormous desk.

"Even better than you know, yet," he agreed, gripping firmly. "So, you're satisfied we kept our end of the deal?"

"More than satisfied." I pointed at the chair in front of my desk and settled back into my own.

And that was nothing but the truth, I reflected. It wasn't many men, even with twenty-second-century medicine, who moved as easily and with so little pain on their 130th birthday.

He'd been right about "building my own empire," too. The truth was, I'd actually enjoyed it more because of the occasional setback. I might not have if I hadn't had that wallet in my pocket, like the shoebox of hundreds stuffed under the bed, but it had been so *satisfying* to know when I'd made the right decision, backed the right hunch.

It had been even more satisfying to spend some of that money paying back . . . and paying forward, I thought. I'd become the patron Sam and George needed to do things *right*, and as their retirement gift, I'd created the Dellinger Foundation for the Homeless, built around their philosophies and work ethic, with a $200-million endowment. They'd both been members of the Foundation's board until their deaths, and their funerals had been attended by thousands of the people they'd helped.

Including me. That had been important, because I knew damned well where *their* souls were going, and I'd needed to say goodbye properly. They'd shown me there was light even in very dark places. I was going to miss them, a lot, but I was incredibly grateful that I'd gotten to know them well enough *to* miss them.

Sometimes we get far more than we deserve out of life. Like George and Sam.

And like Emily. My God, *Emily*. To know she'd loved me for myself, for who I was, not because someone had shoved her into my arms or my bed. Emily, who'd fallen in love with me long before I was one of the youngest billionaires in the world. To have eighty-six glorious years with her. To see her kids—*her* kids—grow to adulthood, have kids of their own. Every one of them, an individual miracle in my life and hers. And their grandkids. Even a half dozen of their *great*-grandkids. Every single one of them his or her own person, and every one of them an echo of Emily and how much I loved her.

"No regrets?" Ninazu probed gently.

"Only that it has to end," I said. "And thank you for Emily, too. She never knew, but I did, and you kept your word about her, too. I don't think she was ever sick a day in her life, not even a *cold,* and she went so peacefully, in her sleep. I'd've sold you my soul for just that."

"I know you would," he said. Then his nostrils flared as he inhaled deeply. "I know you would have, but now it's time."

"Trust me, I'm ready. The kids are ready, and I don't really want to hang around here without Emily. So, let's do this thing."

"Of course."

He smiled a bit crookedly, stood, and walked around to put one hand on my shoulder.

I blinked. There was a moment of vertigo, and then I found myself standing beside him, in a T-shirt and cargo pants that smelled slightly of cut grass, raked leaves, and damp earth. A tall, broad-shouldered, still-muscular old man with a neatly clipped, snow-white beard, dressed in an elegant leisure suit, slumped in a custom-made wingback chair behind a huge desk. The skin was wrinkled, with the lived-in textured of someone who'd spent his life *doing* things—and there was an incredibly peaceful smile on that lined, hawk-like face.

I looked down at my own hands, saw the same calluses they'd borne the day Ninazu and I met, then looked across—and down—into his eyes.

"That was painless," I said wryly.

"Of course, it was. I promised Emily."

"What?" I blinked at him.

"Don't worry about it." He shook his head. "The way she loved you, I knew what she would have wanted, just like you wanted it for her. So, I promised her, whether she knew it or not."

"I have to say this isn't what I expected," I said. "I mean, promises of no eternal torment aside, I don't think anybody would have expected *this*." I waved a hand at the office and my discarded corpse, then at myself. "By the way, I'm assuming we *are* invisible at the moment? I hate to think what this'll do to the security guys when they examine the video, if we're not!"

"Don't worry about it. *Would* be amusing, though wouldn't it?" he chuckled.

"You have a very strange sense of humour," I told him.

"So I've been told." He shrugged. "Give me your hand."

I reached out once more, and he touched it.

I don't remember actually leaving the office, but suddenly we were in midair, outside its 200th-floor floor-to-ceiling windows, looking down, down, down on the glittering lights of the city streets and up at the running lights of air cars. The regular midnight shuttle to the L5 habitats had just lifted off from the downtown airport, and I watched it streak into the heavens.

Then we were in flight ourselves, streaking across the cityscape at a speed to dwarf the shuttle's. We burst up and through the clouds, flashing above their moon-silvered mountain crests, the air cold and thin and bracing. Faster we flew, and still faster, until the cloud summits were a blur, until there was only that vast, enormous sense of motion, of flight, of boundless travel.

And then, with a transition that was sensed more than seen at our stupendous velocity, it was no longer clouds below or the moon above. There was only blackness above us, and a pulsing glow beneath.

We slowed abruptly, and I realized the blackness was the roof of an unending cavern. And that the glow came from lambent pools far below us. Pools of lava, I realized, as we slowed still further and I saw their viscous flow. The smell of sulphur filled my nostrils, but not with the *stench* I would have expected. It was strong, pungent, unpleasant, and yet somehow... exhilarating.

We continued to soar across the landscape, and I saw what could only have been distant towns on promontories surrounded by those glowing seas of molten rock. They rose against the background glow, lifting spires far above the ground, and tiny bat-winged shapes circled some of them. I glanced at Ninazu, half-expecting to see the hand I held turned into a taloned claw, the exquisite tailoring into bat wings and a barbed tail. Nothing had changed, and he smiled at me, almost mischievously, as if he'd read my mind.

I looked down again as we slowed still further, and it occurred to me that I didn't see *anyone* undergoing "eternal torment." Surely all of those lakes of lava should have been filled with unwilling swimmers, shouldn't they?

I started to ask Ninazu about it, but he pointed ahead, and I swallowed as the castle loomed before us. It towered upward, raising crenellated battlements high into the windy dark. Banners flew from tall staffs—black, and if they bore any device, I couldn't make it out—but there was something about the architecture. Something . . . grand to its sweep, to its proportions. It crowned a mountaintop, the tallest point I'd yet seen, looking down upon those fiery lakes, those distant towns, as if to proclaim its authority. There was something arrogant about it, but not . . . malevolent.

It was an odd thought, but I didn't have long to reflect upon it.

We landed in a courtyard. The magnificent marble structure at its centre reminded me of Ninazu's gazebo all those years ago, and the courtyard was gorgeously landscaped, although I didn't recall having ever seen roses whose petals were living, dancing flames, or fountains whose spray was literally liquid light.

Ninazu didn't release my hand, and I found myself walking down long corridors at his side. The floors were polished marble, inset with mosaics in bright colours, not the unyielding obsidian I might have guessed from outside the castle's walls. The torches burning in wall sconces gave off no soot, no sense of heat, and a lot more light than I would have expected from simple combustion.

The long, straight sweep of the corridors—they were obviously longer than the outer dimensions of the castle—appealed to me, and some of the wall art we passed was magnificent. I didn't have much time to study it, but a lot of it looked Renaissance, and I wondered how many "lost masters" had found their way here.

We came, finally, to a pair of massive wooden doors, at least eight or nine feet tall. They *were* as black as I would have anticipated, carved from single, enormous slabs of gleaming ebony and marked in a flowing silver script. I didn't recognize any of the glyphs or letters or whatever formed that script, yet something stirred within me—something both frightened and eager—as I saw them.

Ninazu waved one hand, and the doors opened smoothly before us. We stepped through them into an immense chamber.

Chandeliers of polished iron hung from its high, vaulted ceiling, and a dais against its rear wall held a high-backed throne.

We strode across a polished floor of glittering black marble, adorned with more of that same strange script, until we reached the dais. We climbed the steps and halted before the throne.

I looked around nervously. I could think of only one person who might own a throne at the heart of a castle at the heart of Hell, and however calm I might have thought I was, the notion of meeting the King of Hell personally was . . . mildly alarming.

All right, maybe a little more than *mildly*.

I waited for Ninazu to do or say something, but he only glanced at the golden watch on his left wrist, and I swallowed.

"Should I—" I began, but he shook his head sharply.

"It's not time yet," he said.

I shut my mouth. Not *time* yet?

I decided it didn't matter what he meant, and kept my mouth shut while I looked around that stupendous throne room. Its architect had captured the same arrogance—or maybe the same *confidence*—as the castle in which it was located, I thought. Yet, there was a sense of abandonment about it. As if it was seldom actually used anymore.

I looked back at the throne. It was canopied, and the canopy was of gleaming black, embroidered with silver. The throne itself had a richness that seemed at odds with the plain, unadorned crown of what looked like iron resting on its cushioned seat.

Minutes trickled past, and I stirred. "Not time yet" or not, just standing around was—

"And now," Ninazu said in a voice that was suddenly deeper and far more powerful, "it *is* time."

I flinched as he released my hand at last. Then he reached

forward, lifted the crown in both hands, and wheeled back toward me.

In that moment, in a way that I couldn't have described, he was still as short as he had ever been and yet towered above me. That awareness whipped through me, and then his hands descended in a flashing arc and slammed that iron crown down upon my head.

I staggered back, my own hands rising to the sudden heavy weight, and my eyes flared wide. A meteor seemed to streak directly into them and erupt in the centre of my brain, and a wall I'd always known was there but never been able to breach exploded into splinters.

Memory roared through me. Lost memory, surging like the sea, vaster and far greater than I could ever have imagined.

Memory of the backlash. The blocked communication attempt from my journey to Earth. The energy surging through me, wiping memory, locking ability. Leaving me so much less than I had been . . . and yet, in some ways, so much more.

I looked at Ninazu and recognized him then.

"Welcome home, My Lord," he said, falling to one knee before me.

"Asmodeus." It was my voice, yet deeper, more reverberating, then I'd ever heard it, and I laid one hand on his shoulder. "Well done," I said.

"I thought it would be what you wanted," he said, looking up at me, and I saw a flicker of Ninazu's mischief in his eyes as we both remembered what he'd told me that long-ago day . . . *exactly* one hundred years ago, to the minute.

He'd been right about that, just as he'd been right that I had, indeed, become a pristine soul. One that very well might not have ended up here, where it belonged, left to its own devices.

"That was . . . an unexpected side excursion," I said.

"An unwelcome one, My Lord?"

"No." My voice softened. "Not unwelcome at all, my friend."

"I'm glad," my oldest confidant, my most trusted lieutenant, said to me.

"Yes," I replied, and hid a sharp, unexpected stab of pain.

It wasn't unwelcome, that pain, but pain it was. The pain that is the other side of joy. The loss that memory only makes more precious. Emily. The person who'd loved me solely for *who* I was, not what.

"My Lord?" Asmodeus said quietly, and I looked at him.

"Yours was not the only pristine soul in play," he told me. "And there's always choice for a pristine soul."

I frowned down at him, and then froze as another voice spoke from behind me.

"Lazarus?" it said, and I whirled in disbelief.

Emily! Emily, as young, as straight and tall and *beautiful*, as the day we first met. Emily—Emily herself, not the apparition of her I might have summoned with merely a thought—standing before me in the throne room of Hell.

"Emily?" I whispered. "I can't . . ."

"You're the King of Hell," that familiar, beloved voice said. "You're telling me there's something you can't do? *Here?* After everything I saw you do back on *Earth?*"

The laughter was in her eyes, the laughter I remembered so well, and she opened her arms wide. I wrapped mine around her, tucking her under my chin as I had so many times before, holding her like the most precious thing in the universe, and closed my eyes.

"You shouldn't *be* here," I whispered. "Not in *Hell*, love. You should be—"

"Exactly where I am," she interrupted, hugging me tightly.

"Asmodeus explained everything when he came for me. He gave me my options, and *days* to think them over. How could you ever think I would have chosen something else?"

"But now you're trapped here, forever," I told her, shaking my head slowly. "I *chose* to be here, but I knew exactly what I was choosing. Exactly *why*. You couldn't have—"

"Oh, yes I could have." I'd never heard such assurance in a human voice before, and I knew now just how many, many human voices I *had* heard over the millennia. "I told you, he explained *everything*. And he didn't have to tell me that no one was getting tortured here—not if *you* were in charge of it. Besides, it doesn't matter."

She put her hands against my chest, pushing, and I loosened my embrace until she could lean back far enough to look up into my eyes.

"They say 'home is where the heart is,' Laz." Her own eyes gleamed with unshed tears. "Well, in that case—" she laid the palm of one hand on the centre of my chest "—I'm home, sweetheart. I'm *home*."

TRICENTENNIAL

By Joe Haldeman

December 1975

S cientists pointed out that the Sun could be part of a double
star system. For its companion to have gone undetected, of
course, it would have to be small and dim, and thousands of astronomical units distant.

They would find it eventually; "it" would turn out to be "them";
they would come in handy.

January 2075

THE OFFICE WAS opulent even by the extravagant standards of
twenty-first century Washington. Senator Connors had a passion
for antiques. One wall was lined with leather-bound books; a large
brass telescope symbolized his role as Liaison to the Science

Guild. An intricately woven Navajo rug from his home state covered most of the parquet floor. A grandfather clock. Paintings, old maps.

The computer terminal was discreetly hidden in the top drawer of his heavy teak desk. On the desk: a blotter, a precisely centred fountain-pen set, and a century-old sound-only black Bell telephone. It chimed.

His secretary said that Dr. Leventhal was waiting to see him. "Keep answering me for thirty seconds," the Senator said. "Then hang it and send him right in."

He cradled the phone and went to a wall mirror. Straightened his tie and cape; then, with a fingernail, evened out the bottom line of his lip pomade. Ran a hand through long, thinning white hair and returned to stand by the desk, one hand on the phone.

The heavy door whispered open. A short, thin man bowed slightly. "Sire."

The Senator crossed to him with both hands out. "Oh, blow that, Charlie. Give ten." The man took both his hands, only for an instant. "When was I ever 'Sire' to you, heyfool?"

"Since last week," Leventhal said. "Guild members have been calling you worse names than 'Sire.'"

The Senator bobbed his head twice. "True, and true. And I sympathize. Will of the People, though."

"Sure." Leventhal pronounced it as one word: "Willathapeeble."

Connors went to the bookcase and opened a chased panel. "Drink?"

"Yeah, Bo." Charlie sighed and lowered himself into a deep sofa. "Hit me. Sherry or something."

The Senator brought the drinks and sat down beside Charlie.

"You shoulda listened to me. Shoulda got the Ad Guild to write your proposal."

"We have good writers."

"Begging to differ. Less than two percent of the electorate bothered to vote; most of them for the administration advocate. Now you take the Engineering Guild—"

"You take the engineers. And—"

"They used the Ad Guild." Connors shrugged. "They got their budget."

"It's easy to sell bridges and power plants and shuttles. Hard to sell pure science."

"The more reason for you to—"

"Yeah, sure. Ask for double and give half to the Ad boys. Maybe next year. That's not what I came to talk about."

"That radio stuff?"

"Right. Did you read the report?"

Connors looked into his glass. "Charlie, you know I don't have time to—"

"Somebody read it, though."

"Oh, righty-o. Good astronomy boy on my staff; he gave me a boil-down. Mighty interesting, that."

"There's an intelligent civilization eleven light-years away— that's 'mighty interesting'?"

"Sure. Real breakthrough." Uncomfortable silence. "Uh, what are you going to do about it?"

"Two things. First, we're trying to figure out what they're saying. That's hard. Second, we want to send a message back. That's easy. And that's where you come in."

The Senator nodded and looked somewhat wary.

"Let me explain. We've sent messages to this star, 61 Cygni, before. It's a double star, actually, with a dark companion."

"Like us."

"Sort of. Anyhow, they never answered. They aren't listening, evidently; they aren't sending."

"But we got—"

"What we're picking up is about what you'd pick up eleven light-years from Earth. A confused jumble of broadcasts, eleven years old. Very faint. But obviously not generated by any sort of natural source."

"Then we're already sending a message back. The same kind they're sending us."

"That's right, but—"

"So what does all this have to do with me?"

"Bo, we don't want to whisper at them—we want to shout! Get their attention." Leventhal sipped his wine and leaned back. "For that, we'll need one hell of a lot of power."

"Uh, righty-o. Charlie, power's money. How much are you talking about?"

"The whole show. I want to shut down Death Valley for twelve hours."

The Senator's mouth made a silent O. "Charlie, you've been working too hard. Another Blackout? On purpose?"

"There won't be any Blackout. Death Valley has emergency storage for fourteen hours."

"At half capacity." He drained his glass and walked back to the bar, shaking his head. "First you say you want power. Then you say you want to turn off the power." He came back with the burlap-covered bottle. "You aren't making sense, boy."

"Not turn it off, really. Turn it around."

"Is that a riddle?"

"No, look. You know the power doesn't really come from the

Death Valley grid; it's just a way station and accumulator. Power comes from the orbital—"

"I know all that, Charlie. I've got a Science Certificate."

"Sure. So, what we've got is a big microwave laser in orbit that shoots down a tight beam of power. Enough to keep North America running. Enough—"

"That's what I mean. You can't just—"

"So we turn it around and shoot it at a power grid on the Moon. Relay the power around to the big radio dish at Farside. Turn it into radio waves and point it at 61 Cygni. Give 'em a blast that'll fry their fillings."

"Doesn't sound neighbourly."

"It wouldn't actually be that powerful—but it would be a hell of a lot more powerful than any natural twenty-one-centimetre source."

"I don't know, boy." He rubbed his eyes and grimaced. "I could maybe do it on the sly, only tell a few people what's on. But that'd only work for a few minutes . . . what do you need twelve hours for, anyway?"

"Well, the thing won't aim itself at the Moon automatically, the way it does at Death Valley. Figure as much as an hour to get the thing turned around and aimed.

"Then, we don't want to just send a blast of radio waves at them. We've got a five-hour program that first builds up a mutual language, then tells them about us, and finally asks them some questions. We want to send it twice."

Connors refilled both glasses. "How old were you in '47, Charlie?"

"I was born in '45."

"You don't remember the Blackout. Ten thousand people died . . . and you want me to suggest—"

"Come on, Bo, it's not the same thing. We know the accumulators work now—besides, the ones who died, most of them had faulty fail-safes on their cars. If we warn them the power's going to drop, they'll check their fail-safes or damn well stay out of the air."

"And the media? They'd have to take turns broadcasting. Are you going to tell the People what they can watch?"

"Fuzz the media. They'll be getting the biggest story since the Crucifixion."

"Maybe." Connors took a cigarette and pushed the box toward Charlie. "You don't remember what happened to the Senators from California in '47, do you?"

"Nothing good, I suppose."

"No, indeed. They were impeached. Lucky they weren't lynched. Even though the real trouble was way up in orbit.

"Like you say; people pay a grid tax to California. They think the power comes from California. If something fuzzes up, they get pissed at California. I'm the Lib Senator from California, Charlie; ask me for the Moon, maybe I can do something. Don't ask me to fuzz around with Death Valley."

"All right, all right. It's not like I was asking you to wire it for me, Bo. Just get it on the ballot. We'll do everything we can to educate—"

"Won't work. You barely got the Scylla probe voted in—and that was no skin off nobody, not with L-5 picking up the tab."

"Just get it on the ballot."

"We'll see. I've got a quota, you know that. And with the Tricentennial coming up, hell, everybody wants on the ballot."

"Please, Bo. This is bigger than that. This is bigger than anything. Get it on the ballot."

"Maybe as a rider. No promises."

March 1992

FROM *FAX & PIX*, 12 March 1992:

ANTIQUE SPACEPROBE
ZAPPED BY NEW STARS

1. Pioneer 10 sent first Jupiter pix Earthward in 1973 (see pix upleft, upright).
2. Left solar system 1987. First man-made thing to leave solar system.
3. Yesterday, reports NSA, Pioneer 10 begins a.m. to pick up heavy radiation. Gets more and more to max about 3 p.m. Then goes back down. Radiation has to come from outside solar system.
4. NSA and Hawaii scientists say Pioneer 10 went through disk of synchrotron (*sin-kro-tron*) radiation that comes from two stars we didn't know about before.

A. The stars are small "black dwarfs."
B. They are going round each other once every forty seconds, and take 350,000 years to go around the Sun.
C. One of the stars is made of antimatter. This is stuff that blows up if it touches real matter. What the Hawaii scientists saw was a dim circle of invisible (infrared) light that blinks on and off every twenty seconds. This light comes from where the atmospheres of the two stars touch (see pic downleft).
D. The stars have a big magnetic field. Radiation comes

from stuff spinning off the stars and trying to get through the field.

E. The stars are about 5,000 times as far away from the Sun as we are. They sit at the wrong angle, compared to the rest of the solar system (see pic down-right).

5. NSA says we aren't in any danger from the stars. They're too far away, and besides, nothing in the solar system ever goes through the radiation.

6. The woman who discovered the stars wants to call them Scylla (*skill-a*) and Charybdis (*ku-rib-dus*).

7. Scientists say they don't know where the hell those two stars came from. Everything else in the solar system makes sense.

February 2075

WHEN THE DOCKING PHASE STARTED, Charlie thought, that was when it was easy to tell the scientists from the baggage. The scientists were the ones who looked nervous.

Superficially, it seemed very tranquil—nothing like the bone-hurting, skinstretching acceleration when the shuttle lifted off. The glittering transparent cylinder of L-5 simply grew larger, slowly, then wheeled around to point at them.

The problem was that a space colony big enough to hold four thousand people has more inertia than God. If the shuttle hit the mating dimple too fast, it would fold up like an accordion. A spaceship is made to take stress in the *other* direction.

Charlie hadn't paid first class, but they let him up into the observation dome anyhow; professional courtesy. There were only two other people there, standing on the Velcro rug, strapped to one bar and hanging on to another.

They were a young man and woman, probably new colonists. The man was talking excitedly. The woman stared straight ahead, not listening. Her knuckles were white on the bar and her teeth were clenched. Charlie wanted to say something in sympathy, but it's hard to talk while you're holding your breath.

The last few metres are the worst. You can't see over the curve of the ship's hull, and the steering jets make a constant stutter of little bumps: left, right, forward, back. If the shuttle folded, would the dome shatter? Or just pop off?

It was all controlled by computers, of course. The pilot just sat up there in a mist of weightless sweat.

Then the low moan, almost subsonic shuddering, as the shuttle's smooth hull complained against the friction pads. Charlie waited for the ringing *spang* that would mean they were a little too fast: friable alloy plates under the friction pads, crumbling to absorb the energy of their forward motion; last-ditch stand.

If that didn't stop them, they would hit a two-metre wall of solid steel, which would. It had happened once. But not this time.

"Please remain seated until pressure is equalized," a recorded voice said. "It's been a pleasure having you aboard."

Charlie crawled down the pole, back to the passenger area. He walked, *rip, rip, rip,* back to his seat, and obediently waited for his ears to pop. Then the side door opened, and he went with the other passengers through the tube that led to the elevator. They stood on the ceiling. Someone had laboriously scratched a graffito on the metal wall:

Stuck on this lift for hours, perforce;
This lift that cost a million bucks.

There's no such thing as centrifugal force;
L-5 sucks.

Thirty more weightless seconds as they slid to the ground.
There were a couple of dozen people waiting on the loading
platform.

Charlie stepped out into the smell of orange blossoms and
newly mown grass. He was home.

"Charlie! Hey, over here." Young man standing by a tandem
bicycle. Charlie squeezed both his hands and then jumped on the
back seat. "Drink."

"Did you get—"

"Drink. Then talk." They glided down the smooth macadam
road toward town.

The bar was just a rain canopy over some tables and chairs,
overlooking the lake in the centre of town. No bartender; you went
to the service table and punched in your credit number, then
chose wine or fruit juice, with or without vacuum-distilled raw
alcohol. They talked about shuttle nerves awhile, then:

"What you get from Connors?"

"Words, not much. I'll give a full report at the meeting tonight.
Looks like we won't even get on the ballot, though."

"Now, isn't that what we said was going to happen? We shoulda
gone with Francois Petain's idea."

"Too risky." Petain's plan had been to tell Death Valley they
had to shut down the laser for repairs. Not tell the groundhogs
about the signal at all, just answer it. "If they found out, they'd sue
us down to our teeth."

The man shook his head. "I'll never understand groundhogs."

"Not your job." Charlie was an Earth-born, Earth-trained
psychologist. "Nobody born here ever could."

"Maybe so." He stood up. "Thanks for the drink; I've gotta get back to work. You know to call Dr. Bemis before the meeting?"

"Yeah. There was a message at the Cape."

"She has a surprise for you."

"Doesn't she always? You clowns never do anything around here until I leave."

———

ALL ABIGAIL BEMIS would say over the phone was that Charlie should come to her place for dinner; she'd prep him for the meeting.

"That was good, Ab. Can't afford real food on Earth."

She laughed and stacked the plates in the cleaner, then drew two cups of coffee. She laughed again when she sat down, a stocky, white-haired woman with bright eyes in a sea of wrinkles.

"You're in a jolly mood tonight."

"Yep. It's expectation."

"Johnny said you had a surprise."

"Hooboy, he doesn't know half. So, you didn't get anywhere with the Senator."

"No. Even less than I expected. What's the secret?"

"Connors is a nice-hearted boy. He's done a lot for us."

"Come on, Ab. What is it?"

"He's right. Shut off the groundhogs' TV for twenty minutes, and they'd have another Revolution on their hands."

"Ab . . ."

"We're going to send the message."

"Sure. I figured we would. Using Farside at whatever wattage we've got. If we're lucky—"

"Nope. Not enough power."

Charlie stirred a half-spoon of sugar into his coffee. "You plan to . . . defy Connors?"

"Fuzz Connors. We're not going to use radio at all."

"Visible light? Infra?"

"We're going to hand-carry it. In *Daedalus*."

Charlie's coffee cup was halfway to his mouth. He spilled a great deal.

"Here, have a napkin."

June 2040

FROM *A SHORT HISTORY OF THE OLD ORDER* (Freeman Press, 2040):

". . . and if you think *that* was a waste, consider Project Daedalus.

"This was the first big space thing after L-5. Now, L-5 worked out all right, because it was practical. But *Daedalus* (named from a Greek god who could fly)—that was a clear-cut case of throwing money down the rat-hole.

"These scientists in 2016 talked the bourgeoisie into paying for a trip to another *star!* It was going to take over a hundred years— but the scientists were going to have babies along the way, and train *them* to be scientists (whether they wanted to or not!).

"They were going to use all the old H-bombs for fuel—as if we might not need the fuel someday right here on Earth. What if L-5 decided they didn't like us and shut off the power beam?

"*Daedalus* was supposed to be a spaceship almost a kilometre long! Most of it was manufactured in space, from moon stuff, but a lot of it—the most expensive part, you bet—had to be boosted from Earth.

"They almost got it built, but then came the Breakup and the People's Revolution. No way in hell the People were going to let them have those H-bombs, not sitting right over our heads like that.

"So, we left the H-bombs in Helsinki, and the space freeks went back to doing what they're supposed to do. Every year they petition to get those H-bombs, but every year the Will of the People says no.

"That spaceship is still up there, a skytrillion-dollar boondoggle. As a monument to bourgeoisie folly, it's worse than the Pyramids!!"

February 2075

"So the Scylla probe is just a ruse, to get the fuel—"

"Oh no, not really." She slid a blue-covered folder to him. "We're still going to Scylla. Scoop up a few megatons of degenerate antimatter. And a similar amount of degenerate matter from Charybdis.

"We don't plan a generation ship, Charlie. The hydrogen fuel will get us out there; once there, it'll power the magnetic bottles to hold the real fuel."

"Total annihilation of matter," Charlie said.

"That's right. Em-cee-squared to the ninth decimal place. We aren't talking about centuries to get to 61 Cygni. Nine years, there and back."

"The groundhogs aren't going to like it. All the bad feeling about the original *Daedalus*—"

"Fuzz the groundhogs. We'll do everything we said we'd do with their precious H-bombs: go out to Scylla, get some antimatter, and bring it back. Just taking a long way back."

"You don't want to just tell them that's what we're going to do? No skin off . . ."

She shook her head and laughed again, this time a little bitterly. "You didn't read the editorial in *Peoplepost* this morning, did you?"

"I was too busy."

"So am I, boy; too busy for that drik. One of my staff brought it in, though."

"It's about *Daedalus*?"

"No . . . it concerns 61 Cygni. How the crazy scientists want to let those boogers know there's life on Earth."

"They'll come make people-burgers out of us."

"Something like that."

———

OVER THREE THOUSAND people sat on the hillside, a "natural" amphitheatre fashioned of Moon dirt and Earth grass. There was an incredible din, everyone talking at once: Dr. Bemis had just told them about the 61 Cygni expedition.

On about the tenth "Quiet, please," Bemis was able to continue. "So, you can see why we didn't simply broadcast this meeting. Earth would pick it up. Likewise, there are no groundhog media on L-5 right now. They were rotated back to Earth, and the shuttle with their replacements needed repairs at the Cape. The other two shuttles are here.

"So I'm asking all of you—and all of your brethren who had to stay at their jobs—to keep secret the biggest thing since Isabella hocked her jewels. Until we lift.

"Now Dr. Leventhal, who's chief of our social sciences section, wants to talk to you about selecting the crew."

Charlie hated public speaking. In this setting, he felt like a Christian on the way to being cat food. He smoothed out his damp notes on the podium.

"Uh, basic problem."

A thousand people asked him to speak up. He adjusted the microphone.

"The basic problem is, we have space for about a thousand people. Probably more than one out of four want to go."

Loud murmur of assent. "And we don't want to be despotic about choosing . . . but I've set up certain guidelines, and Dr. Bemis agrees with them.

"Nobody should plan on going if he or she needs sophisticated medical care, obviously. Same toke, few very old people will be considered."

Almost inaudibly, Abigail said, "Sixty-four isn't very old, Charlie. I'm going." She hadn't said anything earlier.

He continued, looking at Bemis. "Second, we must leave behind those people who are absolutely necessary for the maintenance of L-5. Including the power station."

She smiled at him.

"We don't want to split up mating pairs, not for, well, nine years plus . . . but neither will we take children." He waited for the commotion to die down. "On this mission, children are baggage. You'll have to find foster parents for them. Maybe they'll go on the next trip.

"Because we can't afford baggage. We don't know what's

waiting for us at 61 Cygni—a thousand people sounds like a lot, but it isn't. Not when you consider that we need a cross-section of all human knowledge, all human abilities. It may turn out that a person who can sing madrigals will be more important than a plasma physicist. No way of knowing ahead of time."

THE THREE THOUSAND people did manage to keep it secret, not so much out of strength of character as from a deep-seated paranoia about Earth and Earthlings.

And Senator Connors' Tricentennial actually came to their aid.

Although there was "One World," ruled by "The Will of the People," some regions had more clout than others, and nationalism was by no means dead. This was one factor.

Another factor was the way the groundhogs felt about the thermonuclear bombs stockpiled in Helsinki. All antiques; mostly a century or more old. The scientists said they were perfectly safe, but you know how that goes.

The bombs still technically belonged to the countries that had surrendered them, nine out of ten split between North America and Russia. The tenth remaining was divided among forty-two other countries. They all got together every few years to argue about what to do with the damned things. Everybody wanted to get rid of them in some useful way, but nobody wanted to put up the capital.

Charlie Leventhal's proposal was simple. L-5 would provide bankroll, materials, and personnel. On a barren rock in the Norwegian Sea, they would take apart the old bombs, one at a time, and turn them into uniform fuel capsules for the *Daedalus* craft.

The Scylla/Charybdis probe would be timed to honour both the major spacefaring countries. Renamed the *John F. Kennedy*, it would leave Earth orbit on America's Tricentennial. The craft would accelerate halfway to the double-star system at one gee, then flip and slow down at the same rate. It would use a magnetic scoop to gather antimatter from Scylla. On May Day, 2077, it would again be renamed, being the *Leonid I. Brezhnev* for the return trip. For safety's sake, the antimatter would be delivered to a lunar research station near Farside. L-5 scientists claimed that harnessing the energy from total annihilation of matter would make a heaven on Earth.

Most people doubted that but looked forward to the fireworks.

January 2076

"THE HELL WITH THAT!" Charlie was livid. "I—I just won't do it. Won't!"

"You're the only one—"

"That's not true. Ab, you know it." Charlie paced from wall to wall of her office cubicle. "There are dozens of people who can run L-5. Better than I can."

"Not better, Charlie."

He stopped in front of her desk, leaned over. "Come on, Ab. There's only one logical person to stay behind and run things. Not only has she proven herself in the position, but she's too old to—"

"That kind of drik I don't have to listen to."

"Now, Ab . . ."

"No, you listen to me. I was an infant when we started building *Daedalus*; worked on it as a girl and a young woman. I could take you out there in a shuttle and show you the rivets that I put in myself. A half-century ago."

"That's my—"

"I earned my ticket, Charlie." Her voice softened. "Age is a factor, yes. This is only the first trip of many—and when it comes back, I *will* be too old. You'll just be in your prime . . . and with over twenty years of experience as Coordinator, I don't doubt they'll make you captain of the next—"

"I don't want to be captain. I don't want to be Coordinator. I just want to go!"

"You and three thousand other people."

"And of the thousand that don't want to go, or can't, there isn't one person who could serve as Coordinator? I could name you—"

"That's not the point. There's no one on L-5 who has anywhere near the influence, the connections, you have on Earth. No one who understands groundhogs as well."

"That's racism, Ab. Groundhogs are just like you and me."

"Some of them. I don't see you going Earthside every chance you can get . . . what, you like the view up here? You like living in a can?"

He didn't have a ready answer for that.

Ab continued. "Whoever's Coordinator is going to have to do some tall explaining, trying to keep things smooth between L-5 and Earth. That's been your life's work, Charlie. And you're also known and respected here. You're the only logical choice."

"I'm not arguing with your logic."

"I know." Neither of them had to mention the document, signed by Charlie, among others, that gave Dr. Bemis final authority in selecting the crew for *Daedalus/Kennedy/Brezhnev*.

"Try not to hate me too much, Charlie. I have to do what's best for my people. All of my people." Charlie glared at her for a long moment and left.

June 2076

FROM *FAX & PIX*, 4 June 2076:

SPACE FARM LEAVES FOR
STARS NEXT MONTH

1. The *John F. Kennedy*, which goes to Scylla/Charybdis next month, is like a little L-5 with bombs up its tail (see pix upleft, upright).

A. The trip's twenty months. They could either take a few people and fill the thing up with food, air, and water—or take a lot of people inside a closed ecology, like L-5.

B. They could've gotten by with only a couple hundred people, to run the farms and stuff. But almost all the space freeks wanted to go. They're used to living that way, anyhow (and they never get to go anyplace).

C. When they get back, the farms will be used as a starter for L-4, like L-5 but smaller at first, and on the other side of the Moon (pic downleft).

2. For other Tricentennial fax & pix, see bacover.

July 2076

CHARLIE WAS JUST FINISHING up a week on Earth the day the *John F. Kennedy* was launched. Tired of being interviewed, he slipped away from the media lounge at the Cape shuttleport. His white clearance card got him out onto the landing strip, alone.

The midnight shuttle was being fuelled at the far end of the strip, gleaming pink-white in the last light from the setting sun. Its image twisted and danced in the shimmering heat that radiated from the tarmac. The smell of the soft tar was indelibly associated in his mind with leave-taking, relief.

He walked to the middle of the strip and checked his watch. Five minutes. He lit a cigarette and threw it away. He rechecked his mental calculations; the flight would start low in the southwest. He blocked out the sun with a raised hand. What would 150 bombs per second look like? For the media, they were called fuel capsules. The people who had carefully assembled them and gently lifted them to orbit and installed them in the tanks, they called them bombs. Ten times the brightness of a full moon, they had said. On L-5, you weren't supposed to look toward it without a dark filter.

No warm-up; it suddenly appeared, an impossibly brilliant rainbow speck just over the horizon. It gleamed for several minutes, then dimmed slightly with the haze and slipped away.

Most of the United States wouldn't see it until it came around again, some two hours later, turning night into day, competing with local pyrotechnic displays. Then every couple of hours after that. Charlie would see it once more, then get on the shuttle. And finally stop having to call it by the name of a dead politician.

September 2076

THERE WAS a quiet celebration on L-5 when *Daedalus* reached the mid-point of its journey, flipped, and started decelerating. The progress report from its crew characterized the journey as "uneventful." At that time, they were going nearly two tenths of the speed of light. The laser beam that carried communications was red-shifted from blue light down to orange; the message that turnaround had been successful took two weeks to travel from *Daedalus* to L-5.

They announced a slight course change. They had analyzed the polarization of light from Scylla/Charybdis as their phase angle increased, and were pretty sure the system was surrounded by flat rings of debris, like Saturn. They would "come in low" to avoid collision.

January 2077

DAEDALUS HAD BEEN SENDING BACK recognizable pictures of the Scylla/Charybdis system for three weeks. They finally had one that was dramatic enough for groundhog consumption.

Charlie set the holo cube on his desk and pushed it around with his finger, marvelling.

"This is incredible. How did they do it?"

"It's a montage, of course." Johnny had been one of the youngest adults left behind: heart murmur, trick knees, a surfeit of astrophysicists.

"The two stars are a strobe snapshot in infrared. Sort of. Some ten or twenty thousand exposures taken as the ship orbited around the system, then sorted out and enhanced." He pointed, but it wasn't much help, since Charlie was looking at the cube from a different angle.

"The lamina of fire where the atmospheres touch, that was taken in ultraviolet. Shows more fine structure that way.

"The rings were easy. Fairly long exposures in visible light. Gives the star background, too."

A light tap on the door and an assistant stuck his head in. "Have a second, Doctor?"

"Sure."

"Somebody from a Russian May Day committee is on the phone. She wants to know whether they've changed the name of the ship to *Brezhnev* yet."

"Yeah. Tell her we decided on 'Leon Trotsky' instead, though."

He nodded seriously. "Okay." He started to close the door.

"*Wait!*" Charlie rubbed his eyes. "Tell her, uh . . . the ship doesn't have a commemorative name while it's in orbit there. They'll rechristen it just before the start of the return trip."

"Is that true?" Johnny asked.

"I don't know. Who cares? In another couple of months, they won't *want* it named after anybody." He and Ab had worked out a plan—admittedly rather shaky—to protect L-5 from the ground-hogs' wrath; nobody on the satellite knew ahead of time that the ship was headed for 61 Cygni. It was a decision the crew arrived at on the way to Scylla/Charybdis; they modified the drive system to accept matter-antimatter destruction while they were orbiting the double star. L-5 would first hear of the mutinous plan via a trans-mission sent as *Daedalus* left Scylla/Charybdis. They'd be a month on their way by the time the message got to Earth

It was pretty transparent, but at least they had been careful that no record of *Daedalus*'s true mission be left on L-5. Three thousand people did know the truth, though, and any competent engineer or physical scientist would suspect it.

Ab had felt that, although there was a better-than-even chance they would be exposed, surely the groundhogs couldn't stay angry for twenty-three years—even if they were unimpressed by the antimatter and other wonders . . .

Besides, Charlie thought, *it's not their worry anymore.*

As it turned out, the crew of *Daedalus* would have bigger things to worry about.

June 2077

THE RUSSIANS HAD their May Day celebration—Charlie watched it on TV and winced every time they mentioned the good ship *Leonid I. Brezhnev*—and then things settled back down to normal. Charlie and three thousand others waited nervously for the "surprise" message. It came in early June, as expected, scrambled in a data channel. But it didn't say what it was supposed to:

> *This is Abigail Bemis, to Charles Leventhal.*
>
> *Charlie, we have real trouble. The ship has been damaged, hit in the stern by a good chunk of something. It punched right through the main drive reflector. Destroyed a set of control sensors and one attitude jet.*
>
> *As far as we can tell, the situation is stable. We're maintaining acceleration at just a tiny fraction under one gee. But we can't steer, and we can't shut off the main drive.*
>
> *We didn't have any trouble with ring debris when we were orbiting, since we were inside Roche's limit. Coming in, as you know,*

we'd managed to take advantage of natural divisions in the rings. We tried the same going back, but it was a slower, more complicated process, since we mass so goddamn much now. We must have picked up a piece from the fringe of one of the outer rings.

If we could turn off the drive, we might have a chance at fixing it. But the work pods can't keep up with the ship, not at one gee. The radiation down there would fry the operator in seconds, anyway.

We're working on it. If you have any ideas, let us know. It occurs to me that this puts you in the clear—we were headed back to Earth, but got clobbered. Will send a transmission to that effect on the regular comm channel. This message is strictly burn-before-reading.

Endit.

It worked perfectly, as far as getting Charlie and L-5 off the hook—and the drama of the situation precipitated a level of interest in space travel unheard-of since the 1960s.

They even had a hero. A volunteer had gone down in a heavily shielded work pod, lowered on a cable, to take a look at the situation. She'd sent back clear pictures of the damage, before the cable snapped.

Daedalus: AD 2081 | Earth: AD 2101

THE FOLLOWING news item was killed from *Fax & Pix*, because it was too hard to translate into the "plain English" that made the paper so popular:

SPACESHIP PASSES 61 CYGNI—SORT OF
(L-5 Stringer)

A message received today from the spaceship *Daedalus* said that it had just passed within 400 astronomical units of 61 Cygni. That's about ten times as far as the planet Pluto is from the Sun.

Actually, the spaceship passed the star some eleven years ago. It's taken all that time for the message to get back to us.

We don't know for sure where the spaceship actually is, now. If they still haven't repaired the runaway drive, they're about eleven light-years past the 61 Cygni system (their speed when they passed the double star was better than ninety-nine percent the speed of light).

The situation is more complicated if you look at it from the point of view of a passenger on the spaceship. Because of relativity, time seems to pass more slowly as you approach the speed of light. So only about four years passed for them on the eleven-light-year journey.

L-5 Coordinator Charles Leventhal points out that the spaceship has enough antimatter fuel to keep accelerating to the edge of the Galaxy. The crew then would be only some twenty years older —but it would be 20,000 years before we heard from them . . .

(Kill this one. There's more stuff about what the ship looked like to the people on 61 Cygni, and howcum we could talk to them all the time even though time was slower there, but it's all as stupid as this.)

Daedalus: AD 2083 | Earth: AD 2144

CHARLIE LEVENTHAL DIED at the age of ninety-nine, bitter. Almost a decade earlier, it had been revealed that they'd planned all along for *Daedalus* to be a starship. Few people had paid much attention to the news. Among those who did, the consensus was that anything that got rid of a thousand scientists at once was a good thing. Look at the mess they got us in.

Daedalus: sixty-seven light-years out, and still accelerating.

Daedalus: AD 2085 | Earth: AD 3578

AFTER OVER SEVEN years of shipboard research and development —and some 1,500 light-years of travel—they managed to shut down the engine. With sophisticated telemetry, the job was done without endangering another life.

Every life was precious now. They were no longer simply explorers; almost half their fuel was gone. They were colonists, with no ticket back.

The message of their success would reach Earth in fifteen centuries. Whether there would be an infrared telescope around to detect it, that was a matter of some conjecture.

Daedalus: AD 2093 | Earth: ca. AD 5000

WHILE DECELERATING, they had investigated several systems in their line of flight. They found one with an Earth-type planet around a Sun-type sun, and aimed for it.

The season they began landing colonists, the dominant feature in the planet's night sky was a beautiful blooming cloud of gas that astronomers had named the North American Nebula.

Which was an irony that didn't occur to any of these colonists from L-5—give or take a few years, it was America's Trimillenial.

America itself was a little the worse for wear, this 3,000th anniversary. The seas that lapped its shores were heavy with a crimson crust of anaerobic life; the mighty cities had fallen and their remains nearly ground away by the never-ceasing sandstorms.

No fireworks were planned, for lack of an audience, for lack of planners; bacteria just don't care. May Day, too, would be ignored.

The only humans in the Solar System lived in a glass-and-metal tube. They tended their automatic machinery, and turned their backs on the dead Earth, and worshipped the constellation Cygnus, and had forgotten why.

ABOUT THE AUTHORS

EDWARD WILLETT is the award-winning author of more than sixty books of science fiction, fantasy, and non-fiction for readers of all ages. His most recent titles include the *Worldshapers* series for DAW Books and the five-book young-adult fantasy series *The Shards of Excalibur*, just re-released by Shadowpaw Press. Ed won Canada's Aurora Award for Best Long-Form Work in English in 2009 for *Marseguro* (DAW Books) and the Aurora Award for Best Fan Related Work in 2019 for his podcast *The Worldshapers*; he's been shortlisted for Auroras multiple times. He's currently working on *The Tangled Stars*, a new space opera for DAW. He lives in Regina, Saskatchewan. Find him on Twitter @ewillett, on Facebook @edward.willett, and at edwardwillett.com.

TANYA HUFF lives in rural Ontario with her wife, Fiona Patton, six cats, two dogs, and an increasing number of fish. Her thirty-two novels and seventy-nine short stories include horror, heroic fantasy, urban fantasy, comedy, and military SF. Her *Blood* series was turned into the twenty-two-episode *Blood Ties*, and writing episode nine allowed her to finally use her degree in Radio & Television Arts. Many of her short stories are available as eCollections. She's on twitter at @TanyaHuff and Facebook as Tanya Huff. Since she hasn't done anything about it, she probably still has a LiveJournal account . . .

JOHN SCALZI lives in Ohio and metabolizes through the use of oxygen and some other compounds and components.

JOHN C. WRIGHT is a retired attorney, newspaperman, and newspaper editor, who was only once on the lam and forced to hide from the police. He is the author of some twenty-two novels, including the critically acclaimed *The Golden Age* and *Count to a Trillion*. He has published anthologies, including *Awake in the Night Land* and *City Beyond Time*, as well as nonfiction. His novel *Somewhither* won the Dragon Award for Best Science Fiction Novel of 2016. He holds the record for the most Hugo Award nominations for a single year. He presently works as a writer in Virginia, where he lives in fairytale-like happiness with his wife, the authoress L. Jagi Lamplighter, and their four children.

L.E. MODESITT, JR. is the author of more than seventy-five science fiction and fantasy novels, nearly fifty short stories, and technical and economic articles. His novels include four fantasy series, including the *Saga of Recluce* and the *Imager Portfolio*. His first story was published in *Analog* in 1973. His most recent book is *Quantum Shadows*, and his next book is *Fairhaven Rising* (Tor, February 2021). He has been a U.S. Navy pilot; a market research analyst; a real estate agent; director of political research; legislative and staff director for U.S. Congressmen; Director of Legislation/Congressional Relations for the U.S. EPA; and a consultant on environmental, regulatory, and communications issues.

Since 1997, award-winning Canadian author/former biologist JULIE E. CZERNEDA has shared her curiosity about living things through her SF and fantasy novels, published by DAW Books. Her latest fantasy is the standalone *The Gossamer Mage* (2019).

Currently, Julie's returned to her beloved character, Esen, in her *Web Shifter's Library* series, featuring all the weird biology one could ask, with *Mirage* out August 2020 and *Spectrum*, spring 2021. Julie's edited/co-edited award-winning anthologies of SF/F, including SFWA's 2017 *Nebula Award Showcase* and *The Clan Chronicles: Tales from Plexis*, featuring stories by fans of her series. Her website is www.czerneda.com.

SHELLEY ADINA is the author of forty-two novels published by Harlequin, Warner, Hachette, and Moonshell Books, Inc., her own independent press. She holds an MFA in Writing Popular Fiction, and is currently at work on a PhD in Creative Writing with Lancaster University in the UK. She won RWA's RITA Award® in 2005 and was a finalist in 2006. She appeared in the 2016 documentary film *Love Between the Covers*, is a popular speaker and convention panelist, and has been a guest on many podcasts, including *The Worldshapers* and *Realm of Books*. When she's not writing, Shelley is usually quilting, sewing historical costumes, or enjoying the garden with her flock of rescued chickens. Find her on the Web at shelleyadina.com, on Twitter @shelleyadina, and on Facebook @magnificentdevices.

After leaving molecular biology, DEREK KÜNSKEN worked with street kids in Central America before finding himself in the Canadian foreign service. He now writes science fiction in Gatineau, Québec. His space opera novels *The Quantum Magician* and *The Quantum Garden* were published by Solaris Books. The first was a finalist for the Aurora, the Locus, and the Chinese Nebula Awards. Solaris released his "Godfather in the clouds of Venus" novel *The House of Styx* in ebook and audio in August 2020, with the hardcover coming in April 2021. Find him at DerekKunsken.com.

THORAIYA DYER is an Aurealis and Ditmar Award-winning Sydney-based writer and veterinarian. Her short science fiction and fantasy stories have appeared in *Clarkesworld*, *Analog*, *Apex*, *Cosmos*, *Nature*, the anthology *Bridging Infinity*, and boutique collection *Asymmetry*. Thoraiya's novels *Crossroads of Canopy*, *Echoes of Understorey*, and *Tides of the Titans* are published by Tor books. Find her online at thoraiyadyer.com or on Twitter @ThoraiyaDyer.

GARETH L. POWELL is the author of the BSFA Award-winning novels *Embers of War* and *Ack-Ack Macaque*. He can be found online at www.garethlpowell.com.

SEANAN McGUIRE is the author of the *October Daye* urban fantasies, the *InCryptid* urban fantasies, and several other works, both stand-alone and in trilogies or duologies. She also writes under the pseudonym "Mira Grant." Seanan was the winner of the 2010 John W. Campbell Award for Best New Writer, and her novel *Feed* (as Mira Grant) was named as one of *Publishers Weekly*'s Best Books of 2010. In 2013 she became the first person ever to appear five times on the same Hugo ballot. Her novella "Every Heart A Doorway" received the 2016 Nebula Award for Best Novella, the 2017 Hugo Award for Best Novella, and the 2017 Locus Award for Best Novella. Seanan lives in an "idiosyncratically designed" labyrinth in the Pacific Northwest, which she shares with her cats, a vast collection of creepy dolls and horror movies, and, she says, sufficient books to qualify her as a fire hazard.

FONDA LEE is the author of the epic urban fantasy *Green Bone Saga*, beginning with *Jade City* and continuing in *Jade War* and *Jade Legacy*, and the science fiction novels *Zeroboxer*, *Exo*, and *Cross*

Fire. Fonda is a winner of the World Fantasy Award, a three-time winner of the Aurora Award, and a multiple finalist for the Nebula Award and the Locus Award. Her novels have garnered multiple starred reviews, been included on numerous state reading lists, and appeared on Best of Year lists from NPR, Barnes & Noble, *Syfy Wire*, and others. Fonda is a former corporate strategist, black-belt martial artist, and Eggs Benedict enthusiast. Born and raised in Calgary, Alberta, she currently resides in Portland, Oregon.

CHRISTOPHER RUOCCHIO is the author of *The Sun Eater*, a space opera fantasy series, as well as the Assistant Editor at Baen Books, where he has co-edited four anthologies. He is a graduate of North Carolina State University, where he studied English Rhetoric and the Classics. Christopher has been writing since he was eight and sold his first novel, *Empire of Silence*, at twenty-two. To date, his books have been published in five languages. He lives in Raleigh, North Carolina, with his wife, Jenna. He may be found on both Facebook and Twitter with the handle TheRuocchio.

DAVID BRIN is best-known for shining light—plausibly and entertainingly—on technology, society, and countless challenges confronting our rambunctious civilization. His bestselling novels include *The Postman* (filmed in 1997) plus explorations of our near future in *Earth* and *Existence*. Other novels are translated into more than twenty-five languages. His short stories explore vividly speculative ideas. Brin's nonfiction book *The Transparent Society* won the American Library Association's Freedom of Speech Award for exploring twenty-first-century concerns about security, secrecy, accountability, and privacy. As a scientist, tech-consultant, and world-known author, he speaks, advises, and writes widely on topics from national defense and homeland security to astronomy

and space exploration, SETI and nanotechnology, future/predic-
tion, creativity, and philanthropy.

D. J. (DAVE) BUTLER has been a lawyer, a consultant, an editor,
and a corporate trainer. His novels published by Baen Books
include *Witchy Eye, Witchy Winter, Witchy Kingdom, Serpent
Daughter,* and *In the Palace of Shadow and Joy,* as well as *The
Cunning Man,* co-written with Aaron Michael Ritchey. He also
writes for children: *The Kidnap Plot, The Giant's Seat,* and *The
Library Machine* are published by Knopf. Other novels include *City
of the Saints* from WordFire Press and *The Wilding Probate* from
Immortal Works. Dave also organizes writing retreats and anar-
cho-libertarian writers' events, and travels the country to sell
books. He plays guitar and banjo whenever he can and likes to
hang out in Utah with his novel-writing wife and their three
children.

DR. CHARLES E. GANNON's *Caine Riordan* hard-SF novels have
all been national bestsellers. Four have been Nebula finalists, two
have been Dragon Award finalists, and the first was also a
Compton Crook winner. An overlapping series, *Murphy's Lawless,*
launched in 2020. His epic fantasy series, *The Vortex of Worlds,*
debuts in 2021. He collaborates with Eric Flint in the *New York
Times/Wall Street Journal*-bestselling *Ring of Fire* series, has written
solo novels in John Ringo's *Black Tide Rising* series, and has
contributed to the *Starfire, Honorverse, Man-Kzin,* and *War World*
universes. Other credits include a lot of short fiction, game
design/writing, and scriptwriter/producer. As a Distinguished
Professor of English, Gannon received five Fulbrights. His book
Rumors of War & Infernal Machines won the 2006 ALA Choice
Award for Outstanding Book. He is a frequent subject-matter

expert in national media venues (NPR, Discovery, etc.) and for various intelligence and defense agencies.

DAVID WEBER was born in Cleveland a long, long time ago, and grew up in rural South Carolina, with a father who collected autographed copies of every E. E. Smith hardcover and a mother who ran her own ad agency and encouraged him to write. From that start, with a love of history (and as a practitioner of RPGs before the world ever heard of something called *Dungeons & Dragons*), it was inevitable he would embrace the dark side and become a sci-fi writer himself. He sold his first novel to Jim Baen, his enabler at Baen Books, in 1989. Since then, he has perpetrated more than seventy solo and collaborative novels and an unconscionable number of anthologies. He is perhaps best known for his character Honor Harrington, whom he hopes never to meet in a dark alley, given all the bones she has to pick with him. Casual acquaintances are warned never to press his "talk button."

JOE HALDEMAN is the Hugo and Nebula Award-winning author of *The Forever War*, *The Hemingway Hoax*, *Forever Peace*, and many others (more than two dozen), a SFWA Grand Master and a member of the Science Fiction Hall of Fame. Joe has also won the John W. Campbell Memorial Award, the Locus Award, the Rhysling Award, the World Fantasy Award, and the James Tiptree, Jr. Award. For thirty years, Joe was an Adjunct Professor teaching writing at the Massachusetts Institute of Technology, which is also the fictional setting for his 2007 novel, *The Accidental Time Machine*. His most recent novel is *Work Done for Hire*. A painter and poet as well as author, Joe resides in Gainesville, Florida, with Gay, his wife of fifty-five years.

ACKNOWLEDGEMENTS

This anthology would not have been possible without the generous support of the many people who pledged to back it on Kickstarter. You not only made this terrific collection of science fiction and fantasy stories possible, you've set the stage for more *Shapers of Worlds* anthologies in the future. This anthology only includes guests from the first year of *The Worldshapers* podcast. With luck and supporters like you, there'll be a Volume II next year featuring guests from the podcast's second year—an equally stellar collection of authors. Huge thanks to everyone listed below (the names they backed under), and to those who chose to remain anonymous, for helping to bring this book to life.

KICKSTARTER BACKERS

Adam Eaton, Adam Rajski, Adderbane, Adora Hoose, Alex Claman, Alex McGilvery, Allan Harsmann, Amy Blume, Amy Kimmel, Andrea Fry, Andrea R, Andrew, Andrew I Renshaw,

ACKNOWLEDGEMENTS 353

Andrew MacLeod, Andrew Maletz, Andrew Miller, Andromeda Taylor, Anna Fultz, Anne Hueser, Anne Walker, Arthur Slade, Aura Roy, Barbara Butler Long, BCurtis, BE Stewart, Beebs, Ben H, Ben Janseen, Benjamin Wheeler, Benoit Chartier, Beth Lobdell, Bradley Hogland, Bren Hawk, Brendan Coffey, Brendan Rose-Silverberg, Brian Bygland, Bruce Trick, Byron Aytoun, Camille Lofters, Carl Swan, Caroline Kierstead, Caroline Westra, Cata Mari, Catherine Fiorello, Catherine Gross-Colten, Catherine Seeligson, Cathy Green, Celeste Stuart, Cern McAtee, Chawin Narkraksa, Chris, Chris Gerrib, Chris Lisy, Chris McLean, Christer Boräng, Christine Schmidt, Cindy, Cindy Ferguson, Claire Sims, Connor Bliss, Corey, Craig Neumeier, Cristina Alves, Curt Frye, Cyn Wise, D.J. Schreffler, Dagmar, Dan Pollack, Daniel Blatt, Daryl Putman, David Butler, David Edmonds, David Hopkinson, David Perlmutter, David Rowe, David Schumacher, David Strutton, David Teare, david wilkerson, Debbie Matsuura, Deodand, Devin, Diego Elio Pettenò, Dino Hicks, Donna Levett, Duane Warnecke, Dwight Willett, Edgar Middel, Edward Ellis, Edward Kuruliouk, Elizabeth Doherty, Elizabeth Farley-Dawson, Elizabeth Furr, Elizabeth Lundquist, Elly Carlson, Elyse M Grasso, Emily, Emily Collins, Eric Brown, Erin, Erin McLaughlin, Ernesto, Ethaisa, Evan Ladouceur, Faye Onley, Fazia Rizvi, Felaguin, Fiannawolf, filkferengi, Frank Nissen, Frankie, Fred Bailey, Gareth JOnes, Garth Rose, Gary Moore, Gary Phillips, Genevieve Fitzsimmons, GMark C, Gregory Cherlin, Hayden Trenholm, Heather Nickel, Heidi Lambert, Ian H., Ina Gur, Ira Nayman, Isaac 'Will It Work' Dansicker, Jackson Yuen, Jaime Bolton, Jakub Narębski, James Alan Gardner, james coates, James Gotaas, James Lucas, James McCoy, Jarrod Coad, Jeanne Hartley, Jeffrey Carver, Jen & Eric, Jennifer Berk, Jennifer Brozek, Jennifer Della'Zanna, Jennifer Flora Black, Jennifer Pease, Jennifer Whitworth, Jeremiah Johnston, Jermaine Kanhai, Jeroen Teitsma, Jess Turner, Jesse Klein, Jessica Enfante, Jessica Williams, Jessica Willson, Jill Keppeler, Jim Willett, Joann Koch, Joanne Burrows, Joe Geary, John, John McCann, John Tilden, Jonathan Mansfield, Josh Levin, Joshua Palmatier, Jowen, Joy Auburn, JT, juli, Julian White, June m downey, kamalloy, Kamara Willett, karen, Karen McGee, Kari Blocker, Karl Mehler, Kat Munro Glass, Kate Mackay, Katharine Kolb, Kathryn Taylor, Kathy Magruder, Katie Schmirler, Katya, Keith, Keith West, Kenneth Patterson, Kent Pollard, Kerry Kuhn, Khristian McCutchan, Kim, Kim Stoker, Kris Vasquez, Krystal Bohannan, Krystal Windsor, Larry Strome, Lawrence Amrose, Leah Webber, LexiBanner, Lily Connors, Linda Bruno, Linda Cox, Lisa Johnson, Liz M, logosshadow, Louise DiMarcello, maileguy, Manuel Tants, Marc D. Long, Margaret Anderson, Margaret Bumby, Margaret Chambers, Margaret Hodges, Margaret St. John, MARGOT HARRIS, Mark Newman, Mark Thompson, Martin Beijer, Martina James, Martyn Smedley, Mary Alice Wuerz, Mary Haldeman, Maryrita Steinhour, Mate Beljan, Matt, Matt Knepper, Matthew Gaglio, Matthew Runyon, Matthew Wang, Max Kaehn, Max Smolev, Melanie Marttila, Melissa Hawley, Michael Bernardi, Michael Esparza, Michael F. Stewart, Michael Fedrowitz, Michael Feir, Michael Kirpes, Michael Spath, Michael Weckworth, Michael Yigdall, Michala, Michelle, Mike Mancini, Mike Miller, Mike OBrien, Miranda Floyd, Monica cormier, Nancy, Nancy Steffan, Nancy Tseng Glassman, Ned Donovan, Nicholas Trandem, Nicole Hunter, Nina Hill, PABrown, parkrrrr, Pat, Pat H, Patricia Anne Wilson, Patricia Miller, Patrick Curtis, Patti Short, paul, Peggy Kimbell, Peter Friedman, Peter O'Meara, Poisontaster, Rachel Hagen, Rafe Richards, randomscrub, Rethyn, Richard L. Hamilton, Richard Norton, RIchard W Maxton, Rick Straker, RipL, RJHopkinson, Rob Easton, Rob Elderkin, Rob Menaul,

Robert, Robert Claney, Robert Gottlieb, Robert Woods Tienken, Roberta Webb, Ross Qualls, Russell J Handelman, Russell Ventimeglia, Ruth, Sandi Pitura, Scott Kohtz, Scott Kuntzelman, Sean CW Korsgaard, Shael Hawman, Shana, Shannon Mason, Sharon Eisbrenner, Sian, Simo Muinonen, Simon Matthews, Software Bloke, Stephanie Lucas, Stephen, Stephen Ballentine, Steven Callen, Steven Lord, Steven Peiper, Stu Glennie, Stu White, Sue Archer, Susan Baur, Susan Forest, Susan K Jolly, Susan O'Fearna, Susanne Schörner, Sven, T R Jacobs, Tania, Tanja Wooten, Tara Zrymiak, Tero Heikkinen, Thomas Bull, Thomas Hendricksen, Thomas Lockett, Thomas Wiegand, Tiff Reynolds, Tiffany Hall, Tina Good, Tom, Tom Knapik, Tony Calidonna, V Joy Stang, vincentursus, Vivien Limon, Wade Waldron, William McKissack, William Woodford, Yankton Robins, Zachary Williams, Zara.